MEMOIRS OF A HEADBANGER

MEMOIRS OF A HEADBANGER

A Rock Novel

KIRK ANTHONY VOLLACK

Anthony Shelton Publications, LLP
ASP

Dedicated with all my love to my father and mother,
Anthony and Imojean Vollack
…and to all the bands that never made it.

PROLOGUE

This is a story about an American dream.

It was the eighties. The nineteen-eighties. The decade we all lived through but don't seem to remember. The decade of money and poorly made music videos, multiplex mall cinema and big hair. The decade when America reflected for a brief moment upon all the issues and problems of the prior two decades and then said: "Screw it, what's on TV?"

It was the eighties, and we were headbangers. Rockers. Heavy metal heads.

Big hair and tight pants, fog machines and meaningless lyrics. The forgotten genre. We were young suburban little shits. Big-haired, ripped-jeaned, tightly wrapped, cheetah-spandexed headbangers. Dreamers, just like everyone else.

Heavy metal. The silly, obscure music of the silly, obscure decade.

But it wasn't just music. It was a lifestyle. A pastime. A symptom of the eighties. If the real historians want to know the essence of the eighties, they'd be wise to examine the hard stuff. Heavy metal was about excess and hedonism, sex and drugs and power, hype and glamour--everything the eighties were about.

The eighties were mass merchandise and mass promotion, taking any product and selling it through carefully analyzed demographics and profiling, producing four or five new flavors of slushy beverage and advertising the hell out of them until we were either drinking, or at the very least familiar with, the Slushy brand name. The eighties were about MORE. More of everything. Everything bigger, better, improved. Everything louder, brighter, tastier.

MORE.

From this environment, metal music was born. The gluttonous eighties leaned back, still fully sedated, and gave birth to heavy metal. Her own latch-key bastard.

Bastard? You ask. Didn't heavy metal have a father?

Yes, but not one who would claim it. Two fathers, actually. The DNA test shows that the seventies were half responsible. The other half belongs to music video. Heavy metal was the son of a single mother.

Our older brothers and sisters listened to good ole' seventies rock like Led Zeppelin and Foghat, Ted Nugent and Molly Hatchet--greasy hippie guys who performed twenty-minute guitar solos and dosed acid, wailing away in their own little universes. The legend was bigger than the promotion, and the message more vital than the look.

In the eighties, this was no longer adequate.

Message was out. We took Nancy's advice and just said no.

Metal took the rock legacy and spray painted it pink and black, added a few mirrors and a good dose of fog, gutted it, cleaned it, dressed it, fluffed it and wrapped it up with a shiny silver bow. Sure, the meaning may have all been drained out in the process...but metal isn't about meaning. It's about spectacle.

Cable television would soon explode all over America like a carefully hurled corporate water balloon, changing music forever.

No longer did reasonably ugly guys get famous because they were brilliant lyricists making a statement. Music video was upon us. Our eyes now laid claim to something our ears formerly coveted as their own. Suddenly, bands were being seen as often as they were heard. Like books to movies, the old radio rockers came off a bit long-winded and weak compared to the pre-packaged pyrotechnics exploding on the TV screen. And when you have pure spectacle, who needs meaning?

Headbangers don't relate to meaning. Headbangers just want to rock. Headbangers need only the glorious grind of a power cord and the meaty thump of the kick-drum shaking their bones. Headbangers look back at the sixties and see drugged out freaks trying to change the world by singing about peace and flopping around naked in the mud. This is too complicated. Headbangers don't want to change the world, and flopping around in the mud will stain their suede and flatten their hair. Headbangers look back and see Joan Baez strumming a guitar and laugh their asses off. What, no light show? No fog? Her guitar isn't even plugged in!

Headbangers are tired of fighting the system and hoping for a better day. They don't want to join or protest anything. They're sick of meaning and message. Headbangers just wanna party. Oh, and rock. All night long.

So grubby was out. We wanted to rock, but we had to look good doing it. Long hair was still around, but the headbangers took the long hair they inherited from the hippies and washed it thoroughly. They blow dried it upside down and sprayed it with a generous dose of aerosol schpritz to remove every bit of floppy hippy flexibility. They dyed it and bleached it, paraded it around with platinum ends and ebony roots, chopped it into mullets and teased it mercilessly, dominating like beauty pageant parents who slop makeup on their five-year-olds and force them to sing "Tomorrow."

Don't be mistaken. It wasn't a movement. Not by a long shot. Movements have somewhere to go. Metal may make a lot of noise, but the only movement is the unusually satisfying feeling of banging your head to the undeniable beauty of a four-four beat. Besides, last I checked, you needed an altruistic purpose to qualify for movementhood. Unless you count partying as a purpose...

The eighties were stylishly inane and arguably vacant of historical significance, but history should know better than to exclude the silly.

Not that I knew much of history. This was the eighties, and it was also the suburbs.

In the suburbs, history doesn't exist. The buildings, the streets, the schools, the very roof over your head, they're all less than fifty years old. The families are transplants, and the restaurants franchised. Everything around you, including the grass growing beneath your feet was idealized, paid for, shipped in on a panel truck and set up as ordered. Instant neighborhood--just add money. (History not included.) Myriads of homes, city-planned and zoned into a creative confusion of swirls and clusters, all serviced by winding, freshly-paved roads that don't really go anywhere and have a tendency to dead end into quaint, block-party-perfect cul-de-sacs.

Nearby are strategically placed clusters of brightly lit service stations, overpriced convenience stores and video rental outlets, built to help fuel, feed, and provide a steady supply of slushy ice beverages to the thriving populace within the domicile clusters. They must be kept happy so they'll reproduce and create more consumers who will, in turn, need their own cluster homes and their own slushy ice beverages.

The gods of Suburbia sit in lawn chairs on high, pleased with their creation. They look down from their mountainous redwood decks and see the sprawling promised land stretching out endlessly before them, consumer after consumer, procreating and sucking down slushy beverages in their pastel colored domiciles until the end of time. And why not? The gods have provided everything a human could ever want, all within five minutes of home! The suburbs were designed for consumption. Amen.

The American melting pot? The soup is a little thin out here. Someone took the melting pot and poured it all over the place--a chunk here, a chunk there, all lightly coated with the gravy of humanity. But in the burbs, our chunks aren't steeped in the same flavorful depths. And nothing truly melts.

The American lukewarm broth.

Not that the suburbs are entirely void of culture...no more than the eighties were. As with the eighties, however, one must examine the suburbs with scrutiny to find the redemptive qualities, the essence of this mysteriously void community, the unique subculture that sprang from the head of this lawn-mowing Zeus.

The eighties were our inspiration, our benefactor and support...our media pusher, injecting fame-lust and dreams through a syringe known as the box. We were headbangers, and heavy metal was our theme music. The soundtrack of the suburbs.

A fad? Possibly.

A trend? Probably.

Inane? Arguably. Just like the eighties.

But it was me, and it was us.

It was the coolest thing my fifteen-year-old suburban mind had ever assimilated. It was about love and anger and belonging. It was life in every extreme, and to a scrawny loner watching the videos as he strummed his new-used electric guitar, it was the real deal. The American dream, eighties-style.

We just wanted to be heroes. Rock-gods. Legends, like the rockers we watched in videos. And with time stretching out before us, there was no doubt that we'd eventually arrive.

MOB RULES

"Choose yah!"

It began with a fight.

Well, we didn't actually fight, but we were planning on it.

It was a suburban sunny Tuesday at Orion Junior High, the boxy linoleum fortress that serviced the local high school. Three o'clock was the historically established fight time, just as school let out for the day.

Here's how it worked. To lay down a challenge, a kid needed only to walk up to his opponent and utter the time-honored phrase: 'choose you'.

Choose yah.

Who knows the origin? Perhaps it was meant to stand for 'I choose to call you out' or 'You either choose to fight or be forever labeled a coward'. Whatever the specifics, the phrase was always uttered in public, most commonly in front of a disputed young female. It seems ironic that the word 'choose' would be involved in any way, considering the fact that after being chosen, one had very little choice at all.

On this particular day, I was unfortunate enough to be smitten with a feather-haired blonde named Christie. She was soft and tan, and looked great in her gym shorts. Christie was hot enough to be pursued by upperclassmen and was in all likelihood out of my league.

The guy who sat behind me in history class was an unfamiliar dude named James who walked with a bench-press strut and was reputed to actually be friends with a couple of the tenth grade girls. He had curly permed blondish red hair and a stocky build that, when coupled with his challenged height, could only be described as 'squat'. We didn't know each other. As fortune would have it, he was similarly smitten with Christie.

To put the last first, she didn't like either of us and wound up dating someone infinitely more popular. At the time, however, we were still both enrapt in a note passing and late afternoon phone call bonanza to win her curvy blonde affection. I would spend fourth period knowing he was behind me, burning holes through me with his gaze as I passed back handouts and quizzes.

On this day, I dropped the pile of papers back on his desk, inadvertently spilling the lot on the floor. James responded by promptly gripping the back of my neck with his hand.

I knocked away his arm. We both stood, eye to eye.

"Choose yah!"

Good God, he'd actually said it! I'd been 'chosen'!

Having heard the hallowed words, the entire class turned in unison to log my response.

"Fine," I told him instinctively. "Three o'clock, by the tracks."

"Pshht. Fine."

My form was questionable; the time and location were a given and didn't need to be mentioned. James didn't look a bit intimidated.

Following an appropriately prolonged glare, we both sat back down, surrounded by the smirks of our classmates, knowing that as soon as the bell rang, the halls would be buzzing with fight talk. I was too unsettled to bask in the fleeting moments of notoriety.

I plodded out of the classroom ahead of him, watching as the glossy-lipped gossip patrol burst out of class and began spreading the word of the afternoon's coming festivities. I didn't look back.

By the time I reached my locker, my neighborhood buddies were waiting for me, already placing bets. My perpetually tan buddy Kevin was the first to speak up.

"You fighting James Graves?"

"Yep," I answered, my stomach already double-knotting. It was an odd thing to say. I didn't even know his last name.

"I got ten bucks on James," he grinned.

"Yeah? Thanks for the support."

"Just kidding, man."

"Yeah."

Kevin was amused. He'd been around long enough to know that I was pissing my pants.

"Don't worry, Mark. We'll be there to drag you home when it's over."

My own friends were betting against me. I suppose that tells you what you need to know about my God-given toughness. Not that I couldn't fight…in fact, I had no idea. I simply hadn't done it before. I'd seen dozens of brawls out by the railroad tracks, but so far had never been a lucky contestant. Size can be inherited and reputation fabricated, but toughness is earned through experience, of which I possessed none.

Untested, I had no clue about the extent of my destructive capacity. Judging by the junior high odds-makers, I didn't have a chance.

Until then, my method had been to surround myself with a couple of really tough friends--dudes who *liked* to fight. Basically, the idea is to hang out with people tougher than yourself, gain loyalty and then delegate. If successful, your tough friends will perceive threats against you as a call to duty and defend you instinctively. Tom Sawyer-ing is a truly effective means of survival for those charismatic enough to implement it.

And yet, once the hallowed phrase 'choose yah' has been uttered, you're on your own.

The school set alight with fight talk. Many were planning to ditch class during final period to get advance seating. You could count on a quarter of the school to show up for a football game. Nobody ever missed a fight.

It's a bit strange to see the giddiness and amusement created by the thought of your own demise--everyone seeing you in a brand new way, imagining for the first time the image of you black-eyed and bloodied...and liking it.

Popular or unpopular, people are always willing to watch you get your ass kicked. These are the life-lessons they didn't teach in school.

Fear of Humiliation 101. The World Has No Pity 200.

Perhaps not as significant as algebra, but they're pass/fail, and never forgotten.

So I couldn't bail. Not even.

At least I was bright enough to realize that avoidance would only make the situation worse. I had to go through it now or be forever penned with the Scarlet P. The small part of me without fear was wondering what the worst could really be.

So I strutted out the heavy steel doors and into the afternoon autumn sun like a prize fighter in the spotlight, heading to the ring with twenty-some people following directly in my wake. I was puffed up like a revolutionary on his way to the guillotine, oddly enticed by the thought of the whole school paying attention to me. This, I sensed, was probably as good as it would get.

It felt great, too--until I saw James tromping out and rolling up his sleeves, followed by an entourage twice the size of my own. The mob was gaining members as it crept toward the railroad tracks, heady fight fans hopping the chain link fence in numbers like soccer hooligans rushing the field.

The tracks were the popular fight spot for two reasons. Being just outside official school property, we couldn't be suspended for fighting if caught. The most our beleaguered vice-principal could do was break up the fight and disperse the crowd. And the dirt lot in the shadow of the bridge was roomy and accommodating, holding the school's population far better than the gymnasium, complete with a hill for stadium seating and a towering cottonwood tree for the sky-box elevated view. These seats were distributed on a 'king of the hill' basis.

Everyone showed. It was an impressive array, a demographic masterpiece that crossed all boundaries and classes. This was as much of a melting pot as we'd ever find. Jocks and band geeks, cigarette-puffing freaks and undersized underclassmen coming together, united for a common purpose. The trend-setters and the outcasts side by side, the classes swirled and mingled, the cliques and ostracism momentarily forgotten in deference to the promise of free live violence.

Fist-violence, that is. No guns, no knives.

It was the eighties, and the suburbs. Ye olden days. A simpler time and a simpler place, before the advent of automatic weapons in the classroom.

These were fistfights, old style. Plain and simple, traditional 'fist meets face' dukers, two young bulls pounding it out in clouds of dirt. No death, no hospitalization. Bloody noses and black eyes were the war wounds--public humiliation did the lingering damage.

It sounds mild. By most standards, it probably was. But when taking the long walk for the first time, it didn't feel so peachy.

Comely Christie was in her element. She enjoyed her part in the chaos, bragging how the fight belonged to her and using the stage to impress the studly upperclassman she'd been pining over. In the midst of my plague of self-doubt, I'd almost forgotten about her. The sight of her dyed blonde hair and perfectly straight nose offered little inspiration; she seemed an utterly different girl when surrounded by her friends. They pointed and stared with amused contempt, as though knowing I was headed for defeat.

And yet there was no choice. At the very least, I had to make an appearance and get my ass kicked.

Yes, I would undoubtedly wind up the butt of many jokes, but at least I could say that I didn't back down. Butt-kicking would be forgotten. Chickening out, however, was the height of pitiful form, something that could do irreparable damage to a reputation. I'd have to take my blows.

I faced off with James, the mob forming a tight circle around us. Christie, secure in her role, took her position at the front of the circle, equal distance between.

I noticed he was shorter and not much heavier than I was, remembering something about 'the fight in the dog'.

"So…you been saying crap about me?"

James began with a question instead of a push.

I was stunned. The ball was suddenly in my court. Seeing a light to run toward, I pursued the discussion angle.

"You're the one who's been talking…"

"I didn't never say nothing," James replied, demonstrating his belief in communication over grammatical correctness.

"Well, same here," I told him. "I don't even know you, dude."

"No doubt. You neither."

"No doubt."

"So?"

I shrugged. "So…Christie was the one who told me."

We turned to look at the mischievous goddess. Christie seemed disappointed, her gloss-lipped jaw falling fast. She wasn't the arguing type and hadn't expected this much information to be exchanged.

The crowd was beginning to sense the stall. From the midst came repeated shouts of 'hit him!'. I assumed they meant me.

James puffed out his chest and balled up his fists, staring at me for a moment longer before turning on our fluffy culprit Christie and pointing a finger.

"You caused all this," he said.

She shrugged her petite little shoulders and picked at her press-on nails. "Huh-uh. As if!"

Coming from that face, 'as if' was almost hard to argue with. Still, I persevered and took my turn.

"What do you mean? You told me last night on the phone that he--"

"Tch, I'm sure," she interrupted, flexing her vocabulary. "I'm SO sure. You guys are such losers. Are you gonna fight, or not?"

I looked to my opponent. The spell broken, neither one of us felt like taking a swing anymore.

Christie flipped her hair and turned her back, not interested in defending herself. I should have known she wouldn't take the blame.

The crowd dispersed moments later, disappointed, lamenting the lack of blood. Christie was among the first to leave, her friends in tow, tailing her new target. Neither James nor I would ever really speak to her again--at least nothing beyond superficial hellos.

It was notably odd for us to begin our careers by failing to please the crowd, but we left that slathering bunch of Romans walking away from the coliseum without having even seen a blow landed or a single drop of blood.

As James and I turned back to face each other, we seemed to realize the disappointment. I thought for a moment he was going to haul off and hit me anyway--instead, he said something I never expected.

"I hear you're a drummer..."

"Well, yeah."

"You're not in school band, are you?"

I scowled. "No way."

School band, particularly marching band, was the only real way that you could play an instrument and still maintain full-on geek status. No self-respecting headbanger could even consider the thought of participating in an organized board-of-education-approved music class. The entire concept of 'band class' runs contrary to everything that is rock--you might as well just join the debate team and the chess club and forget about it.

Would Eddie Van Halen or Ozzy Osbourne play in the school band? Would our heroes have ever willingly participated in such a pseudo-fascist display of regimented horn-blowing? Would they deign to wake up at five in the morning and march around on a frozen field tooting their trumpets, giving up so much just for the opportunity to look like an even bigger geek marching around in absurd, matching uniforms at halftime of the football game? Not a chance.

Headbangers don't play in marching band. Headbangers ridicule band geeks, even the ones who are musically superior. The band geeks may very well have been better musicians and they undoubtedly possessed a higher combined grade point average...but why take on the towering stigma just to improve your skill? In rock music, skill counts for only a third of your total score--style points are far more important. Private lessons were cool. Public ones were not.

I had no idea that James was a guitarist. He didn't look much like a rocker to me. Then again, my own hair was yet to truly embrace my collar, so I suppose I had no room to talk.

"You got a kit?" he asked.

"Yeah."

"So what kind of stuff do you play?"

An important question.

"Well…hard rock," I answered. "AC/DC and stuff like that. Priest, Maiden. Metal, mostly."

The truth was, I practiced my drum kit in the basement with puffy headphones screaming, mimicking along to everything from The Beatles to Styx. This, however, was a loaded question. As it turns out, he replied:

"Cool. I'm a guitarist. We thought you listened to Journey or something…"

I chuckled. "Why is that?"

He shrugged without malice. "Dunno. Not too many true headbangers around here."

"I hear you, dude."

It turns out that we walked home in the same direction, and so we fell in step.

"We're looking for a drummer," James said to me. "You should come jam with us sometime."

And that was that.

By the way, I did listen to Journey…but it's not the kind of thing you tell people.

Hell Ain't a Bad Place to Be

I walked into the house only a day later, lugging my black Vista-lite drum kit down the stairs into an unfinished basement belonging to James' buddy Derek.

Concrete everywhere, with squared silver vents connecting to the furnace. A couple of neglected moving boxes and a third-hand couch in the corner. In the middle of the room, a square piece of old carpet, upon which rested two small amplifiers and a weathered mic stand. The air smelled of stale beer--the cheap kind.

James busily chunked around on his guitar, a red Destroyer with an ebony neck. Nice axe. I couldn't help but be impressed.

Unlike their Clapton-esque Stratocaster counterparts, Destroyers are jagged, asymmetrical beasts. Not the state of the art, of course...but cool-shaped. Kick-ass. A guitar destined to spend its days being caressed by two-note power chords, fated never to know the gentle callouses of a country musician.

Next to James stood Derek Ellis. Healthy guy. Fit and angry. Taller than either of us, light blonde, the perpetually mischievous look on his face alleviating the necessity for long hair. Derek was a punker at heart.

His guitar was an unnamed beauty, six strings stretched across a cherry red cartoon lightning bolt. Cheap quality. The cheapest, actually. Likely constructed in a sweat shop somewhere across the globe. The thing was never quite in tune. It DID, however, look like a lightning bolt.

They were busily hacking their way through an old AC/DC tune called "Hell Ain't a Bad Place to Be."

Derek looked up first. "Dude."

James made a sour face as he let the grind resonate into feedback, grinning at the squeal.

"Dude," I replied.

"Alright!" James pulled the strap over his head and leaned his axe up against his amp, pocketing the pick. "Nice, man--you can set up right over here. You need some help?"

"Well, I still got the cymbals and hardware out in the car...and everything else."

"Your dad bring you?"

"Yeah."

"Cool."

The three of us bounced up the stairs, plodding past Derek's single mother in the kitchen. Nice lady. Attractive, I guess, but perpetually work-weary. I was told to call her Renee. She smoked constantly and never seemed to mind the noise, smiling without comment as we bounced back through with the equipment moments later.

I set up my drum kit while James and Derek banged away on another three-chord AC/DC favorite called "Whole Lotta Rosie," a tribute to large women and indiscriminate sex.

"42–39–56 - you could say she got it all!"

Derek screeched into the microphone in manufactured falsetto, his Bon Scott impression falling a bit short. I had to admit, though, what he lacked in talent he more than made up for in attitude. Derek bore a thug-next-door smile, and his clothes always looked like he'd just been in a fight. Nicely dressed, but always untucked or unbuttoned, one sleeve up and the other down as though he'd been shopping at Macy's 'delinquents' section.

My ears were ringing before I ever hit a cymbal. Apparently, volume was an important facet of their playing--these guys really had their priorities straight.

Volume…the friend of amateur guitarists, the beloved bene-factor of the marginally talented. The louder the better. Screaming high end mostly, without the advent of the bass filling the bottom end, pedal-manifested distortion crunch, levels turned to full bleed and pushing the pre-owned speakers to the limits of clarity. All mistakes would be disguised, entire missed chords swept away in the churn of sweet ear-bleeding decibels. Singing, playing, soloing--everything sounds better with a little bit o'butter.

Chunk-a chunk-a chunk chunk.

Ahh, the bliss of a properly dirtied guitar and a muted power chord going chunk-a chunk in your ear and begging for a beat. Crunchy und dandy.

"Wait, wait. How about this one?"

Chunk-a chunk…Chunk-a chunk.

James scraped out the intro to "Highway to Hell."

Chunk-a chunk, chunk-a chunk, daa cha-chunk.

I picked up the beat quickly, reverting to the good old standard four-four 'boom, tap, boom, tap'. To their ultimate surprise, I rec-ognized the song they were attempting to play.

Chunk-a chunk - boom, tap - chunk-a chunk - boom, tap.

Adolescent nirvana. Pure exaltation as the guitar chunks and the drum beat connect for the first time, coinciding to sound like something very closely resembling the actual song.

Derek barked stunted lyrics into the microphone, his face glazed with the sweetness of the moment.

James chunk-a chunked faithfully, banging his head.

Never had the song sounded so sweet. I'd heard "Highway to Hell" at least a hundred times and never before had I enjoyed it as much as the mind-splittingly loud version we managed to produce that day.

OUR version, complete with train-wreck ending. Horrible, but ours.

We reveled in the growling glory of the Destroyer and the cheap lightning bolt. My inspired cymbal crashes left bright dents in our eardrums. The chunk-a-chaos music leapt out, rebounding off the walls like cannon-fired pink and black racquetballs, colliding in an explosion of crunchy metal-goodness.

The song ended before it was supposed to, crashing as Derek searched for the chords to the bridge. It's a rare thing for a new group of rockers to make it all the way through a song the first time. Inevitably, the confounded bridge is the tripwire that sabotages the mimicry. Playing the beginning of a song is simple--continuing through to the end requires practice.

Bridge or no bridge, we were ravenous. We wanted more.

"Kick ass! What else?"

"What else?"

"Something harder?" Derek suggested.

I assumed that he meant 'harder' grittier, and not 'harder' more difficult.

Realizing that my drumming was still under scrutiny, I wanted to suggest something appropriate. I played along with the albums at home, so I was familiar with quite a few songs. The selection, however, was a different matter. Few of my practice selections were cool enough to be blurted out.

Tom Petty, respectfully, would have been too mild.

REO Speedwagon? Huh-uh.

Styx? A genuine risk--Derek didn't seem like the Styx type.

Pat Benatar would have been my ticket out, the ultimate embarrassment. Good God, I would never have even admitted I LISTENED to Benatar, much less that I knew the drum parts.

I couldn't look like a pussy. I had to choose something that lived up to the burly metal reputation--after all, there was much more than my drumming being judged here. With Derek and James still under the impression that my musical tastes were a little too wimpy for their standards, this was my chance to prove myself.

"How about Judas Priest?" I asked, coming upon the perfect suggestion. For crunchy metal goodness and butch simplicity, Judas Priest was the ringer. Easy to play and cool enough to let them know exactly where I was coming from.

Derek and James looked up from their humming amps, grinning in unison. With two words, I'd passed the cool test.

In that moment, the band was formed.

"What song?"

"'Breaking the Law'," I breathed, squinting like Josie Wales.

Derek nodded, his lip curling. "Hell yeah…"

Another excellent choice. Totally.

The Number of the Beast

Naming the band. In theory, a seemingly simple task. In practice, an absolute bitch, especially for musicians.

Imagine yourself left with the opportunity to choose your own name, to mark yourself with a brand of your own, a title by which you will now and forever more be known.

Now imagine having to accomplish this task with the mandatory cooperation of three or four other people--each of whom would themselves be required to bear the name as well.

Now imagine that these people are musicians. The horror.

Naming the band. It's harder than you might think. Band names always seem easily concocted for others, and yet impossible to think up for yourself.

So you brainstorm. You find a piece of paper, sit down with your ballpoint and make a list. You jot, you think, you jot. You write down every animal and mythical beast you know, leaving out the obvious and the uncool. You add colors to the wildlife. You write down single-word concepts and afflictions like faith and suicide. You write down dark Tolkien-esque words like sabre and moonblade. You jot like hell.

And then you stop and take a look at what you've written. You try to imagine yourself being in a band named Orc's Bane. You try to picture how Whyte Wolf will look on a T-shirt.

Thank you, goodnight…we're Steel Falkon!

Horrifying. You begin to realize that perceived cool and actual cool are not the same thing. When you take a moment to picture yourself performing under the name Hot Stuff or Explosive Heir, it becomes sickeningly ridiculous.

That's the word for it: ridiculous. Naming a heavy metal band is a ridiculous act.

Suddenly, you're struck with inspiration. Go with the ridiculous thing. You've always admired the bands that didn't take themselves too seriously, and you're a musician, so surely you can come up with something that's undeniably clever. Go clever.

So you jot, you think, you jot. You write down lesser known clichés and bathroom wall innuendo. You jot, thinking of The Rolling Stones, Cheap Trick, The Who. You try to go creative and only manage to jot down moderately clichéd things like Sudden Death and Fair Game. The jotting quickly degrades into Summons, Bastard Four, and Pickle Whip.

Ack.

Despite the fact that you're a musician, your brainstorm has netted a steaming pile of brain turd. You've drained yourself of profound notions and are forced to return to the group with little direction.

Now imagine three musicians in a basement, spewing out moronic ideas. They all have a vision. The world is at stake, and nobody brought a pen.

So you mentally jot. You encourage the collective brainstorm, and the turds begin to fly.

"Furious."

"Doomsayer…"

"Stryker X!"

"Hell's Breach."

"What?"

"Hell's Breach. Hell's Breach!"

"Wait, wait. What's a Hell's Breach?"

Derek shrugged. "Well…it's like a breach, dude. In hell. Self-explanatory."

"Do you even know what a breach is?"

"Yeah. You know, a breach. A breach in your shorts."

"Now there's a song title," I couldn't help interjecting. "Breach in my shorts…"

"Okay, how about Hell's Chosen?" Derek offered, sticking to the devilish theme.

James crunched up his face. "Nah. Too evil, dude."

"A bit…"

So we brainstormed on, calling upon the dark clouds of our imagination to summon forth mighty lightning bolts of inspiration. We grabbed the muses by their supple glowing throats and demanded that they bring down the raining storm of brain. In reality, we provoked little more than a light cerebral drizzle.

The titles all fit in one of five simple categories: 'too cheesy', 'too evil', 'derivative', 'weak, but not horrible' and 'utterly stupid'.

The band resumed spewing out the best ideas they had to offer, and the categories began to fill up with wet dogs.

"Equalizer."

"What? Pshht. Weak."

"You think? Equalizer is weak?"

"Yeah. How about Three Man Gang?"

James shook his head. "Yeah, but we're adding a bass player."

"Oh yeah…only…Four Man Gang doesn't sound right."

"Better than three, dude. Three isn't even a gang. Three is like, a trio."

"Dude, I think you have to have at least five people to be a gang…"

"Is that true?"

"Think so. Four would be a quartet."

"How about Skin Tight?" I ambushed them with one of my better ideas.

They paused.

"I like that," James told me, airing a guitar riff. "But not for the band. Good name for a song. I got you skin tight, baby…vrrrt, vrrrt vrttt, dow-da vrrrt!"

"Yeah, good song name," Derek seconded. "Just not with those rank lyrics. And I'd have to sing it…"

James rolled his eyes. "Your singing bites."

"So?"

"I got one…how about Squealer?"

"Squealer?"

"Yeah."

"That's an AC/DC song, dude."

"Well, yeah. Kicks ass, too. But it's a song name, not a band name."

"People would know we stole it from them."

"Some people would…but it would be like a tribute thing."

Derek shook his head. "No way, dude. I'm not paying tribute to shit. Besides, they'd think we were trying to copy--"

"Pshht." James rolled his eyes. "No, they wouldn't."

"They would, dude."

"Yeah, right…"

"Well then, why don't we just name ourselves 'Highway to Hell'?" Derek asked, crystallizing his point. "How's that?"

"Fine, fine--I get it."

"Let's just move on," I said, struggling to come up with a suitable alternative. At this rate, we were likely to hobble away with a name like Black Ruby of Death.

"Greed Mongers," I said, pulling it from the extreme shallows of my imagination and throwing it aground.

Another pause.

My ideas were less frequent, but seemed to have a calming effect.

"Not bad..."

"Another great song name," James vetoed. "Mark, you rule at coming up with the song titles."

"Assault!"

"Nah. There's already an Assault. From Denver. How about The Thorn Birds?"

"It's a novel," I piped in.

"Nah--that's a mini-series with Burt Reynolds," Derek corrected.

"Richard Chamberlain, dude."

"Whatever. What about Dragon's Scab?"

This was too dumb for words. James and I stared back.

"Seriously?"

"...Yeah."

"Too...Dungeons and Dragons-y," James answered. "And the 'scab' part is too punk. Bloody Scab, on the other hand..."

"Nah. Serpent's Kiss?"

"Too cheesy," I said.

"Something with serpent, then..."

"No serpents, man. The Dirty Boys?"

I winced. "No way. Not even..."

"No doubt. That's way too wussy." Derek was the barometer. He wasn't the best at thinking them up, but he knew a dog when he smelled one.

"How about something like Demolition?"

"Eh….almost, but no," James said. "No verbs. A band can't be a verb."

"Demolition isn't a verb," I spoke up. Some mistakes I couldn't bear.

He rolled his eyes. "Well, it sounds like one…"

Derek paced, thinking so fervently that we could almost smell the smoke.

"Agent Orange?"

"Better…but it's taken, I think."

"It's taken, dude."

"White Tiger?" I offered, knowing it sucked.

"Hell no!" Derek hated it. "Are you kidding? No chick band names! And no colors in the name, either. Everybody does that."

Granted, colorful names were popular. Rock already had a Whitesnake and was soon to include White Lion. But it was among local bands that the colors were truly coveted. White Night, Red Death, Black Roses, Whyte Lightning. Yecch. I should have known better.

As per the budding heavy metal tradition, misspellings were wholly encouraged, as long as they included proportionally cool letter replacements, e.g.: Def Leppard, Stryper, Kix. 'Y' replaces 'i.' 'Z' replaces 's,' as in Boyz, Whyte Noyz, Girl Toyz. Kewl spelling.

"Come on, dude. Don't tell me you can actually picture yourself playing in a band called White Tiger…"

I chuckled at the thought. "Well, no."

Derek produced a can of chew and snapped it with his finger to pack it down. He opened the lid, and the unmistakable stench of Copenhagen wafted out, distinctive and pungent. Derek took a big pinch and inserted it into his bottom lip, brushing the sticky sweet clingers from his face. He picked up a formerly abandoned soda can and spit into it.

"I don't like cans," he commented. "I can't see the spit."

"Have you showed Mark your spittoon?" James asked.

Derek grinned proudly, p-tewing the bits of chew from his lips. "Not yet. Lemme get it."

He bounded up the stairs and returned moments later carrying a two-liter bottle full of what was unmistakably chew spit.

Jug o'spit. Viscous, putrid, semi-transparent brown expectoration...in volume. The previously chewed bits floated in the mouth syrup like tiny flakes in a crystal snow globe. Thankfully, the cap was on. One whiff would have been enough to clear the room.

"I've been saving this since last summer..." Derek held up the bottle to the light, proudly examining the contents.

"That's just plain nasty," James chuckled. "That thing is a health hazard just waiting to happen."

Derek nodded, p-tewing. "My pride and joy, man."

"I thought your guitar was your pride and joy..."

"Well...yeah. Ok. I guess the guitar is the joy and the spittoon is the pride. Wait, wait--I got it!"

"What?"

"Naked Doom!"

Naked Doom. Two words, which, when put together, evoked a smorgasbord of unsettling images. I laughed out loud.

Derek didn't laugh. He wasn't joking.

"Naked Doom?" James asked, repeating as though merely saying the words was a rebellious act. "Nah."

He hated it. So did I. Original, but horrible. Uniquely bad.

"Why not?"

James shrugged. "I don't know...it just sounds to me like a bunch of naked gay Vikings with swords."

Derek didn't see it that way and the implication offended him. "No way. Naked Doom is fucking cool. And there's no such thing as a gay Viking."

It took us two weeks to convince Derek that Naked Doom sucked. We eventually settled on the name Blind Faith.

Oops.

Two weeks later, we were informed by Derek's sister that Eric Clapton had used the name Blind Faith long ago, with considerable success. Bastard.

Youth Gone Wild

K eg parties.
An American tradition.

Keg parties are means by which young minds wean themselves from mere childish mischief and begin committing more adult forms of naughtiness like binge drinking and promiscuous sex. A pre-school for the bar circuit, a kindergarten for clubbers, a way to prepare ourselves for the rabid local club scene.

The band had been jamming garage-style for months, performing for exclusive groups in the basement and honing our chaotic craft to a dull edge before deciding to finally branch out. We needed a bigger stage and a real audience. Keg parties seemed the next logical step.

And so our debut gig was performed in the cozy confines of a middle-class suburban domicile, surrounded by affordably priced furniture and matching throw pillows. A residence. Somebody's home, bordered by a neatly trimmed lawn, labeled with a hand-crafted plaque on the door that read 'The Smiths'. The place was loaded with quaint little knick-knacks and country kitchen kitsch.

The parents, of course, were on a short vacation, leaving their responsible teenage daughter Sherrie home and in charge of the house. We arrived about four-thirty, long before the party was set to begin.

"Where do you guys want to set up?" Sherrie's pudgy-lidded eyes always seemed bright, as though a black-lite bulb was burning inside her head.

We looked around, acting as though we knew what we were doing.

"Ummm," Derek stood in the family room, looking for a decent stage. "The dining room looks good."

"We'll move the table and chairs."

"Okay," Sherrie chirped without hesitation. "We can put the furniture in the garage, I guess."

Sherrie was a big girl. She was round and friendly, usually dressed in bright colors under faded denim. Never risking anything too tight or revealing, Sherrie always did her best to keep up with the skinny little pretty girls while attempting to conceal her weight. Riding the preppie fence, she was neither heavy-metal nor new-wave, taking no fashion risks that would detract from her warmth or risk drawing ridicule.

Sherrie would be best described as semi-popular. Quasi-popular. One of the chunky but amiable chicks who were generally liked despite the extra pounds, known for being friends with everyone and girlfriend to no one. A blind-date candidate.

I always liked Sherrie because she smiled a lot. She beamed like she couldn't help it. Not in a fake way, either. Her smiles were genuine and contagious. Sherrie was a survivor, using her indefatigable personality and propensity for alcohol to counter any ostracism. Everyone likes a big happy drunk, I suppose.

I guess she'd be called normal. And, like any normal girl, Sherrie had been anticipating her parents' absence for weeks.

Keg-party time.

Sure, it was risky. By allowing eighty-some drunken teens into her home, she was likely to find serious trouble with her parents.

But the tremendous upside was well worth the gamble. By holding a successful keg party, she stood to gain scores of cool points and respect, not only with her own class but also with the hallowed upper classmen and the pretty girls she had to contend with every day in the halls.

For the moment, at least, Sherrie would be the focal point of the entire school's attention, the most talked about individual of the weekend. Her reward would be a moment in the glorious sunlight of popularity, a far greater accomplishment than her spot on the high school yearbook staff or her recent election as student body vice-president. If done right, people would remember Sherrie's rager for years to come. Our band was to be the icing on her popularity cake, insuring that hers would be the event of the semester.

We were just happy to play.

She waved a hand like Vanna White turning letters, allowing us unrestricted access to her house and granting full license to move whatever furniture we wished. We set to work moving the dining room set into the garage, using reasonable caution not to nick or scratch it, placing it with care beside the lawnmower.

"What about that dish display thing?"

"Nah, leave it," James replied, staring down the china cabinet. "Too much trouble."

"Yeah."

Sherrie appeared visibly relieved, bouncing off to answer the doorbell.

As we set up the equipment, Sherrie's closest friends arrived, already primped and primed for the night's festivities. She gave big hugs. They pulled super-thin cigarettes from their little purses and glommed in high-heeled mini-cliques in the kitchen.

The keg, otherwise known as the guest of honor, was yet to make its appearance.

Band or no band, beer was the lure. It goes without saying.

The trick, however, was obtaining the keg. It would have to be purchased and transported from the local liquor store, a steep challenge even in the liberal 'no ID required' eighties. After all, it wasn't every day that a seventeen-year-old could march into a liquor outlet and purchase a six-pack, much less pay for an entire keg of beer. Sherrie, however, knew its ultimate importance and wouldn't let a minor obstacle like age deter her from her moment of triumph.

For Sherrie had an older brother, an invaluable resource in the burbs. Her brothers were not yet old enough for the hard stuff, but this was the eighties, when there existed a fine concoction known as 3.2 beer. A subject worthy of discussion.

3.2 beer.

Thanks to the beer companies' masterful plan to facilitate beer sales to those UNDER the age of twenty-one, we were not only allowed, but encouraged to drink. The drinking age for hard liquor and the well-respected 'adult' 6.0 beer was twenty-one, but the State Legislature had been generous enough to make the drinking age only eighteen for the 3.2 variety.

Eighteen was the promised land.

Good for business, good for America. 3.2 beer. 3.2 bars. 3.2 commercials in which studly young men danced on beaches with bikini clad models and a little white pit bull named 'Spuds McKenzie' lounged on a blanket, flanked by cleavage. The beer companies had found their new demographic group, and the government approved.

Sherrie's elder brother Trace had been eighteen for more than two months, finding himself in the enviable position of being able to buy as much 3.2 beer as he wanted without any repercussion. Her little brother was only fifteen, but he possessed a passable fake I.D. and was more than gutsy enough to accompany the treasure hunt.

It took both of them to transport the golden prize and bring it back. They stood to make around three hundred bucks for the effort, more than enough to cover the cost and pay the small deposit. We were just completing our setup as the brothers returned with the keg and a few hundred plastic cups.

The younger of the two, John, would be the cup-man. As the party guests stumbled in, he would collect a five dollar cup fee and mark the paying customers with a magic-marker star on the back of their left hands. Five bucks a cup.

Trace would be the keg marshal. His duties would include hawking over the keg, selectively pouring cups and determining when pumping was necessary. He would defend the treasure and its plastic tap, doling out lukewarm froth to whoever had the patience to wait. One tap, and one dude to service all those cups. They lined up like Sneetches. But stars or no stars, Trace determined who would drink and how often they would be re-filled. He could serve his own friends first and the rest of the crowd at his discretion.

The keg was set up in the backyard, placed carefully in a trash can and surrounded by a couple of bags of supermarket ice. Trace sat on a stool beside it, smoking cigarettes and holding a SuperSlushy cup filled with beer.

I gripped my complimentary cup and approached with some trepidation, not knowing what Trace would think about the long-hairs set up in his mom's dining room. I was actually worried that he'd snub me. You see, I didn't yet realize the first benefit of rock band membership: People you don't even know will pretend to be your friend. And they'll give you things for free.

Things like cups. And beer.

As soon as Trace saw me, he lifted his arm to wave me forward, parting the crowd with a flick of his hand. As shocked as the rest of the keg crowd, I strolled up and handed him my cup. They were all watching me.

"You guys about ready to jam?" he asked, mouthing his cigarette as he poured my brew.

"Oh yeah."

"Kick ass. Jam good, buddy."

He handed it back, well-filled. The crowd parted to facilitate my exit.

Trace couldn't have helped me more. He was out of school and had been the one to acquire the keg. Suddenly, twenty-some witnesses were thinking Trace and I were friends from way back or that I routinely hung out with him. I was his buddy now. I hadn't even played a single beat, and I'd already been transformed. A nice feeling, by the way. I returned to the setup and immediately told James and Derek to go get some beer.

Without the dining room table, there was just enough room for our equipment. I set up the drum kit at least a foot away from the china cabinet, far enough that I'd have to fall back into it to do any damage. Sherrie didn't seem to mind.

As the sun faded away and the kids escaped in their dads' vehicles, the cul-de-sac filled with slow moving traffic, drive-by lookers and parked cars. Word was spreading quickly, from the parking lot of the Gas-n-Go to the smoking section of the Taco Shack. Before the night was over, the parking would be three blocks thick.

The house soon filled up with jean-jacketed dudes and their heeled female counterparts, the initial wave of close friends already having downed their first beer and working on their second. All of them stopped to look at us as we tuned our guitars and tried to act as though we'd done it all before. Even then, almost as if by instinct, we learned that professionalism and bullshit are hard to distinguish sometimes.

Not to say that we could really call ourselves a band.

Two guitarists, and one drummer. That's all. No vocals, no singing…no bass guitar. With the immaculate exception of The Doors, it is metaphysically impossible to have a rock band without a bass player. Skill is optional. Presence, however, is generally required.

The crowd grew thick at the sound of distorted guitar. James chunked a power chord, a rippling murmur spreading through the ranks and setting off a couple of whistles. The upperclassmen were starting to arrive. The older girls were watching from a distance, red-lipped and curious.

I hit the kick drum a couple of times and drew a few more whistles.

Now was the moment of truth. Two guitars and a drummer. No band, no vocals. No problem.

Derek cranked his amp, turning away from a piercing squeal of feedback and scratched out the intro chords to "Highway to Hell."

And they cheered. Cheered like we were real.

Daa daa chunk. Daa daa chunk chunk da chunk…Daa daa chunk

Boom, tap, boom tap--I hit my cue on time, sending another murmur through the crowded living room.

James followed, pointing the head of his guitar at the crowd and joining Derek in the riff. He banged his head along with the beat. The dudes in the front followed suit.

They were buying it. I realized it almost immediately.

The whole room was watching us, watching and waiting--some undoubtedly waiting for us to screw up, others apparently giving us too much credit for what we were doing. We held the attention of both friends and rivals, braving the risk of looking stupid.

James focused on his fingers, not caring if he looked stupid. I would later realize that this was a big part of his success in heavy metal. He was so worried about his playing that he didn't think too much about looking good.

Derek was more punk in his stance--rigid and pronounced. He always looked like he was snarling when he played, as though the music was bringing something bestial to the surface. He chunk-a-chunked with crusty regard.

We managed to work our way through the song with no major screw-ups, train-wrecking the ending...and receiving an ovation beyond our wildest imagination. The cheers of a hundred half-drunk minors, crammed into the living room, whooping and whistling as they peered their heads out around the dining room wall.

I wasn't kidding myself. They were cheering for the song as much as they were for the band. But something about hearing a bunch of local dudes jam "Highway to Hell" in someone's dining room just makes you want to whoop and whistle.

I wanted more. We all did.

"What's next?" Derek bounced up and down. "What's next?"

"'Livin' After Midnight'," I said with confidence.

"Sweet."

James started the riff this time, drawing another round of appreciation as soon as the crowd realized what he was playing.

We kicked into the Judas Priest song with twice the energy, rushing the tempo in our eagerness to feed the crowd, blasting through the screw-ups without thinking twice. I could hear our friends singing along in unison and wished I had a microphone.

Heads bobbed.

Bimbos bounced.

China rattled.

Beer spilled.

Utter joy. Unabashed bliss. Hell yeah.

We continued to churn out the melody-less tunes, the chunk-a-chunk doing its job to keep the curious faces coming. Sherrie's brothers stood talking by the screen door in the kitchen, dividing up the cash. I looked over to see them gesturing back with the devil-horned headbanger salute.

Sherrie was enjoying her moment in the sun--perhaps a bit too much. She was breaking one of the cardinal rules of throwing a kegger: Don't be the biggest drunk at your own party. She was bouncing around with the best of them, downing liberally with her own keg privileges. Sherrie was a pleasant drunk, a happy, bubbling, charming little chirp of a drunk. None of us had the heart to tell her she was bordering on foolish; it was her moment after all.

The band, however, was loud. Enormously loud. Disturbingly loud. It seemed impossible that the neighbors could tolerate this kind of noise for very long. Combined with the parking lot in the cul-de-sac, our siren song was certain to lure the police. And when they arrived, everyone knew whose head would be on the block.

Sherrie didn't mind. She was oblivious to consequence at this point, polishing her fourth cup of beer and joining the other girls in their coy appraisal of our act.

Ravenous for more attention, we kept playing. I hit the cymbals with purpose, staring past their dirty copper edges at our crowd. I saw newfound admiration in some of the eyes. Others offered budding envy, disguised as a smirk. The wrestling lettermen chuckled and pretended not to notice, but I saw the second glances their girlfriends were passing back to me.

No doubt.

Upperclassmen. Girls to whom I'd been invisible hours earlier, suddenly giving me second and third thoughts. What had changed? I looked the same as I had that morning. I was the same person, with the same scrawny arms. I was still an underclassmen to these mature beauties. And yet, tonight I was notable.

Notable. Cuter. More popular. And all it took was a bad, lyrically absent version of "Ain't Talkin' Bout Love" to put my virginity in serious jeopardy. My libido did pushups, the kind where you clap in-between.

The rager continued at perilous pace. Things were beginning to get broken. Sherrie was busy now, drunkenly chasing amorous couples out of her parents' bedroom and cleaning up the broken remnants of her mother's corn husk dolls. Little brother John was out of cups and was no longer taking money at the door. Trace was still dutifully marshalling the near-depleted keg, determined to get his deposit back and pocket a few extra bucks.

But as word spread around town, the crowd kept coming. Sherrie's cul-de-sac looked like a high school car show--filled with rows of shining muscled Mustangs and Camaros, jacked up pickups and open-air Jeeps, the collective display of sweet sixteen automotive gifts proudly exhibited, windows down and tunes pumping.

It didn't last.

The police arrived just as our set-list began to dwindle. Four cruisers with rollers flashing.

The authorities went by the suburban kegger playbook. First, they blocked off the cul-de-sac and set up an impromptu DUI checkpoint, trapping the myriad of unfortunates who lacked the foresight to park on the next block over. Then, in suburban swat formation, the cops walked up the street toward Sherrie's house.

Sherrie came running down the stairs, beet-faced and screaming at us to stop playing. We relented, bringing our reckless train to a halt.

"Oh my God, you guys, I am SO busted!" Sherrie wailed big time, as though she hadn't been expecting this.

"Nah, you're cool," James told her, unable to hide his disappointment. "You're a girl, so they won't do anything to you. This party's toast, though."

Brother Trace was already in motion, hiding the keg in his father's pre-fab aluminum tool shed. Distributing alcohol was a more serious offense than drinking it, but despite the proliferation of plastic cups, nothing could be proven without the presence of actual beer. No keg, no bust. He'd done this before.

We stared down at our warm equipment, disappointed but still riding the high. With all our gear in her dining room, the band certainly wasn't going to escape the police. It didn't matter. We were underage and numerous. Experience told us that the police posed no threat.

Nobody ran. Nobody really even moved until the police were actually in the house. There would be no arrests now, but the cops at the end of the street would certainly manage to plaster a few DUI's on the stragglers of the retreating horde. Like reluctant protesters, the rager dispersed slowly, the guests knowing that there was safety in group lawlessness. The only person who really had anything to fear was Sherrie.

Poor, inebriated Sherrie. She was in no condition to be talking to the cops, and all but her closest friends were bailing on her.

One of the officers cast an amused look and approached. His belt squawked with white noise.

Derek let loose with one final power chord, grinning.

"Shut it down, guys," the cop ordered, appropriately stiff.

"Yessir," Derek answered with another grin, flicking the switch on his amp. "I didn't know it was still on."

"Load it up and get out of here."

James looked out the front window. "Too many cars out there, Officer. See, we gotta pull our truck in to load up. You guys will have to clear 'em out before we can pull in--"

"Just get moving." The officer scowled back, seemingly not too happy about taking orders from a kid in an Ozzy T-shirt. "We'll clear the street."

Apparently, this was the 'serve' portion of the 'protect and serve' job description. The cops had cleared the cul-de-sac in less than fifteen minutes. Soon the only people left in the house were Sherrie, her best friend, the authorities, and us. First to arrive, last to leave. Band members get to see both ends of a party.

Sherrie cried and blubbered her way out of serious trouble; the keg was missing and no one had been hurt. The cops had done their duty to the neighborhood, and all that remained was to leave Sherrie with a ticket for disturbing the peace and possession of al-cohol. They departed before we finished tearing down the gear, tipping their hats and promising to stop by and have a talk with Sherrie's parents later that week.

The coffee table glass was shattered and laying in thousands of crystals on the floor. The carpet was stained in places and burned by cigarettes in others. One bathroom smelled of vomit and the other of urine, and someone had dropped a beer bottle in the fish tank. All in all, the damage was rather light.

Still, we expected Sherrie to be in emotional turmoil. There would certainly be a few harrowing moments of explanation in her future, and she seemed relatively inexperienced where trouble was concerned. But as the cop cars finally pulled away, Sherrie lit a ciga-rette, reached for her beer and returned quickly to her bubbly self, as though knowing the punishment would be well compensated. She'd been kissed earlier, and nothing was going to spoil the moment.

We went home that first night riding on a mild beer buzz and a potent shot of pure ego. We babbled and rambled, vocalizing our enthusiasm over and over again, enjoying every fresh memory and wanting nothing more than another taste of glory. It was late, but the adrenalin was still racing in my veins, leaving my stomach in contented knots and my eyes wide awake.

I ran to my room and closed the door behind me, single-minded.

I strapped on my guitar, not bothering to plug it in. I threw a red T-shirt over the lamp and put on my headphones, setting needle to vinyl and cranking the volume. Then, standing before the full length mirror, I proceeded to air-guitar the entire first side of KISS's *Alive II* album, mouthing every word.

The audience stretched out before me, hands raised in exaltation. The upper class girls I'd fantasized about were there, watching in admiration as I jammed along with Ace Frehley and Gene Simmons. In my mirror there lurked a world of endless arenas and stadiums, all of them begging for the sound of my voice.

LOSERS AND WINNERS

left my drum kit in Derek's basement, my new home away from home.

It was a beauty of a practice space by any standard, decorated with rock posters and Derek's impressive collection of empty beer cans from around the globe. The concrete walls sounded acoustically perfect to our perpetually ringing ears, and the lack of air conditioning only served to fan the flames within. A giant piece of white cardboard was tacked to the wall with song titles scribbled on it--big letters in black marker.

The finishing touch was a banner, lovingly created with a bed sheet and house paint, depicting our new logo. Blood red letters spelled out SKIN TIGHT, jagged and splattered on clean linen. It looked like hell, and we loved it.

We began practicing three times a week and soon on weekends as well. The rehearsals themselves became contagious. We were leaping and bounding home from school every day, chomping at the bit to punish our ears and get our fix of jamming.

Sherrie's rager had been an overwhelming success. She'd been soaking up the attention and reminiscing at a continuous pace, reveling in the afterglow of her victory and promising another party as soon as her parents went away again. Judging by the harsh sentence she'd received, we assumed it would be a while.

And yet, after hearing about Sherrie's live entertainment, the standard of rager excellence had been permanently raised. Live music was now a must.

Suddenly, everyone wanted a band--and we were the only game in town.

Julie Dennis, Arie Martinez and Greg Daugherty were prompted by Sherrie's success to throw ragers of their own, featuring us. We played on Mike Laughlin's back lawn, in Laurie Peters' apartment clubhouse, and behind Rena Mason's garage. Kenny Richards even paid us fifty bucks to show up for his birthday party, an event that started small but grew to legendary riot-size status.

The fetching Andersen sisters were the latest to request our services. Based on the foundation of their popularity, we knew the party would be the event of the season.

"We need a bass player," James announced one afternoon, saying the words we all knew to be true.

"No doubt."

"The Doors never had a bass player," Derek countered, apparently not overly bothered by the prospect.

"Really?"

"Seriously."

James smirked. "Yeah, but they were all on acid. And they're the ONLY ones."

"Jim Morrison was cool."

"He was," I seconded, picturing old Jim flopping around on the stage as though he'd been shot.

"Jim used to whip it out on stage…and the lyrics were pretty cool."

"He was the whole band, man. You could put a bunch of chimps on stage with Morrison and he'd make them look cool. They could all jam."

"Yeah," James rolled his eyes, unimpressed, "But they still suck. And we need a bass player. We can't play songs like "Metal Health" without a bass. Besides, we don't look real without one."

It was true. There's no such thing as a band without a bass player, all Doors rhetoric aside.

"He doesn't have to be that good," James added, conceding the obvious. "It doesn't take much to play the bass."

"True."

"A, A, A, A, A, A, A, A...E, E, E, E, E, E, E, E--simple," he continued, mocking. "Anybody could play the bass. I'd do it, but I'm the lead guitarist."

Derek scowled in revelation. "Dude...I thought I was the lead."

"Well, we're both lead."

"We can't both be lead guitarist, dude. That's why it's called lead guitar. You know? Cause there's only one. Somebody has to be the rhythm guitar."

"Dude. Judas Priest has two leads..."

Derek considered it, nodding. "Okay, true."

"Iron Maiden has two leads."

"Yeah, okay."

"Yeah, and we still need a damn bass player, or else we're BOTH rhythm."

"I get it, I get it," Derek said. "So what about a singer?"

James shrugged. "I dunno. I thought you were gonna sing."

Derek picked up the empty pop can on his amp and spit into it. "Yeah--but only in practice. I'm not singing in front of people."

"But you're in choir class. Both you and Mark. Right?"

"Yeah."

"Shit," Derek chuckled. "I take choir class cuz it's an easy A, dude. I don't really sing at the recitals."

I pictured Derek in choir class, hiding behind his libretto as he pinched a dip of Copenhagen into his bottom lip. I was only marginally more serious about choir, but unlike Derek, I didn't take it for the easy grade. I took it because of the nine to one girl to guy ratio, and because I loathed P.E..

"Well, we need a bass player worse than a singer," James warned.

"Yeah."

After seeing Joe Perry of Aerosmith jamming with a cigarette propped between his lips, James had adopted a smoking habit, for image if nothing else. He lit one, practicing, talking with it between his lips like Keith Richards. "And we'd better hope that the cops break this party up, too--or else we're gonna have to repeat songs."

"Man...Jody Andersen is totally hot," Derek mused.

"Totally," I responded, forced to agree. "Jenny's not bad, either."

"Yeah...she's alright. Though her butt is like, flat, you know? It's like a foot long but it doesn't stick out at all..."

"Those kind of asses look good naked," I told him, possessing no personal knowledge on the subject beyond *Playboy* magazine.

Derek's brow furrowed in deep contemplation. "Yeah, I can see that. Do you think supermodels have flat asses? Like, for instance, does Cheryl Tiegs have a flat ass, too?"

I thought about it. "Probably. She looks like it."

"Cheryl Tiegs is too skinny, though," Derek added. "Jenny Andersen's got chubby arms. I like chubby arms."

"Derek likes 'em big."

"Not big...just chubby," he countered. "Like the angels in those art museum paintings. You know--sexy-chubby. But they've got to have tits or else the whole chubby thing gets wasted, and--"

"Were you guys even listening to me?" James burst out, insta-pissed. "Who cares about fucking Cheryl Tiegs and flat asses! Shit, you guys! We only got three weeks!"

Derek shook his head. "Dude, settle down. We're just talking. We'll find someone."

"What about Paul Lowder?" I offered. "I heard he plays bass."

"He plays in the jazz band," James said, frowning. "And he's still a freshman."

"He's a pussy," Derek chuckled. "I mean, seriously. Just looking at him makes you want to kick his ass."

"That could be a problem."

"Besides, it has to be a guy who we don't mind hanging out with. Someone who's already cool, right? I mean, I have to like the guy, you know?"

I nodded. "Yeah, I guess I couldn't stand Paul Lowder for long, either."

James shrugged. "Yeah, yeah--all well and good, you know, but you guys are missing the most important thing."

"What's that?"

"Ability?"

James shook his head. "Nah. He's gotta have the look. If he doesn't look right, it won't matter how good he is."

Derek made a disagreeable face. "The look? What, like he's supposed to be some foofed-out pretty boy?"

"I didn't say that," James replied. "But he has to look good enough to be on stage, and in photos and stuff. Seriously. Can you picture yourself standing on the cover of *Cream* Magazine beside some idiot like Paul Lowder or Alan Anderson? Or maybe some guy who's three hundred pounds, or--"

"Alan Anderson plays bass?"

James' jaw did a double clench. "No! Of course not! But he sure as hell--"

"I'm just screwing with you, man." Derek laughed, delivering a punch to James' left arm. "I hear what you're saying. Mellow out."

"You ass…"

Derek waved the headbanger salute. "Thank yah."

"So he has to look good," I said.

"That, and good equipment," James added. "His gear can't be all dime store and shit."

"Yeah," Derek seconded.

"So he has to look good and have good gear."

"And a good attitude."

"Look good, good gear, good attitude."

"Totally."

"No doubt."

We paused in a moment of collective reflection.

"Oh yeah…and he has to know how to play."

"Well…given."

"Yeah."

Rainbow in the Dark

The next Friday afternoon I had a dentist appointment and didn't get to Derek's house until just before dinner. James had officially cancelled rehearsal, but I knew that they'd be in the basement screwing around and hoped to get a few songs in before I had to go home.

As I knocked on the front door, I heard the distinctive, tonal rumbling of an electric bass.

Paul Lowder, surely. Pussy or not, James had apparently invited him over for an audition.

I tried again, my knocking utterly drowned out by the sound.

And then, another noise--a disturbing, heart-dropping sound: my drums, being played by someone else.

Played well.

Boom, tap – buggadugga tap – boom, tap – buggadugga tap.

Good God! I'd never played a buggadugga.

I could hear them laughing. I could hear the excitement of gigs to come. They were jamming with someone else...on MY drums.

Like any relationship, fidelity is important to a band. Being in a rock group is like dating two or three other people at once-- all the tempers and passions, all the planning, the future and the past, your heart and soul poured into endless hours of shared experience.

Bands are like marriages without sex.

That's not quite right. Actually, the jamming itself could be considered the sex--after all, no matter what problems or arguments are present, jamming makes it all better. It's hard to remain angry at someone when you're bashing your way through a bouncy tune. Jamming, like sex, requires the participants to forget about everything else for a while and simply enjoy the moment.

Thus, if jamming is like having sex, then jamming with an imposter on my drum kit would equate to sleeping with someone…in your old lover's bed. Insult to injury.

It wasn't the act itself that folded in my gut. When you catch your lover in bed with someone else, it isn't really the action that becomes the crime. It's the notion that your dream is being shared with a stranger. It's the broken dream that kills you.

At first, I didn't know whether to knock a second time or simply turn around and leave. My first thought was that I should leave, that I was dreaming and imagining the whole thing.

I took a breath, rationalizing.

There were, after all, rational explanations for this. There had to be. I didn't know too many other drummers, and it was entirely possible that the individual buggaduggaing in the basement was somebody's father, someone too old to be a member in the band. It could have been a cousin, visiting from out of town, or perhaps the sales guy from Drum Town stopping by to jam for a diversion…

My sixth sense told me this wasn't the case. I knew the moment I heard the first buggadug that I was about to be replaced.

The initial rush of despair was soon drowned in a flood of anger and betrayal. The thin hairs on my arms stood straight. My stomach double-clenched, faked, and clenched again. I wanted to throw up all over Derek's welcome mat and grind it in with my clean white Nikes.

They couldn't hear the doorbell. They couldn't hear the knocking. I would have had to wait until the song was finished to pound on the door, and I didn't have time to wait. Couth or not, I opened the door and stepped into Derek's house.

I raced to the basement door, imagining what I'd say, picturing the guilty looks on their faces when I marched down into the midst of this egregious infidelity.

I stomped down the stairs, trying to disguise my anger with a calm expression, eager to see who was playing the drums.

They saw me--and didn't even stop playing.

James and Derek wore their axes, crunching away with diligent pride.

Playing the bass, a lanky longhair named Tommy Hoff. He played a black Fender Precision through a shitty old amp, banging his head, posturing as he plunk-a plunked along with the guitars.

And behind my kit, a guy I'd never seen before, a tall, thick guy wearing a half-shirt and jeans. He had long, dirty blonde hair. Longer than mine.

"Hey dude!" Derek was the first to acknowledge me, and he screamed his greetings above the din.

He didn't look the slightest bit guilty. For a moment, I thought I was merely over-reacting.

James, however, looked at me, looked over at the drum kit, and then back at me. His awkward grin came slowly, and he stopped playing. The room fell quiet, only the steady buzz of an ungrounded amp accompanying us.

"Hey man," James said. "Mark, dude."

"What's up?" I asked.

That was it. None of the tirade I concocted in my head ever made it down to my lips. Raging, fuming, hurt--and all I could seem to muster was a 'what's up'.

"Nada, dude," James replied, finding his composure. I could almost smell the smoke from his working mind as he formulated an explanation. "Just jamming."

"Sup, Mark?" Tommy spoke as though he knew me. The old whassup reversal.

I shrugged. "I got done early. I thought I'd find you guys here."

"Dentist? Are your lips numb? I love that feeling."

"Nah. Just a cleaning."

My drums were being violated, and I was discussing my dental appointment.

"You love the dentist?" Derek asked, incredulous. "Not me. Man, I'd rather have surgery! At least they put you under."

"Mark, you know Tommy, right?"

"Yeah," I replied, unable to grin politely. "I didn't know you played bass. Sup, Tommy."

I shook with Tommy.

"The wild man behind the drums is Randy. He goes to East."

"Sup, Randy."

Randy raised his chin in recognition. "Sup, dude."

I could see the competitive fire burning in his eyes. Buggadugga betrayal was written all over his face.

"So…are we expanding the band, or what?" I asked, knowing James would likely never reach the point on his own.

"You never know," he answered cryptically. "Tommy's not playing with anybody right now."

He knew damn well that I could care less who Tommy was playing with. We needed a bass player. A drummer, we already had.

"I hope you don't mind me jamming on your drums," Randy commented. "They said you wouldn't mind."

"Nah," I shrugged, poker-faced. "No biggie."

No biggie. My metal heart was coming unscrewed, and I said 'no biggie'.

Randy threw in a quad on the floor toms before rising from the drum throne. "I like your kit. I'm used to playing on more drums, though…"

"Randy's got a massive double kick," James said, "and like ten toms."

"Well, yeah, only eight."

Good God, his kit was bigger than mine. As with adultery, size matters.

"It's not how big the kit is…it's what you do with it."

"Funny. What kind of kit?" I asked, compelled to know.

"A Gretsch. Purple mahogany. With Zildjian cymbals."

Purple mahogany, no less. I'd never even seen a mahogany kit, much less a purple one. My kit was constructed of fine, formed black plastic; reputable, but a far cry from colored wood.

"Wicked," I said, tensing. "You play with a band?"

Randy looked to James. "Not right now."

Tommy pointed at the clock radio and unplugged his bass. "I gotta go. My step-dad told me to be home by five."

"Yeah, cool," Randy seconded. "I should probably go, too."

I should have been happy that they were leaving, but I sensed a band discussion coming on.

I was about to be axed. James could barely look at me.

"Later, dudes," Derek shook with both of them, offering his customary guy-hug and pat. "We'll go party this weekend. My sister's going to let me take her car. We'll get a shitload of beer and go cruise."

"Sounds good to me. Later."

"Cool. Later."

Randy and Tommy echoed their laters and walked back up the stairs, leaving the three of us alone. Almost instinctively, I walked over to my kit and sat down, picking up the drumsticks. I could swear they were still warm.

James unplugged and took off his guitar. Apparently, he was through jamming for the day. He looked at me and said, "We gotta talk, dude."

The kiss of death. Rock musicians are so rarely serious. When someone calls for a band discussion, you know something bad is about to happen.

I knew what was coming, and I didn't even really require an explanation. Randy was obviously good--better than me. He had long blonde hair. He had the look, AND the skill. He had a gazillion purple mahogany drums. His kit was bigger, and he could buggadugga.

"Ok, we'll talk."

Derek reached for his can and pried a dip of chew into his lower lip. He was already working on the endless toon, part four.

"So, am I out of the band, or what?"

No need to waste time. I wanted to get right to the point.

Both James and Derek balked for a second, looking at their shoes.

"We never said you were."

"It sure seems to look that way…"

"Look, dude--I understand if you're pissed about Randy playing your drums, but we didn't think you'd mind. He didn't break nothing."

"I know."

James was thinking of a way to break it to me easily. His mastery of the language was apparently failing him.

"It's not what you think," Derek told me, spitting.

"But I'm not the drummer anymore?"

"Well, yeah...but it's not what you think."

At least Derek was being honest. He wasn't making sense, but he seemed honest about it.

I threw the drumsticks.

James shook his head. "You don't have to get all pissed, man."

My calm broke like a new toy tumbling down the stairs. "No? What the hell do you expect me to do, dude? You want me to be fucking happy, is that it?"

"You just gotta let us explain."

"What's to explain? This dude is better than me, and so while I'm at the dentist, you decide to kick me out of the band! Screw you guys..."

I started tearing down the drum kit.

"Settle down, man! We never said we were kicking you out of the band."

"What?" Now I was confused. "Derek just told me you were! He just said it, James!"

"Look--we said we needed a bass player, right? And Tommy is the best one we know. He's not that good on his instrument, but he has the look."

"So what does that have to do with the drums?"

James hesitated. "He said he wouldn't join unless we brought in Randy, too. It was both, or nothing."

"So you sacrifice me?" I shouted at him, the anger flooding forth. "This is bullshit. We could find another bass pl--"

"Randy kicks ass, and his kit is huge. Dude--he's from England."

English, no less. What else would I have to compete with?

"I didn't hear any accent."

"He was born in England, then moved to Texas when he was like two or something. He's English-Texan."

"So?" I shouted back. "Who gives a shit? I'm the drummer in this band!"

Derek walked over and put an arm around my shoulder, his tobacco breath unbearably rank. "No," he said calmly, "You're the lead singer."

The words stopped me in mid-defense.

Lead singer?

Associative visions flashed in my mind. Diamond David Lee Roth screeched like a hyena, bending backward. Mick Jagger flapped his arms like a chicken, pointing to the crowd. Steven Tyler flipped his scarf-covered mic stand around, dancing. Jim Morrison jumped as though reaching for the moon, then collapsed in a heap on stage.

I didn't reply immediately.

"We need a singer, too," James appealed to me. "You're the front man type, dude. You don't deserve to be cooped up behind a drum kit all night…"

He bore the slightest tone of condescension, as though he thought I was actually dumb enough to buy the ego ploy.

"You can sing, dude," Derek said, patting me on the back. "I hear you in choir class, and you actually sing. Besides, you're not swole enough to play drums. Drummers are butt-kickers. You're a scrawny dude, and the chicks like you. You're perfect for lead singer."

Lead singer. Lead singer. Lead singer. The words tempered my rage down to insignificance, dulling the anger and making me feel almost ridiculous. I pictured myself standing in front of the mirror, commanding the stadium full of devoted fans. I could see myself leading the band, stretching out my lungs, reaching down with my non-mic hand and touching the yearning fingers of the devotees in the front row. I thought of my voice amplified to ear-splitting volume, my picture on an album cover, centered and posed among my band mates.

"The lead singer is the whole damn show, man. We need a singer worse than anything else. Besides, you're smart, Mark. You can write lyrics."

I could. Or at least I thought I could.

"Are you guys serious?"

"I'm serious," Derek replied without hesitation.

"Totally," James echoed, reaching for his cigarettes. "You're the man, Mark. I know you can do it. So do you."

The idea of fronting a band would be exciting to anyone. The reality of it, however, is a bit terrifying. Bands are made and broken on the strength of their vocalists. A barely competent bass player could pass. A mediocre guitarist was acceptable. But a bad singer would bring the whole thing crashing to the ground like a zebra-striped Hindenburg.

"We're not saying you're a bad drummer, cuz you're not," James continued, exhaling. "But to be honest, dude, Randy kicks ass. You should see his kit…"

"He's the drummer type. You're the lead singer type. At least give it a shot. Think about it, man. We'll be a REAL band, then. Well, once we get a decent P.A., that is."

"Besides, being a singer isn't about being talented--it's about having big enough gonads to command a crowd, dude. Don't tell me you haven't thought about it…"

"Course he has," Derek chuckled, patting me on the back. "Course he has. Look at him--he's thinking about it now! You can see it in his eyes."

"I don't know…"

"Sure yah do, Mark! I think you already made up your mind."

Truth be known, other than in my bedroom mirror, I hadn't actually considered singing. But often, the oddest fantasies have a way of suddenly becoming reality.

I looked back at my kit, feeling surprisingly little remorse.

I wasn't being dumped--I was being promoted. It didn't matter that they were trying to play on my ego or lure me on stage as though it were a trick. I knew James' 'you deserve better' line was meant to provoke. Sometimes, smart is stupid. I would have been an idiot to get offended by these persuasive compliments.

James extended a hand. "So whaddya say? Are you ready to rock, dude? Are you our fucking lead singer or what?"

Jim Morrison stood center stage in my mind, bare-chested and drunk, bathed in red light, his finger extended and pointing at me. Jim dude beckoned me to join the leather-clad fraternity.

"Yeah. I'll do it," I replied simply. "I'm there, dude."

"Hell yeah!" Derek balled up his fist, hooting.

"We're a real band, now, dude!" James moved toward his guitar. "I'll call Tommy and Randy, and we'll jam all weekend! We can be ready in time for the Andersen sisters'! Start writing down lyrics, bud."

And so I became a lead singer.

Looking back, I see I really had no choice; I would probably have played friggin' tambourine if it meant staying in the band. As it turns out, my friends handed me the reins, lifting me and placing me atop the band hierarchy. They discussed it and voted me in. Singers are not born--they're nominated. Elected.

At that point, it was all in my head. Talent, be damned. I didn't even know if I'd be any good. I was untried, untested, and un-auditioned.

Lead singer, however, is not a position to be turned down.

WHAT'S NEXT TO THE MOON?

I arrived at practice early, my lyrics scratched out on scraps of notebook paper, my newly purchased Shure SM58 microphone firmly in hand. I'd been listening to the songs on tape, over and over again, trying to absorb every word in preparation.

My parents sprung for the mic, but only after I'd promised that my grades wouldn't slip. It would be an easy bargain to fulfill. Thus far, public school offered little challenge, if any. I barely needed to study and securing straight A's posed no difficulty. James and Derek were prone to occasional ditching, but I hadn't missed a day of school since my metamorphosis. I was notable now, after all, basking in the notoriety of rager afterglow, and the time spent socializing in the halls was well worth the boredom in the classroom.

My status was about to swell again. I could sense it. As lead singer, I'd be even more recognized.

Clout extension. All I had to do was pull through and sing well.

I conducted my own private rehearsals at home, accompanied only by a boom box and the loving audience that lived within my mirror. I posed and postured, holding the microphone and practicing my cool facial expressions.

Embarrassment, however, prevented me from singing out. Thus far, I'd only been able to belt a few lines in the shower. Going into rehearsal, I still wasn't sure if I could hack it.

I wanted to amaze them. I wanted the guys to realize that they'd made the right choice. I possessed more than just the look and wanted to prove it. As an ex-drummer, I knew that tempo would always be my companion. Pitch remained my only adversary.

"Sup, dude?"

"Nada. Sup?"

Derek was already banging away on his guitar, bursting into an ear-splitting, spastic solo. His style would be best described as chaotically devoted, and what he lacked in talent, he made up for in volume.

Volume. The friend of the inept, the savior of the less than talented. If there's one thing we excelled at, it was volume. I plugged the mic into our trailer-made P.A., testing it with the customary call:

"Check. Check. Two, two. Suey-eee-aaah. Suey-eee-aaah."

Derek stopped playing to listen. "Sweet mike."

"Thanks."

"We're gonna kick so much ass."

"No doubt, dude."

"So I saw Jody Andersen in the hall today. She was ditching fifth period to print up some flyers."

"Flyers? Nice."

"Two kegs, I hear."

"Sweet."

James bounded down the stairs, still wearing his school football jersey.

"Hey man!" Derek shook with him, punching James in the shoulder. "I thought football practice didn't let out till five…"

"It doesn't," James answered, grinning.

"Ahh--you ditched?"

"Nope," he replied, puffing up. "Coach told me to take an extra lap, so I told him to screw himself."

"You quit?" I asked.

He nodded, pleased with himself. "Hell yeah. He kept making little smart-ass comments about my hair. And he's like 'we don't have a girls' team, Graves' and 'you get purrrdier every day'--shit like that. Well, anyway, he's making me run extra hills on a daily basis. I swear, as soon as he sees me, he watches for something he can bust me for!"

"Coach Vigil is an ass," Derek complied.

"Seriously, dude! I swear I was only about five minutes late--but he doesn't even say anything at first. He just points over at the hills and blows that stupid fuckin' whistle like fifty times. So I walked over there, and all the time I was thinking what bullshit the whole football team thing is, right? And the last thing I wanted to do was run hills, man. So I didn't. I just stood there."

"You what?"

James nodded, his eyes hot with mischief. "Totally--but get this: like five minutes later, Coach looks over to the hills and sees me standing there talking to Sherrie Coleman and her sister through the fence. I swear, dude--he came sprinting over in his little yellow shorts with that whistle planted in his bald-ass head! Damn, I didn't know whether to crap my pants or laugh!"

"So what did you say?"

"Well, he says something about quitters and totally grabs me by the jersey--dudes, I seriously thought he was gonna hit me. He probably would have if Sherrie hadn't been watching...anyway, he tells me I'm a worthless punk and asks what the hell my problem is. I tell him my problem is running hills and he's just as worthless as a coach!"

"Seriously?"

"Totally. I swear, dude. He said I'd be running hills until spring, and I'd better get started. So I told him to screw himself and walked."

"You walked?"

"Hell yeah."

Derek grinned, extending a hand to shake. "Told you, man. Good job."

James huffed. "Who needs football, anyway? Pain in the ass… it's all about, like, taking orders and shit. Screw it--my mom won't care. Besides, I don't want to hurt my hands. I need 'em both to play."

It made sense. Football was for jocks, not headbangers. On the field, James was just another grunt, one of fifty. As a lead guitarist, he was indispensable.

I was proud of him. However exaggerated the retelling, his symbolic act was not lost on us. James was choosing the band over the rest of the world. He had an alternative now, something of his own creation, and it felt pretty damned good not to be just partici-pating anymore.

Little by little, the rest of the world was falling away. My child-hood friends seemed suddenly banal and unimportant, and I'd re-cently moved out of Kevin's locker to share with James. We postered the thing with guitar heroes and held court in the halls between classes. Not that we were suddenly popular, mind you--just differ-ent and proud of it. Recognized. Without realizing it, we'd formed our own headbanging clique.

Randy and Tommy arrived together, with the Jefferson High School Pom-Pom Squad in tow.

Well, ten of them, at least. Perky little beauties with matching pleated skirts. Their bronze legs ended in dainty sport socks and clean white tennis shoes, fuzzy pink balls tied into the laces. Lip gloss, pony tails and cheerleader uniforms. Oh, the humanity. Any other day, it would have been a gift from heaven. On this day, I was petrified.

My first attempt at singing would be witnessed by an entire cheerleading squad. No pressure. I didn't know whether to thank Tommy or to cuss him out.

As advertised, Randy's drum kit was impressively beefy, the copper cymbals polished and clean, the kind of kit I'd only seen in music stores. And he could play it. Even his warm-up routine was notable.

Buggadugga dump buggadugga dump.
Buggadugga dump, buggadugga dump.

Oohs and aahs from the cheerleaders. The Jefferson chicks were music lovers.

"What's first, chief?" Derek asked me, crunching out a power chord.

I flipped through pages of lyrics, searching for something easy.

"'Livin' After Midnight'," I said, shakily confident, a diamond about to be formed under the pressure of solid rock.

Randy counted off the beat on his hi-hat.

The guitars kicked in, grinding the riff on cue. The volume was formidable, crunchy metal goodness ricocheting off the bare walls.

Here went nothing.

I sang the first lines of the song into the microphone. My voice barked out of the speakers.

Acceptable. Not bad. Good, even.

Disguised by the volume, my voice almost sounded authentic.

The Pom-Pom squad focused their peppy attention on me. I tried to look disassociated and cool, as though I'd done it a thousand times before. Beneath the exterior, my heart did the cha-cha.

Derek looked up at me with triumph in his eyes, as though he'd just won the lottery. I knew exactly how he felt. Sweet adrenalin. A rush of potent fear, tempered by ego and exaltation, spurred on by the creamy-skinned spirit squad.

I was doing it.

Singing for chicks. Hell yeah.

I became brave on the second verse, dropping the lyric sheet and singing from memory. I could feel the weight of every glittered eye.

"Yeah!" James shouted at me over the noise. Had he been at football practice, I suppose he would have slapped my butt.

Randy pounded away, impeccably timed, driving the beat.

Derek sneered contentedly and hacked away at his lightning bolt, leaning his head back as he chunk-a-chunked.

Tommy banged his head like a good bassist, hamming it up for the cheerleaders. His curly hair flopped around but attracted little attention. The pep squad was focused on me.

The transformation had begun.

Driven by the sweet four-four beat and the demurely cast affection, I became a singer. A front man. A fetal superstar.

Did I sound good? Did it really matter?

My voice was holding up and that was good enough. Disguised by the din of distortion, good was a relative term. That day I learned my first lesson of rock singing: Presence is everything.

Looks That Kill

Damn, Tommy! You got enough hairspray on, or what?"

"Not yet," he answered. "It's not standing up the way it's supposed to."

"You gotta blow dry it upside down...and then re-spray it. Repeat as necessary."

We stood in Tommy's bedroom, gazing with admiration at his magazine-cutout wallpaper.

Home-postered. Wall-to-wall, ceiling-to-floor, every inch of drywall plastered with glossy magazine photos and unframed posters. Eddie Van Halen, Ozzy, KISS--they surrounded us, every worthy member of the heavy metal fraternity, guitars gleaming and pyrotechnics blazing. Stage shots, interview candids, publicity photos, each one of them carefully placed, connecting in an endless metal mural.

I was notably impressed. My own meager postering job was put to shame by Tommy's obvious dedication; it must have taken fifty magazines to fill the whole thing.

Not only that--he had a theme, and order. Singers on the west wall, guitarists to the east. Tommy even managed to separate the poser bands into their own section, a mural on the sliding closet door. The only window in the cell-size bedroom had been covered to keep out the light, and on the back of the shade was painted an inspired but artistically bereft drawing of Iron Maiden's skeletal mascot Eddie embracing a scantily clad vixen with big hair. Classic.

On the wall behind Tommy's bed were displayed his most prized possessions: a signed photo of bassist Steve Harris, a genuine Maiden guitar pick and part of a broken drumstick shattered by Neil Peart of Rush. Being a bass player, the signed photo was his favorite.

The only unrelated item in the room was a framed portrait of a long-haired Jesus, with an inscription below that read: 'Grow your hair as long as you like…just tell them I said it's okay'.

I wondered about Jesus' using contractions, but kept the comment to myself.

"This is way cool," James said, nodding his approval. For him and me, it was the first time in Tommy's sanctuary.

"Thanks, dude." Tommy beamed with pride. "I used to put 'em up with tape, but I switched to a staple gun. Way easier, and I don't destroy anything…least not too much. That way, I can rearrange them if I want. I can take 'em down without wrecking the pictures. It helps out when you move a lot."

"That wall is like Swiss cheese, I bet."

"No doubt."

Tommy shrugged. "No biggie, really. It's not our wall. When we move, we'll have to paint it anyway--to get back the deposit and stuff."

"Yeah? You moved a lot?" I asked.

"Three times in the last three years." Tommy sounded almost proud. "This is by far the best place of all three."

By comparison, I'd only lived in two houses my entire life, both in the same city. I was a local veteran, and the new kid thing always intrigued me.

"Three times in three years? What other states did you live in?"

"Didn't," he replied, chuckling at the thought. "I never been out of Denver...but I've been all around it. Lakewood, Aurora, then Federal Heights, then Capitol Hill with my mom's boyfriend, then here. The dude was a total asshole. Serious dick. Bob's way better than the last guy."

"I thought Bob was your step-dad."

"Nah," he replied. "He's just her new boyfriend. I call him my step-dad sometimes, but not to his face or anything..."

"Is he cool?"

Tommy shrugged again, staring down at the Steve Harris photo. "Yeah, I guess. He drinks a lot, but he's pretty alright. He's got a wicked .38."

Cool photos or not, Tommy's room seemed almost claustrophobic to me. The bedroom was no bigger than our storage room at home--the whole apartment consisted of three cells and a miniature kitchen, encompassing far less square footage than the main floor of my parents' two-story house. It made me feel fortunate.

"Care if I play your bass, dude?" Derek asked, eyeing the amp setup.

"That was my Uncle Pete's bass. Go for it."

The black Fender Precision Bass sat in its own treasured corner of the room on a stand, perpetually plugged into a small Peavy practice amp. It had undoubtedly seen a few gigs, the battle scars on the pick guard only adding to our reverence. Derek eagerly rushed to pick it up, lifting the broad leather strap over his head. He cranked the volume and proceeded to bang out the infamous "Smoke on the Water" riff.

"You gotta turn it down, man," Tommy protested immediately. "The neighbors will start bitching."

"Screw 'em if they don't like it," Derek sneered, continuing to play.

James reached for the knob, turning down the amp. "Don't be a dick."

Derek chuckled between notes. "Whatever. Hey, Tommy, get some tunes going here--I wanna play along. This bass shit is easy!"

Tommy moved to the boom box on his dresser, pausing to check his hair before pressing play. Iron Maiden's "Die With Your Boots On" filled the room. Derek plunked along contentedly at low volume.

"So what are you wearing for the gig?" James asked.

"My Maiden concert shirt. You?"

"I guess my AC/DC shirt."

"The one with no sleeves?"

"Yeah. Half-shirt."

"Sweet. What about Mark?"

I shrugged, considering it. "I don't know. I was thinking about wearing my Ozzy shirt."

James shook his head. "Nah. That's no good."

"Why not?"

"It's not even a real concert shirt," James protested. "It's store bought, man."

"Pshht," Derek offered, banging his head. "Don't listen to James. That Ozzy shirt is cool."

"Yeah," James continued, "but Mark is the front man. He has to wear something different, you know? He has to stand out."

Derek and Tommy agreed with him.

Standing out. Front man.

It may sound silly, but I never considered it before. Like the rest of them, I'd been taking a pair of scissors to all my favorite clothing, cutting off sleeves and midriffs, turning my T-shirts into I-shirts as a matter of course. The ripped-jean uniform I wore was intended to blend away my bookish smart-kid reputation with conformed coolness. Now that I was singing, however, I was somehow supposed to stand out.

"We should just all go without shirts," Derek said, apparently still following his Naked Doom theme.

The idea horrified me. Half shirts were one thing; showing nipple was entirely another.

"No way," I told him. "We're not the Sex Pistols."

"Okay, then. How about a leather jacket with no shirt on underneath?"

"Isn't that the same thing?" I asked.

James frowned. "I don't want to get my leather all stinky with armpit sweat."

"True. Leather pants would be cool, though."

I thought of Jim Morrison. Good 'ole leather-clad Jim. Sometimes the pants wear the man. Jim never had that problem.

"No doubt."

"They have to be tight though," James added. "You have to have them tailored so they, you know, fit right around the crotch."

"Well, yeah."

"Given."

Tight pants. Next to big hair, tight pants were the fashion trademark of our generation. We wanted them squeeze tight. Skin tight. So tight that we could be the visual aid for an anatomy class. Tight enough to display your package and your thighs at once. Men, women, boys, girls. Tight.

Gonads under pressure. Thighs in bondage. Big hair. This is the way of my people.

Big pants were for old people. Big pants were for dishwasher repairmen and aging farmers. In the eighties, there wasn't a single butt crack in sight.

Rips, tears, frayed edges--all acceptable. Preferable, even. Between stretches of strained paled fabric, an occasional hole would show a bit of flesh. We still embraced the worn hippie look, but the standard was a size too small.

For the girls, it was no different. There was nothing more attractive than nubile young flesh squeezed into jeans so tight they could have been painted on. Even the grubby Iron Maiden chicks wore them frayed and tight, and whether nature or nurture, I was raised to love the look of thighs straining against tired denim.

Given all that...I wasn't concerned with my ass. I was so thin as to barely have one at all, and given the fact that I didn't have to look at it in the mirror, my butt was just aces with me. The issue of my attire remained unresolved.

Later, we sat around Tommy's television, watching the "Like a Virgin" video on MTV. Tommy's mom was still at work, and having already watered down her vodka to the point of uselessness, we'd resigned ourselves to a quiet evening.

"Would you do her?" Derek asked, spitting into a pop can.

"Who, Madonna?"

"Yeah."

"I would," James answered without hesitation. "Pshht--of course."

The rest of us nodded our agreement.

"Yeah," Derek agreed. "She's hot, in a new-wave kinda way--but she's a flash in the pan. Like a virgin? Yeah, right."

"No doubt."

"Okay, okay--who would you rather do? Madonna or Joan Jett?"

We all gave the issue serious thought. The question was near-moot, considering that none of us had 'done' enough to form a valid opinion. Still, lack of experience never prevented enlightened discussion.

"Joan Jett doesn't have any tits," Tommy said plainly, offering his expert analysis.

"Yeah. Madonna don't have much more."

"True, but still…"

"Joan Jett," I answered definitively. "Way."

The choice seemed simple. Madonna was cute, but Joan was cool.

"Mark's right," Derek answered. "Joan Jett rocks. She'd be much better in bed. Rocker chicks are way better."

I liked Derek. He had his priorities in order.

Derek grinned. "Okay, here's a tough one. Joan Jett or Lita Ford?"

Tough one. Lita was blonde and had bigger…hair than Joan.

"Lita," Tommy said. "Bigger boobs."

"Right again," Derek answered. "Lita is the shit--and not just because of the boobs. I mean, blonde is better, right?"

I still preferred Joan Jett, but couldn't argue with his assessment.

"Lita seems like she'd be high maintenance."

"No doubt."

James shrugged. "I wouldn't kick either one of them out of bed…"

A knock on the door.

Tommy leapt to his feet, hiding the ashtray and waving away the clouds of smoke.

"You expecting someone, dude?"

Tommy shook his head. "Nah. It's probably just Alex."

The door opened and Tommy's Uncle Pete walked in. He was thirty-something going on forty-something, still side-burned, distinguished by his mullet and a bulbous, alcoholic nose. He wore dirty jeans and a leather vest over a T-shirt that read: 'I don't have a drinking problem: I drink, I get drunk, I fall down. No problem!'.

"Ay! The whole crew is here, eh, Tommy?"

Tommy gave his uncle a hug. "Almost. This is James, Mark, and Derek."

"Alright, guys. Alright. Tommy told me a lot about you guys."

We moved to shake hands with Uncle Pete, biker-style. He smelled like Aqua Velva and filthy denim.

"Tommy, you're going to be happy when you see who I brought with me…"

The screen door creaked open again, and in walked the epitome of eighties femininity. Three of us lost our breath.

Tommy grinned widely. "Cousin Tabitha!"

Tabitha. A name sexy enough not to need a 'y'.

Tabitha was a Scorpio, with light eyes, dark hair, and smooth caramel skin. Seeing was believing. Beauty that commanded attention. Her presence was sweet and potent, like drinking Hershey's chocolate syrup straight from the can.

At the time, she could be found in my personal dictionary under 'ideal'. Two years our senior, Tabitha possessed the mystery of an older woman. Our jaws collectively dropped at the sight of her.

We looked on jealously as Tommy gave her a prolonged hug. The competition would be stiff indeed.

"All these cute guys," she said, her voice dripping with sweetness. "This must be your band, Tommy."

"Everybody except Randy," he said.

She walked into the room, filling it with her divine, perfumed scent. "Oh yeah? Well, are you going to introduce me?"

"Yeah…James, guitarist. Derek plays guitar, too. And Mark here is the lead singer."

Lead singer. I loved the sound of it.

Tabitha flashed me a smoky glance, staring into me.

"Lead singer, huh?"

"Yeah," I answered brilliantly, dumbfounded by my own libido. She tilted her head. "I can see it. You look like a singer."

I was staring and didn't care. Good God--even her ears were gorgeous! My heart and my mind traded places. Words failed me.

"Yep, he's the man!" Derek patted me on the back, slightly more immune to her charm spell. I appreciated the assist.

"So what are you doing in town?" Tommy asked. "Mom didn't say you were coming."

Tabitha smiled. "I'm just visiting Uncle Pete--I came into town to see Grandma. I thought I'd better get out here before it started snowing."

"Tabitha's from California," Tommy said, filling us in. "She's going to dental school."

California. No wonder. At that age, it seemed every woman from Cali was a babe. As far as I knew, it was a fact.

"Well, dental assistant school," she corrected him. "I'll be a hygienist."

"You can clean my teeth anytime," James told her, grinning with lecherous pride. He seemed to have a limitless ability for vaguely tasteless comments, though I failed to locate the innuendo in this instance. Tabitha giggled politely.

I looked at her.

She looked at me, and looked at me looking at her.

I looked away, then looked back.

She looked at me again, her gaze lingering. I likewise lingered.

The time for looking had passed. Now was the moment to unleash my arsenal of witty repartee.

Guh.

Guh, I was thinking.

Lead singer or not, I was having trouble fronting the conversation when she was involved. Shyness muzzled me, but I doubt my eyes ever left her face, waiting for the moment when she'd grace me with another glance.

Uncle Pete cast me a crusty familial glare, looking as though he'd been reading my mind.

"So you guys been practicing a lot, or what?"

"Yeah."

"Yeah."

Tommy nodded. "Oh yeah--all the time. We got a gig coming up. A kegger."

"Oh yeah? Alright." Pete squinted approvingly. "You gotta work hard, bud. Trust somebody who knows."

"Uncle Pete used to have a band. He was a pro musician."

"Yeah, well, you know--back in the day we were pretty good. Played all over this town. Whiskey Dan's, The I-70 Saloon, shit--all up and down the front range. Hell, we were good. We were right on the verge of getting discovered, too, you know, but our damned singer ran off with his little slut girlfriend. Bastard got married. Lost interest. Can you believe that shit?"

"He chose a chick over the band?"

"Straight away," Pete lamented. "That woman got in his head and killed all his hope. You gotta keep it tight, boys. Don't let the girls get in the way. Take it from me, nothing kills a good band quicker than love. Yo, Tommy--your mom leave anything good in the refrigerator?"

"Yeah, sure." Tommy flopped back down on the couch. "Chili Rellenos."

Uncle Pete moved the five steps required to reach the kitchen and opened the fridge. He chuckled and patted his gut before extracting the food.

"Ahh..." He sniffed the dish and squinted his eyes. "Just like I remember. Boy, I miss your mom's cooking, Tommy. She used to cook for all us kids when we were your age."

"I know."

Derek ignored the chili talk, still focused on Tabitha. "So…are you still gonna be here on Saturday?"

She nodded. "I leave Sunday."

"Then you should come see us play on Saturday night."

"Oh yeah?" Demure smile. "Sounds great."

I fielded another glance from her, looking away to keep my knees from buckling.

"Yeah, we're gonna jam," Derek nodded. "Major kegger. Mark's singing debut."

"Oh yeah?" Another sultry glimpse. "Well, I wouldn't want to miss that."

I smiled bashfully. Did Tabitha and I already have chemistry? I didn't see her staring at James or Derek…well, at least not the love-smothered type of looks I was fielding. The lead singer reputation was working like Spanish Fly. I may have been mistaken, but--

No, I wasn't.

Tabitha sat with us on the couch and watched videos while Tommy and Uncle Pete reminisced. I didn't really hear a single word, tongue-tied but blissfully breathing in the scent of bronze California flesh, her fine features already etched into my memory. When she talked to me, she'd reach out a hand and touch me on the leg or the shoulder, her fingers tactile bliss.

I would have to kick ass on Saturday. There was no other option.

NOTHING ELSE MATTERS

It was a nice thing--to see myself as something different. To see other people seeing me as something different...and to know that it was all my own doing.

It may sound funny, but they'd been making me. Until that moment, the entirety of my existence had been designed, produced and directed by the powers that be.

Not some Big Brother thing or some kind of government or religious conspiracy. No, my indoctrination was not unlike that of millions of others, an almost invisible process of grooming and channeling me in the direction they wanted me to go, running like a little white mouse in a maze and knowing that, in a maze, I possess only the pretense of choice. In a maze, there are only two directions: right and wrong.

It was my life, presumably.

And so they trained me and set me out with the reassurance: We trust you to make the right decisions. We know that you'll do the right thing.

And, of course, I knew what that was.

The right thing was the thing they expected. The thing they wanted. The right thing was finishing the maze. No pressure at all.

Not that finishing the maze was my concern. I could run the damned maze backward and forward. I was invincible, and I could ace every test and get into college without trouble. They'd have their graduate, their famous son and their grandkids someday. No big whoop.

I was a lead singer now. I was a hot shit front man, something they'd never truly understand.

I knew that just the idea of the band scared my folks, much less the reality. And not the kind of situation-comedy type parental worry, the 'my kid is mixing with dangerous types' or 'my kid is going to become a drug addict' fear. They figured I'd leave all the dangerous types behind when I graduated and went to college. They assumed that their genius son was way too smart to consider drugs. So what scared them about the band?

They knew I loved music, and I suspect they thought I was talented. They'd dished out countless dollars over the years on private lessons and trips to the theatre and the symphony, determined to see that I was cultured and well-rounded. They'd provided fertile ground for rock and roll dreams and were now seeing the results.

That's what scared them. The thought that everything they'd done, all the parenting books and cautious restraint, all the lessons and carpools and den meetings--all of it could have ultimately been leading me to a dead end, and not to the end of the maze as they'd intended.

When they started realizing how important the band was to me, they acted disappointed in me. But I knew that, in part, they were disappointed in themselves and scared to death of the thought that they'd somehow erred in their parenting. They hadn't spanked me enough, or had done it too much. They'd demanded too much, or not enough. They searched their memories trying to think of what it could be, what they'd done to make me choose such an unlikely path. I was taking wrong turns, following some long-haired neighborhood buddies into a dead end.

But I wasn't lost yet. Not in my parent's eyes.

I was merely expressing myself. Going through a phase. A transitional period in which the child asserts individuality, blah, blah, blah. This whole rock and roll thing was just a short-term passion that would have to be endured, passively discouraged whenever possible. I was merely broken and in need of fixing. The maze was big enough to allow for a few errors, and their ninth-inning parenting techniques could surely pull out the big win.

I remember that day because I'd come home in a great mood. Derek's new girlfriend brought a couple of cute friends to practice, and the little brunette had been decidedly interested in me. We'd gone to Taco Shack after rehearsal, so I didn't get home till after six. In itself, this was no big deal. Mom and Dad were pretty flexible about dinner.

So I stepped through the door with a smile on my face, the brunette's number in hand, ready for a little television and telephone sweet talk. Mom was waiting with hands on hips.

"Don't worry," I told her. "I already ate."

"Well, your aunt and uncle are coming for dinner at seven-thirty," she replied, giving me the look. "So I guess you're eating twice."

"I guess I forgot."

"Apparently."

She was mad about something. Mom's presence radiated parental irritation, and I suspected that it was much more than tardiness.

"Rehearsal ran late," I told her, hanging my leather jacket.

"Did you get a lot done?"

I shrugged. "Yeah, I guess. It sounds a little better every time."

"Doesn't Derek's mom get tired of your making noise in her basement?"

Another shrug. "Not really. Renee's pretty nice about it. She says she likes to listen."

Mom raised an eyebrow. "You call her Renee?"

"She said to."

"Ah. What does Derek's father do?"

"They're separated, or divorced or something," I answered, headed for the kitchen for a soda. "I don't know what he does. I never even thought to ask. He's never there."

Mom followed close behind. "Well, if you have any homework to do, you'd better get it done. They'll be here in less than an hour. I didn't see you bring any books home..."

"I don't have any homework."

"You know, Mark, you never seem to have any...I rarely see you studying anymore."

I shrugged. "Well, I get it done in class..."

"Aren't you supposed to be paying attention in class?"

"I am! Mom, it's so easy--I can do it in like five minutes!"

"That's not the point, Mark."

This was one of her favorite remarks. I excelled at making points of the general variety, but routinely failed to see THE point.

"Well, I don't have any homework!" I told her, trying to end the conversation. "Alright?"

Not alright. The whole homework issue was only bait to lure me into a conversation about 'the point'.

Mom served up a frown. "I was looking at some of the papers that you brought home from school the other day. You could do better."

"What? On the history homework?"

"Yes."

"But I got an 'A' on that!"

She shook her head. "Yes, but it's not 'A' work, Mark."

I was smart enough to know that this simply didn't make sense.

"He wrote the grade right on the top of the paper, Mom."

She gave me the look. "Don't be smart with me, Mark. I'm being serious."

"I know you are...but I don't know what you want from me! Mom, I'm getting A's!"

"But you're barely even studying..."

More odd logic.

"So? That makes me smart, right?" I asked, feeling suddenly defensive. "I do enough studying to get an A on almost everything! That's the highest grade, Mom! You know they don't do plusses and minuses anymore--"

"But it's not enough, Mark. We're afraid that you're not pushing yourself academically--and the school's not doing a thing to prepare you for college."

"What? Mom--when they send out the transcripts to colleges, my GPA is going to be just as high as everyone else's!"

"That's not what I'm saying--"

"I'm taking the hardest classes, too! No P.E., no shop--"

"I suppose we should have put you in private school long ago, but most of them were parochial. It may have been better, though..."

"I didn't want to be in private school," I told her.

She nodded. "I know. We didn't want it, either. Call it foolish belief in the public school system, I suppose. They're well-intentioned, but they're teaching to the slower kids, and not to the smart ones. They figure kids like you will do just fine, and the curriculum doesn't challenge you at all. College will be much harder, Mark."

Prophetic words. At the time, I thought she was saying things to keep me on point. She was threatened by the band and wanted to scare me into focusing on college.

But I was already focused. Totally, dude. I'd never encountered an academic mountain I couldn't climb, and I knew exactly where I was going. I only needed one letter of acceptance, and Mom and Dad would be off my back.

I'm The Man

"This is sweet!" Tommy announced, surveying the backyard from Jody and Jenny Andersen's elevated deck. "From here, we can look right down their shirts! This is prime cleavage watching territory, bud."

I nodded, though I was looking forward to more than cheap glances. Tabitha was supposed to show, and I'd devoted an extra thirty minutes to my primping routine in her honor. Without the benefit of leather pants, I'd settled for my coolest pair of ripped jeans and a black Jack Daniels T-shirt.

The chunky redwood deck was built around the second story of the house, looking over an expansive, treeless backyard that sloped downhill to a tall wooden fence. Chateau du Andersen. A suburban palace, by most standards, complete with a propane grill and a keg already on ice.

A near-perfect location for a rager, the house was located in the semi-rural part of town, a hundred yards or so between the Andersens and the nearest neighbor. Odds on police intervention were five to one. For the first time ever, we faced the prospect of the party going the distance. With Jody and Jenny's parental units present, it seemed a lock.

"Anything left in the truck?"

James shook his head, shuffling past with his prized Marshall amp head. He'd been uptight all day, demanding that we run over the songs twice before the gig. "Has anybody seen Jody's parents yet?"

"Nah, not yet," Derek answered, looking to the keg. "They're inside, I think. Pretty weird."

"No doubt. Jody said they get drunk together all the time. They let her have guys stay the night and shit..."

"Seriously?"

"Yep. She says they told her--get this--they told her they know she's going to do it anyway, so they figure it's better to have her do it at home."

"They're definitely cool," Derek said. "Still seems weird, though. Somehow, I don't think it would be as fun if you didn't have to sneak anything."

Tommy lit a cigarette, offering one to James. "This is gonna be sweet, man. Major babes."

Tommy's hair was still the most impressive of our lot. Already past his shoulders, it was naturally curly and bushy. Tonight, he'd taken the time to blow-dry it upside down and added enough Aqua Net to make it a fire hazard. I was fortunate to have thick hair, and mine usually stood up without the necessity of too much spray.

In terms of length, however, Tommy still had us all, hands down. Looking at him, I developed a case of follicle jealousy and vowed it would be a blizzard in hell before I'd let anyone cut my hair again.

"Time?" James asked, plugging his amp into the power strip.

"What?"

"What time is it?"

Derek shrugged. "I don't have a watch, man. You know that."

I produced a plastic digital from my pocket, having thought ahead. "Almost eight-thirty."

I'd carry a watch, but wouldn't wear it. Watches make you look like you care, and somehow I didn't want people thinking that.

I'd been confident all day, psyched and ready, driven by Derek's relentless optimism and the knowledge that Randy would be bug-gaduggaing behind me. When I saw the crowd begin to pour into the Andersen's back yard, however, I suddenly began to feel ill.

Nauseous, like a cat about to hack up a fur ball.

"You okay, Mark?" Derek asked. He wore a faded orange Denver Broncos shirt with the words 'Fuck Oakland' written in magic marker on the back.

"Think so…"

"You're looking kinda pale."

I waved him off. "Yeah, I'm okay. No biggie."

"You need a beer, dude."

"Not just yet…"

He slapped me on the back. "Don't sweat it, man. Whatever you do, don't sweat it. A crowd is like a mean dog. A crowd smells fear. If you don't want to get your ass bitten, then you have to walk out there like you own the place. Seriously. Remember, you're the man. If you get nervous, then just bang your head a few extra times or something!"

I don't know where Derek gained the enlightenment to become a singing guru, but his advice made me feel better. I thought of the old Brady Bunch episode where Marsha relaxes by picturing her audience in their underwear.

"Get a beer," he offered again. "It'll settle your stomach."

"Yeah, okay" I replied, taking a deep breath. "Maybe you're right."

"Course I am."

Derek was the only one of us without long hair, and yet it didn't matter. His short cut was mussed and unattended, and his reputation already established. Derek never had been, and never would be, a pretty boy. He needed no mullet, no hairspray, no mesh tank top. He'd kicked ass enough times behind the school to establish himself as a tough guy, and fashion consciousness would only serve to dilute his image. Not that Derek cared about image, either.

To distract myself from the fading nauseous lurch, I helped Randy finish setting up his drums. He'd been using money from his part time job to pump up his kit and had just purchased two new cymbals. Gleaming bronze, spun copper brilliance, and a weight that made them feel like trophies in your hands. New cymbals are gorgeous things.

Randy's kit was looking good. Piece by piece, he was building a monster to mirror that of his heroes. Bigger was better and, short of having enough money to buy a new kit, Randy was forced to make frequent enhancements. The size of it alone was impressive, and I was surprised to find that, as I placed the polished cymbals on their respective stands, I didn't miss drumming at all.

The crowd continued to flock in, diverted from the front door around to the gate, filling their blue plastic cups and mingling in anticipation of the band. The volleyball net had already been knocked to the ground and the volleyball booted over the fence. I could hear the flatulent rumbling of a Harley in the front yard.

"Set lists?"

I nodded, producing a scrap of paper for each band member, the song titles lovingly printed in big letters.

"Cool," Tommy said, looking it over.

Randy frowned a bit. "I don't see 'Queen of the Reich' on here."

I couldn't sing "Queen of the Reich." Way too high. Way.

"Oh yeah…well, see I'm not so sure about that one," I wavered. "I didn't get all the lyrics memorized. We're not too tight on that one, either. I'd kinda rather not play it."

"Whatever."

He didn't mind.

Truth be told, I intentionally left the song out. As with many of the metal standards, the vocals were intended for a tenor--or, in some cases, for a soprano. This is ridiculously high for a confirmed baritone, and the last thing I wanted was to embarrass myself by going falsetto.

The second lesson of singing: Don't attempt anything beyond your range. Regardless of talent, nothing is worse than a singer out of range. Fool them by singing where it's easiest. Ask Elvis and Frank if you don't believe me.

At the moment, singing was the least of my worries. Gig time was upon us, with no indication of settlement in my gastric tract.

"If I fart up here," I announced, "you guys are gonna have to take it."

"Do it on the other side of the stage," Derek warned. Jugs of expectoration didn't bother him. Flatulence, however, was apparently not his thing.

Randy teased the crowd with some quads and snare hits, drawing the occasional whoop. James crunched a couple of power chords, the beautiful distortion and feedback lingering in the night air.

"'Metal Health' first, right?"

I nodded, my sweaty hand holding the live mic.

"Remember," Derek whispered, patting me on the back, "You're the man, Mark. You're the fuckin' man. Let's show 'em what we do."

I nodded, feeling better.

"Talk it up," James told me. "Work the crowd."

I nodded again, feeling worse.

We launched into the opening bars of Quiet Riot's "Metal Health," and the crowd responded. The guitars were in tune.

I closed my eyes, letting the music blow past me. As I opened my mouth to utter the first lines, I wasn't quite sure whether it would be the lyrics or my lunch that would come out.

My voice blared from the speakers, filling the backyard. Not great, but not bad, either. Loud. The crowd didn't seem to know the difference. I paid silent homage to the gods of volume, the decibels disguising the imperfections and missed notes.

Derek sneered his guitar face, stepping over to where I stood frozen center-stage. "Move around," he yelled in my ear. "You sound good, dude…"

I remembered what he'd said about dogs in the yard, flipping my hair and forming a fist.

Jim Morrison lounged inside me, drinking from a bottle of Wild Turkey and grinning. He stood shirtless from his chair and threw the bottle to the ground, glass shattering at his feet. Jim stared at me and faked a punch, laughing. 'You're on, man…'

I was on. I couldn't just stand there and sing.

I'd mimicked it hundreds of times before in the mirror. Now it was time to apply my experience. Snarling, I imagined myself standing before a packed stadium, thousands of raised lighters beckoning me.

The guitar solo approached, and James stepped to the front, pointing his guitar at the mass of humanity. He twitched like Warren DeMartini, shredding up the neck in an imperfect but pas-sionate solo. His eyes blazed.

I banged my head, turning to look at Randy. Enrapt in the groove, he grinned back and dashed the cymbal closest to me.

I turned and grabbed the mic again, pulling it from the stand and brushing the hair out of my eyes. The horde stood before me, facing forward in silence like an enraptured flock at church. I narrowed my eyes and belted into the final verse.

The song ended as soon as it had begun, wrapped up with a lingering final chord.

Silence, for just a moment.

And then, just as I thought we'd bombed, the glorious sound of cheering and applause.

I went on auto-pilot. "Hell yeah!" I shouted over the P.A., my adrenalin red-lining. "Who's ready to party?"

Another roar. I could see Jody Andersen grinning like a trucker in a brewery.

Better than beer. Better than sex. Better than anything.

"Hell yeah!" James shouted at me.

Derek slapped me on the shoulder. "You're the man, bud. You're the fuckin' man!"

Randy cued the band, counting off the next song on his hi-hat. "Looks That Kill" was a timely selection.

I pumped my fist in the air, my fear fading with every note, the divine ringing sound already gracing my ears. For the moment, I actually WAS the man.

...And the Cradle Will Rock

We wrapped up the first set with a rousing version of KISS's "Rock and Roll All Night," the packed yard chanting the 'and party every day' refrain as they worked toward inebriation. We train-crashed the ending.

"Beer break," I told the crowd, brushing my sweaty bangs out of my eyes. "We'll be back soon..."

The applause died quickly, the party goers looking toward the keg in anticipation. No one, however, was leaving.

"Kick ass," Derek said.

"No doubt, Mark. Good job, man."

"I'll get better," I told them, vowing to do so. It seemed the worst part was over.

"How's your stomach feel now?"

"Better."

"Thought so," Derek beamed. "Let's go smoke a joint."

"You've got weed?"

He nodded. "My sister gave me a little present. Come on--it's guaranteed to get rid of that stomach ache."

There was a first time for everything. Apparently, tonight would be a night of firsts.

We all crammed into Derek's car, having floated all the way from the stage. He popped open the ashtray and produced a single joint, holding it up for inspection.

"It's Mexican," he lamented, "but it'll do."

He popped in a cassette tape and cranked the stereo. "Just installed my new equalizer. Hold on to your asses..."

The tape rolled, the hiss of pre-song white noise telling of imminent assault. We braced ourselves.

"I WANNA ROCK!"

Dee Snider's metal-perfect wail pounded our eardrums, setting all five heads to banging. Derek's stereo was loud enough to break the snares off our eardrums. He lit the joint, the skunky sublime haze filling the car.

We didn't talk strategy or song list. We didn't ruminate over the abundant crowd or the friendly reception. No words were necessary. Twisted Sister said it all for us.

We chanted along with the song, passing the joint and pumping our heads, chomping at the bit to re-take the stage. Had we been headlining at Madison Square Garden, we couldn't have been any more psyched.

We poured out of the car only minutes later. My brain was baked, the virginal high like skating on thin air. My eyes were bloodshot, my ears ringing, and my heart three sizes too big. Any and all signs of illness were far behind me now, smothered by the reassuring buzz and the inspiration of cymbal clatter.

I was alive, and I could feel it. Living inside the mirror.

We trotted back up the street like junkies running for a fix, passing through the crowd without noticing, without thinking, without anything but jamming on our minds. I didn't care who was in the crowd, or what they thought. I didn't care how we sounded or whether the Andersen sisters were happy. I wanted only to drink in the high octane mix of fear and ego.

More than ever before, we wanted to rock.

We leapt up the stairs to the redwood deck and resumed our positions on stage, feeling like big fish in our own spoon-sized pond. The rabble responded at the sight of us with sporadic whoops and whistles, juiced up and ready for another round of loudness. In our absence, someone had placed a tray of beers by the kick drum. Membership has its privileges.

"Brew. That's what I'm talking about," Randy announced, handing them around. "I've got major Mojave-mouth."

"Looks like no cops tonight, so let's do it," James announced, taking a swig and spilling on himself. "Just keep 'em coming and don't wait for too long between songs. Let's rip their faces off!"

Randy took his place behind the monster kit and gave us the warm-up buggaduggas, rousing the yard and drawing the audience back to the stage.

Flacka-du blug. Flak. Flak.
Flacka-du blug. Buggadugga.

"Jam on, dude," Tommy said to me, strapping on his bass. "My cousin's supposed to show tonight. Uncle Pete's car is in the shop, so he's taking her to the airport tomorrow in my mom's car. She's staying the night at my house."

Revelation. Before the gig, I'd been preoccupied with the prospect of seeing Tabitha again. When Tommy said the words, I couldn't believe that I'd forgotten all about her. It didn't seem the night could get much better.

"She's got the hots for you, Mark," he added.

The hots. She had them. For me.

The night immediately improved.

"No. Really? Seriously?"

"I shit you not," he declared, smiling an eerie caste of not-so-familial jealousy. "She was asking about you…"

As if I needed any more inspiration.

Suddenly, it wasn't just my heart that was leaping. My libido joined the mosh pit in full stride, shirtless and arms swinging. Inside me, Mr. Morrison grabbed his crotch and let forth a guttural 'Whoop'.

"What's first, dude?"

"What else?" I answered. "'Ain't Talkin' Bout Love'."

"Sweet."

Randy polished off his cup of beer, pointing a stick at James and belching. "Hit it, dude…"

As James played the intro, I spotted Uncle Pete making his way through the crowd. Behind him walked Tabitha, dressed dangerously in a one-piece red sleeve. Her lips matched the outfit, parting to reveal a blinding smile as she stared up at me.

Inspiration overload.

Suddenly, I wanted to kick ass. Not for the crowd, or the Andersen sisters, or the band. I only wanted to put the lead singer's whammy on this girl and make her mine.

I grabbed the mic and sang into it, doing my best David Lee Roth impression. From below, I could hear someone scream 'shit yeah'!

I'd expected to feel like Dave. I'd imagined that if I sang his words, I'd finally know what it was like to BE Dave. But it wasn't like that--it was better. I was Dave, Elvis, Mick, Frank, and Bon. I was every singer who had ever performed, all of them wrapped up in a new package known as Mark. Van Halen may have been reaping the royalties, but for that moment, the song was mine.

The metamorphosis continued. My inhibitions fell away, invisible now, the wall of trepidation splitting down the middle and crumbling to dust. Inside my head, Jim Morrison writhed and screeched, commanding the crowd with a wave of his hand. Wild-eyed, he swiveled on his heel and pointed at me.

I belted it out like I didn't know I could.

I stood fearless for that moment, reveling in the rush of solid steel adrenalin, feeling like somebody important for the first time in my short life. Never had I been so close to Jim.

Cherry Pie

I t was almost 4 a.m. when I left for Tommy's apartment.
I'd made the obligatory trip home to satisfy the parents before slipping out the door and back into the night, determined not to let this glorious evening end so soon. There were still two hours left before sunrise, and I didn't intend to let Tabitha down. No one could have kept me at home. Not even Jim himself.

Then again, Jim would have approved. Of course, Jim probably wouldn't have gone home in the first place or bothered to leave his car in the street or pillows under his sheets...but I was still far from achieving one with the Jim-ness...full front man nirvana. Grasshopper Mark still had much to learn.

My lead accomplice Derek was waiting down the street, engine off, headlights out and listening to the Sex Pistols at a considerately low volume.

Derek seemed to enjoy being a part of anything rebellious, however mild it might be. I suppose he possessed more of the punk spirit than any of us--that chaotic tendency toward excess, the ability to dive down deep and come up expressing real emotions, angry or kind. There was no pretense and no posturing to Derek; if he hated you, he'd kick your ass, and if he liked you, he'd go to the wall for you. Always.

He offered me a beer from the twelve-pack in the back seat and we headed for Tommy's, banging our heads to "Anarchy in the U.K." I'd never heard the Sex Pistols before I met Derek, but his passion for them was contagious. And while the music itself sounded coarse and unrefined to my pop-trained ears, I could undoubtedly appreciate the barbaric yawp of raw grinding guitars, the pointed lyrics and the 'who cares' delivery of Johnny Rotten.

I would be a liar, however, if I said I was thinking about the Pistols that morning. My mind was centered, floating gently in a warm bath of beer and THC, focused on the images of Tabitha's face.

I would again be a liar if I failed to mention that I was not merely focused on her face. She was a well-rounded girl and, out of fairness, my libido was giving all portions of her equal billing.

We parked down the street from Tommy's place, so as not to wake mothers and uncles with Derek's muscled steel.

"You kicked ass tonight, dude."

"Thanks, man--so did you. I screwed up in a couple places, but I don't think anyone noticed."

"Hell no," Derek replied, tossing his empty into a bush and producing another from his jacket. "Pockets on the inside," he bragged. "I can carry like six beers in here if I have to. Perfect for shoplifting, I guess. You got a couple beers to take with you?"

"Just this one," I held up my half-finished can.

He fished around inside his jacket and produced two more cans. "Here--take these."

I accepted gratefully. I'd already had my fill, but Tabitha was likely to want one. It couldn't hurt.

We moved around the side of the building to Tommy's bedroom window and knocked quietly on the glass. A flutter on the shade and the light inside went out. Moments later, Tabitha and

Tommy appeared around the corner. My stomach clenched at the sight of her, my breath struggling to stay inside me.

"Sup," Tommy whispered, still radiant with the night's afterglow, success written all over his grinning face.

"Sup, Mr. Rock God!" Derek slapped him on the shoulder and handed him a beer. You ready to take a ride?"

"Sure. Where to?"

"Amy Douglass…es," Derek answered proudly. "Her and Missy Jacobs are waiting for us."

"We're there," Tommy approved, looking to Tabitha. "You guys want to come along with us?"

Tabitha looked at me, knowing the answer.

"Sounds like a couples thing," she said. "I think me and Mark will just go for a walk or something. That way you can come home when you want. Knock on the window and I'll let you in."

Tommy shrugged, looking a bit reluctant to leave me alone with Tabitha. Thankfully, the lure of Missy Jacobs' company was simply too strong.

"Okay. That's cool…"

"Let's go, dude!" Derek beckoned from the driver's seat. Tommy lit a cigarette and hopped in.

Moments later, Derek's car was out of sight.

Finally, the California siren and I were alone. Now…what to say?

I looked at Tabitha, still a bit overwhelmed by her, suddenly wanting to be far away from the apartment and the sleeping Uncle Pete.

She tilted her head, brown locks spilling over good-God soft tanned shoulders. "You looked good up there tonight. I love watching you sing. You sounded good, too."

I looked down, still caught in the initial straightjacket of shyness, wanting to respond with humble denial and tell her I was a mere apprentice. I remembered some quote about keeping your shortcomings to yourself and decided to play the role instead.

"Thanks," I replied, looking into her expertly lined eyes. "I don't ever remember having that much fun."

"I could tell! Tommy was practically floating all the way home--I've never seen him so happy about anything."

"Let's walk," I said.

She grabbed my hand without provocation, holding it as we moved toward the park, through the empty streets.

Between midnight and dawn, the suburbs are like a ghost town, serene and desolate, a nightly Twilight Zone episode where the people cease to exist until morning. Some cities never sleep. The suburbs get at least eight hours every night.

So we strolled down the blacktop, arm in arm, feeling like the king and queen of our own darkened kingdom. My libido was running the hundred meter hurdles, but I managed to keep the exterior rocker cool, hoping I didn't do or say something she didn't like. Tabitha slipped off her heels and walked in bare feet on the cool asphalt, her height advantage thankfully quashed.

"I'm glad you showed up tonight," she spoke through glossy lips. "I thought for sure you'd have a girlfriend."

"Nah, not right now. I mean...I'm glad I didn't."

"Well, you will," she told me. "Once they see you sing, those little groupies will be all over you. You'll be fighting them off..."

Groupies. I could only hope. She was overestimating my popularity, but who was I to complain?

"I wasn't really thinking about any of the girls tonight," I confessed. "I was really just waiting for you to show up."

She smiled like I was a charming liar. "That's sweet of you. I knew you'd be a sweet guy--I could see it in your eyes. Tommy says you're really smart, too."

"Oh yeah?"

She nodded. "He said you're like a straight 'A' student, and you don't even have to try. He said you know something about everything, but you don't try to rub it in anyone's face or anything."

"That's cool of him," I replied, thinking aloud. "I'll go to college after I graduate, provided..."

"Provided you don't hit it big before then?"

"Right," I conceded, thinking of the prospect. There were goals, and there were dreams. With me, the latter always seemed to take precedence. "If this thing with the band takes off, then I'll follow it."

"So you don't want to be a doctor or a stockbroker or something?"

"Nah. Being a rock star will be more than enough."

She smiled admiringly. "Well, you'll have to remember me when you're a big star traveling the world. Promise me that."

"Remember you? You'll probably be backstage with us! And when it happens, I won't forget anyone or anything. I'll be like Elvis. I'll buy everyone cars and houses."

We stopped walking when we reached the moon shadows and cool grass of the public park. Still holding my hand, Tabitha sat down and patted the ground next to her.

"Come sit next to me, Mr. Singer."

I obeyed, breathing in the oddly arousing scent of baby oil and cheap perfume. She leaned in before I even considered making a move, kissing me softly.

"Mmmm. That was nice. You're a good kisser."

"I am?"

Tabitha nodded. "Mmmhmm. Let me check, just to make sure."

She kissed me again. I responded this time, my libido doing the Moonwalk.

Glory. Divine headbanger glory. The night's victories were too awesome to assimilate. It was as though the karmic deities had re-paid all my strife in a single, brilliant night of gratification, one for which I would surely someday pay.

"You're amazing," I told her, utterly smitten. "I don't even be-lieve I'm sitting here with you right now."

"You're the amazing one," she replied smokily, playing the se-ductress role to the hilt. "Tommy told me you were shy, and I didn't know if you'd show up. I'm glad you did."

"You're leaving tomorrow, aren't you?"

Tabitha nodded. "I have to. But let's not talk about that now…"

I kissed her again, growing bolder with the sugary sound of her words. Her soft lips beckoned me, the touch of her hand on my thigh too much to tolerate. Within moments we were locked in embrace, lips moving, hands exploring, libidos doing the tango. She was soft and sweet and perfect.

We lay in the grass, kissing and whispering, laughing and hold-ing until the sky grew light. The moment arrived far too soon, forc-ing us make our way back to the apartment and reluctantly say our goodbyes. I would have given my soul to keep the sun from rising that morning.

Shot Down in Flames

"Did you make it with my cousin?"

I wanted to say yes.

"No. We just talked…"

Tommy grinned back at me, bearing an oddly jealous look. "Sure, sure. That's not what Tabitha said. She was all grinning and happy."

"Right," Derek chuckled. "Mark's been walking around all day like he won the lottery."

"Okay," I proudly admitted, "So we did a little more than talk…"

"I knew it," Tommy said. If he wanted to believe, then I wasn't going to stop him. Still, I didn't want to taint the memory with cheap talk. Tabitha wasn't just another piece of ass. She was special.

"I got the lyrics for 'Jamie's Cryin' down," I said, changing the subject. "We can try it today if you guys are ready."

"I'm ready," James announced. "Except for the solo, I mean. I'll fake it for now."

"Tabitha's getting married." Tommy said in my direction. "Did she tell you that?"

"Married?" My heart shrank.

"Yep."

"So when is the wedding?"

He shrugged. "Next spring I think, but she's engaged. Her fiancé is a pretty cool guy. He's rich, too."

A serious blow. I tried to remind myself that nothing was forever. After all, she'd given me her California phone number, and I intended to use it.

"Let's try the song," I said.

Randy rumbled the intro, but James waved him off.

"Wait. I wanna try something else…"

James scratched out a power riff, something I'd never heard before.

Randy picked up on it quickly, pounding out a back beat.

"That's cool, James! What song is that?"

"It's mine," he said, continuing. "Just play along."

Watching James' hands, Tommy found the note and plucked in tune. I found a note and began singing, making up the words as I went along. Relying on the time-honored tradition of clichéd lyrics, I repeated the phrase 'seeing is believing' and added some innuendo.

Derek watched for a moment, studying the four of us before following the repetitive riff and bobbing his head.

Instant song--just add passion. It repeated tirelessly, and we held with the pattern for five minutes before James stopped playing.

"Hell yeah, man," Derek nodded his approval.

James looked proud. "I figure if we ever want to get into The Tank, we need at least a half-hour's worth of originals. I got a bunch of 'em like that."

"Sweet."

"Nobody will ever take us seriously if we don't have our own shit," he pressed.

"Totally…"

"We need like six songs, I figure. At least six for the gig. To fill the rest of the time we can play a couple covers. But most albums have ten songs, so I figure we should shoot for ten."

"Double guitar solos," Derek added, ruminating over the prospect. "And Mark can write the words."

"Exactly," James echoed. "Whatever you come up with, Mark. Make it cool."

And so it began. Writing our own songs felt like the next logical step. It seemed simple enough; play a riff, set it to a beat, and put a few appropriately cool words to it. We promised to scratch out one new song a week.

I went home that night harboring mixed feelings, hiding my romantic disappointment over Tabitha's engagement behind the prospect of original songs. I stayed up late, scratching heavy metal poetry on notebook paper and wondering if I should call her.

I relented, of course, finally mustering enough courage to pick up the phone and dial the numbers. Engagement or not, I knew we'd shared something unique, something Tabitha wouldn't be able to deny.

It rang and rang.

'Hi, this is Tabitha. I'm sorry I missed your call. Leave me a message, and I promise I'll call you back. Wait for the beep...'

Beep.

I hung up, realizing I didn't know what to say.

Back to the lyrics, promising myself that I'd wait till I could hear her voice. If the fiancé was around, he wouldn't appreciate another guy's voice on the machine. Besides, Tabitha and I needed to keep this thing discreet, at least until she was ready to break the bad news to her husband-to-be.

She'd tell him everything, confess her love for me and come running back. I had no doubt...almost.

Of course it was unrealistic. So was the idea of becoming a rock star, and the notion of writing good lyrics. Unrealistic, however, was not a concept with which I was familiar. 'Unrealistic' sounded like a cop out, a concession, a lack of confidence. Had Jim ever used the word? I seriously doubted it.

I suppose I knew it was unrealistic--all of it. I was bright enough to see that fame, fortune and romance were nothing but tidal waves and breakers. I guess I realized the depth of the water and had seen the rocks near the shore.

But it mattered so little. I just wanted to surf.

Jim nodded to me, looking gnarly in his leather Bermuda shorts. He flashed the hang ten sign and toasted me with a bottle of spiced rum. I closed my eyes and waded out to jump a wave.

METAL GODS

Upon assuming the post of lead singer, I gained the positions of lyricist and songwriter as well.

Prestigious tasks, I thought. Prime band clout, handed over like an extra taco. Songwriting credit? Why yes, thank you very much.

At the time it seemed like they were tossing me the keys to the Mercedes and brushing off the driver's seat. I thought that sooner or later one of them would figure out what they'd just given up and change tune. Still, none of them seemed the least bit concerned about making me the words-and-melody guy. They wanted me to do it, and I was more than happy to accommodate.

I would name the songs.

I would come up with snappy, non-clichéd choruses.

I would make lyrical decisions that would shape the band's image, and ultimately affect the history of the modern world. Or something like that.

It seemed a large responsibility. To write lyrics, I'd have to look at the bigger picture.

Even then, I was acutely aware of the fact that the lyrics set the tone, the tenor, and the gimmick of a heavy metal band. You are what you sing. And, since it had been placed solely in my hands, I realized before I started laying down words that I'd need to envision and embrace some kind of greater theme.

You see, there were shades to heavy metal, even in the embry-onic days.

The dark and the light. The hard and the fluffy. The pissed and the horny.

As with any artistic genre, there would, of course, be excep-tions, bands who managed to cross the line from hard to fluffy with-out difficulty. But for identification purposes, every one of them could still fit into one of two categories.

If we wanted identity, we would have to make our choice at the proverbial fork in the composition road. As the instant lyricist, I would call the turn.

The dark bands were the staple of heavy metal, the devilish-ly good archetype that the non-educated used to pigeonhole hard rock. These were the bands that managed to bunch up Tipper Gore's panties and provoke the creation of the PMRC. In the grand tradi-tion of metal founders Black Sabbath, the dark bands sang about demons and war, swordplay and atrocity. Anti-pop. Walking where Elvis and Sinatra feared--or tastefully declined--to tread.

The rebellious allure of such ideas was marketable and dis-tinct, appealing to the testosterone-provoked aggression of most young rockers. Freedom of speech at its grisly best. Nothing says 'anti-establishment' like a song about the devil, and young rock-ers like nothing better than thinking they're sticking a fiery trident into the buttocks of civilized society. Dark albums were confiscated by morally paranoid parents and labeled the harbinger of Western Civilization's decline. What could be more attractive?

Hunted. Persecuted. Hated by some and loved by others. The trademark of good hard rock music. Infamy can be a sign of success. It's been said before, but there's no such thing as bad P.R. Tipper and her censorship-happy crew had no idea that they were validating, giving credence to, and putting cash in the pockets of the individuals they tried to persecute.

The dark side would soon branch out into Death Metal, Speed Metal, Thrash Metal, and eventually, with a little help from the punk community, Grunge. Dark side headbangers know what they like and accept no substitutes. They are single-minded and loyal, and most of them won't even acknowledge the validity of the light side.

By light, I don't mean to imply 'light-sounding'. In reality, the music of the light side bands is strikingly similar, concocted of the same mix of crunchy riffs, drum calisthenics and intensity. But the two sides aren't defined by the music. They're defined by theme.

Light Metal. MTV Metal. Bubblegum chaos, if you will. The theme discards the devilish motif in favor of tangible, everyday things like alcohol and warm female flesh. They sing about partying, first and foremost, and everything that goes along with it. Drinking, sex, cars, sex, thrill-seeking, sex, drugs, sex, turning up the music, and drinking. Did I mention sex? These are time-honored rock and roll topics, going all the way back to the stone age of popular music. The Neanderthals were likely grunting and chanting about the same thing.

Light metal's roots are far less distinct than those of the dark side. Since the beginning of music, love songs have been a standard. Symphonies and operas, folk music and soul music. Innuendo is the essence, the timeless theme. Glenn Miller was in the mood. Elvis had a case of burnin' love. And Muddy Waters was a hoochie coochie man.

Light metal was born from blues and good old seventies rock. And though it started with hard rock giants like AC/DC and Aerosmith, it soon devolved into a monstrous, unholy union between metal and mass marketing. Light Metal would eventually become the bane of the whole genre.

And as much as I would have liked to be a dark metal-head, when the music began and I started singing, evil things didn't emerge from my mouth. I felt ridiculous writing songs about dragons and battleaxes. My pop inclinations and healthy libido would inevitably put us on the lighter side. Van Halen was the standard, and becoming the biggest party band on the planet was the idea.

You've Got Another Thing Comin'

"So what are you, dude? Irish?"

Derek paused, thinking. "I guess so."

"You don't know?"

"My mom was from Wyoming."

"And your dad?"

"He's from the pit of hell, I think."

I chuckled. "So, you're Hellish?"

"Half Hellish, half Wyomish."

"Nationality can't be a state, dude. It has to be a country."

"I know...unless it's Texas."

"Okay, true. But you have to be like Irish or Italian or Swedish or something. I mean, like, originally."

"I think we're just mix-breeds, dude. Mutts, like most people."

"Yeah."

"I'm Muttish, man." Derek nodded. "That'll work. It's all bullshit anyway. All that crap just separates everyone. I mean--who gives a crap if your great-great-grandma was from Italy? You know?"

"No doubt, but people like to identify with their roots," I told him, feeling like the devil's advocate. Not that I had any roots of my own.

"Yeah, I guess," Derek replied, still unconvinced. "But most of us don't really have any roots. Shit, dude--I'm from the suburbs. Rootless. So what are you, Mark? English?"

"Don't think so," I told him. "I'm a Muttish-Scottish, with a dab of Norway."

"Yep. You're a mutt, then."

"Yeah. I'm suburban."

"Listen--right here dudes!" James reached down to turn up the stereo. "This solo is godly."

Tommy, Randy and I banged our heads in the backseat, Derek's flapping woofers mere inches away from our battered but grateful ears. James rode shotgun, marshalling the tunes. He made guitar faces over the seat, airing the solo as Vivian Campbell jammed on Dio's "Rainbow in the Dark."

Still glowing with the sweat from another inspired practice, we rolled past landscaping and convenience stores on our way to Taco Shack in search of crisp bean burritos. Unlike their corporate competitors, Taco Shack was grateful for their alternative patrons and allowed teenage loitering. On Friday nights, the place doubled as a party command center, a beefy smelling outpost where groups could gather and share updated kegger recon. We'd become some-what addicted to the menu, and the post-practice scarf sessions had gone from habit to ritual.

We stepped through the doors red-eyed and ravenous, squint-ing in the bright fluorescent white. The line was empty, and we almost tripped over each other trying to get to the register. Tommy lagged behind, scanning the place for friendlies. Derek won the race to the front, clutching a five dollar bill.

Kimmy Everett stood behind the counter, saddled in her brown Taco Shack uniform, her cheeks glowing shiny with a lacquer of airborne grease. She looked surprisingly hot wrapped in the layers of polyester, a single lock of her golden hair having escaped from the paper Taco Shack hat.

Despite the uniform, the Taco Shack counter job was one of the best in town. Kimmy was the queen of the information syndicate, a position she inherited from her older sister. Kimmy was privy to every break-up and backstab, every kegger and house party--from her illustrious post behind the register, she could dish out the gossip and get paid for her time. On Friday nights she'd often post a list of the weekend's keg parties to relieve the burden of answering so many questions.

"Hi, Kimmy."

"Hey Derek. Hey guys."

"Sup?"

"Not too much," Kimmy cocked her blonde head, shrugging. "Boredom, mostly. Everybody's resting up for the park party this weekend, I guess. Kennedy Park. You guys going?"

"Probably. Yeah, I guess."

"There's supposed to be another one off Miller Court, too. It's a Jefferson party, but I hear it's gonna be totally huge. Greg Martin was in here, and he said that him and Mike and Russ and those guys might go over there after they check out the park party. I wish you guys were playing."

"Me too. Are you going?" James asked.

Kimmy shrugged. "Well, I'm working, of course. Greg said they'd check it out and see if it was cool or not, then they'd come back here to get me and Denise after work. You guys can meet us here if you want to. Anyways, what can I getcha?"

"The usual," Derek said. "Three crisp bean and a medium Pibb."

The phone behind the counter rang. Kimmy held up a long-nailed finger and answered it. We held our salivating tongues and waited patiently for the phone call to end.

"Hey, dude," Tommy tapped me on the shoulder, lowering his voice.

"Yeah?"

"Hey, um," he looked down at his feet. "Do you think you could buy me a burrito, man? I don't got any cash right now…"

Tommy needed a burrito, and it wasn't the first time. It wasn't even the third time. Tommy had a perpetual cash flow problem. Since he'd been fired from the shoe store for refusing to cut his hair, he'd been running on next to nothing.

"Sure, dude," I answered. "Order what you want."

We'd all fallen victim to the amiable begging.

Burritos had been mooched. Fries had been coveted. Still, I didn't have it in me to deny him--Tommy was part of the band and sweated along with the rest of us. Free enterprise or not, it seemed shameful to have him sitting there empty-handed while we stuffed our faces. Besides--the whole hair issue made Tommy's firing seem like a noble act worthy of reward. I should give him credit; he ordered modestly.

Two crisp bean burritos, a large Mr. Pibb, and an order of spicy tater-tots that they insisted on calling Border Fries. The ordering process was lengthy, but soon we were seated around our usual table, reveling in the warm smushiness of refried beans and lard, inhaling burritos and laughing at Derek's Jeff Spicoli impression.

"You do that good, man."

"I've seen that movie like four times," he said between bites. "There's like a ten second slo-mo of Phoebe Cates' tits, dude. Case closed. My sister's got a laser-disc player."

A two-fisted eating experience, we held our burritos in one hand and little plastic packets of hot sauce in the other, using the alternating squeeze and chomp technique.

"I'm hooked on these things," I announced, only halfway through my first one and already considering seconds. "They must put something addictive in the sauce."

James held his burrito out and looked at it. "When we're rich, man, we're going to have Taco Shack fly 'em in by the crate."

"Nah--we'll be eating steak and crab legs and expensive shit like that."

"Yeah right, Tommy. Have you ever even tasted crab legs?"

Tommy nodded. "Course. I been to Red Lobster..."

"I wonder if we'll come back here after we graduate," I said, thinking out loud.

"That's right...three more months."

"There's no Taco Shack in Boulder?"

"Not even," I told him.

"I'm enjoying it while I can," James said, sliding Tommy a second burrito. "Once I graduate, I'm never coming back to this town again."

We always ordered more than we could eat, and when Tommy started looking pitiful, we'd graciously sacrifice one of our burritos. Tommy mumbled his thanks and tore into it.

"I'm skating through this last semester," James continued, belching thoughtfully, "and then it's bye bye. I won't even look back. After graduation, it'll be embarrassing to be seen in here. Maybe... and I mean MAYBE our classmates will be lucky enough to see me pull up in a limo at the class reunion..."

"No doubt, dude! A huge stretch limo with like a hot tub in the back!"

Tommy liked the idea. It sounded pretty good to me, too.

"So, do you think they'll ask us to come back and play?"

"Course they will," Derek answered.

"Well, yeah...only they won't be able to afford us!"

"Totally."

James swallowed his last bite and pushed the tray away, reaching for his cigarettes. "The way I figure it, with all the parties we're not gonna have time to worry about food. Not to mention the babe market," he added. "Between jamming, partying and getting laid, we'll be pretty damn busy."

"Our own place," Randy said. "Band house, dudes. Jamming, day and night. Dwell on that."

We did as he said, and dwelled. We'd been chasing the future like a stampede of cartoon pigs after a turnip truck, and finally it seemed as though we were nearing the edge of the cliff. No more rules, curfews, or decibel limits. We'd jump willingly and freefall in the chaotic breeze of bachelor living, confident that we'd eventually sprout wings on our soft piggy backs. These swine would fly in Boulder.

"Lots of chicks up there, too," James said. "Classy chicks. College chicks."

"You know it."

"Good luck--college chicks don't go for headbangers." Derek shook his head like we were crazy.

"Sure they do, man."

"Right..."

"Shit, some of 'em do! Some straight chicks totally get into bad boys. How do you think Mark wound up with Carrie Wallace at that party last week? I mean, nobody would have pegged her for that."

"I guess you got a point. Hey Mark, what's up with you and Carrie Wallace?"

I shrugged. "Nothing too notable," I answered. "She's okay, but she chews gum all the time. She tastes like Big Red…"

"Yeah, and you're one of the few who ever got a chance to find out!"

"True," I answered, slurping from my straw. "She's not my type, though. Too…something. Too normal."

James rolled his eyes. "Listen to Mr. Stud over here! Mark'll go through the whole junior class before he finds one he likes!"

"Well, I always heard I should keep a lot of irons in the fire…"

Granted, my libido had been running itself ragged since we'd formed the band, taunted by an over-abundance of opportunity. I'd dated older, younger, rocker, and preppie. I'd dated girls from other schools and even managed a couple of flings with the not-so-straight-laced jock babes like Carrie Wallace. Between the five of us, we'd virtually combed the area clean of exciting new prospects and were ready to seek more expansive hunting grounds. Rock music would be our bait.

No sharing. This was the only rule regarding girls. If your buddy hooked up with someone, the girl was off limits. Forever.

"Look who's here," Randy said, tilting his head toward the glass door. "Mr. Regional Wrestling Champion."

We craned our necks to see Joey Desiato's custom black pickup truck rumbling into the lot. He parked it and hopped out, dragging Carrie Wallace's ultra-popular friend Tracy under his arm. Joey was a thick jock, stump-necked and sporting the kind of wussy short mullet that said he lacked rebel commitment.

The jock couple walked through the swinging glass door and into the shack, Joey lifting his chin in the time-honored 'sup' gesture. Usually, a 'sup' was about all we could expect to receive from the uber-jocks, but as Tracy leapt forward to get the news from Kimmy, we looked up from beans and cheese to see stud-boy Joey headed our way.

"Hey guys," he said, hands tucked into the pockets of his letter jacket. Like a four star general, his jacket told of the accolades. A gold 'C' was embroidered into the sleeve.

"Sup, Joey…"

"What's goin' on tonight?"

"Not much," we collectively mumbled, shrugging. The rarity of Joey's attention made us all eager to dismiss him.

"Hey Joey--I heard you got a scholarship."

"Yeah."

"For football?"

"No," Joey replied in athletic monotone. "Wrestling."

"Oh. Well…that's still pretty cool."

"Yeah. You guys still got your band?"

"Course. Jammin' as always."

"Yeah. I saw you at Sean Schneider's kegger. You guys rock."

"Yeah, thanks dude."

"Hey James, buddy," Joey blocked out the sun as he leaned suspiciously over the table, lowering his voice to a conspicuous whisper. "I need you to get me some weed."

Randy looked at me as though he smelled something nasty, I almost broke out laughing. It was, after all, laughable. Joey Desiato, captain of everything, asking us to get him a bag? When I looked over at James, I realized he wasn't sharing my amusement.

"What makes you think I know where to get it?" James snapped back at him, his tone suddenly and undeniably confrontational. "You think I'm a dealer or something?"

"I just figured you could get ahold of some…"

James clenched his jaw, then rubbed his forehead in a suppressive show of anger. "You figured that we're longhairs, so we're automatically stoners, right?"

Apparently big Joey hit a nerve. James glared at him with Mike Tyson intensity, lit up and full of attitude. This wasn't the guy I almost fought at the tracks...

Joey snorted back at him. "Yeah, funny. Look, bud--can you get it or not?"

"Well yeah, actually," James fired back, "I could. But not for you, BUD."

Joey Desiato was no hockey star, but he recognized a face-off when he saw one. In moments, his slope-headed visage metamorphosed backward from Cro-Magnon to Neanderthal.

Jock-boy pulled his ham-hock fists from his jacket. I looked across the table to see Derek flashing a 'you got burned' grin Joey's way.

"You got a problem, James?"

A rhetorical question.

"Yeah, I think I do," James answered without flinching. "You know, Joey, you talk shit behind our backs and call us freaks! You told Carrie we were just a bunch of fuck-ups!"

Joey offered a condescending huff. "Fine, forget it--"

James pressed. "Shit, dude--we've been in the same class since we were in third grade, and the only time you ever bothered to talk to me was five years ago when you kicked my ass! Oh, but now you want to come over here and act like we're all fuckin' friendly, right? I guess you figured freaks like us can score you some dope, right? Well, too fucking bad, buddy."

Joey was bristling but slightly stunned, apparently unaccustomed to being challenged. "Screw you, James! You little prick! I was right--you guys are all freaks."

"Tell you what, Joey--I'll leave your bag of weed with Coach, and you can pick it up in his office!"

James was on a roll.

Joey took a thunderous step forward. James stood from the table, pushing away his chair. I stood as well, though I did it through no conscious effort. I found myself between the two, looking up at the colossus.

"Cool it, you guys," I said.

Cool it? Admittedly lame, but at least it was an attempt.

"Sit down, dick," Joey ordered me.

Not knowing who dick was, I remained standing. I no longer felt like cooling it.

"Don't you have somewhere better to be, Joey?" I asked, stewing in James' contagious courage. "Like running a lap…or maybe showering with the rest of the team?"

The rhythm section snickered out loud. For that moment, the joke was worth the risk. However, I was relatively certain that Goliath was going to club me.

Joey moved into me, bumping chests and lifting Derek from his chair. Derek put an arm out straight between us, his glare telling Joey that the next move would be for keeps.

With Derek in his face, Mr. America deflated a bit, taking a regressive step backward. Joey may have been strong and fast, but Derek was higher on the violence food chain.

"You longhaired faggots and your lame-ass band," Joey burst out, his cool breaking. "You walk around acting all cool with your band and shit, but deep down inside you're still the same fucking geeks you always were!"

"You better shut your mouth about the band," James barked from behind me. Drawn by the growl of machismo, Kimmy, Tracy, and the rest of the Taco Shack patrons were now looking on.

"Your bullshit little band sucks. You losers will never make anything out of it…"

This time, the stricken nerve was mine.

"We're in better shape than you, dude," I snapped, the anger-fueled words emerging without discretion. "Mr. Captain of the team--hey, guess what, Joey? In just a few months, you aren't going to be Captain of jack shit anymore!"

"Gee," James joined in, "I bet losing out on that football scholarship really hurts, too. Hundreds of damn colleges out there, and none of them want you? You can't even get into Podunk State! Shit, Joey--you're already washed up!"

We'd poked the caveman one too many times. His face flushed pork n' beans red.

Joey wound up a ham-hock.

I think the punch was intended for James. In the end, it didn't matter--the blow never arrived at its intended location.

You never know when you're going to run into those special moments, the ones you know you'll truly never forget. We had no clue, no way of knowing that a legendary memory was upon us.

Derek caught the punch.

Zip thwap.

Caught it.

I shit you not, my friend. Bruce Lee couldn't have done it better. Kung-fu city. Joey's fist was literally stopped in mid-throw, held in place by Derek.

Looking back, I remember the whole thing in widescreen slow motion, but in reality, I know the pectoral standoff lasted for only a moment before Derek exploded forward, clotheslining Joey with his free arm.

Joey was leveled, flat on his hairy back. The champ was down for the count.

And then, as though knowing he was about to step into the pages of local Taco Shack mythology, Derek uttered an action-movie perfect phrase:

"Fourth down, bud. I think it's time to punt."

2 Minutes to Midnight

Maiden was coming.

We were cruising with Lonnie when we first heard the Iron Maiden at Red Rocks show announced on the radio. Following the initial round of high-fives and smiles, Lonnie popped Maiden's *Powerslave* into the tape deck and cranked it. Heads banged.

We'd seen the videos and listened to the songs hundreds of times. We'd purchased the posters, the T-shirts, and the backstage candid photos. We knew the names of every member and had already conducted our own informal panel discussions on what version of the lineup kicked the most ass.

Now it was time for the concert. Time to pay homage to our heroes and sacrifice at the holy sandstone altar known as Red Rocks Amphitheatre. The first show of the year, a triple header with King's X and Accept filling the opening slots. Sure, it probably wouldn't compare with the rain-drenched Aerosmith/Dio show we'd seen the year before, or be as memorable as the majestic Van Halen arena concert two months earlier, but it didn't matter. This was our event. This would be graduation summer, the year of our blissful release from public school and the beginning of the rest of our lives. Two of us would attend prom. No one dared miss the concert.

Step one--acquisition of tickets.

Lonnie was the best of our non-musical friends, an honorary member of the band who never missed a party. He was a gear-head at heart, a loyal guy who lifted weights, worked on his truck and smoked record amounts of dope. He'd been there through all the backyard parties and late nights, often providing the truck in which we hauled the equipment to and from gigs. Lonnie stood about five-five, but was wider--and tougher--than any two of us put together. And the guy could drink.

Perhaps a little Tom-Sawering involved here...but Lonnie wanted to go to the show as bad as the rest of us.

So Lonnie slept outside overnight in the ticket queue, our money stuffing his pockets, wondering why the line wasn't longer. It was only after arriving at the ticket window that he realized that the concert would be general admission. Seats would be first come, first served, the day of the show.

General freakin' admission.

This was a revelation. If we were resourceful enough, the front row could actually be ours. Sometimes, brushing with greatness requires work.

Even at a general admission show, landing the front row was a bitch. The park didn't allow ticket line campers until noon, two days before the show. Being first would mean getting there early, and that would require a constant physical presence in line for at least forty-eight hours prior to show time. Even at that, being first in line wouldn't guarantee the front row.

We sat around the Formica table.

"There's two entrances to the park," James reminded us, "so we'll have to run."

Two lines of voracious fans, slathering and drooling over the prospect of front row seats. To complicate things, the entrances were located at the top of the towering stone amphitheatre and the front row in the belly of the beast. Thus, after breaching the row of ticket takers, the unwashed hordes would pour down hundreds of stone stairs in a Rollerball free-for-all sprint for the front. And even if fate and intimidation somehow managed to land us in the front row, the territory would have to be jealously guarded against would-be seat burglars and the swells of pressed flesh. Many an overconfident concert-goer had fallen victim to general admission shoving matches.

It would take dedication and perseverance, planning and foresight. A masterful group effort would be required. Like expert thieves with a job at Fort Knox, we assembled our team and talked line-camp strategy.

"Okay, so Lonnie, Derek and me get there on Thursday," James continued. "We'll park in the campground north of the amphitheatre and hike up to the gates from there. I figure they'll be opening the lots around noon, so if all things work out, we should be first, or close to it."

"Sweet..."

"Mark and Randy, you guys will be second shift. Get there when you can, sometime after dark. Tommy and Alex will spell you on Friday morning, and then by five or so we should all be back to stay. Tommy and Alex can get some sleep or whatever, and then come back when they're rested."

"Shouldn't we try to get spots in both lines?" Tommy asked, experiencing a rare moment of cerebral activity.

James shook his head. "No way. My brother and his friends tried that last year at AC/DC. No good. It's too hard to save seats with only a couple people. I'd say we need to all be together when we make the run."

"Besides," Derek interjected, "Line-camping is the best part. Hell, the line-camping is almost better than the show! Besides, Lonnie's got something special planned."

Lonnie smiled deviously, nodding and scratching his chiseled chin. "Oh yeah…" He pulled a sizeable joint from his shirt pocket and passed it to Tommy. "You do the honors, bud."

"You got a lighter?"

"Here."

Tommy lit the spliff, double-hitting. He held it in for a moment, raising a finger before deflating in an exhale that filled the room. Coughing ensued.

I took a drag and passed it. "So what happens after that, Master James?"

James narrowed his eyes, thinking it over like General Patton on the shores of Sicily. "Well, after all that waiting, we've got to have a plan. Course, all this doesn't mean crap unless we get a good placement. But as long as we're close to the front of the line, we've got a shot. So…the fastest runner is the first to hand off his ticket. I guess that's you, Mark."

I tensed. "O--kay. But I've never been the fastest anything--"

"No sweat, dude. Seriously. Derek and Lonnie will be right behind you, ready to lay down some damage if it gets rough. They're like the muscle."

I nodded, wondering if I was coordinated enough to sprint down a flight of concrete stairs after drinking rotgut for twelve hours. I could already picture myself going down face first or catching a clothesline and being flown off the mountain in one of those paramedic helicopters. For the moment, I would hang my positive outlook on the fact that the enforcers would be behind me.

Derek glanced at me, mischievously confident as always. He undoubtedly welcomed the thought of the general admission mayhem. I envied him.

"Now Mark, we're all going to be coming in behind you, so once you hit that front row, you gotta stand your ground for a second or two. Alex has volunteered to run interference, so if we see any threats, he'll eat pavement and throw a couple blocks."

I felt relieved to hear that Alex would be the designated pavement eater.

"I can do it," I told him.

And so the plan was set.

Fate grinned at us, but was yet to show any teeth.

STILL LIFE

Line-camping.

Fourth in line, west side. Not bad at all.

Three people managed to beat James and Derek to the line, fellow headbangers whose genius apparently surpassed our own. They'd been camping in the wilds for three nights and were by right and respect the undisputed line champions.

By the time Randy and I arrived on Thursday night, the entrance path was well camped, and the line stretched thirty or forty people long. With no sign of James at the back, we continued up-line, proudly passing the campers as we headed toward our place at the front. Still forty some-odd hours away from the gig, the line-camps remained very subdued.

Despite James' guarantees of first place, I had actually been predicting them to land somewhere between fifth and tenth. Line campers were clever survivalists, and some of these concert goers were serious die-hards so it wouldn't have surprised me to see James and Derek even farther back.

Admittedly, I was praying for failure.

I wanted to see the concert as bad as anyone and would have been thrilled to find myself sitting front row...but sprinting and jockeying for seats? Competing for our prize? General admission line placement would become a moot point after about the first twenty rows, and I was hoping to find Derek and James frowning in spot twenty-five.

No such luck. We found them waiting fourth in line.

My fate was sealed. I'd be running for the front row.

"Mark, dude! Sup Randy!"

Randy shook with Derek. I shook with James. Derek shook with me. James shook with Randy. So on.

"Maiden, dude...this is it!"

"No doubt! Totally stoked, dude." Derek leaned back and looked around, holding out his jean-jacketed arms. "So what do you think?"

"Damn!" I said, truly impressed. "Nice line placement. You're way close."

"We should've gone to the east gate," James commented, sniffing. "I heard there were fewer people--I bet we'd be first in line over there."

I shrugged. "It looks good to me, dude. This is perfect."

Perfect for taking a tumble down a flight of stone steps...

"You guys did it," Randy nodded happily. "Shit, we only have three people in front of us. This rules, James. Front row should be a lock, eh?"

"Huh-uh. Wrong," Derek interjected. "See, these three people in line are just holding spots, like us. For all we know, each of them could have ten friends on the way. We could wind up fifteenth or twentieth by the time it's over."

"Not only that," James added, "But we have the other gate to think about. It could get pretty hairy when we're sprinting for the front row on Saturday." He looked to me. "I guess we're relying on you, dude. You sure you want to lead the rush?"

He made it sound like my choice. And I was miles away from sure. I had serious doubts about the chances of actually landing front row, and even less faith in my ability to remain free of injury while trying to do so. Still, I couldn't stand looking like a wuss.

"I'm sure," I told them, trying to sound sincere. "But you guys better be hauling ass behind me…"

"Oh, you know it," Derek answered, clapping his hands and rhythmically nodding his head. "I'll be there two seconds after you. And so far, these guys in line look like pussies. We're too close to lose it now. I mean…this is important, man! I swear, I'll take somebody out if I have to."

Derek was ready. More than any of us, he wanted this concert-- and the front row. And whatever the peril waiting for me at the stage front, he'd be there to follow me down the mountain. It didn't make my task any less perilous, but it was better knowing that if I went down, Derek would make someone pay.

James nodded, re-inspired. "Totally. We can still do this thing."

"No doubt…"

"We'll see you guys tomorrow," James reaffirmed, "hold the line."

"Cool. You know where we'll be."

"Cool."

Derek and James said their laters and took off, promising to be back by five the next day. Before leaving, James gave strict orders that we should infiltrate the surrounding camps and obtain reconnaissance data on their numbers and firepower. We said 'yes sir, dude sir,' and gave him the headbanger salute.

And so our shift began, another peaceful spring evening in leather-land.

I stared up and down the line, chuckling at the sight of weathered rockers. A thin mist of chilled wetness descended with the setting sun, leaving the hair bunch looking like soaked cats. Three spots down, a girl pulled a can of spray from her purse and added another coat to the dark brown tumbleweed that rested atop her head. The wet wind was wreaking salon havoc with her look, causing the over-treated strands to clump and wilt pitifully. She looked up at me like a troll doll, pulling on her bangs, the grim spectre of follicle defeat etched in her eyes.

Flat hair, and soaking wet leather jackets. Seeing the bar crowd transplanted into the mountainous setting was a lot to absorb at once. The headbanging faithful looked oddly out of place here, like one of those old sepia brown photographs where the cowboys are dressed in suits.

We weren't outdoorsy types. Unlike country music fans, headbangers didn't generally ride horses, own ranches, or worry about getting in touch with nature. We passed the time in neon-lit clubs and concert halls, two-room unfurnished apartments and one story starter homes. The items on our 'to do' lists were primarily indoor activities, and the vast majority of them required electricity.

The exception was our headbanger cousins, the bikers and Harley fanatics. They were as comfortable inside as out and would often throw outdoor parties up in the canyons. The bikers' culture and traditions were completely their own, yet they shared hard rock music with us, and thus our clans would regularly pow-wow. They treated the younger and trendier longhairs as their illegitimate offspring and tolerated our differences because we were musical kin. This being the foothills, the bikers were well-represented in line, settled in like amiable pit bulls.

Randy and I said hello to our immediate neighbors and rolled out our sleeping bags on the cold pavement, setting our bony butts down on hallowed concert ground as thousands of line-campers had done in the past. We reclined, smoking cigarettes and looking up at the huge red rock wall, recounting our favorite Monty Python lines and discussing the finer points of dude philosophy. Someone up the line cranked their boom-box and Zeppelin's "Kashmir" saturated the night air, reflecting off the mountains and back down to our casually grooving heads.

Our neighbors seemed nice enough.

On the right, in spot number three, was a furry guy who called himself Rowdy. His mom must have been psychic. He went for the Charles Manson look, sporting a beard and comb-deficient hair, looking every bit his name. Not without a sense of irony, Rowdy dozed the entire first night.

The neighbor on our left was Ruth, a six-foot-three redhead bruiser of a woman who wore army boots and an oversized leather jacket. She didn't seem to give a crap whether her hair was flat or not and had a habit of clearing her throat. Every now and then, she'd let loose with a bit of low humor and, though she didn't say much, her comments indicated that she was tuning into our conversation. Ruth was alone for the moment, but talked about her old man joining her later. We expected a biker, and by the looks of her, a big one.

I was beginning to get cold. Even in the early summer, the nighttime Rocky Mountain temperatures plunge into the seriously chilly range, and as card carrying members of the headbangers' union, we refused to wear anything heavier than our leather jackets.

Leather. Too warm in the spring and summer, and never warm enough in the winter. When we'd purchased our jackets, we'd focused on look and not lining, and now we were paying for it in shivers. On the upside, we looked cool as we lay there freezing.

Randy brought some odd-tasting peach-flavored brandy and we passed the bottle back and forth, the conversation growing deeper by the minute.

"So dude, check this out," Randy reached for his smokes again.

"Can I bum a shreed?"

"Sure," he passed me one. "I brought a two extra packs so I don't have to buy any all weekend. Pretty damn responsible, don't you think?"

"No doubt," I replied. "You get the smoker's merit badge, dude."

"Merit badge? Sweet."

"It's a little silver pin that looks like a black lung."

He laughed. "So what does the drinker's merit badge look like?"

"Hmm...I think it's called the 'Grey Liver'."

Randy laughed, pulling from the bottle. "And the weed badge is the fried cerebellum! Speaking of...James told me you got accepted to college, dude."

"Yep," I answered. "The letter of acceptance settles it."

"Congrats, man--that's huge."

I shrugged. "Yeah, I guess so."

"Boulder bound. I bet your parents are happy..."

I shrugged again. "Yeah, I guess. They'll be happy when I have the degree. Getting accepted doesn't mean much by itself."

"Yeah it does. Damn, I can just see you up there--walking around the campus with your screamin' long hair, and you'll be like, 'In your face, yuppies!'. You'll kick ass up there, Mark. School comes easy to you."

I didn't like talking school with the dudes. I always sensed a 'you think you're better than me' vibe coming from my headbanger buddies, so I usually de-emphasized any academic successes.

"You did pretty well in class," I said, attempting to re-direct the conversation. "You didn't even send out one application?"

"No need for it now." Randy pulled from the bottle. "No college for me. Shit--I'm better at drums than anything else. Do what you're best at, right? I'll be drumming one way or another. Drummers don't get any better as they get older, and I'd bet you I'm a hell of a lot smarter five or ten years from now, you know? I can go to college later…if I need to."

Now in most situations, this would be the place where a good friend would put his foot down and amiably tell his buddy that notions like blowing off college for the promise of drumming money were idiotic at best, and that attempting to cover at least a few bases was not always a bad thing.

But this was Randy. And as much as I would have liked to pitch the value of a college education, his mind was made up. Besides, Randy hated real work.

"My drum teacher Justin says I'm good enough to go to college for music if I wanted," he continued on cue, "but I figure I'd just be wasting time. Not that the degree is a waste or anything…I just think I've learned all I need to. I'm better off jamming. With any luck, we'll hit it big, and we won't have to worry about any of that."

With any luck. What a depressing phrase.

With ANY luck. Okay, so it's better than 'with all the luck we can get', but still…strange, how people always use it when they're being optimistic.

"I just want to get on stage," I told him, staring up at the clouds. "I want to stand on one of those big stages, look out and see the place packed wall-to-wall with metal-heads!"

Randy chuckled, taking another drink. "We're gonna slay 'em. Given. Hey, dude…look at this…"

Randy pointed, and I followed the trail of his finger to a rough-edged silhouette moving up the hill toward us.

It was a shirtless drunk guy, staggering so dramatically as to make it dangerous. He slanted in wavering, diagonal steps, toppling forth wildly in one direction before leaning back in the other. The result was a skidding lurch that drew a round of chuckles from the waking souls in line.

The guy had screaming long hair, but its elevation had long ago been defeated by the rain, leaving the greasy strands drooping, parted flat in the middle like an Allman brother. His jeans were embarrassingly dirty, holes worn in the knees and pockets, a tourniquet-tight bandana encircling his thigh.

He staggered closer, teetering toward us.

We sat mesmerized by the human train wreck, watching as he took one misstep too many and landed with a fleshy thud at our feet.

Laughs erupted from the line. Biker Ruth croaked a throaty guffaw and shook her head.

"You okay, man?"

We both stood up, moving quickly to either side of the fallen drunk. The guy was on his hands and knees now, head down.

"Hey," Randy tapped him on the shoulder. "You okay?"

The guy sat back on his heels, shaking it off. Fresh pavement burns colored his elbows and chin, and his front teeth had apparently been rotting for a while. His hair was so dirty that the raindrops were beading up. No shirt, a padlocked chain choker, and one of those pen-knife home tattoos that said OZZY. The guy looked like he grew up UNDER a trailer.

The guy looked up at Randy. "You got a cigarette, man?"

"Yeah, sure. Stand up, bud."

We lifted the guy back up on his shaky legs and, surprisingly, he remained afloat. Randy pulled out his new smokes and made the mistake of opening the pack and holding it out.

"Can I take two?"

Randy chuckled some more. "Sure."

"Thanks, man."

"Sure."

The guy took the smokes and lit one before offering a giant war whoop.

"MAIDEN, MAN! MAIDEN!"

Disturbing the peace, but in a good way. From down the line the guy's outburst was seconded with a few whistles and responding whoops, the line-camping wolves baying at the thought of the concert.

The guy was pleased at this and tipped an imaginary hat like a gunfighter before wobbling on past us. Biker Ruth laughed until she coughed.

We sat back down, re-situating ourselves.

"That guy was messed up, dude." I leaned forward, no longer seeing him.

Randy nodded in agreement. "Did you see his face? Damn, he was fucked up--in every way! If somebody saw that guy on the street, they'd think he was criminal. Kinda sad if you think about it, man...at least, like, twenty percent of all headbangers are sketchy dudes like that, right?"

I shrugged. "Yeah, probably."

"Well, when most normal people think of heavy metal, they picture that guy. It's like when we go into the department store and the security guards tail us like we're ready to rob the place! Most people think headbangers are scumbags and morons...."

I shrugged again. "Yeah, but once people know you, they make a decision based on who you are," I said, rationalizing. "I remember going into classes and seeing the teachers look at me like I was a screw-up. I didn't care, because once I started getting good grades, they'd be forced to change their minds about me. By the time the semester was over, I'd be the teacher's pet."

"Yeah, but most people don't get a chance to know you enough," he replied, "and other people's bullshit is buried too deep to change."

"You're still thinking about that crap with your cousin, aren't you?'

"Nah...I don't know," Randy offered. "I guess so. Not like I should really worry about taking shit from him or anything..."

"What did he say again?"

"Same old. He got into this trip about my hair, telling me I'd never get a decent job and telling me how many other people have to struggle against discrimination--all that. He said he doesn't know why I'd choose to grow my hair when I know people will give me shit for it. He says if you choose discrimination, you can't bitch about it."

I frowned. "How much older is he?"

"Ten years," Randy answered. "And he's a total geek."

"He's probably jealous of you, dude."

He nodded reluctantly. "Maybe, but he's a realtor or something like that. He makes good money--good enough, at least. When him and my grandma and everybody look at me, all they see is that fucked-up guy. Oh, get this--he asked me why we have to grow our hair! He asked why we can't just play without all the bullshit."

I raised both eyebrows. "Did you tell him we WANT to grow it?"

"I didn't know what to say. I said it looked cool."

I pondered the issue, wondering how I would have responded in his place. I looked to my inner lounge, asking Jim why he always took his shirt off, and why he grew that Grizzly Adams beard toward the end of his career.

Mr. Morrison stared me down like I was crazy. While giving me the finger, he told me I should know the answer.

"Maybe we do it BECAUSE it pisses people off," I told Randy. "Maybe we do it because we found something that's our thing, you know? And when we walk in the damned department store, we don't even have to say a word because they can tell with one look that we're not playing the game...at least not all the way. I guess I do it because I can, and because they can't really stop me. We just... explore our personal freedom a little more than some people. Screw 'em if they don't like it. They're not supposed to."

Randy grinned. "I should've said something like that..."

"I mean--rock music isn't supposed to be liked by everyone," I continued, now inspired, "especially heavy metal! It's supposed to be unpopular with most people. That's the point! Do you think that guy would have carved Ozzy into his chest if his mom was a fan? No way. Seriously--if some little old lady doesn't hate it, then it's not rock, dude. That's why crossing over is the kiss of death for a true rock band..."

Randy nodded his agreement, but wasn't satisfied. "I just hate people looking at me and thinking I'm stupid."

"Pshht," I responded gracefully, basking in ignorance, "opinions are harmless. You've just got to ignore it and find people who can see through. People's bullshit opinions can't change your life."

"Yeah, I guess," he conceded, lighting a cigarette and exhaling a cloud up into the night. "But rocker or not, guys like that give headbangers a bad name..."

"So why'd you give him the smokes?" I asked.

"It was only human."

The warm peachy petrol was heating me from the inside now, and I began to think the night wouldn't be so long. Strains of Iron Maiden's first album drifted down the line like a four-four iron lullaby.

"Pretty soon we won't have to take shit anymore," he said, "from anybody. In a couple of years, we won't be sleeping out for tickets, dude--we'll be giving them away. One way or another. We've got to improve, and all...but we're getting there."

"It's getting to be a drag loading all my shit in and out of keggers all the time," Randy said. "My kit sounds way better with a real sound system, I guarantee."

"We'll all sound better," I said, picturing ourselves on stage at The Tank. "We'll kick ass down there, I think."

"Oh, that's a given, dude. You'll see. We'll be jamming in Denver like three nights a week and turning away the chicks!"

"Yeah, hopefully--some of them, at least. To be honest, dude, I just want to get on stage. Huge crowds, lights and fog and all..."

He looked over at me. "Look at you, man--all Mr. Confidence. I remember the first time you sang."

"The Andersen sisters' party?"

"Yep--you were so worried that we all thought you'd lose your lunch on the first song! Sounded good though."

"I still feel sick sometimes," I said, chuckling. "I just don't tell you guys anymore."

Randy smiled, reminiscing. "Man, that party was wicked. That raised deck, no cops--we jammed 'till like one o'clock or something. You never know when you'll have one of those nights you'll never forget. You know what I mean?"

"No doubt, dude."

I thought back to the Andersen sisters' party, my memory skipping immediately to visions of Tabitha.

"That was the night you got together with Tommy's cousin, wasn't it?"

Apparently, Randy was reading my mind.

"Yep," I answered, nodding wistfully. "Tabitha. No doubt, man--that was a good night all the way around."

"Whatever happened to her, anyway?"

Shrug. "I wish I knew. We got along great and everything, and she gave me her number in California. So I called her and chickened out the first time--left a message the second time. Nothing. I called again about a week later, thinking she didn't get the message. So I left another one, you know, acting all nice. ...still nothing."

"Shit." He shook his head, grinning. "So...you called back about twenty more times instead of giving up?"

"Well, not that many...but yeah," I admitted. "You know, it's not like I actually expected her to be with me or anything like that. It's just after all the calls I made, the point now is how uncool it is for her not even to call me back."

"Harsh, dude," he answered, shrugging. "It happens, though."

"I called her about once a month for the next few months. At some point, I just stopped. I just have to remember that when a girl gives you her number, it doesn't necessarily mean she wants you to call."

Randy smirked. "You don't need that chick--she's the marrying type, and you're not. Besides, you can do way better. Look at it this way: you saved a buttload of money on long distance charges!"

"Yeah, but I liked Tabitha."

Randy laughed. "Yeah, and you liked Amy, who you dumped when you decided you liked Tracie, who you liked until you met Missy, who you dumped when you de--"

"Alright," I smiled, holding up my hands in surrender. "I get it."

"You just wait," Randy said, slurring a bit. "Pretty soon you're going to have half the chicks in town wanting to come home with you. They always go for the singers, and you're gonna be fronting the best band on the circuit!"

It was reassuring to hear Randy talking in such prophetic terms. If I was deluded, then at least someone else was similarly afflicted. His confidence seemed to validate my own, and things seemed to be rolling along just as they should. With any luck, we'd get there.

As fortune would have it, we both passed out soon after, carried away by the gentle strains of Zeppelin IV and the smell of wet asphalt.

When the Night Comes Down

"Dude, wake up. Dude…"

Disoriented, I sat up, realizing I was sleeping on the side of the mountain in my leather jacket and jeans. The breeze was wicked cold.

"Mark, dude…"

Derek crouched next to me, his voice bearing weight, his lower jaw quivering with the chill.

"Hey man" I squinted, trying to get my bearings. "What are you doing up here? What time is it?"

Next to me, Randy was rolling awake.

"Like two-thirty or something," he answered. "Man, I'm glad you guys are up here…"

I could hear tears in his voice. This was Derek, and he wasn't the type of guy who cried.

"Derek, man--what's wrong?"

"Fuck it, man…I just had to come up here." Derek ran a sleeve across his eyes, his lip curling in anger. "Fuck him if he doesn't like it--like I had any choice my whole life…now he thinks he can fucking tell me what to do when he doesn't even give a shit about me… or anybody or anything--"

"Dude, slow down! What happened?"

Derek stood back up, his rage provoking him to pace. "He'll probably call the fucking cops on me now! Piece of crap never did shit, and now all of a sudden he acts all like he knows what best for everybody... I swear dudes, all I wanted to do was cave his face in with the heel of my boot!"

His voice cracked as he ranted, losing composure with every word, the quivering lips slowly being replaced with a vicious, depressed look. Randy and I were both on our feet now.

Derek took a breath, spitting angrily. "Fucker doesn't know me at all! He wasn't there when any of the important shit went down! And screw it, because my mom doesn't care--she wouldn't even let him see me if it wasn't for the court order!"

"Derek--what is it? Something happen with your dad?"

"Of course! Shit! I swear to fucking God man, once I graduate I'm out of that fucker's life forever! No shit--he'll never see my ass again!"

His eyes were lined with bloodshot red, his face puffy and etched with distress. I'd seen him angry, but not a single tear had ever emerged from Derek's eyes in our presence before. He wasn't the kind of guy to break down, and I admit, I had no idea how to calm him down.

Randy produced a cigarette. "Dude...here."

Derek pushed away the offer and yelled 'fuck' at the top of his lungs. The snoozing line-campers responded with a few New York admonitions.

"Shut up, you little shit!"

"People trying to sleep here, dumb-ass!"

Derek spit again, and looked over at me. "Fuck it, man. Just fuck it all!"

He turned and started walking.

Away from the line, into the darkened foothill forest surrounding the amphitheatre, without another word to either of us.

"Derek, dude--come back, man!"

"What are you doing? Derek--tell us what happened! Where are you gonna go?"

"Away!" he shouted, holding up his middle finger.

He kept going. I could hear the mumbled rage as he ranted to himself, planting one foot firmly in front of the other, marching away from us.

Randy and I looked at each other. His face bore the same sleepy-eyed shock as mine.

"What do we do?" he looked down the line. "Wait for him to come back?"

And then, with absolutely no regard for line etiquette, general admission or Iron Maiden, I stepped out of line.

I followed Derek's steps, away from the row of cozied concert-goers and into the cold mountain wind.

"Derek! Hold up!"

"Mark!" Randy yelled at me, clinging to our spot as though held by a magnet. "What's up?"

"I'm gonna go get him," I shouted back. "Wait here if you want…"

I kept walking, trying to focus on Derek's shadow ahead. A few seconds later, I heard Randy running up behind me, falling in pace.

"Screw the line," he said.

Derek must have known we were following him, because he picked up his pace as though trying to lose us. We kept after him, willing our sleepy legs to move.

When we finally caught up, Derek was engaging in a little de-struction therapy. He'd picked up a fallen branch and was whacking trees like a baseball player, swinging hard and grunting with each crack. The tears were coming now, and he whipped and struck as though trying to beat down the forest.

"Derek! Dude!"

"Come on, man--just tell us what the hell happened!"

With a grimace, he tossed the branch. "Oh, nothing big--I just punched my fucking dad...that's all..."

"What happened? Did he hit you or something? Just sit down for a second and tell us! Randy, man--you have any of that brandy left?"

Randy shook his head. "Tapped out."

Like a melancholy wind-up doll, Derek was slowing down bit by bit, his rage replaced by a look of hurt. He wiped his eyes, raising a hand. "Don't worry...I brought my own..."

He found a rock and sat down, finally winding to a stop. Pulling a pint of vodka from his jacket, he twisted the top and took a swig. I figured Derek had probably already had enough, but said nothing. Just holding the bottle seemed to calm him down.

"It's not like I even see him much anymore," he began, taking a drink. "He only gets visitation like once a month on weekends, and even then, he cancels half the time. So--do you think he could give me a fucking break this weekend and let me come to the show? Fuck no!"

"Your dad wasn't gonna let you come?"

"Of course not! But not because of any good reason, man. He knew this was important, and he put his fucking foot down to spite me! All these other weeks he's too damned busy, and now suddenly he has to see me? Bullshit! Some fucking coincidence!"

"So I told him I was going," Derek continued, now inspired by the need to talk. "I told him he was being unfair and that he could kiss my ass. He caught me at the door and had his finger all in my face pointing--he said I'm a big fucking disappointment to my mother, and I don't respect anything...I mean, what the hell is that? He's the damn disappointment! Shit!"

"So he tried to stop you?"

"He was leaning against the door. I pushed his arm away, and he smacked me with a backhand. So I hit him."

"In the face?"

"Yeah, I guess," he answered guiltily. "Though I wasn't trying to hurt him. Seriously. It was like instinct, I swear!"

"Oh shit...but he's okay, right?"

"Yeah--he's too fucking dense to get hurt by a single punch."

"He hit you first," Randy added. "Wasn't the first time, either."

Derek wiped his eyes. "Yeah, but don't get me wrong--he hasn't really hit me in a long time. It's not like I had some vendetta or something against him--"

"Oh, I know, dude. I wasn't saying you're, like, some battered child or something...just that he started it, and all..."

"I don't deny that I'm pissed off at him," Derek said, passing the bottle and rubbing his eyes. "We've been at each other's throats for years...but it's not because I'm mad for myself, you know? I don't care. Personally, I can deal with the shit he did to me--I can take it. My mom, though--that's different."

We remained quiet, knowing how rarely Derek opened up. He stared at the ground as he talked, as though watching a movie on the pine-needled ground.

"It's like...when my mom and dad first got divorced, we moved away from him and my mom got a new job and everything--she was happy, you know, like she'd started a new life. And everybody told us how happy they were for us and how much better our lives would be without him...but my mom's not happy. She's not fucking happy at all, and it only gets worse. He broke more than her nose, you know? Her whole life got broke, and there's no way for her to fix it. I have to watch her smoke a million cigarettes and hear her crying in her bedroom and there's not a fucking thing I can do!"

"It's alright, man--"

"No! See, that's the thing, dude! It's NOT alright, and it never will be again! My mom didn't want to be famous or anything--her dream was just some simple, regular shit like getting married and being in love and having a couple kids! Well, that's gone. Fucking done. She just works and sits around now…it's like there's no such fucking thing as a new beginning, you know? We always have the old shit hanging over our heads, whether we admit it or not!"

I looked down, not knowing what to say. Derek's hands shook with cold, his face now reflecting a dying look of regret.

"Nothing ever stays the same," I told him, trying to think of a way to talk without saying things would be alright. "Just like the way it changed when they got divorced. Soon, things will change, and your mom will be happy again. Time helps to heal things…"

I don't know if this was good advice. I didn't even know if it was remotely true. But Derek needed to hear something, anything-- and he didn't like to be bullshitted.

"Time is all screwed up now," he replied angrily. "My mom's life might get better, but it won't be because anything healed, dude. If we can just forget it a little bit, that would help--but my family's wasted now, especially after tonight. He's gonna call the cops, I bet."

Randy shook his head. "No way, dude. He wouldn't do that."

"Fuck, man, I don't even know why I'm here. You know? I just cause my mom problems. Like he said, a disappointment."

I couldn't stand it. The sight of Derek dipping so low was spurring a kind of indignant anger in me, and I didn't know what to do. I'd been the peacekeeper and the emotional middle man of the band, and now it was my duty to pick him up.

"You're not a disappointment to your mom," I told him. "And you're not a disappointment to us, man. And you're family's not wasted, because WE'RE your family."

"Yeah, and I'm practically sober," Randy added, smiling at his own joke. "Get it? Get it?"

Derek couldn't help himself, and his frown broke into an amused grin. "You fuckers left the line…"

I shrugged. "Screw the line."

Randy laughed. "I'll go find that stick, and you can release a little tension getting us our place back."

"I'd do it, too." Derek took another big pull from the bottle, his eyes growing calm. "You guys left the line for me--I suppose it's my fault."

I shrugged. "No biggie. General admission, man. The concert's not important."

Derek sniffed, grinning. "Like hell it isn't!"

He leaned his head back, taking a deep breath as he stared up into the sky. We sat for a few long moments without speaking.

"You're right, Mark," he said finally. "I never had any brothers, you know? I never even knew what it was like to have a brother until I started hanging out with you guys. My sister's cool and all, but she never had my back. Not like you longhairs…"

"That's what we're here for, man."

"That's what a band is, dude."

Derek nodded and punched me affectionately in the arm.

Randy laughed, jumping to his feet and reaching down a hand. "Okay…so who's freezing?"

"I think Randy needs another drink."

Derek brushed himself off, checking the bloody scrapes on his hands. "I feel like an idiot now…just don't say anything about this to James. Okay?"

"No problem," I said. "Forgotten."

"We'll get over it," Randy told him. "It won't be the first time you embarrassed us!"

"Yeah, fuck you guys," Derek smiled, spitting. "I'm ready to rock."

We walked back to the queue with an oddly fortified sense of confidence, knowing we'd get our place in line back. Derek's moment of weakness had somehow strengthened us all, and the future was once again brightening for three longhaired brothers.

Hope rules all, I suppose.

That's what a band is, dude.

At the time, I actually believed it.

BALLS TO THE WALL

Derek was pretty quiet through the night, but the chill of morning seemed to find him in a surprisingly good mood. I decided it was best to avoid anything too serious, and he wasn't eager to revisit the events of the night before. Whatever the repercussion, Derek had wisely decided that he'd deal with it later. I suspected he would.

We played hacky-sack that morning with Rowdy and his barefoot wife, enjoying the clean air and morning sun. Tommy and Alex arrived around noon, and Randy and I found our trip home to be a mere turnaround, an opportunity for a quick shower and change of clothes.

When we returned to the line, the quiet little camp had changed considerably. The line was growing in width and length as rockers of all makes and models joined the effort. Bikers and headbangers, posers and dinosaur rockers, and even some individuals who didn't have tickets but simply wanted to attend the line camp party. Twenty-four hours until the concert, and the festivities were already beginning. I looked down the line to see a much more congested view, a cornfield of leather and wind-flattened hair.

"Hey dudes."

"Ay! There they are!"

We found Tommy and Alex. They were sharing a beer with Biker Ruth.

"Guys, this is Ruth."

We all mumbled our heys. Ruth looked up and waved.

"Yeah, we met Ruth earlier. No sign of your old man?"

It felt strange saying old man. Ruth shook her head.

"You ready to party, or what?"

"You know it," she snorted.

"Sup, Mark!"

I shook with Lonnie. "Ay, man! Sup?"

"This is what…"

As promised, Lonnie bore a special surprise in the form of a two liter bottle filled with a dubious brown liquid. Within the liquid floated indistinguishable chunks of what appeared to be fruit. Near the cap it foamed with a light brown head. It immediately reminded me of Derek's infamous spittoon.

"What's in the bottle?"

"A special mix," Lonnie said proudly, holding the bottle up to the light. "Basically everything I could find. Rum, vodka, apricot brandy, orange juice, and Dr. Pepper. In that I put some orange slices, a few melon balls--scooped 'em myself--and some cherries. I call it 'Nam' juice, dude…"

Knowing about the glass bottle restriction, Lonnie found resourceful ways to provide for his drinking habits. He handed me the bottle, and I reluctantly unscrewed the cap and took a sip.

The mix tasted like circus peanuts and gasoline.

"Whoo! Duh-ay-am!!!"

"Kinda grabs you by the boo boo, don't it?" he asked, doing his best Chong impression. "That's why it's 'Nam' juice…the buzz will wear off, but you'll be having flashbacks for the rest of your life! I've got another one in the truck."

"Lonnie's all ready."

"Hell yeah I am," he belched, taking another sip before handing the bottle to Tommy. "The line party--this shit right here--is the best part, man. What's gonna suck is waiting for the concert to begin. We hit the gates at noon, but the concert don't start till seven. So...drink up, I guess. Any hotties around?"

"A few."

The 'Nam' juice made a trip around the circle and we were off to Saigon, not bothering to pace ourselves as we loped into the eighteen-hour odyssey of fresh air and inebriation. The tunes pumped steadily from the boom boxes down the line, and the windbreaker clad park officials were finally kind enough to set out porta-potties for the guests. No longer would we have to use the downwind trees.

Concert stories were compared and bullshit was served up. A new show always made you reminisce about the old ones, and we'd stand around for hours comparing quarter notes. Of course, to musicians, concert stories are like fishing tales and seem to get bigger every time they're told. Everybody wanted to be able to say 'I was there when' or 'I saw so and so back in such and such'. You could gain extra esteem if you had, for example, seen a Led Zeppelin concert or witnessed a Randy Rhodes performance. Now that Dave was out of Van Halen, it was becoming trendy to claim having seen the old VH live.

Fish tales of the leather-clad. Our mythos.

Many of the concert stories were greatly fabricated. Others were completely and unabashedly contrived, told to you by people who hadn't even been to the shows they claimed. This was quite common, as it was virtually impossible to prove that someone hadn't been at a show. However, proof would sweeten your story, and proof came in the form of a concert T.

An investment in the future. When first purchased, the T-shirts seemed common, overly black and itchingly new. Time passes and the shirts become faded and worn. They get lovingly hacked with scissors and take on a sentimental quality as half-shirts or muscle shirts. The more years that pass, the more valuable the T is, both in terms of proving your concert claims and proudly displaying your long-term membership in the headbanger club. Weekends like this were made for showing off your oldest concert shirt, and from the looks of things, the line boasted an impressive variety.

As nine rolled into midnight, the crowd grew a bit more, with biker Ruth's boyfriend finally showing up. As predicted, he was a huge guy with steel-toed boots and a mullet. I would have to outrun him.

Derek had done the recon on Rowdy and claimed that there were only four in Rowdy's group. Rowdy, in turn, had done a little investigation of his own, finding that spot number two would have only two people, and spot number one would have five. Including Rowdy's bunch, that would make eleven people in line ahead of us. My task suddenly didn't seem so easy.

I considered faking an injury on the way down. A fake injury, however, would likely require actually falling down--risking a real injury. That, and I'd be forced to fake throughout the show and didn't know if I could maintain the charade.

By two a.m., Tommy's neighbor Alex was puking in the bushes and wishing his tour of duty would come to an end. The rest of us lay against the short stone wall, holding the place in line and trying to stay warm. We'd finished the first bottle of 'Nam' juice and a twelve-pack of beer.

By four a.m., everyone was asleep on the asphalt with the exception of Tommy and me. We walked a half-conscious Alex up and down the hill to wear off some of the liquor. He proclaimed his love for us both, puked, and then passed out.

By eight a.m., we were all roused from stiff-necked slumber to the sounds of the Bullet Boys…everyone but Alex, of course, who remained mercifully unconscious. On the verge of cannibalism, Lonnie offered to sacrifice his parking spot and make a run down the hill to pick up some fast food. Money was collected, orders taken, and he returned about an hour later with some prime grub.

Scarfing helped. Energized by the food and the warm sunshine, we discussed Ginger vs. Mary Ann, Suzanne Somers vs. Joyce DeWitt, Wilma Flintstone vs. Betty Rubble and Barbara Eden's Jeannie vs. Liz Montgomery's Samantha. The only thing we could seem to agree on was Betty, though somehow James always seemed like a Wilma man to me.

The moment of truth approached.

By eleven a.m., we were discussing strategy. The final horde of gate-rushers was arriving, filling the road and craning their pale necks to gauge their chances. The line-stealing was already being plotted, and Tommy was assigned to stand guard, insuring that eleven, and only eleven people stood between us and the gates. Alex had recovered enough to stand on his own, but it was apparent that he wouldn't be much use in claiming the seats.

We would have to do it ourselves. Derek gave me a pep-talk, and James figured out a few last minute line changes. Randy volunteered to look after Alex, who was still having mountain-spins. I regretted not having volunteered myself. We clutched our tickets and waited, squinting beneath the unbridled mountain sun.

My chest tightened. The gates opened and the line began to slowly filter past the ticket takers and into the park. As the lucky front campers passed the entrance, we could see them breaking into a run and heading for the stage. Next to me, James shifted impatiently and agonized over each one.

Finally, Rowdy stepped through ahead of me, and it was my turn. I handed over my ticket and started running.

"Go dude!"

I went. When I traversed the entrance path and reached the top of the amphitheater, I saw the east gate bangers already massing near the stage. Front row was highly unlikely, but Derek and James were coming right behind me and expecting me to run, so I ran.

My path was not clear. As expected, Rowdy and his portly girlfriend were slow, and moving down the center aisle. I was moving fast enough to run by, but didn't want to try pushing my way between them after they'd been friendly with us all morning. In the heat of battle, I let it get personal.

I surged past Rowdy and moved down the flat seat rows toward the stage, a perilous but lucrative option. Unlike the aisles, running down the seat tops required rhythm and coordination, as one had to leap with each step.

One did. At least for a while.

Step…step…step…

I was moving well, zeroing in on my target, a thin spot in the crowd around the third row.

Step…step…

I had rhythm now. My momentum increased as I leapt with confidence, never knowing if the others were behind me.

Step…step…step…

The front approached.

I tried to slow down, but I couldn't stutter my steps without falling.

Big…bikers…ahead…can't…stop…

Thud.

I collided with an enormous, hairy lumbar region, the massive lower back of a pale but dense biker who stood in the second row.

Little cartoon birds circled my head.

I don't recall precisely what happened, because I was down on the ground for most of it. I do, however, remember the gelatinous rocker turning around and punching me hard in the left kidney.

Derek and James ran to my aid, screaming and ready to rock. A mild fracas ensued, characterized mainly by gestures and threats between Derek and the kidney-puncher. Fortunately, the general seat claiming chaos was enough to prevent the security guards from reaching the burgeoning conflict in time. Threatened with imminent expulsion, everyone simultaneously backed down. Seconds later, Randy and Tommy were pulling me from the wreckage.

"You okay, dude?" they asked, laughing 'with me and not at me'.

"Yeah…I'm fine. It probably hurt him more than it did me…"

"I doubt that, man. You should have seen it! It looked like you were trying to run THROUGH that guy! I swear, man, that was the funniest fucking thing I've seen in years!"

"You're just lucky that guy's ass wasn't made of brick!"

"You should've seen it, dude…everybody stopped running and just watched!"

"I couldn't wait to give my first performance at Red Rocks," I said, rubbing my shoulder. I was just glad it was over. Now I could stop thinking about the seats and start thinking about the show.

Our seats? Fifth row was where we eventually landed, and no one but my kidney complained. The stage was in spitting distance; we would avoid some of the close-in shoving matches by being a bit farther back. I knew everyone wanted to be closer, but thankfully they were considerate enough not to bitch. James was probably kicking himself for letting me lead the charge; he would certainly think twice before including me in any other tasks requiring physical coordination.

We hurried up and waited some more, now on the final leg of our marathon park party. Six hours until the show, and we were acting as though it would start any minute, provoked by the amphitheater P.A. system's tunes and the sight of the stage. I calmed a headache with four aspirin and only sipped at the 'Nam' juice.

Tommy brought over some cute girls he'd met at the concession, and we squeezed them into place. At Red Rocks, there are no 'seats' per-se, just curved rows of stone with numbers on them. Assigned air, basically. It was no problem to accommodate more people, especially if they were as talented as the friends Tommy delivered.

The fluid nature of the seating situation required resolute vigilance, an awareness of the immediate neighbors and the territorial seating lines. Lonnie and Derek would be our anchors, flanking our territory and insuring that the borders were not breached. The rest of us took our places between them, knowing our responsibility would be to hold against attacks from the higher rows. When the surges came, we would also assist Lonnie and Derek with a group shove.

The group in our immediate area seemed to be a generally docile bunch, but it was still early. The buzz of reaching our seats faded a bit when we saw a roadie come from backstage with a bucket of paint and a long-handled roller. Acting as though he didn't even see the thousands gathering before him, the roadie slowly set to the task of painting the stage.

Painting the stage. We were literally watching paint dry for the majority of the afternoon.

Still, the time seemed to pass without notice. The bowls fried and the second assault of 'Nam' juice made its rounds until there was nothing left in the bottle but alcohol-swollen fruit. Lonnie proudly passed out the treats, and we wiped our sticky hands on our jeans, shaking off the potent effects.

The house system pumped metal tunes all afternoon long, and the crowd swelled with anticipation, the anxiety relieving itself in the occasional spontaneous brawl. James witnessed a chick fight near the restrooms, a memorable event in which one of the girls emerged without a shirt and was promptly booted from the park. It felt good to know I wasn't the only one embarrassing myself.

The clouds stayed away. At around six, the fires atop the Rocks sprang to life, stirring a cheer from the crowd. One hour to show time, and the remainder of the crowd was arriving. Other than a single pushing episode, the seating borders had not yet been breached.

Alex finally recovered from his all day retch-fest, claiming that he needed 'some hair of the dog' to make him feel better. Needless to say, he would relapse into dependent intoxication, and by the end of the warm up, he'd be passed out. That night, we would drive him home and quietly place him on his front porch swing for his mother to find the next morning. Two weeks later, Alex would claim that Iron Maiden put on an incredible show.

Seven o'clock. Show time. Oh hell yeah. We raised our hands and shouted toward the empty stage, the quest finally nearing its culmination. Scores of sunbaked rowdies raised their voices, the parting sun sending a glorious orange-pink caste across the sky above.

At long last, the lights went up, bathing the stage in red. The ominous intro to "Metal Heart" sounded through the speakers, provoking a roar of blissful recognition from the faithful. Low-lying clouds poured from massive fog machines, filling the stage. Randy tapped my arm and pointed, watching as the drummer took his place behind the gleaming kit.

Flash!

Accept stepped from the wings. The glorious grind of power chords saturated the air, drawing the crowd immediately to its feet.

Kick drum impact shook our bones and loosened our jaws. Like a video come to life, the stout Europeans cranked forth with precision and grunting intensity. The crowd surged and pushed, but we shoved back, banging our heads and laughing.

The peak came during "Balls to the Wall," thousands of hands clapping in time and shouting the title as singer Udo addressed the crowd in his thick accent. Like disciples in church, we chanted along with him, overcome by the deafening mood.

I looked over to see Derek banging his head with reckless intensity, fist raised and punching at the sky. He had his eyes closed and was mouthing every word.

The set ended all too soon.

Being close to the stage is a completely different experience than witnessing a concert from the cheap seats, and as I looked around the group, I saw a hunger in their eyes. Our minds were thinking the same thoughts, wondering what we'd have to do to get on our own stage.

"That rocked so majorly…"

"Told you guys!"

We stood with our backs to thousands of fellow headbangers, collectively exhaling the rush of one show and gearing up for the next. My heart beat twice as fast in my chest, swollen and provoked by inspiration.

Derek was still breathing heavily as he wiped the sweat from his grinning face and punched me affectionately in the arm. The light in his eyes was genuine this time, and I knew that the head-banging had been like therapy for him. Derek had opened up and allowed the torrid hurricane of music to wash over and through him. He was cleansed--at least for the moment--and that was all that really mattered.

"Hey, Mark…" Derek reached out and shook with me, leaning in to reach an arm around my neck. "Thanks for everything, man."

I swore I saw tears forming in his reddened eyes, but I never said a thing about it.

"Forget it, dude. I've got your back, and you've got mine. That's the way it's supposed to be, and that's the way it goes…"

"You know it, bud."

I could see it all so clearly now. The guy who'd always done everything himself, the kid who wrecked the grading curve and thought he could do anything better…like a bolt of pink lightning, I realized that the success of the band had nothing to do with our skill, or our hair, or even the people who listened.

Struck by inspiration, I reached out to grab Randy's shoulder. "Dudes, listen. Dudes! I have something to say--band meeting, right now."

James grinned. "Cool. Band meeting. Hey Tommy, dude--Mark wants a band meeting."

"What?"

The five of us formed a motley little huddle in the midst of the horde.

"What is it, dude?"

"Right here it starts," I told them, too inspired for my own good, my path suddenly seeming so clear. "Dudes, I want a promise. I want an oath that we'll keep this thing together. Like the Three Musketeers' 'all for one and one for all' thing. We can't sweat the little shit, and we can't let money, or gigs, or women stand between us. I'm fucking serious, too. This is what's important, dudes! The five of us--we make a vow to each other, and all the other shit will fall into place." I held out an open palm. "Now, what about you guys?"

"Hell yeah," Derek slapped my hand with force. "I swear it."

"No doubt."

"You know it, dude. The Five Musket-dudes!"

James grinned at my initiative, as though a question had been answered in his mind. "I'm already there, man."

At that moment, I didn't see anything that could possibly stand in our way.

Peace Sells

The future was upon me.

Less than a week after graduation, I moved out of the suburbs and into the metaphysically correct environment of Boulder.

College town plus, the legendary bastion of front-range liberalism and all-around partyness. Boulder was home to the coolest bars, the best live shows and a University chock full o' liberated coeds. To a bunch of aspiring rebels who'd been gnashing at the suburban bit, the place seemed like heaven.

This was not our parents' Boulder. The acid-dosing, deadhead hippies and single-minded radicalism were faded like an old tie-dyed shirt, now visible only in coffee-shop corners and used book stores. Boulder was getting wealthier, and with the money came the migrating herds of Yuppies and wealthy Californians. The town we inherited was less hippie and more Skippy, a wannabe Aspen.

We didn't know, or care. Compared to the neatly trimmed lawns and covenant-controlled nicety of the burbs, it seemed like a carnival of freedom. In the cracks of the new yuppie-dominated community, coolness still existed.

Young people stood behind the counters and clerked the stores. A chick with a red Mohawk would make your falafel sandwich while a horn-rimmed Goth handed you the change. The guy with the face tattoo could sit in the commons and beat African drums with a Texan-Korean new waver and his French-Canadian girl-friend. Debutantes and homeless Rasta guys peddled on the same streets, and if you listened hard enough, you'd hear more than one language.

Difference was everywhere.

Our blow-dried martyrdom seemed at an abrupt end. Political correctness held more sway here than the law itself. In this town, you would sooner rob a bank than throw a cigarette butt out your car window.

We'd made a few forays into the college town during our se-nior year and were surprised to find that our rocker motif didn't stand out so much among the punkers and enlightened eccentrics. Nurtured by the college community, even the local kids our own age seemed worldly and accepting, shocked by little and copa-cetic with almost anything. They'd been weaned from a very dif-ferent mother's milk, raised on radical thought and Grateful Dead tunes, an earthy bunch who accepted our pretty boy style without a blink.

Beyond the obvious escape from parental observation, there was a purpose in moving.

Somewhere in the midst of the concerts, basement jam sessions and sexual exploration of my senior year, I'd managed to get accept-ed at the University of Colorado. I was still successfully towing the line and doing quite well considering I hadn't attended any classes yet. Despite the distraction of the band, I'd managed to wind up in the top ten percent of my class and believed that college would be no different. I saw no bumps in the road and was more than willing to take a few classes if it meant extending the excesses of my youth for a few more years.

College, after all, was my destiny. That, and mega-stardom.

Derek and James somehow managed to graduate on time, but neither intended to pursue further education beyond guitar lessons. Randy had been a decent student, but thought of little more than finding his way to the cover of *Modern Drummer* magazine.

And Tommy? I honestly don't know how Tommy managed to get his diploma--his grades were meek at best and his attendance spotty. A beneficiary of public school overcrowding, he was handed his diploma to help facilitate low class sizes. Tommy's family threw him a big party, acting as if he'd won the Pulitzer.

I guess that's how I knew I was smart. Smart kids didn't get 'we're so grateful that you graduated' parties or any other credit for a measly little high school diploma. My accolades, apparently, waited somewhere up the road.

I would be the only college student in the band. And though we never sat down and specifically discussed the reasons, it was accepted that the band would simply follow me to Boulder and exist where I existed. I was the only one who'd made reservations for his future, and they all seemed to accept the fact. Besides, Boulder was cool. For the rest, the lure of house parties and promiscuous co-eds would be more than enough.

We rented a single story house in the cheap part of town and moved the entire band in. Five headbangers, two cats, one cocker spaniel and James' new girlfriend Sandy. The whole grass menagerie. Green Acres meets Easy Rider.

We soon realized that we owned more music equipment than we did furniture.

We gladly made it work. Two stereo speakers served as quaint end tables for our second-hand sofa, and a lovely coffee table was created using cinder blocks and plywood. A fortuitous trip to the junkyard provided us with a wobbling kitchen table and a set of mismatched but reasonably steady plastic chairs. As for bedroom furniture, Tommy was still snoozing nightly on a sleeping bag and dirty laundry cot; the rest of us purchased used waterbeds from the newspaper want-ads.

The Spartan accommodations didn't bother us. This was the adult world, and creating our own reality was a more than adequate trade off. Who needs curtains or couches when you have ultimate personal freedom? Besides, the basic necessities had been taken care of: posters for the wall, color television, and stereo equipment that kicked major ass.

As the months rolled by, we'd accumulate a plethora of hand-me-down pity furniture. James, Derek and Tommy would take the three bedrooms upstairs, and Randy and I would occupy the basement rooms. Personally, I liked it downstairs. Our area was colder than the boxy main floor accommodations, but the remainder of the half-finished basement was to be our new rehearsal hall, a place where we could jam anytime we wanted, day or night. I would be able to step from my bedroom into the practice space.

Life was good.

"Set up the drum kit over here, dude." James was directing traffic, surveying the basement like a realtor.

"All the way back there?"

"Yep. Gotta be. You wanna have parties, don't you?"

Randy delivered a sarcastic nod. "Well, duh."

"So we need to clear as much space as possible. We'll make it like a bar set-up. We can put the amps on either side and the P.A. speakers in the corners. The keg'll go back there..."

"As long as the drums are out of reach," Randy returned. "I don't want anybody getting behind the kit. Kristi spilled a beer on my floor tom at Brett's rager--remember?"

"Yeah."

"And not just a little, either. She set her cup on it like it was a coffee table, then knocked it over."

"We cleaned it up good, though."

"Still…"

"Yeah, I get it."

Randy sniffed at the air. "And keep your cats out of my kick drums, dude. This foam smells like cat piss already."

"He's just marking your kit, dude."

"I'd better not catch him doing it…"

"We'll get some incense," I offered.

"Incense? Then my drums will smell like sandal foot."

"Sandal root."

"Whatever."

I shrugged back at him. "So you'd prefer the stench of cat wiz to incense?"

"That's a tough one…"

Tommy came bounding down the stairs, a cigarette propped between his lips. "I just met the neighbors."

"Oh yeah? What's the story?"

He flipped his hair. "Three chicks. College students."

"Hot?"

"Well…sure, as long as you're not looking directly at them."

"Ahh…drag."

The truth hit me like naked chicks falling from the clouds.

"No way," I told them, freshly inspired by the thought. "We're psyched…"

"Yeah, right! Leave it to Mark to be psyched about ugly chicks! So much for college!"

"No," James interjected, "He's right. Think about it, dude--the house across the street is empty. It's still for sale."

"What?"

"Think about it, man. No neighbors, no trouble. We can have a party every night if we want to. We'll just make friends with the chicks next door and invite them every time we do something. No neighbors means no one to call the cops on us."

Tommy got it. "Oh yeah...good thinking. Endless ragers!"

Endless ragers.

I stood in realization that we were now the masters of our own party destiny, left to our own dude devices, suddenly in complete control of our own fun-time discretion. A harrowing thought.

Back in the burbs, we'd wait for someone's parents to go out of town to have a kegger. We had to borrow a home and suffer the inevitable fallout. But this was our house. Our home. Our own personal nightclub. Suddenly, a voluptuous new world of rocking possibilities was unfolding before our bloodshot eyes.

I went upstairs to see Randy lugging more than he could carry, weighted down with hardware. With no equipment to haul, I was overcome with the rare affliction known as singers' guilt and helped Randy with the drums. It seemed so long ago that I'd been playing a kit myself, but I well remembered the tedious horror of setting up and tearing down.

You see, anyone can play drums.

But to be a drummer, you must be a slave of more than the rhythm. You have to love the equipment, too--and there's a lot to love.

Drum heads, rims, beaters, snares, bolts, clasps, sticks, et cetera—endless collecting and spending. Drummers are devotees of steel and copper, connoisseurs of the balanced maple drumstick, versed in the gear-speak and eternally looking toward their next purchase. They're continually assembling and disassembling their musical erector sets, becoming intimately familiar with every bolt and rim. Randy had the love--he actually enjoyed it.

When we got back downstairs, we found Derek standing in the middle of the room, scowling.

"Something ain't right down here," he announced ominously. "It doesn't feel right. These cement walls are depressing."

Tommy looked around. "We could hang up a few centerfolds…"

"Nah," Randy shook his head. "Everybody does that. Have some class. Let's go with some cool posters or something. Or we could paint the walls black."

"Yeah," Derek agreed. "We'll paint it all black! Just paint the whole damned basement, then put in some black lights and hang fluorescent posters. We'll call it 'The Pit!'"

"Now THAT is a good idea."

A bolt of lightning hit me. This was my second epiphany in mere moments.

"No, wait! I know! Let's get a bunch of spray paint--all different colors. We'll spray it up like a subway."

The comment froze the room. In unison, the band nodded their approval.

"That's it, dude." James looked around, envisioning it. "That's perfect."

"No doubt."

"The Cistern Chapel, dude."

Randy raised an eyebrow, eyeing his drums. "Fine with me… but you guys are gonna help me take all this gear back upstairs."

We each hoisted a drum and carried it upstairs before digging in our pockets for enough cash to buy spray paint. Like housecats on new carpet, we were suddenly struck with an instinctive desire to mark our territory. Admittedly, spray paint in the house was one of my better ideas.

We piled into James' hollowed-out Chevy van and sought out our local hardware store, our mouths flowing with design ideas. The red-smocked girl behind the counter cocked an eyebrow, but didn't say anything as we handed over the remnants of our taco money for colored spray lacquer.

Soon we were standing back in the basement, each of us brandishing a different colored can. We paused for moment as we stared at our massive concrete canvas, relishing the rush of creative lust and imagining the possibilities. The wall beckoned, already primed virginal grey by the last tenants.

"So where do we start?'

"The band logo," I told them. "Huge. On the back wall, behind the drum kit. Permanent backdrop. From there, we'll improvise."

Derek sneered. "You guys go ahead and start the logo. I'm gonna paint a big anarchy symbol right here by my amp."

"Ooh--good call."

And so we set to work. Dude decorating, interior style.

In less than an hour, the entire wall was covered.

Flames leapt from the floors. Purple clouds kissed the ceiling. Logos and skull heads stretched across the bodies of crudely rendered cartoon vixens. Like a sun shining over the room, a giant yellow rasta-haired smiley face grinned back through fanged teeth. Beside it was a sign that read 'To Hell' with an arrow for directions.

It was inspired, epic, created with the kind of artisanship and loving care that only beer-buzzed headbangers can provide. Trailer-park beautiful. Designated degeneration. Tacky, colorful, and ready to rock.

It wasn't until we were finished that I realized we'd neglected to open a window.

"I feel dizzy, dude…"

Randy looked clammy.

I stood from a crouch and my head swam.

"Yeah…me too."

The smell was overpowering. Atomically small particles of toxicity saturated the air around us like a cotton-candy fog. Like bulls on bubble-wrap, you could almost hear the brain cells popping as we set the paint cans down and slowly stepped away, driven to cease our revelry before passing out.

We staggered up the stairs and stumbled into the cool grass of the front yard, laughing our long-haired asses off.

Heaven's Trail

We sat in the Technicolor practice space, eating squeeze-cheese from a can as we waited for James. I don't think he'd ever been late for rehearsal before.

"Where is he?" Randy was utilizing the spare time, polishing his drums with a combination of spit and elbow grease. He eyed the cats suspiciously, sniffing at the foam inside his kick drum.

"He'll be here," Derek reassured, abandoning the liquid cheddar in favor of a bowl. "He probably got stuck at work again--boss man asked him to hose off the pavement or something."

"He knows we're rehearsing today, doesn't he?"

"Course he does," Randy replied. "Double standard, man. James bitches us out when we're not on time, but if he doesn't show, I guess it's okay, right?"

"Ease up. He'll show." Derek passed the loaded bowl to Randy. "You do the honors, dude. I'm sensing you could use a little attitude adjustment today."

Randy nodded, accepting it with a grin. "You got that right."

"Randy's a true drummer," Tommy watched as Randy put a flame to the pipe. "If he doesn't get to beat on something every twenty-four hours, he gets all excited and shit..."

Randy chuckled, holding in the hit until we thought he'd explode.

"Randy, you look like that guy in 'Scanners'! The veins in your neck are like popping out!"

He laughed, exhaling and filling the room with sweet smoke. A short coughing fit later, he broke into the lizard face.

"Look out," I said. "Here comes the lizard man…"

"Geeble. Reeble. Geeble sneeble." Randy contorted his face and lapped his tongue in mid-air, doing his trademark routine. The sight of it kicked off a Cheech and Chong line dropping session.

"Sir, can I see your license, please."

"Uh, my license? Isn't it on the back of the car?"

"No, your driver's license, sir."

"Oh yeah…here it is."

"What is your name, sir?"

"My name? Isn't it written there on the license?"

We turned at the sound of high heels.

James' girlfriend Sandy clickety-clacked down the stairs, her mop of abused blonde hair appearing around the corner.

Sandy was pretty, in a domestic way. She was one of those girls who tried hard, but was fighting a losing battle against her hometown look. Pretty but indescribably mild, cute but not even close to gorgeous. Even in the most banal of situations, the girl never seemed to be without high heels. Apparently, the pot smell had lured her from upstairs.

"Sup, Sandy."

"Hey guys. The kitchen is clean, finally."

"Thank God for that."

She smiled, feeling needed. "So…you gonna play a song for me?"

"If James ever gets here, sure."

"I know." She shrugged. "It's weird. He should be here by now. You guys should play something anyway."

Derek shook his head, passing her the bowl. "Nah, not without James."

Sandy popped her gum. "So did you guys hear about David Lee Roth getting kicked out of Van Halen?"

"Yeah. Only he didn't get kicked out."

"Oh yeah?"

"I heard that he had a blowout with Eddie and quit on his own. They couldn't fire Dave. You don't just kick out the most important member of the band, man. I'm tellin' you, they're gonna regret it."

I nodded my agreement. "Dave WAS Van Halen."

"Nah," Tommy protested. "Eddie was and still is Van Halen. I mean, it's his name, right?"

"The name doesn't make the band," Derek mused, chiming in on my side. "Dave is the man. Straight up. Do you think they ever would have got famous in the first place if it wasn't for Dave?"

"I guess not..."

"Eddie's good, no doubt. But when you go to a Van Halen concert, who's carrying it? Dave, man. I don't care if he can sing or not--Eddie just doesn't get it. You can't just kick out your singer and expect it to be the same."

"They say David Coverdale might take his place," Sandy added, nursing the bowl.

"That won't work," Derek said simply. "David Coverdale is English, and Van Halen is like the ultimate American band. Besides, Dave blows him away as a front man."

Randy cupped his hands over his mouth, eyeing the bowl. "Nurse Sandy. Nurse Sandy, report for surgery..."

"Oh, sorry." She took a toke and passed it.

"It still won't be the same," I commented, remembering how completely good ole DLR commanded the stage. "It's like, you picture a band as a tight group of friends, you know? It's about the friendship. I mean, sure there are fights and shit, but kicking Dave out is just harsh. Now when I see Eddie jumping around and laughing…it just won't be the same, that's all."

"Totally," Randy echoed. "But I bet Dave will have his own band soon. I hope they blow Van Halen off the stage."

"They probably won't," I said, "But I'll go see Dave's band before I'll see Van Halen again. Without Dave, their careers are over. Toast."

"You never know. AC/DC lost Bon Scott, and they still rock."

"True," Derek said, "but Bon died. That's different. He died just when he finally hit the top--never even got to enjoy it. If you die, though, you're famous forever. I like Brian Johnson and all, but he's not better than Bon Scott. Bon is a legend…Bon's a role model."

"Bon drank himself to death, didn't he?"

"That's how rock legends go out…hell yeah. All hail King Bon."

Tommy shrugged. "Well, duh. I didn't say they were better. I just said they still rock."

"That much is true." Derek turned up his guitar and scratched out the riff to AC/DC's "TNT."

"Oy! Oy! Oy!"

The song was contagious. Randy jumped behind the kit, picking up the beat. Tommy and I looked at each other for a moment before leaping to join in. Soon, we were cranking out our own impromptu version, playing from memory. Sandy was our audience of one, bobbing her head as she lit one of her super-thin girly cigarettes and listened.

The lyrics were buried within me and they sprouted out as soon as I heard the riff. Ahh, the joy of spontaneous jamming!

It seemed like months since we'd turned it up without calling it rehearsal. I hate to say it, but James' absence nurtured the moment.

Just as we were reaching the 'Oy' break, he appeared at the bottom of the stairs.

James pumped his fist and sang along, stealing a kiss from Sandy before dropping the Bugerland bags he was carrying and running for his guitar. We botched a couple chords, but made it unscathed to the end. The improv headbanging ended with a minute-long rumble, the kind where the music doesn't stop until the feedback gets too loud to tolerate.

"You guys learning new songs?" James asked as soon as the noise died down.

"Nah. Just screwing around," I said, feeling oddly guilty. "Doing a little tribute to Bon Scott."

Derek was already unhooking his guitar strap. "You brought food?"

James grinned. "Major grub."

"Dude!"

We swarmed the take-out bags like bulimic Ethiopian hyenas, tearing into the shiny wrappers and indulging. Sandy stood back so as not to be injured, laughing at the sight of group munchies.

"I'll go get the twelve-pack out of the fridge," she said, heading back up the stairs.

We looked up, mumbling our appreciation through mouthfuls of beef and special sauce. It wasn't until we'd satiated our hunger that James broke the good news.

"So, I bet you guys are wondering where I've been…"

"If you were picking up food, then your absence is forgiven."

"No doubt," Randy agreed. "New rule: If you bring food, you're never late."

James smiled like it was Christmas morning. "It wasn't just the food that made me late. I got us a gig, dudes."

"We got one, too," Derek joked. "Friday night, right here--"

"Seriously--it's way better than that," James teased, pausing dramatically. "Way."

A gig? This was what we'd been waiting for.

"Dude--what's up? Tell us already!"

He chuckled, supremely pleased with himself. "Okay, okay. We've got the first slot at The Tank. We're there, dudes. One week from Friday."

We sat, our momentary loss for words soon replaced by kudos and righteous exclamations. Fives were high. The reverberation from Tommy's 'whoop' made the cymbals ring.

"Dude!"

"The Tank! Seriously?"

"Dead serious," James beamed. "We're there, dude."

"That place is filled with babes," Tommy brushed his hair back, musing over the possibilities. "We're so psyched…"

"And headlining!"

"Headlining?"

James shook his head. "No. Huh-uh. I said first slot. As in, we play first. Seven to seven forty-five. It's our first time and all."

Apparently, 'first slot' meant first to play, as in: 'warm up act for the warm up act'. It's like batting eighth in the order or singing opera in the chorus. We'd be on stage, but that early in the evening, the audience would be meager to non-existent. Not wanting to be the first to complain, I kept my comment to myself.

After all, a gig at The Tank would be the next big step. It was the spot of local legend and served up all the best local bands. It was the hot spot for B-minus bands passing through town and A-list metal stars on their way to and from the strip joints. We'd be driving down to compete on the somewhat mean streets of Denver, leaving the sanctity of our home field advantage.

We were about to meet our competition.

"Oh well…who cares what time we play? No biggie. The main thing is--we're in. We'll work our way up."

"Originals or covers?" I asked, thinking ahead to the song list.

"Either," James responded, "But I figure we should do at least three originals if we want to pass the audition."

"Audition?"

"Well, yeah. I mean, they don't call it that or anything, but that's pretty much what it is. This guy named Dan owns the place, and he'll be watching. If we ever want to get a second gig, we have to blow him away. A lot of bands don't get asked back."

Pressure and music. The two, together. It seemed a shameful combination, but this was just the beginning. And I'd never failed a test in my life.

"We'll kick ass," I told them, gaining confidence from merely saying it. "We've got the ultimate practice space and enough time to get it tight."

Derek nodded his agreement. "Easily! Have you heard some of the bands that play The Tank? We're better than most of those bands…"

"But that's not good enough," James snapped back, his words sounding oddly familiar. "We have to blow away ALL the bands, not just some! Shit, if we want to get any of the really good gigs, we have to be in the best of the best! I'm not doing this just to be some middlin' half-ass band!"

Derek raised his hands in surrender. "Damn--don't be so defensive!"

"I'm not," James replied, cooling. "Just trying to get shit to-gether, that's all. We gotta be tight."

"We will, man."

"I hope so…you guys ready to rehearse?"

Collective nods. It seemed strange that on the day we finally score our first Denver gig, James would be so uptight. Better to stop talking, I figured, and start playing. Jamming had always proven an able remedy for whatever ailed us.

We set to work with rocker diligence, far more serious than before, each one of us hammering out the tunes picturing ourselves on the wide Tank stage. We ironed out the mistakes and discussed the breaks, tidying up our messy endings and repeating the rough spots. Jamming had suddenly become rehearsal. No longer would we be performing for throngs of unassimilated friends and school acquaintances. This time, our gig would be performed in the molten core of the local metal universe.

Welcome to the Jungle

Competition. A new word for us. A new concept. Yet even in the depths of the music world, the river bottom sludge of the local bar scene, there lurked a vicious competitive spirit.

On any given night, The Tank's audience would be composed of at least one entire band, ten other musicians who themselves played in bands, and at least twenty other significant others who were currently dating, had dated, or were related to musicians in bands. All tallied, we could easily expect ninety-five percent of the audience to claim intimate affiliation with the band scene.

In other words...everybody was hooked up.

A bunch of experts, our fellow musicians were paranoid and predacious, devoted enough to their own cause to jealously defend it. Constant scrutiny was the name of the game, and every performance would be judged. Lips would move. Slights would be delivered. One way or another, the crowd would buzz with something--we'd have to make certain it was envy and admiration.

Several factors opposed such success. Kicking ass was not enough.

The rival band members would lounge in the audience during our set, cuddling their girlfriends and watching with glares of amused contempt. Pre-disposed toward criticism, they would gladly pass judgment on our style and ability.

Then again, style and ability were actually considered secondary.

As with any headbanger criticism, the first and most important question was a strictly instinctive one: Does this band suck?

This was the defining question. A phrase that actually possessed the power to split the entire universe into two neat and clean categories.

The foundation of all dude philosophy. A means by which the path clears, and answers may be found to every one of life's questions. It is the center of the dude, the unifying question:

'Is it cool, or does it suck?'

There are no equations or formulas. This is the purest of gut reactions.

'Is it cool, or not?'

A Zenfully thoughtless moment delivers the answer, a response that comes straight from the lips of the inner child. The answer will flash, the correct answer, an instinctive and honest response to the question. No thought required. No second guessing. A true dude knows what is cool.

Of course, some things are cooler than others. Accordingly, the opposite statement 'some things suck more than others' is also quite true.

These, however, are issues of little concern. The dude is only concerned with two sides--and one decision. After drawing a line down the middle of everything known to man, the dude has efficiently made every other decision much easier.

The foundation of the dude philosophy is written in four ancient phrases, composed with Zeneriffic simplicity in mind:

Dude.
Some things are cool.
Others Suck.
You'll know.

This was the criterion upon which our band would be judged at The Tank. After all the practice and songwriting, all the promotion and gigging, it would boil down to a split-second of stoner Zen.

And so goes the game, the survival of the coolest.

Those who suck can take solace in the fact that sucking is, in most cases, a curable condition. Change happens. It is fully possible to improve and, conversely, to degenerate musically. But whatever the sound or the style, your fate would be sealed with the initial question.

The dude can take solace in the fact that a significant percentage of the audience can't actually tell a good band from a bad one in the first place. This is good news. Even if you suck, there will inevitably be those who fail to recognize it and continue to think you're cool. God must have a soft spot for bad musicians.

But we didn't plan on sucking. After countless hours grinding away in the basement, we were ready. Our breaks were tight. Our backup vocals were acceptable. And damn it, our hair was cool.

With Dan the bar owner watching and the jealously enlightened criticism of the musician-filled audience lingering in the air, we knew we'd have to come off tight or get the axe before we ever had the chance to improve.

MEAN STREET

The lead singer role was getting a bit more complicated.

Thankfully, I felt safe with the material. As long as I didn't forget lyrics, I felt relatively confident with the singing side of the job. The front man part, however, was a little more challenging. Warming up a hostile crowd at The Tank would be far different than playing house parties for drunken friends.

In truth, James and Derek were the ones to pity. They were guitarists, after all--members of the most competitive and hyper-critical colleague pool of them all. Guitarists are the worst.

Drummers had a kind of fraternity.

Guys who like to beat on things seem to have this affinity for others who have similar interests. Like two prize fighters who punch each other in the head for twelve rounds and then hug after the final bell, the rock drummers were family by profession. Drummers generally got along with other drummers.

Similarly, bass players generally liked other bass players.

In our world, the majority of the bassists were in reality under-achieving or lazy guitarists who enjoyed the company of anyone who didn't make them feel technically inferior. Needy and amiable by nature, they were people persons.

Singers, however, generally hated other singers. At least on the inside.

The act of singing is the most insecure of the roles and requires irrational defenses to combat. This could be a result of the fact that singers carry their instrument within their bodies and cannot simply buy a new voice if the old one doesn't sound good. With no strings to change and no drum heads to replace, the voice would seem an ideal, economically sound instrument to play. It is, however, a gamble.

It's a paranoid craft. Your beautiful instrument is highly susceptible to disaster. Someone can sneeze on you in the checkout line at the supermarket and change your world. The morning of the gig, you can wake up to find your instrument flaming with strep or covered in thick yellow goop. And if you sound like a stuffed up warthog when you belt lyrics through your aching throat…too bad. You're only as good as your last crack.

So the insecure singers privately hated each other. Rarely, however, did we show this hatred, unable to get personal for fear of exposing our own apprehension. Most of us would have liked to have the kind of honest fraternity that the drummers had, but by nature we were too self-absorbed and neurotic to truly warm up to each other.

Why? The truth be told, most singers can be simply defined by the unifying question, making all other questions moot. Singers are either praised or endangered.

Guitarists were different. The wolves of the club circuit, they neither held affection nor hid their contempt for those they found inferior. They hunted in packs and didn't worry about leaving a carcass or two. They judged on ability first and foremost, but had a style requirement as well. Hyper-critical and overly technical, the metal guitarists held their contemporaries to a high standard, a level of expertise beyond that of other band members.

The stage was set by guys like Hendrix and raised by Eddie Van Halen and other greats, players who made 'better, faster, tastier' the norm. The standard was carried by countless amateurs who then sat for hours in their basements, pouring over tablature and learning the masters' solos note for note. If imitation is the highest form of flattery, then our guitar legends are some of the most heralded individuals in history.

This was the decade of fireworks and exact imitation. When a band played a cover song, they would be held responsible for making every note sound like the original, the closer, the better.

Duplication. For some, this was a relatively easy task. For a guitarist in the eighties, it was a feat. James had his work cut out for him.

Sound like Eddie--every note.

Sound like Yngwie Malmsteen--don't miss a note.

Jam just like Randy Rhodes, and don't you dare try to fake the solo because there will be someone in the audience who knows it by heart. There was no escaping judgment--a budding guitar hero either started practicing his licks or got out of the game. Sink or swim.

For the fallen, there was hope. The wonderful world of bass players would gladly embrace any and all guitar washouts, but a guitarist moving to bass is like a shortstop moving to right field or a former movie star pitching infomercials on television.

The other option for failed soloists was becoming a rhythm guitarist, a lesser position in terms of both prominence and pressure, but a respectable position nonetheless. As rhythm guitarist, Derek wouldn't be subject to the same harsh rhetoric as James. He would be judged, but not as an elite.

Derek was fine with that. From what I could tell, he never really cared much for technical precision as long as the feeling was there. Having conceded his lack of riff-mastership, Derek rarely soloed anymore and was better for it.

James, however, seemed intent on success. He'd never been a studious guitarist, but in the week leading up to The Tank gig, he began buying back issues of *Guitar Player* magazine and tearing out pages of tablature, studying them despite not knowing what he was really looking at. I had to admit, he was making a supreme effort.

But there was something different about James. He changed after landing that first gig at The Tank.

Personally, I wasn't worried at all about his playing. None of us were. We weren't foolish enough to think we were the best musicians in the world, and we recognized the gallons and gallons of polish it would take to eventually buff us up. No one was about to blame James for not kicking ass. He was dedicated, passionate, and he was our buddy.

Our guitarist, in our band. That was enough. One for all and all for one, as we'd promised.

I found James in his room that night, hunkered down over his amp and soloing his brains out. Eyes closed and tongue lolling, he shook his head and concentrated, playing the same lick over and over again. His orange hair stuck up in odd spots, wavering in mid-air. The ashtray in front of him was overflowing.

"Sup?"

"Hey Mark. Have a seat."

"Sounds good, man."

He rolled his eyes, striking one last chord before turning down the amp. "Yeah, right. I don't even understand most of this tablature crap. It's so much easier to just play the tape and sound it out. Look at this shit--I swear, guitar wasn't meant to be written down…"

"It sounds rough," I sympathized, glancing around at the chord charts and the guitar tablature, a language unkind to novices.

"Majorly harsh, dude. These guys are like all over the neck, doing shit I can't even figure out, much less play. Modes and shit. You think you can keep it all in pentatonic, and then some guy like Randy Rhodes comes along and I can't even figure out what the hell he's doing! Thank God for Angus Young, man."

"Don't worry about the gig, man. We're gonna kick butt."

"I ain't worried about the gig," he snapped. "I just figure I have to get better if we're gonna improve."

"But we ARE getting better…"

"It's not like I'll hate myself if I can't play the things note for note, but I wanna say I can do it, you know? I've seen how good Scotty Jennings and those guys are. Not that I care what they say, or anything. It don't matter what anybody thinks, but I want to show well, you know?"

I nodded. The competition was on his mind, even when he denied it. I wondered if Eddie Van Halen and the other guitar heroes knew what kind of misery they were dispensing on guys like James when they concocted a wicked new solo.

"We all feel that way," I commiserated. "Shit--I'm going out there without a guitar to hide behind, just hoping my voice doesn't crack. And then when you go into a solo, I have to stand there and bang my head or something to use the time until I sing again. I always feel stupid during the solo."

"You do a good job," he told me, lighting a cigarette. "But I see what you mean. All the great singers have to do something during the solo. Like how David Lee Roth stalks the stage…"

"Steven Tyler dances and works the mic stand."

"Right! And Ozzy stands there in one spot, just banging his head and clapping like an idiot. You'll find your thing eventually. As long as you stay centered stage-wise, you'll do good. We have faith in you, dude."

"You too, dude," I told him, feeling grateful. "We're all in this together. Besides, being anxious is one of the reasons we gig in the first place. It's a thrill-seeking thing. Some people sky dive, and other people play guitar in front of crowds of flammable posers!"

He laughed a bit. "So what do you think we should wear?"

I shrugged. "What's wrong with what we wear now?"

James paused. "Well...nothing, really. I mean, jeans and T-shirts are cool and everything, but this is a whole new level, man. Seriously. The big bands at The Tank all wear spandex and leather. That singer from Tempting Feast has this sweet pair of red and black zebra-striped spandex."

"Spandex?"

Visions of Hamlet came to mind.

"I don't know, man...I don't think I'd look too good in tights."

"But it looks cool. You know all the pro bands wear it. Think about Iron Maiden, or Mötley Crüe. It looks professional. Not tights, dude--spandex."

An odd business, this, where donning a pair of zebra-striped tights was considered professional. I still didn't see myself in spandex. Jim Morrison would never wear spandex. Leather pants would be where I tried to draw the line.

Knowing James wasn't a Doors fan, I tried to think of a no-tights guy he liked.

"Joe Perry never needed spandex," I told him, considering it a good defense. "And neither did Bon Scott. Besides, there's no way you're going to get Derek to hop into a pair of spandex by Friday."

"I guess you're both going to take some convincing," James responded, his tone cooling. "I just want what's best for the band. I hope you do, too."

"What?" I was more than a bit surprised at the comment. "Dude. Of course I do--but we don't have to look like clones. And who decided that spandex was best for the band? You?"

James rolled his eyes. "It's just what we need to do, man. We've got to keep up with those guys, or we'll never get any of the good gigs!"

"Dude, we're gonna do fine!"

"You don't know that," he told me, nearly shouting. "You don't know that! We could bomb out and screw ourselves into house parties for another year or two...or five or ten! Shit, man--you got your classes and everything. You're not worried. I know how it is, Mark."

I frowned back. "What do you mean by that?"

"You know. If this doesn't work out for you, then you just go back to college and it's no big loss! For me--this is all I've got, dude! I don't have shit to fall back on. I'm not as lucky as you!"

The turn in the conversation stunned me.

"That's not fair, man..."

"I'm not trying to put you down or anything," he said as soon as he saw my reaction. "Don't get me wrong--I'm not saying there's anything wrong with what you got. You're smart as hell...but you don't know what it feels like to have nothing to fall back on but a lame bank job or collecting cash at a gas station! You've got, like, this little foundation of security that you've always stood on. Your family, your looks, your smarts--"

"And that's my fault?"

"No, no--nothing like that, dude." James shrugged, looking at me. "But I think it changes your outlook on things, you know? You don't have to worry the same as I do--about the same things. Remember when you were going with Darcy Taylor, and I asked you if she was a keeper? You said that she was good enough for now, but you'd never marry her."

"So?"

"So it's like--you think to yourself that you don't have to be serious because there'll be other, better chicks--because there'll be better jobs! And that's because you got college, and you'll have a sweet job either way. You want the band to do good--but you don't NEED it."

This wasn't the conversation I intended to have. I felt deflated and didn't know what angle to use.

"You don't think I'm committed to the band?" I asked, wanting to hear it clearly. "You think that because I'm in school I don't want the band to succeed?"

"I didn't say that--"

"What, James? Do you think I look at this band like some two-month girlfriend? Yeah, sure--I've got college. I've got to! But do you think I really want to be some stupid fucking accountant or some business prick? You think I'd be just as happy sitting behind a desk all my life? I've got pressures too, man. Different ones than you!"

I was ranting and didn't care. James eyes widened, but he didn't seem angry. It had been a while since he'd seen me upset; my role as peacemaker demanded an even temper. Some issues, however, were touchier than others.

"I don't even know how we got on this topic in the first place," I continued, holding back the stream of toxic comments in my head. "But I'm in this thing just like you are, James! This is my band too, dude. We all have faith in your guitar playing. Fuck the other guys, man--we're gonna get there."

"Whatever, man." He looked down at his guitar. "It's cool."

I wanted to keep talking. I wanted to shout at James and question him for doubting me. I wanted to tell him that he was all wrong about the girlfriends, and that I didn't look at the band like I did the girls, that I had the kind of commitment to the music I'd need to persevere. I wanted to, but I couldn't.

Sometimes you get so angry about the accusation that the defense becomes meaningless. James was obviously in the midst of a major league bum trip, and I figured he needed the support more than I needed to prove my point.

"Five years plus we've been jamming," I told him, bouncing my head to the sound of Derek's stereo in the next room. "Scott and them, Wicked Smile, Bohemia--none of those guys have been together as long as we have. We're tighter than you think, James. No need to be worried before we even know how we stack up..."

James nodded, then shrugged, responding immediately to the de-escalation of hostilities.

"That's true...and I'll be psyched to see how we sound through a good sound system."

"No doubt! Can you imagine Randy's kit through a good P.A.?"

He grinned a bit. "Yeah--that'll kick ass."

"We'll jam, man," I told him, flexing my vocabulary. "I have a good feeling. We'll talk about the rest later."

"Okay--I won't push the spandex thing on you guys so close to the gig, but after five years, we should really have our shit together as far as our look."

I raised my hands. "You're right. Look, after the gig we can just sit down and have a band meeting. We'll figure out what we want to wear--all of us, together. As for Friday, let's just stick to our jeans and stuff. Okay?"

James thought about it, staring coldly for a moment before nodding his agreement. "Okay. That's cool, but I want you to think about it seriously. I mean, did you really think you'd make it big playing in your ripped jeans?"

"I don't know...maybe I did."

"Just think about it."

"I will," I promised, knowing what I'd think. "I understand what you're saying."

"I don't want to sound like a hard-ass, but I'm trying to do what's best for the band, you know?"

"I know. It's cool."

James looked at the clock. "When does Derek get home from work?"

"About six," I answered.

"Good deal. I told Tommy to be here by seven for practice." He turned his attention back to the tablature, still irritated. "That means I still have almost two hours to work on this shit."

James needed to relax, and I felt responsible for insuring it.

"Ack! Give yourself a break, dude. Let's go get something to eat."

He hesitated. "Nah, I think I'm just going to stay here and--"

"I know! That Mexican restaurant up the street! Let's go up and get a couple of those fat burritos smothered in green chili." My mouth was watering at the thought.

He hesitated again. "It sounds tempting, dude, but nah. Nah. I should stay."

"Dude."

"Randy will go with you."

"Randy will go with US," I told him. "You're coming with us."

"Nah, dude."

"Dude: smothered burritos."

He paused.

"Smotherrrrrrred burrrrrritos," I pressed, rolling the 'r's for effect. "I'm buying. Come on--I'm a friend of Sarah Connarr. Come wit me if you vant to live."

"No way."

Not even the Schwarzenegger impression was working.

"DUDE!" I let out the big artillery, tossing James his jacket.

"Okay! Fine!" he relented, ambition battling with hunger.

He stood and followed me out, chuckling and shaking his head. Some people have to be coaxed out of the house.

I suppose I was a bit green at the time, for I couldn't even conceive the notion of The Tank crowd not liking us. We had presence and chemistry, and what we lacked in talent, we made up for in enthusiasm. They were bound to like us, spandex or not. How bad could it really be?

Blind in Texas

Bad.

I'd been successfully repressing my anxiety all day long. When I got home from class that Friday, I found Derek, Tommy and Sandy doing shots of tequila at the kitchen table. They'd even gone to the trouble of borrowing a lime from the chicks next door. It struck me as a bad omen.

"Mark dude!" Derek grinned, looking up at me. "Sup, man?"

"You guys warming up?"

Derek raised the bottle and looked at it, chuckling. "Hell yeah! No salt, though. You ready to kick some ass tonight?"

"You know it."

He pushed out a chair. "Sit down, man."

"Fix Mark up with a shot," Tommy urged.

I held up a hand to decline.

Derek raised an eyebrow. "What's the matter?"

"Nothing," I replied. "I just want to get something to eat first, that's all."

He set the empty shot glass in front of him and unscrewed the bottle of Cuervo. "I'll just pour you a small one, then."

Derek was already lit up. His timing sucked. We had less than three hours to get our equipment loaded and get down to The Tank for a five-thirty sound check. I pictured James' head exploding when he saw Derek drunk.

"Is James home yet?"

"No way. He should be here any minute."

"And Lonnie?" I asked. "When is he supposed to be here with the truck?"

"He'll be here."

"We've got to get down there early because five-thirty sound check means READY TO GO at five-thirty. That means load in and set up and mics for the drum kit. Load in at five. Plus, the half hour it takes to get there, and--"

"Shit, man!" Derek halted my rambling mid-sentence. He stared for a moment, tilting his head. "Relax, bud. You're starting to sound like James!"

Tommy and Sandy enjoyed the joke. Admittedly, it was true. I was beginning to feel like him, too. I waited for Derek to rise from the table and put the bottle back in the cabinet.

The bad omen continued.

An hour and a half later, Lonnie was still missing...along with the truck that was supposed to carry our gear to The Tank.

James had been home for an hour and seriously ranting about Lonnie's tardiness for the last thirty minutes. Overshadowed by the fact that we were about to be late for our own sound check, Derek's inebriation went relatively unnoticed.

Lonnie's black monster finally turned the corner, squealing to a stop. Judas Priest poured from the cab. He looked down from his open window, raising his arms in apology and waving his finger in a circle like John Wayne rounding up the cattle train.

In retrospect, I suppose it wasn't the best idea leaving the crucial element of transportation in the hands of the biggest stoner we knew. Granted, he'd never let us down before.

Time pressed, and Lonnie was a humongous dude--so we didn't bother to scold him. We loaded the truck in record time, hopping in our respective vehicles and speeding down the highway toward downtown Denver.

Rush hour. An accident was, of course, clogging up traffic. The convoy rolled to a running crawl. Our fate was sealed.

Tommy rode shotgun in Lonnie's truck, and I went with Randy. Dead in the midst of the jam, I looked over and saw Derek's car in the lane beside us. He gave me the headbanger salute, window open and singing along with The Sex Pistols' "Bodies."

In the seat beside Derek, James sat brimming. The look on his face was one of ultimate discontent and disgusted calm. He was thoroughly pissed, but generally preferred to bottle up his anger and then unleash it at a less appropriate moment.

I was angry too, I suppose, but I didn't see any reason to dwell on it. I rationalized that The Tank was a first rate gig, and they no doubt treated their artists with respect. We'd explain the situation, and they'd still have plenty of time to fit in a sound check. James' anger would become misplaced, and he'd have to concede to the 'all's well that ends well' cliché and mellow out.

No harm, no foul, right? After all, it was just a sound check.

We arrived at The Tank around five forty-five, a full fifteen minutes late. As we pulled into the small back lot, there was still a dim hope in my naïve suburban mind, a hopeful notion that perhaps our tardiness would go unnoticed. Lonnie backed the truck into the band slot, as close to the stage door as he could get.

We leapt from our cars, feeling the weight of truancy bearing down.

Derek's window had been rolled up, and I could see him arguing with James as they pulled into the lot. Apparently James wasn't saving anything for later. I waited for him to finish with Derek and hop out of the car before I knocked on the stage door.

The steel door cracked, and the mullet-cut head of the soundman appeared from the darkness within. The guy was forty-going-on-twenty, a Tank fixture for years. His name was Dale, and his reputation was deservedly crusty. At that moment, he looked like the Grey Mask of Death.

"We're the--"

"Sound check at five-thirty?" he asked drolly.

We all nodded in unison.

"That figures," he snipped. "Well, you missed it. Load in your shit." Dale pushed the steel fire door open and squinted out at Lonnie's truck. "You can't park there, either."

Dale turned without comment and disappeared back into the club. Stricken but not beaten, we hurried to load the equipment on the stage.

The Tank was taller than it was wide, with two upper levels overlooking a large dance floor and stage. The raised stage dominated one corner, stretching an impressive twenty feet wide, shiny-floored and deep, a black linen curtain pulled across the front. The drum riser was the highest I'd ever seen, topping out at four feet.

There were already drums on the riser. Two kits.

Both Lonnie and I helped Randy with the drums. His set up was time-consuming, and I'd seen his face drop when he realized that he might not be miked properly. He was deservedly mad.

Sound checks, above all else, are about drum mix. The vocal mics are run on the familiar house system and miking the guitar amps is an easy task. Miking a drum kit, however, takes time. Mics in the kick drums. Mics on the snare, the toms, the hi-hat, and if you were lucky, the cymbals. After forcing themselves to play in acoustically inept basements and garages their whole lives, drummers practically cream their pants when they finally hear their kit pumped through a huge sound system. After the first time, nothing else will do-- they will forevermore long for the chest-caving thud of an amplified kick.

But all drum kits are different. Getting a good sound can be a tricky task, even with purple mahogany. A decent drum check requires monotonous slow beating.

Monotonous…

Slow…

Beating…

Drum…

To…

Drum, moving from one to another as the sound is dialed in. Steady monotonous beats are the theme music of the sound check. The soundman's dirge.

If what the asshole sound guy said was true, we weren't going to get any kind of sound check, much less a full blown drum check.

Randy was fuming, but pressed on.

"Don't worry," I whispered to him. "They have to mic your kit. Late or not, the drums are always miked here."

"Yeah, I guess," Randy replied, unconvinced. "It's gonna sound like shit, though."

Derek, James and Tommy worked busily to set up their amps in low light.

Soundman Dale approached, eyeing the drums. "Looks like a nice kit. Why isn't it set up?"

The guy should have had 'bastard' tattooed on his forehead.

"Well, we didn't know if we were supposed to set up on the drum riser, or--"

"Well, does it look like there's room for you on the drum riser?"

Randy's jaw clenched. "Well, obviously not."

Dale tapped his forehead. "Good thinking, Slick. So set up on the floor, right here. I'll do what I can for you with the mics. I'm missing dinner for this shit, just so you'll know…"

Dale turned away again, moving over to talk to James and Derek. I could feel Randy radiating rage like a space heater. The power of the impending gig and the black light kept his mouth quiet, though, and he returned immediately to his setup.

Late for sound check and about to play our audition, we had no room to bitch. Randy reigned in his anger and continued the setup, muttering insults under his breath. James shook his head and tuned his guitar, the first to finish.

We'd pissed off the soundman. Not a good thing.

The others were soon miked up and checked, and we waited while Dale gave Randy a cursory run through on the drums.

"Right kick drum." Dale stood behind the board, his voice booming through the house P.A..

Thud.

Thud.

Thud.

Thud.

Thud. Randy beat the kick in slow tempo. The sound moved from flat to thick, deep reverberation shaking the tables. Most impressive.

"Okay. Left Kick drum…"

The rest of the band stood together beside the stage watching Randy and collectively lamenting our poor luck.

"They're letting people in already," James said, looking to the front. "And if Dale is pissed, then so is Dan. We're fucked."

"Who's Dan?"

"Dan is that guy up there on the second level--the one with the big hair helmet."

"That old DJ dude?"

"The owner, dude," James said. "And he likes to be finished with sound check before he opens the door. That's professional."

Dale and Randy moved to the snare drum. We all craned our necks to look at the cheesily attired rocker in the DJ booth.

"That guy is the owner?"

"Yep. He's a guitarist."

"But...he tucks his pants into his boots!"

"Yep."

"Figures."

"Aw, screw him," Derek chuckled, unphased. "We're okay."

"You don't know shit," James snapped, his aura turning crimson. "We probably won't ever get back in this place, and you're too wasted to care!"

"Who's wasted?" Derek replied, shrugging off the aggression. "Not even. And who gives a shit? Settle down, James."

"That's easy for you to say," James stepped closer, pointing a finger at Derek. "You don't ever give a shit what happens. Ever."

Derek sneered. "Get your finger out of my face, dude."

People were beginning to stare. I stepped between them. "Cool it--here he comes..."

The brief but satisfactory drum check completed, Dale approached. He wore a leather jacket now, carrying a backpack and a motorcycle helmet. "I'm going home for dinner," he announced. "The dressing room is that little black door over there by the stage. You can wait in there or out here--whatever. Just be onstage and ready at ten till seven."

"Will do," James said, sounding like a salesman. "And we're sorry again about being late and everything…"

"Yeah. Be ready. And tell your drummer to tune his drums. They sound like crap."

Round & Round

"He said what?"

Randy couldn't believe his ears. He needed to hear it again.

"He said you need to tune your drums."

"He said they sounded like crap," Tommy clarified.

We sat in the 'dressing room', a six-by-three box which doubled as the utility closet when it wasn't occupied by a gaggle of head-bangers. Sponges and mops tangled our steps. The potent lemony-fresh scent of industrial strength cleaning products saturated the air. The only mirror was a large broken shard that had been duct taped to the wall, face high.

"What the fuck does he mean by that?"

"He means you need to tune your drums," James told him. "Like NOW."

"I like the way they sound," Randy replied. "They're tuned already."

"Dude, don't lie. I never see you tuning your drums."

"Bullshit, James!"

"I think your kit sounds great," Derek added, glancing at James. "I say fuck 'em--you tune it the way you like it, Randy."

James shook his head, pushing the drama. "You guys just don't get it. Shit, until five minutes ago, I thought the drums sounded good, too. But we have to make sacrifices if we wanna make it. This is just the beginning of the pain, and already you dicks can't handle it!"

"What? Dude…"

"That asshole only said that about the drums because we were late!" Randy blasted in defense. Thankfully, the steady bump of house music outside the door would keep anyone from hearing.

"Yeah, so what?" James returned immediately, his face ripening by the second. "He probably did. He was pissed! But instead of being all offended, you should just suck it up and do it. So he wants us to jump through a hoop? So fucking jump! What do we care?"

"Well shit, why don't we just put on some pink tights and play Wham covers, then?" Derek faced James, staring down at him. "I mean, if you want to sell out, James, then you should at least do it right!"

"Selling out?" James was shocked. "You actually think that tuning the drums because they asked us to is selling out? That's stupid, man! You're being stupid! Have another drink, Derek…"

Derek lunged at James, but Tommy and I were already in place to hold him back.

"What the hell is your problem, James?"

"You're my problem," James stood ready, but wouldn't dare hit Derek while we were holding him back. "Kicking my ass won't make you a better guitarist."

"Fuck you! You've got no right saying that to me." Derek surged with alcohol-fueled aggression, and we held against the continued strain. Eventually the tide receded and he relaxed a bit.

"Dudes, let go of me." He turned a cold eye. "Let GO."

Derek easily brushed us off. Tommy flashed me a 'what the hell do we do now?' look.

"Stop this crap!" I ordered, losing a bit of my own cool. "This is bullshit! This is some little bitty bullshit, and you're turning it into a major thing! You guys are friends."

Derek turned away from James, breaking the treacherous glare.

"I didn't say we weren't friends."

"You're fighting over things that don't matter!"

"Bullshit!" Derek scowled, anything but calm. "It matters a lot, man! James has no right--especially James--has no right hacking on my guitar playing!"

James eyes widened. "What do you mean, by 'especially James'?"

"Exactly what it sounds like I mean."

"At least I'm not drunk all the time and slow to learn everything."

Apparently, my negotiation techniques weren't working so well.

"What?" Derek's bristles bristled. "So what are you saying? Suddenly I'm not good enough?"

James rolled his eyes. "I didn't say that--"

"This is such bullshit!" Derek hung his head. "This isn't supposed to be like this. Like, I didn't know we were supposed to be fucking evaluating each other all the time!"

"Don't be a baby--"

"DUDES! Shut! Up!" Randy burst out in staccato authority. "This is a really bad time for this."

Randy was behind Derek on this one, but had apparently heard enough arguing.

I felt both sides on this one. I couldn't blame Randy for being upset--he wasn't exactly accustomed to taking criticism--from anyone--where his drumming was concerned. And then there was the thought of James, sitting at his little practice amp pulling out his hair because he couldn't duplicate some obscure solo.

"Look, we're all pissed," I interjected, taking advantage of Randy's interruption. "We're all disappointed, not just you two! All of us! And we ALL wish we could have been here on time, and we weren't. But we're HERE and we still have a gig to play. This is The Tank, dudes! I mean, all this other bullshit aside--isn't that the point of the whole thing?"

"Exactly," Derek agreed.

James shrugged his consent.

DEFCON 4. Nearly at peace.

"Look, if we go up there all pissed and huffy, we're going to suck. Big time."

"I agree," Randy nodded.

Tommy seconded the nod, and Derek shrugged slightly. We were getting somewhere.

"Randy, I know it sucks, but go out and at least pretend to tune the drums a bit, just so they can see. Derek and James, drop this, and finish it later--or better yet, drop it completely and have a drink later. Right now, you're still two out of five, and you OWE it to the rest of us to get along. Are we cool?"

"Yeah," Randy agreed, shaking my hand. "We're cool."

"That's what I was trying to say," James turned away, checking his hair in the mirror shard.

"Well, Mark says it better," Derek countered, not quite finished. "Maybe you should shut up and listen sometime."

"Derek…"

"Yeah, yeah, whatever," Derek relented, moving toward the door. "I'm cool. I didn't start this shit in the first place."

The door opened, and in walked Todd Vandermeer.

THE Todd Vandermeer. Lead singer and chief stud of 'Vandermeer', bitchin' cool front man and all-around studly local demigod. His band was at the predator pinnacle of the local band food chain, and Todd was reputed to be the second coming of Robert Plant.

Todd Vandermeer looked every bit the part. His bleached blonde mop was adroitly coiffed, possessing both volume and height. His wrists were covered in bangles and friendship bracelets, with rings on every finger. Tonight, the costume ensemble included a see-through red mesh muscle shirt, bandannas around the arms, and…you guessed it…spandex.

Cheetah spandex, with little white boots. Apparently, cheetah and red go together. Not a trace of shame on the guy's face.

He looked us over, a perpetually mocking sneer etched on his fine features. I suppose it takes a lot of clout to sneer while you're wearing lycra tights, but he pulled off a red cheetah kind of intimidation, dark eyes stabbing from beneath his blonde bangs. Todd Vandermeer was my toughest competition. The local standard. My own personal Grendel.

"You guys first slot?" Todd queried, utilizing his well-practiced ability to ask a question and still sound disinterested. He tossed his gig-bag on the floor.

"Yeah, first slot," James answered, disguising all discontent.

"First slot sucks. Good luck."

"What time do you guys go on?"

"Ten," Todd sniffed. "Like always."

Like always. The guy was marking his territory. He may as well have pissed on the wall.

"Well, I'm headed for the bar," Derek announced, moving to the door, predictably unimpressed with the great Todd Vandermeer. "You guys fix your hair or whatever. I'll see you on stage at seven."

"Ten till seven."

"Yeah, yeah."

"I'm coming with," Randy said, stepping around James to follow Derek out. "I have to tune my drums."

Rock City

Quarter to seven, and the babe brigade was arriving.

One by one, they strolled past the cover charge, walking on tall heels and sizing up the place with narrow charcoal-lined eyes. They possessed some of the biggest hair in the entire city and ruled The Tank with attitude, short skirts, and compressed cleavage. Quarts of creamy make-up base covered their faces, filling every crater and pock, removing all signs of blemish and leaving a smooth, glossy sheen. On top of this, gloriously red lipstick, made shiny with something called gloss. The trademark charcoal eyes would be the final touch, lined just enough to look both sexy and mean at the same time.

They continued to file through the entrance, spilling colorfully into the bar like clowns pouring out of a little flowered car--all shapes and varieties, all of them ready to party. A veritable smorgasbord of bar chicks. The primping standard was quite high; even on a weeknight, most were fully costumed and ready to compete.

This was our universe.

First and foremost, there were the glam girls. They were the most easily spotted, decked out in bright skimpiness and proudly displaying their flesh. Generally bleached blonde and customarily tan, the glam girls emulated the 'video chick' look and liked to dance with each other as long as someone was watching. Hobbies: wet T-shirt contests, nail care. See: Tawny Kitaen.

In contrast to the glam girls were the rocker chicks. The rocker chicks, for one reason or another, couldn't stomach the thought of being a glamour girl. Some were in bands themselves. Some were too oddly shaped to look good as a glamour girl. Others simply shunned all things bimbo.

Rocker chicks wore jeans and leather, tough but never too slutty. Boots or tennis shoes, but rarely seen in heels. Sometimes big-haired, but never matching the porn star mega-hair of the glam girls. My personal favorites, the rocker chicks were the queens of eyeliner. Hobbies: laughing at male stupidity, mouthing lyrics. See: Joan Jett.

The biker chicks were closely related to the rocker chicks, with the exception that they carried a sixties/country flavor along with their uniform. On the whole, biker chicks were tougher than rockers. Leather vests, chaps, and always a pair of jeans or leathers. You'd rarely see a skirt on a true biker chick. Hobbies: cruising, automobile repair. See: your local pub.

The remainder of the female talent was comprised of women from many other tribes. The Madonnas, the punkers, the posers, and the yuppies were all represented in smaller but still significant numbers. From my spot behind the curtain, it looked like at least a hundred women.

"I can't believe this turnout!" I summoned James, who was already wearing his guitar. He looked through the gap. "It's still early, too."

"It must be the Vandermeer crowd," he said. "Those guys are mega-popular. The chicks love that band--especially Todd. That dude knows how to work a crowd..."

"They like him 'cause he looks like one of them," Derek said, shuffling in behind us and heading for his amp. "That Todd dude looks like a chick whose sex change didn't take."

James glared at him but said nothing. Admittedly, it wasn't the time or the place to insult Vandermeer. Even with the blaring house music, I feared the walls might have ears. Just as I was about to say something to that effect, Soundman Dale appeared through the curtain, jacket off and wearing his headset.

"Everybody here?" he asked, looking us over.

"Yep."

"Good." Dale eyed the connections. "You guys are on as soon as the song ends."

T-minus twenty seconds and counting.

I looked down at the big lettered song list, trying not to think of the babe quotient, taking a deep breath to calm down. Toothy butterflies swarmed and fed in my stomach, ignoring my pleas. I suddenly wished I'd accepted the shot of tequila when it was offered.

We waited as owner Dan delivered a half-assed introduction over the P.A..

"Okay--don't forget it's drown night on Tuesdays and ladies' night every Sunday. This weekend we've got Dirtwater Fox, Rat Patrol and Assault coming in--and of course, coming up later tonight we got Vandermeer! Keep the tips coming--we don't like to see Tammy angry! Right, Tammy? Yeah…okay, this is a new act here at The Tank--give it up for Skin Tight…"

The crowd offered a bare smattering of preemptory applause.

Focus, I told myself.

"Let's do it."

The curtain slipped open.

James' intro riff cut like a dirty blade, the amplified crunch slicing into the murmuring void.

Derek joined, stepping forward and doubling him, head banging.

Randy and Tommy launched in perfect time, the stage suddenly bathed in red and orange light. Warm brightness blared into my eyes, catching me in a crossfire of debilitating color.

I stepped up to the mic and started singing.

Something was so deafening that I couldn't hear myself. That something was me.

Professional sound. Friggin' loud. My voice screamed back at me from the ballsy black monitors at my feet. I'd been shouting over the band for years. Suddenly, I was the loudest thing on stage.

The lights blared warm in my face.

I couldn't see, but I could hear. Just as well.

I fought the awkward feeling and belted my own lyrics, stomping around a bit. I looked up, feeling the eyes of the crowd but unable to distinguish anything but big-haired silhouettes through the blinding spots.

Synthetic fog began to roll from the machines on either side of the stage, filling the stage floor with breath-stealing clouds of white. The synthetic smell caught me off guard, and I inhaled a lungful.

Choke. The urge to cough was irresistible, and I pulled the mic away from my lips just in time, abandoning the lyric.

Focus, I repeated in my head. Focus.

Cough.

I banged my head a couple times to disguise the gag. James was glaring.

Somewhere inside, good ole Jim Morrison stepped forward, surrounded in a mist of mental fog. He shook his head a bit, looking amused.

'Forget the focus,' he told me. 'Just sing, man. Feel, not focus…'

I recovered, picking the lyric back up. I looked up to the DJ booth and saw Dan standing, arms folded.

We reached the guitar solo, and James stepped to the front. He glanced at me, bearing a manufactured smile. Gratefully, I stepped back and cleared my throat.

I resorted to the Ozzy technique, banging my head and stomping back to Derek's side of the stage. He and Tommy bounced in unison. The solo passed.

Up to the microphone, I finished the final verse and they launched into the drum-heavy ending. Below me, the dance floor remained empty. I looked out again through the spray of colors, wishing I could see the audience.

Bug a Dug.

The ending was relatively tight. We paused a moment, waiting for a response before starting the second tune.

Scattered applause.

Scattered, at best.

It wasn't that the bar crowd was antagonistic…I'd say disinterested would be a better word.

I'd already learned two of the twelve golden rules of club gigging: #7) Start your set with something the crowd knows; and #8) Do not pause after the first song. Always go immediately into a second song. We'd broken rule number seven, and paid for it. Number eight was strictly by the book.

Boom. The second song began with the familiar drum intro. KISS' "Rock and Roll All Night." Our no miss selection. Who could deny the coolness of a band that would cover KISS tunes?

As soon as the first verse began, the lessers in the crowd began creeping toward the dance floor. The floor was nearly full when the song ended. They weren't exactly riveted, but the mood improved.

I could see Sandy and her friends dancing as we plugged right into the third song.

Derek was enjoying himself, and he flashed me a 'what's wrong with you' look.

My fog-filled lungs needed a breather. I walked back to the drums, where Randy worked with flair. He banged his head and his hi-hat.

"You want a drum solo at the end of this one?" I yelled over the monitors.

He smiled vengefully, cueing me for the first verse.

I resumed singing and turned back toward the crowd, but I could hear him shout 'Hell yeah!' behind me. Whether or not they liked the band, this crowd was going to like Randy's drumming.

I knew James would be upset at my calling an audible, but it was the best thing for the band.

Time flies in a forty-five minute set. Soon the third song was behind us, and Randy was rumbling his way into the drum solo.

"And on the drums...Randy 'Psycho' Sanderson!"

James stared over at me as though I'd broken a commandment. The crowd, however, loved it.

Rule #6) People love drum solos. Period.

A couple of stray whoops emanated from the dance floor, eyes looking through me toward Randy. I moved to the side of the stage to allow him full avail of the light.

"What are you doing?" James blurted, his aggression now directed my way.

"I was choking on the fog, dude. Besides, they're loving it."

"It's not on the song list," he replied. "And you don't even know when we're sucking!"

"I know," I told him. "That's WHY he's soloing. We should skip the rest of the originals--they're not going over."

James shook his head. "No way."

He turned away so as to prevent a reply.

Across the stage, Derek and Tommy were enjoying the drumming. Derek grinned over at me and balled up his fist in congratulatory gesture. I don't know if Randy's drum solo saved us that night, but it sure didn't hurt.

DR. FEELGOOD

The set flew past us, ending with a whimper. Our last tune was a cover of "Mr. Brownstone," a song by a new band named Guns 'n' Roses that we thought would go over. Apparently not. A mild rash of scattered applause came from the crowd, the majority of it created by Sandy and her promiscuous posse.

The lights died and the curtain slid closed, leaving us sweating and alone again on the stage. The house music kicked back on.

"Stick around, folks," Dan's voice boomed over the system. "We've got Hot-n-Nasty in twenty minutes and, of course, Vandermeer at ten! So you definitely wanna hang out for that... And just a reminder for you ladies: You're gonna want to be here for our Ms. Metal contest next Thursday! Three events, three hundred bucks in cash!"

Randy was dripping sweat, beaming with satisfaction. Derek walked over and patted me on the back.

"Good job, bud."

"Thanks, dude. That was great..."

"Good job?" James mocked from the other side of the stage. "What the hell are you guys talking about? That sucked!"

Sucked?

I didn't understand. Sure, the crowd wasn't exactly on their feet…but it was still early, and our first time here. We couldn't expect too much. James, however, looked to be on the verge of explosion.

"It didn't suck." Derek snipped, unplugging.

James stepped quickly to oppose him. "How would you know anything? You're fucking drunk, man!"

"Yeah, right. I hit the breaks just as clean as you did, bud. You tell me where I missed…"

"The covers went over pretty well," I added, trying to diffuse the potential of more fisticuffs. "The originals…not so hot, but nobody knows 'em. If we just start out with a cover next time--"

"Next time?" James shook his head at me and let forth a condescending chuckle. "You don't get it, Mark! We'll be lucky if there IS a next time!"

Derek's tone darkened, his eyes meeting James'. "I'm getting pretty damned sick of this…"

"Sick of what?"

"James, dude…you seriously need to settle down, bud."

"They'll ask us back," I said. "We weren't that bad."

"No doubt," Randy agreed from behind me.

"Our originals suck," James lamented, continuing his rant. "They're not gonna re-book us, especially after we were late! I don't know why the hell--"

Discretion halted James mid-sentence.

Dale was on his way up the stairs.

"You guys have ten minutes to tear down," he told us, not bothering to comment on our performance. I didn't really want to know his opinion.

James turned to face him. "So, do you want the stuff out the door, or just out of the way?"

"The stage door is open," Dale answered, kneeling to unplug the drum mics. "Load out NOW."

"Okay," James answered in buddy-buddy tone. "Thanks, Dale."

In ten minutes, the drum kit was disassembled and resting safely in the truck beside the guitar amps. The tear down was perhaps our biggest victory of the evening. The members of Hot-n-Nasty emerged from the utility room and took the stage without acknowledging our presence.

James appeared at the back door, waiting outside as though he wasn't allowed back in. He beckoned me.

"Lonnie's taking me home with the equipment," James said, the frustration still dominating his mood.

I protested immediately. "Don't do that. Stay here for a while, dude. Let's just get a beer, and talk."

"I don't want to right now," he answered, looking away. "I don't feel like it, you know? Besides, I don't want nothing getting stolen..."

"Just leave the truck right there," I said. "It'll be fine, man. Come back in and have a beer. C'mon--let's go check out the scenery. This place is loaded with women tonight!"

He shook his head and flashed a look that told me I'd never convince him. Not even the lure of the bimbo brigade could prevent him from going.

"I can't stay, dude."

"Is this because of Derek?"

James shrugged. "It's just about...everything. I'm just pissed, that's all. I don't want this thing with Derek to get too out of control."

"If it's the originals you're worried about, dude...we'll get better."

"I know. I know that." James looked over my shoulder, into the bar. "You want to be better. I never questioned your heart, Mark. You may not know exactly what it takes, but at least you care. We're in the same boat, you and me."

"You're right," I told him, thinking again of the pressures of lead guitar. "All we know is right now--what we know right now. Sure, I want everybody to think I'm a good singer. Sure, I want to make Todd Vanderfuck look like an amateur. You know it. But we're not gonna win every battle, dude."

"I know, but--"

"For all we know, the soundman gave us a shitty mix, or maybe the Vandermeer guitarists were out there talking trash. There's a ton of shit that we can't do a thing about. Some of those people are going to hate us--not just tonight, but every night! So what? So fuck them, we keep playing! You know I have faith in you, man. We all do."

"I know," he responded awkwardly, pausing. "Tell me, though--how much faith do you have in Derek?"

Dude.

This was serious. James' question carried weighty implications. Until that moment, I would never have thought it possible. Somehow, I knew at that moment. We were headed for the reef.

"A lot," I replied. "I have faith in the band, and that means all of us. Derek's fine, dude. Seriously. He was nervous; you were nervous; we were all frickin' nervous! No biggie. We all just deal with it in different ways, you know? Just give him a break tonight, and I bet he doesn't drink like this next time. You'll see."

I felt uncomfortable defending Derek's budding alcoholism, but the seas needed calming to keep the boat from taking water. The 'nervous' argument seemed to do its job, tempering James' attitude a bit.

"Yeah, I guess so." He looked back over his shoulder. Lonnie and Sandy waited in the truck, waving a joint in the window for James to see. "I still don't feel much like partying. I'll see you guys back at the house."

We shook, said our laters, and I stepped back into the bar just in time to hear Hot-n-Nasty's first tune. Their strong voiced, wide-hipped singer Destiny vocalized her way through Heart's "Barracuda."

I made my way to the lower bar in search of Derek and the others, surprised that I wasn't drawing more attention. It wasn't that I felt like such a stud at the time, but I'd grown accustomed to attracting stares at keggers and parties. I was used to being a fat little fish, and going from the pond to the lake was making me feel a bit small. The Tank crowd seemed to be purposely ignoring me, as a way of letting me know I was still a low rider on the headbanger totem pole.

Androgyny reigned. Guys and girls, all of them prettied up and tough, thriving in their natural habitat. The walls were lined with band members galore, drinking and trying to maintain the 'crazy yet aloof' image as they jealously kept an eye on their girlfriends. Bettys surrounded me on all sides--rocker chicks and glam girls alike, clustered and passing gossip, looking similarly aloof as they puffed on ladylike 100's. The scent of stale beer and stage fog lingered in an airborne soup of cigarette smoke. Concert T's and bangles. Fake eyelashes and ear cuffs. Leather and denim and studs. Oh my. This was headbanger country.

I found Derek and Randy at the bar, somehow managing to save me a seat.

"Where is James?"

"He went home," I said, not wanting to talk about it. "I told him to come in, but he said he felt sick."

"Oh, man..."

"Wuss," Derek commented, raising a beer bottle to his lips. "He's stressing out too much. I'm telling you, I'm getting worried about James. He's getting like this close to pissing me off for real."

Randy shrugged his agreement. "It's like he just can't seem to relax anymore."

"He's just worried about the competition," I explained, wanting them to know. "He knows Vandermeer is playing tonight, so he knows Todd and Eddie Rand and all of them are watching."

"He shouldn't be so freaked. They're not that much better--"

"Yeah, but he IS freaked."

"That's crap dudes! It had nothing to do with the music!" Derek snapped defensively, his enunciation slowed by the accumulation of drinks. "I'm tellin' you--it's Sandy, dudes. Seriously! He's whipped-- straight up. She didn't want him around all these babes, so she faked a headache or acted real horny so he'd take her home."

Blame it on the girlfriend. Sandy didn't deserve this one, but pressing the truth was bound to light up Derek.

My typical dilemma: Do what's right? Do what I feel? Or do what's best for the band? It was nice when all three happened to coincide. Anymore, I was happy to get two out of three.

So I flaked.

"Yeah, probably," I said. "Sandy does get pretty jealous..."

Weak. I folded instead of pushing the issue with a drunken Derek and regretted it immediately. I guess I figured my band policing quota was filled for the night and wanted a break from mending everybody else's fences. I told myself I'd help the band more by keeping my mouth shut.

Unfortunately, I have a tendency to pick at scabs.

The bartender brought me a fresh beer, and I drank.

"Where's Tommy?"

"Upstairs, somewhere," Derek replied. "He saw some chick he knew and took off. We would have gone with him, but her friends were ultra-skanky."

The tables were as full as the dance floor now, dancing to the Hot-n-Nasty version of Zeppelin's "Heartbreaker."

"So what do you think?" Randy asked, motioning toward the stage.

"They're pretty tight," I answered honestly. "That Tama kit is pretty sweet."

Randy nodded. "Yeah, I guess. I like his cymbals. The chick singer? Now THAT I don't know about…"

"You don't like her? Destiny, or whatever? I think she's got a good voice."

"Yeah, but she just doesn't look right," Randy answered. "There's something I don't trust about a rock band with a girl singing."

"And they always play the same shit," Derek chimed in. "I guarantee we're gonna hear more Heart before the set ends."

"No doubt."

Hot-n-Nasty's Destiny was something of an attraction here, and her crowd on the dance floor was considerably larger than ours. Still, I nodded and let the subject drift away, tiring of band conjecture. We leaned back, surveying the crowd and soaking in the talent. The Tank was heating up--soon it would be too crowded to move.

That was the night I met Sara. Or should I say, with all deference to John Lennon and his Norwegian wood, that was the night Sara met me.

The first time I saw her, Sara was coming out of the bathroom, her bobble-headed friends in tow. She looked gorgeous and tough with her leather jacket and patched jeans, walking as though she owned the place. Her raven-touched hair was long but not teased, possessing its own enviable volume. Burgundy lips, and thick circles of eyeliner around curious, cynical almond eyes.

A rocker leading glam girls, Sara possessed the kind of charm that allowed her to forego the glam look without losing a bit of sex appeal. She would have been sexy in a radiation suit. It wasn't a question of perfect features or boob size, either. Sara had a bulletproof charisma and was beautiful because she acted it. Without ever knowing it, she was living a corollary to the first rule of lead singing: Performance is twenty percent talent and eighty percent attitude.

She was fearless, and smart. Her intelligence was obvious on the outside, and before I ever spoke to her, I guessed that she would have a sharp tongue. Sara never got teased or pinched; she intimidated the pick-up artists and general drunks like a beautiful but poisonous fish. The predators sensed her danger.

Not that she didn't get hit on. I watched her from the bar for at least twenty minutes, and she was approached three times. The first two suitors were sent packing quickly with a few choice words from her friends. The third suitor was still in the game, sitting at the table and trying to make time with the diminutive blonde who accompanied her. Sara sipped her drink, not making a fool of herself, not dancing or bubbling over. Exceedingly cool.

Had she seen the set? I hadn't seen anyone from the stage, and there was no telling if she even knew of my performance. Even then--this was The Tank. What would it matter? By the look of her, Sara was well versed in the romantic ploys of headbangers, and this was longhair central. The old standard 'I'm in a band' line would be useless with her.

I'd have to get an angle, an excuse to talk to her.

I turned back to the bar, ordering another beer. Randy sat next to me. Beside him, Derek was talking with a well-shaped stripper with hard nipples and blinding reflective flashes that sparkled on her over-glossed lips.

"You still torn up over that hot chick?" Randy asked, looking over his shoulder to where she sat.

I didn't yet know her name, so she was currently being referred to as 'that hot chick'.

"Yeah. She hasn't danced once."

"That's a good thing," Randy said, pointing to the dance floor. "Look at all those dumb-asses out there, doing the white guy two-step and trying to make conversation. I promise you, not a single one of 'em wants to be out there…"

"It's like some mating ritual. A requirement."

"A hoop to jump through. And look at the chicks! Most of them aren't really dancing. Watch, watch!" He pointed. "They're, like, shuffling back and forth. Just enough NOT to break a sweat. So if your hot chick doesn't dance, then all the better for you."

I nodded absently, still trying to come up with something witty to say.

Being a singer had dulled my predatory skills; I was accustomed to the prey coming to me. I was used to fawning high school girls who fantasized about being the singer's girl. Easy pickings. I usually knew they liked me before I ever spoke a word. Short of extreme rudeness or body odor, I would never lose with those girls.

Sara, however, was different. She'd been there and done that. You could tell that she fawned for no one.

"Easy, dude. Just go over and ask if she saw the set," Randy urged. "And then after you start talking to her, find out if that little blonde is taken."

"And what if she hated the set?"

He smirked. "It doesn't matter. All that matters is that you were the one singing. Dude, go talk to her. Shit…"

Randy nudged my arm with his elbow.

"What?"

He nudged me again, tilting his head.

I smelled roses. I turned slightly back to the right, and in the corner of my eye I saw her standing right behind me. She waited for the bartender.

This was it. A golden opportunity, delivered into my hands. Randy and Jim were watching, and my pride wouldn't allow me to wuss out.

"Don't think, just talk," I heard Randy whisper.

Right. Just talk. Simple enough. I'd play it off the top of my head.

Turning to face her, I uttered the most weary and clichéd of all pick-up lines, the great-grandfather of bad approaches: "So, do you come here often?"

Even as it left my lips, I couldn't believe I'd said it. And yet, there it was, the most overworked phrase in the history of taverns. I might as well have asked her what a nice girl like her was doing in a place like that.

She smiled a bit--the 'you're an idiot' smile--before nodding. "Yeah, I guess you could say that."

Of course, now I was confused. Not only had my first line been ancient and stupid, but it also left me no follow up question. I wasn't fool enough to pursue the 'don't come here much' line any further.

"Does Hot-n-Nasty play here a lot?"

It was still weak and impersonal, but at least I was talking.

"Yeah," she said. "They play about once a month, I'd say. Destiny's good, but we came for Vandermeer."

"Oh yeah? You a big Vandermeer fan?" I tried not to sound jealous.

The bartender appeared, and Sara passed him a five, asking for cigarettes, calling him by name.

"I like 'em," she nodded, sincere but not overly enthusiastic. "They're good. My friend is dating the bass player, so we basically come for her."

"Ah, I see."

"Was this your first time playing here?" she asked.

She'd mentioned the set. She'd seen and heard it. I didn't know whether to feel fortunate or damned.

I chuckled defensively. "Yeah, it was. Did it show that much?"

Sara tilted her head, grinning a bit. "Well, you guys did look a little green."

"Yeah?"

"That'll wear off. It was good, otherwise. I thought you guys were good."

"Yeah..."

"You just have to play the right stuff and you'll be fine. This crowd is picky. I'm Sara, by the way."

"I'm Mark." I shook her hand awkwardly. "So, do you think we'll get asked back?"

"Oh yeah," she mouthed. "Totally. Don't you think you will?"

The bartender returned with her smokes and her change. She tapped the pack and waited for an answer.

"Well, I don't think the soundman likes us too much..."

She rolled her eyes. "Dale? He's a shit, and he's like that with everyone. Tell you what--I know Dan's girlfriend. She's a stripper down at Lucky's, and I'll tell her to put in a good word for you."

"Really?"

She lit a cigarette. "Not a problem."

It was all coming into place. The attitude, the looks, the Marlboro 100's; Sara was a stripper down at Lucky's! Oh fickle fate, must you tempt me thus? Thusly? Something like that.

"Do you…"

"Do I work at Lucky's?" she asked, reading my mind.

I shrugged. "Yeah."

"Two years now."

"Oh…"

"Kidding! Not EVEN," she said, seeming amused with the thought. "Why? Do I look like a stripper?"

I squirmed. "No…of course not. I didn't mean it like that--not that I mean that you don't look good enough to be, because I'm not saying that, either…I just mean, you know, I didn't think you were a stripper. Really."

She grinned as I fumbled through my explanation, chuckling as she let me talk myself into idiocy constructing a dull point. When I was finished, she paused dramatically.

"Alright, then. That's better." Another smile, this time the 'you're cute' variety.

My spirits lifted. Was it time to ask her to breakfast? Too soon?

"I'll buy you a drink…"

"No, but thanks," she waved it off. "I can buy my own. I'm good for now, anyway."

I fumbled for a question. "So…are you going to be here till close?"

She raised an eyebrow, two steps ahead. "Hmm, don't know. What exactly did you have in mind?"

"Well, I thought maybe you'd want to go do breakfast with me and Randy." I tapped his shoulder. "Randy, this is Sara."

"Hey Sara."

"Hi Randy."

He turned dutifully back toward the bar, leaving me to close the deal.

"I have to work tomorrow," she said, "or else I'd go. Do you guys ever come down on Tuesday nights? It's my day off, and I'm always here then. I'll give you a rain check, and you can show up on Tuesday. How's that?"

A rain check? Bueno.

"Can I get it in writing?"

"Sure," she laughed. "I'll send over my lawyer--she's that little blonde in the pink over there. Danni. Or better than that, you guys could come sit at the table and wow us with your pickup lines."

"That sounds good. I could use the practice…"

REMEMBER TOMORROW

Sara kept her word.

After talking all night, even during Vandermeer's well-received performance, she said her goodbyes and led her somewhat bimbotic friends right out of the club. There would be no breakfast. I was far from emotionally defeated, however. I had the promise of Tuesday and a phone number, pressed discreetly into my hand just before she left.

I resolved not to use the number too soon. It was a test, a trick to see just how desperate I was. I'd more than likely wind up talking to a machine, and she wouldn't be calling back. No, the wiser course of action was to simply show up at the club on Tuesday and play the game. She'd dropped the hint, and by the time I finally gave her a call, I wanted her to be expecting it.

So I waited patiently.

By Tuesday, I was spoiling for someone to accompany me to The Tank, eager to get another glimpse of Sara. Randy initially declined the invitation, having fared poorly with Sara's blonde friend on Friday. Derek, however, was more than willing to make the trip, noting that it was drown night, featuring three bands and fifty-cent beers until ten. We planned to go after practice.

On the band front, tempers seemed to be cooling. James had been far less intense the day after the gig, and he and Derek exchanged veiled apologies over Cheerios at the tilting kitchen table that morning. Inspired, I'd been writing new lyrics and thinking over the song list. At least for the time being, we were in need of popular cover tunes.

Practice went smoothly. We played through our normal set and worked a bit on Van Halen's "Unchained" before winding up the rehearsal with a spontaneously nostalgic version of "Whole Lotta Rosie."

At times like these, I could barely hear myself. With two half-stacks and a twin bass cabinet, the volume was formidable indeed. Add to this the pounding of the miked kick drums and the bronzed cymbals exploding like bombs in my ears, and *voila*, the makings of a head-ringer. In rehearsal, I could only stand next to the monitor and try to sing as loud as possible. Even after emerging from the speakers, my voice had a torrential river of noise to travail before it would ever reach hearing.

The trash can ending. Battered 'A' strings. Full-on amp crankage. Cymbals whimpering under Randy's felonious assault. We were all jumping around like Family Feud contestants by the time we finished, sweating and laughing.

"That rocked, man."

"Did you see Tommy fall down?"

"Yep."

Tommy examined his upper thigh. "I was trying to do those James Brown splits, right? But then I realized that if I went down too far, I was gonna hit my bass on the ground. So I did this kind of thing like 'huh' and 'huhh,' and anyways--"

"He fell on his ass."

"I think I pulled my groin."

"Won't be the first time…

"Ugh! Dude, go pull it somewhere else."

James was smiling. He actually seemed to be having as much fun as the rest of us. When we began packing up and talking about the club, however, his attitude quickly mutated.

"You guys are going to The Tank?"

"Yeah," Derek nodded, taking a chew. "Mark's going back to hit on that hottie from Friday night."

James huffed. "You guys weren't going to ask me to go?"

I shrugged. "We just figured you didn't want to, that's all."

"Oh," he shrugged back. "Whatever."

"Well, do you want to go?"

"Nah…"

"See?" Derek grinned. "We knew it."

"Yeah," he said. "But you should still ask. I thought we were gonna work on new material tonight…"

I instantly felt guilty.

"I said 'this week'," I answered. "We'll do it tomorrow, cool?"

James threw up his hands, exhaling. "Tomorrow. Shit. That attitude will never get us anywhere."

"What?"

"You heard what I said, Mark."

I couldn't believe he was actually pulling the old 'duty to the band' thing on me tonight. I wanted to go to the club. I didn't feel guilty about it, either. Derek spoke before I could think of a reply.

"Will you just chill with that crap, James? That's all you fucking worry about."

"Well, shit--somebody's got to worry about it!"

Derek's switch was back on.

"Dude! Get the chip off your shoulder! We're just going to the club--for kicks. No big deal. Mark's meeting a chick, so we're going. If you want to come, then get your coat and let's go. But don't fucking start up with all this responsibility shit."

"All I'm sayin' is that we have to work if we want to--"

"Dude! We just rehearsed for two hours!"

"Whatever." James grabbed his guitar and headed for his room. "You do what you got to…"

"Yeah, whatever."

Tommy waited until James was out of earshot before turning to Derek. "I'm not staying home with the slave-master. I'm going with you guys."

Randy lit a cigarette. "Me, too."

Smooth Up In Ya

"You have to have a certain kind of personality to be a bartender," Derek stated, mid-treatise. "You've got to be part con, part sadist."

We sat at the bar on the main floor of The Tank, watching employee-of-the-month Tammy wash glasses and pour shots.

"Oh yeah?"

"Truth. You see, Tammy and all the other good bartenders--the ones with the knack for it--they like to keep you going until you're drooling on yourself and falling off the stool--and then cut you off and kick you out! They enjoy it. A good bartender always offers another round. Right, Tammy?"

"That's right." Tammy stared his way, red-nailed hands on hips. She was cute yet seemed over the hill to us at thirty-something. A fixture at the club, Tammy had clout; she pulled the best shifts and was tough enough to handle the juvenile-minded rock crowd. Tammy was a pro.

And she could field the compliments like a big leaguer. It was mind-boggling to consider how often this woman was propositioned. At the modest estimate of three a day...let's see, fifteen a week, sixty a month...that would be an average of seven-hundred twenty pickup lines fielded and returned every year. Impressive.

Derek, of course, was flirting with her, never afraid to approach the unapproachable. Derek had guts *d'amour*. He was the kind of guy who could speak to anyone, without hesitation, and endear himself in mere minutes. A small-talk specialist. Not a smooth talker, necessarily, or a player--nothing insincere that would make you doubt him or feel uncomfortable. He was great to have around when girl-hunting; the consummate icebreaker, he could get you in the door without fail. He would get us to the girls' table, and we would work from there. As the initiator, Derek would take first pick.

Perhaps it was something about the way he looked. Or maybe it was the way he never came across as needy or wanting. Derek seemed perennially absent of ulterior motives. He was actually interested. You got the feeling that he was talking to you because he genuinely wanted to. Apparently women like that sort of thing.

Under normal circumstances, Tammy would have been unapproachable for me. Unthinkable. I'd never dared to utter more than a simple blurt and a drink order before tonight. Derek, however, had little difficulty. He didn't feel stifled like I did in The Tank. Somehow, the place didn't intimidate him.

"She enjoys it--don't you, Tammy?"

"What's that, sweetie?"

"Watching us all get drunk. It's a sadist's job."

"That's right," she said, cracking an imaginary whip, "and Mistress Tammy says you WILL order another round--and then you're cut off."

"Yes, Mistress," Derek reached for his wallet. "This round of punishment is on me, as long as I don't have to bark like a dog or anything."

"You're getting there," she smiled, working the tap. Drown night meant draft beer only, no bottles tonight. "You're a pretty good tipper, so I'll let you off easy this time."

It was almost eleven, and still no sign of Sara. I tried not to rubberneck too much, though admittedly my eyes kept wandering toward the neon-encircled entrance in search of her. The phone number remained in my wallet, unused, and I began to wonder if my brilliant man-logic had somehow backfired.

Did she actually expect me to call her? Had someone amended the rules of the phone-number game without telling me?

The answers are always more complicated than they should be. I tried not to think about it and joined Derek's continuing banter, sipping my third beer. Sara would show up. I had to believe it.

A barfly in my mental nightclub, Jim Morrison sat with a bottle of Jack in one hand and a roach in the other. He looked at me, exhaling a cloud and telling me not to sweat it. He then tilted his head back and began reciting a poem full of inspired gibberish, ranting until he passed out. The poem itself isn't worth repeating. Apparently, Jim was taking the night off.

My libido was chomping at the bit, yet I quashed my needy instincts, realizing that calling her presented greater danger in the long run. It was still early enough to believe that she'd make it. I concluded that I was over-reacting. I gave my libido a Rubik's Cube and told it to play quietly by itself.

Randy and Tommy returned from their trip down to the edge of the stage, having inspected the equipment of both bands.

"How did it look?"

Randy shrugged, disappointed. "Lame…I've heard so much about Dana Mills' kit, you know? It's big and all, but it seems kind of old. And he's got his toms set up all flat. Weird. I don't even see how he plays like that."

"I hear he's a stick-twirler," Tommy added.

"Pshht." Randy wasn't impressed. "Everybody twirls."

Thanks to the Crue's Tommy Lee, the stick-twirling trend was monstrous. Randy could actually do it rather well, but was philosophically opposed to twirling. He rejected the showy style and vowed never to spin a stick outside of practice. For drummers, there was no middle ground; you were either with the twirlers or against them.

"Like I said, his kit's big," Randy added skeptically. "But I'm not all that impressed. We'll see how he plays. I hear he's good."

"And what about guitars?"

"Steel Diamond is running all Marshall heads," Tommy reported. "Half-stacks, though the rhythm player is coming out of a Laney cabinet. One Strat up there, one Kramer. The bass player has a sweet Mesa Boogie setup and a black P-bass--pretty nice. I bet it sounds good. As for the other band, Ricochet or whatever their name is--they're running a bunch of crap. A couple little practice amps, and they're running the bass player direct. Should be interesting…"

"Did you see that singer from Ricochet?" Randy asked.

"No, not yet. Why?"

Tommy laughed. "Dude--you'll see. He's just all bleached out and pale with like, this fright wig on his head, white spandex, and little leather tie-offs up and down his arms and legs. I'm telling you, the dude looks totally lame."

"What a douche…"

"An albino ferret in a Barbie dress, seriously. Makeup and everything, like a gay vampire or something!"

"I swear, dude--you're gonna laugh your ass off!"

Ouch. The guy was taking big hits. For a moment I thought Randy and Tommy were jealous, hacking on the guy out of competitive spirit. It seemed impossible that anyone could look THAT bad. After all, this crowd was capable of tolerating some truly bizarre spring collections.

But then, as if delivered for punishment by the gods of gossip... said poser appeared.

"There he is, dude! Look--over by the dressing room!"

I looked, spotting the white spandex. Against the black backdrop, it was easy to see that the guy possessed a pair of wiry chicken legs. Someday, he would make an impressive retiree.

'That bad', however, was an understatement. The bleach tortured hair was screaming for release from its Aqua-net prison. He wore girly chain belts and wristbands up to his elbows. And worst of all, the guy was wearing red lipstick...and totally incapable of pulling it off. In an attempt to emulate his rock heroes, this poor soul had obviously gone mad in a fit of androgynous egotism and poor taste.

"Oh crap, man...that's just sad. Oh man..."

"I told you," Randy nudged me. "Damn, I'm glad you don't look like that, Mark."

"I'd make a terrible blonde," I joked, fluffing my hair. "And the lipstick color is just wrong."

"Seriously, though. How can they jam with that guy? You know what I mean?"

"You'd think somebody would tell him..."

"It's like--they can't all be stupid enough to think he looks good that way. Right? I sure couldn't step on stage with that freak. Hey Mark--after seeing that, I'm giving ultimate thanks you're not a poser."

It was high praise coming from Randy.

"And I'm glad you're not a stick-twirler," I answered in kind.

"Screw that twirling crap," he said proudly. "I won't play shirtless, either. Been done. Hey, look--isn't that Sandy over there?"

We all turned, searching the room for Sandy's hair helmet.

"Where at?"

"Right there by the bathrooms…"

"Yeah, that's her."

"There's her friend--you know, what's-her-name. Right beside her, in the black."

"You mean Nikki?"

"Yeah, Nikki. You see 'em?"

"It's Sandy alright," Tommy verified, tapping Derek's shoulder and pointing. "I'd know that butt anywhere."

"Which butt? Nikki's?"

"No, Sandy's."

"Okay…I was gonna say…because Nikki's butt is just about non-existent."

"No wonder James was so pissed!" I said, thinking aloud. "This is Sandy's bar night!"

Derek swiveled on his stool and glared in Sandy's direction. "Whatever. Look at her, all maxed out and ready to go."

It felt strange that night, having everyone there but James. Despite his promises, I knew that he wasn't at home slaving over his guitar tablature. In all likelihood, he was squatted in front of the television and marinating in his own broth as he waited for us to get home.

"Dude!" Tommy grabbed my arm, wide-eyed. "I just had, like, the best idea."

"What?"

"We should go call James and tell him to get his ass down here!"

"Right," I answered. "But he won't come. I'd bet money on it."

Derek belched. "He'll come--but you've got to give him a reason. You know James, dude. He always needs a reason to do things. He likes to feel like he's getting shit done."

We all pondered the thought.

"Sandy isn't reason enough?"

He chuckled. "Are you kidding? Uh…no."

"How about this, then?" I offered. "Tell him he needs to come and see the bands."

Derek nodded. "Yeah, good. Make it sound like we're scouting the competition. It doesn't have to be a good reason--he'll buy the bullshit as long as you make it sound good. Besides, his wench is here."

"No doubt! Tell him we're all gonna hit on her if he doesn't come down!"

"Not funny, Tommy…"

"Dumbass."

Tommy lowered his eyes. "I was only kidding."

"Well, Private Thomas," Derek straightened, assuming his military voice. "Since you were the one to come up with this mission, then you will be assigned to complete it. Move out and head to point A, then proceed to initiate Operation Phone Home. When you're finished meet us at the rendezvous point. If you are captured, then this mission never existed. Do you understand your orders, soldier?"

"Yes, Sir." Tommy clicked his heels. "May I have permission to take a wizz before I complete the mission, Sir?"

"Permission granted," Derek saluted. "But wash your damn hands afterward, Thomas."

"Right…do you mean I should wash after the mission, or after the wiz, sir?"

"Dumbass," Derek pushed him, laughing. "Go do it."

"Alright. I'll be back." Tommy disappeared into the crowd, headed for the bathrooms.

A tap on my shoulder. I turned quickly, expecting it to be Sara. Close enough.

It was Sara's wee blonde friend, Danni.

"Hey you!"

She reached up and gave me an undeserved hug. I hugged back.

"How goes it?"

"Mahvelous, dahling," she mugged. "Hi Randy. I like your hair…"

"Hey," Randy smiled politely. "Thanks."

"Sara told me to come down and see if you guys were here yet. We've got a table upstairs."

Relief flooded in. Sara was present. And apparently, she knew how to delegate--I knew she was special.

"Sounds good," I answered, "but how did she know I'd be here?"

"Because I told her," Danni said. "I saw it. I'm part psychic."

"Oh yeah?"

"Yep--and I bet you're a Pisces, aren't you?"

I nodded. "You're right. How did you know?"

"I have my ways," Danni twinkled, glancing at Randy. "So you guys come upstairs and I'll tell you all about it. My drink is up there getting watery, and Sara's waiting for you. She's a Leo…so you don't want to keep her waiting."

I didn't.

Don't Tell Me You Love Me

fell asleep that night in a strange but warm bed...and woke up in a relationship.

It's happened since the dawn of mankind, an affliction striking countless men and women. It has shattered families, destroyed empires, and changed the course of history.

The one night stand that takes. I was hooked before I knew it.

Insta-relationship. Just add sex.

I'd known it the night before. Sara was straddling me when she asked if I had a girlfriend. It seemed a rather odd time to bring up the subject, but I would later realize that it was a brilliant move on her part. In such a compromising position, there could be only one answer.

"Do you mean earlier tonight," I replied, "or do you mean right now?"

I'd said it. She'd baited me and I'd walked right in, pridefully, thinking I was reserving her like a table in a restaurant. It wasn't until I smelled the coffee the next morning that I realized: I was the one who had been reserved.

Not that I minded. At least not in the beginning.

I woke up to her kisses and the sound of the clock alarm.

"Ugh--what is that horrible noise?"

"I set my alarm to play country music," Sara replied, sleepy-eyed. "I hate it so much that I wake up immediately. It's like a bucket of cold water."

"You should have told me," I said, kissing her back. She seemed just as sexy the morning after, and I took it as a good sign. "Next time, I'll wake you up personally, with a little selection from Mr. Conway Twitty."

Next time. I was implying another rendezvous.

"Spare me," she laughed. "So…what are your plans for tonight?"

Now she was talking plans. Just add scheduling.

"I've got class till four, and then rehearsal till eight," I told her, thinking only momentarily about James and my promise to put in overtime with him. "After that, I'm free."

"Good," she said, dropping the sheet and my jaw simultaneously. "How about you come back here tonight? I'll cook dinner, and we can rent a couple movies or something."

"Sounds good," I told her. "Great, actually."

"Is a quiet night at home too slow for you?" she teased.

I mugged. "Not at all. Not with you."

"Good answer." Sara walked toward the bathroom wearing only her panties, turning just as she reached the door. "I'm going to take a shower. Don't let me come back to find you gone and a little note on the pillow…"

"Not a chance," I told her, staring. "You'll have to kick me out."

"Oh, so you're like that?"

"That's right, baby. Play Misty for me."

I remember her laughing and feeling so happy that she got the joke.

Sara was my first Leo. She was clever and quick, and the stars smiled upon us. I knew all about it now, thanks to a night in the presence of the underachieving psychic Danni.

To the ultimate delight of both Jim and my dancing libido, Danni proclaimed Sara and I to be a good match. Pure luck, no doubt, but I could do no better than a recommendation sent from the stars, particularly one delivered from the lips of her best friend.

Whew. Thankfully, I'd passed the dreaded astrology portion of the potential-boyfriend screening procedure. A milestone, indeed, when you're dating the sign-conscious. The astrology test can be a relentless and unforgiving process, one by which even the brightest prospective suitors get shafted out of contention.

Here's how it worked.

Once I'd graduated to the spot of serious contender, Sara sent Danni to question me about my astrological sign. I had answered immediately and truthfully, thinking it no big deal. Why lie? Surely, 'what's your sign?' is one of the most reliably answered questions in the universe.

But others were thinking while I was not. Behind the scenes, the wheels of fickle fate were turning. My astrological information was relayed through Sara's network of friends, one of whom reached to her shelf for the hundredth time and pulled down the bible of wanna-be astrologers:

Love Signs.

The book was, and likely still is, inescapable. And despite its light-hearted goodness and innocent appeal, it was the wrecking ball of matchmaking, razing countless foolish dreams. Sooner or later, we're all put through the astrology test.

This test, however, can only be passed through luck. Starry-eyed luck. And though it would no doubt be a feat of devious romantic genius for a pick-up artist to somehow master the correct response for any occasion, I doubt it's ever happened.

And so my sign was taken to the holy book and cross indexed with Sara's sign.

And yea, the prophet spoke, saying, 'Rejoice, my sister, for the two of ye are like totally awesome for each other'.

And the blessing was good. Yea, the tightly-packed subjects did rejoiceth and headbangeth.

On behalf of Jim and my libido…thank you, Linda Goodman. Amen.

GYPSY ROAD

The club gigs began lining up. We hadn't been offered a repeat performance at The Tank, but there were a few other less prestigious dives willing to give us a try.

These places had names like The Grave and Uncle Jake's Rockpile, Bud's Saloon and Kicks Nightclub: A Rock Experience. They were local dives, crammed tightly into shoppette malls between local businesses named Hair's To You and Jimmy's Liquors. Independent bars, ruled with iron fists by aging alcoholics in golf bracelets and Hawaiian shirts, where the lights never came up and the musicians rarely got paid. This was the absolute bottom of the river, the quiet murky depths where fish swim blind and the only light you see is that reflected from the surface, far above.

Home to bottom-feeding headbangers.

But they were gigs. At that point, the grade of venue made no difference. At the moment, dive bars suited us.

Following a shaky audition, we were hired to play weekly at a local dive in Boulder, a bar named J.R.'s.

That's right, weekly. Impressive by our standards.

By some miracle, Thursday night was ours. The owner was trying to boost his weekend numbers and figured live music on Thursdays would provide a good opportunity to promote Jello wrestling on Saturday. We never did outdo Babe-Brawl night; admittedly, bikini clad women flopping around in tasty dessert was always the bigger draw. Some things you just can't compete with.

Still, Thursday nights were fine with us, and the weekly appearances gave us the right to claim, however meekly, that we were a house band. To sweeten our situation, the owner declared it Bladderburster Night, offering ten-cent pitchers until eight, fifty-centers till ten. By the time we hit the stage, the customers were customarily ripe.

The gigs were different here in dive country, both in terms of length and intensity. The single set Tank gigs were like a hundred-meter sprint in the rain, a mad dash to the finish line amidst distraction. The five-set bar gigs at J.R.'s, however, were a thousand-meter run on a sweltering day. Five forty-five-minute sets, with a fifteen-minute break every hour. Mild by Vegas standards, perhaps, but after being primed on transitory gigs, the long nights were formidable.

Our song list needed to be adequately pumped with at least forty or fifty tunes, so as not to require repetition. Nothing felt worse than running out of material, playing something that did well earlier and flopping on it the second time around. Our headbanging crowd did not tolerate repeats. They wanted to be surprised like kids opening presents on Christmas, more elated with each new song than they were with the last. The crowds could be won or lost with song selection alone.

Song selection. Learning the right songs, and then knowing when to play them. It didn't take many gigs before I realized that we could get more mileage out of a chant-along like "Takin' Care of Business" than we could out of any number of technically superior songs.

Once we'd chosen the songs themselves, the task was building sets.

Our game plan. Our playbook. The hairy football metaphors we'd heard so many times were finally beginning to make sense. The team, the positions, the plays.

James and I could talk set list for hours on end. We figured that once we'd created the perfect set lists, we could simply play them over and over again without fail. The beauty of the art form is that there is no perfection, and you never know if your creative input is worth a damn until you start reeling off the songs.

J.R.'s proved to be the ideal location to hone our set-crafting skills. They let us play basically whatever we wanted, as long as we started precisely at the top of the hour and took a break at no earlier than quarter till.

The bar was small by any standard, but the cramped conditions served to give the place a feeling of continuous activity. Compared to the wide spaces and neon glow of The Tank, J.R.'s was a small shack. And yet, it always felt bigger when crowded with regulars. Bladderburster Thursdays were the best thing that ever happened to us.

The crowd was a varied mix, including but not limited to: headbangers, band friends, dead-heads, college students, punkers, bikers, gear-heads and dosers. Here, in the middle of America sat yet another melting pot!

Or lumpy pan gravy, at least. The many faces of Boulder--the grease, the milk, the flour and the sausage, stirred together and heated up. The alcohol was the flour that held them together. The music was the hot pan that forced them to mix. We simmered together as one, united in the name of alcohol and loud music.

We unloaded everything on those crowds. With Sandy, Sara, and the two combined gaggles of demure friends, we were guaranteed a decent babe presence at the gigs and a cheering section every week. They would walk in and dominate the place, high-heeled and dark-eyed, their fleeces white as snow. And everywhere the women went...well, you know the rest.

We were generating a following now. Word soon spread that Thursday was babe night at J.R.'s, and within a month we were playing once again to near-packed houses. Sure, they came to party and not to gaze upon our spectacle--but the crowds showed and were comfortable enough to stay until closing. No band can keep the crowd on their feet for five hours, but we had our moments, always insuring that the last set was our best.

Two songs from the end.

The clock read 12:40, and we were launching into an inspired version of Metallica's "Am I Evil?" A somewhat risky choice, but bouncy enough to keep them out. The crowd seemed to sense the end of the night drawing near and was juicing the pleasure out of every last moment.

We rocked in line, bouncing and banging our heads, breaking away on cue and strutting to the corners of the stage. I grabbed the mic stand and planted it center stage, holding out my arms at my sides and leaning my head back.

I closed my eyes, the warm stage lights soaking me in red, Derek and James hacking away on either side. Waiting in the on-deck circle was our final tune, the no-miss splendor of Aerosmith's "Sweet Emotion." Not a metal standard, but a song no crowd could resist. Perfect and complete, the song possessed an intro, a beat, a hook, a memorable riff, a crescendo, and a screaming guitar solo at the end. An almost perfect song.

Better yet, when the crowd inevitably beckoned for an encore, we could always follow it up with "Walk This Way," another no-miss, maintaining our Aerosmith theme and laying waste to the crowd in one fell swoop.

We jammed our way through it, banging our heads and laughing as James hammered up the exit solo. When the music was playing, we never seemed to have any problems.

As "Sweet Emotion" rolled to an end, James turned and motioned to us, then walked over to say something to Randy. I stepped up to the microphone and said our goodnights, the riff repeating behind me. A particularly large biker chick had already stopped dancing and was beckoning for more.

The crowd was shouting before we finished, sensing the end.

Bug a dug, Bug a dug…Dug, dug..........Dug.

"Thank you guys. See you next week. Don't forget Jello-mania on Saturday, and tip your bartenders and waitresses on the way out…"

The 'one more song' cries rang out in equal measure with whistles and applause, the contents of the dance floor turning their collective eyes toward me. The cheers were like manna from heaven. I paused, looking out at them, juicing the moment for all I could get.

"Who wants more?" I shouted out at them, my amplified voice booming. They roared back at me. Sweet.

The crowd wanted another song, and I wasn't about to be the goat.

I turned to James, finding him already huddled with Derek and Tommy in front of the drum kit.

"'Walk this Way'?"

"Wait--I've got a better idea!" James looked inspired. "Com'ere…"

The crowd beckoned and wasn't going to wait.

"What's your idea, James?"

"Let's play an original," he said, looking at me.

"Last, you mean?"

"Why not?"

It sounded risky, but we had very little to lose.

"Yeah, cool. How about 'G-String'?"

Derek and Tommy nodded their agreement.

"Oh, and one other thing," James said, looking at each of us to insure our attention. "You assholes had better play it right--I called Steven and booked the hours we were talking about. Next week we'll be in the studio recording our demo…"

"No way!"

"Studio time?"

"Totally," he replied, chunking his guitar. "Way."

"Dude!"

It was just like James to spring something like this on us during a gig. His method, however, worked well. We turned back to face the audience with visions of sugarplums in our heads, launching into the song.

Our dream had suddenly taken the form of a plastic cassette tape. Soon, we'd have a recording of our own…and real credibility.

Diamonds and Rust

"Is anybody sitting here?" I asked.

The redhead looked up from her Nietzsche.

"No, actually," she replied. "Go ahead."

I set down my lunch and let my backpack fall to the carpeted floor of the University Memorial Center. Half-cafeteria, half-study hall, the UMC attached to the protest-popular fountain commons and was the best place to hang between classes or get in some eleventh-hour cramming.

I looked down at my tray, realizing I'd chosen the chocolate milk, a bag of Ranchero corn chips and a two-pack of Twinkies. Granted, it all looked good to me when I was purchasing it…but as I glanced over at the redhead's bottled water and bean sprout sandwich, I found myself wishing I'd picked differently.

She looked at my food then up at me, flashing an indecipherable smile.

The girl was classy. From her modern bob haircut to the mellow salmon cashmere sweater, the girl was dressed like a professional debutante. Her nails were painted in subdued pink, and the rings that adorned her scholarly fingers hinted of family riches.

An out-of-stater. The other type of student, the ones that stood across the economic chasm from us. Their mums and dads sent them across the country from places like Connecticut and

Rhode Island. They paid triple our tuition and usually landed in the sororities and fraternities, keeping company with their own kind.

Sorority girls were untouchable to me. They were full to the brim in their own little world and had no time at all for anyone extra. I don't mean to say they were arrogant--I never conversed enough to make any kind of judgment--but the sorority chicks would look right through me. They couldn't even see guys like me, but it wasn't their fault; they'd just been trained differently. To say they were rude would be like blaming them for disregarding a chair or a garbage can.

So, in a general way, in-staters avoided the outs.

But as I sat there trying to discreetly chomp my corn chips and sip at my milk, I began to steal glances of her and soon realized that I was very attracted.

She wasn't my type. At least not my 'official' type. A bit plain, a redhead, conservatively dressed, and short-haired...but there was something amazing about her. When you put it all together and combined it with her face and those pretty Irish eyes...I couldn't explain it. I suppose you could call it smitten.

Smitten with a preppie.

Good God, I hoped Jim wasn't paying attention.

In all fairness, she always sat in the smoking section. She dressed for style, and her expensive leather boots spoke of a potential wild side. Perhaps she was simply waiting for a longhaired dude to offer her the right line so she could fulfill one of her rich girl fantasies by screwing the swarthy peasant minstrel. Good by me.

Not that a one-night-stand was my ultimate goal...but given the task, I figured it was a start. Once she got to know me, she'd see that all her preconceptions were bullshit, and treasure me all the more for my differences.

I'd decided all this before I ever talked to her. I'd been watching her from distant tables, knowing that eventually I'd sit down at hers and begin the charming seduction. I just had to figure out what to say.

In truth, I hadn't been thinking of her that day. I'd come out of the cashier line expecting to quietly nosh munchies and cram for an exam. Fate, however, had filled the UMC to near capacity, leaving me with no other alternative than to sit with the redhead, Twinkies and all.

She continued to peruse her philosophy, seeming genuinely interested. In itself, this was captivating. I decided that I should be doing something intelligent and reached for my backpack.

Decisions, decisions. *The Survey of Psychology* textbook seemed far too juvenile--after all, my class was still in chapter four. Thankfully, I'd registered for an Intro to Western Literature class, and as part of the enormous required reading list, I'd purchased Ayn Rand's *Atlas Shrugged*. I pulled the brick-thick paperback from my backpack and turned to an imaginary bent corner somewhere in the middle.

Granted, I was not that familiar with Ms. Rand's work.

Not at all familiar, actually. I did know, however, that it was recognized for its greatness and suspected it would give the right impression to the type of girl who'd read philosophy and drink bottled water.

Lo and behold...the book worked.

"What do you think of it?" she asked, the words startling me from my feigned concentration.

I looked up from the pages and into her eyes.

"Oh, this? Yeah, pretty good," I replied, certain I was playing it safe. "Really good. Deep."

"Hmm." She made a face. "I didn't like it much at all."

"Well, to be honest...I haven't really been able to get into it."

This statement was technically true. In fact, I hadn't been getting into much of anything besides Sara and the band.

"Are you an English major?" she asked, analyzing me with a glance.

I half-nodded. "Well, yeah, basically. I'm still technically undecided, but it's between English and J-school. And you? You're a philosophy major?"

She chuckled conservatively at the thought, her teeth brilliant white. "Hardly. A person would have to be insane..."

"Yeah, I guess so."

"I'm a poly-sci major." She waved the book. "I guess I just do this for fun. I learned my first year that I should take a couple of easy credits every semester. Not that philosophy is necessarily easy, but you understand. So you're a freshman?"

Not something I wanted to admit.

"Is it that obvious?" I asked in reply.

She shrugged a bit. "Not really--I just saw how heavy your backpack looked and figured you were toting around hundred-level texts."

That, and my hair. She was kind not to mention it.

"Very observant," I said, trying to grin through my nerves. "You should consider criminal science."

Little response. She pulled a hard pack from her little purse and looked inside, disappointed.

"Can I borrow a cigarette from you, please? I ran out..."

I reached into my backpack and produced the pack, glad to see her smoking. Gratitude could be built upon, and it made me feel like less of a dude. It would be hard for her to act condescending

after she'd just bummed one from me. She accepted and lit the cigarette immediately, blowing the smoke straight up, like bookies and
old ladies do.

"Thanks--what is your name?"

"Mark," I answered. "Mark Magruder." I reached out a hand to
politely shake with her.

"I'm Ashley," she said in all seriousness. "Ashley Whitmore."

Ashley Whitmore? It sounded almost contrived, as though a
writer had concocted it.

"Let me guess--you're not originally from Colorado…"

"Is it that obvious?" she mimicked me, smiling.

"No," I answered, lying. "Just a good guess."

"I'm from Vermont," she said with a sense of pride, "though I
live here year-round now."

Vermont. Somehow, the poly-sci major made sense. I assumed
she was a junior but didn't bother to ask for fear of widening the
age chasm.

"And before you ask," she said, pointing, "NO, I didn't come to
CU because of the skiing."

I raised my hands in defense. "I wasn't even thinking it. I don't
ski, either."

"And you're a native?"

Nod. "A Denverite. It costs a lot to go skiing anymore…I guess
I just never got into it…"

"I get invited all the time, but I just haven't gone yet. Too busy,
I guess." She looked at her watch.

The lunch rush was ending, and the UMC was thinning out a
bit. A tall blonde guy walked past with his tray, and I found myself
grateful that he didn't ask to join us at the table.

I looked down at Ayn Rand and then up at Ashley, at a complete
loss for topics of conversation. Mr. Slick Lead-singer was tongue

tied in the face of a debutante, searching for something to say that would make me look brilliant and witty.

With long hair, witty is pretty easy to do. Brilliant, however, is a mountain to climb. I reminded myself that this girl was looking at me with a very different eye, one that already had more than a few pre-conceived notions about headbangers. When she looked at me with her velvety Vermont eyes, what was she really seeing? It was impossible to know without talking her up a bit...but my brilliant repartee was sticking like maple syrup.

She tilted her head, exhaling. "So...I'm guessing you're in a band or something..."

Ahh--the familiar subject. The subject I'd been avoiding. She'd stepped right into my biggest play, but I knew better than to work her like a groupie. Ashley Whitmore simply demanded better.

"Yeah," I replied with eloquence, "I guess the hair is a dead giveaway, huh?"

She grinned. "...And the jacket, and the shirt, and the snake-skin boots..."

I looked down, realizing I'd worn my shit-kickers, pale snake-skin with just enough wear and tear to make them look cool.

I feigned a confident smile. "Well, you've got to look the part, I guess."

"I figured you wouldn't look like that if you weren't in a band or something..."

What?

Was that a crack, or just brutal honesty? I got the feeling that Ashley had just discreetly backhanded me.

"I don't mean anything bad by it," she continued quickly, sensing my offense. "It's just that you have that...look to you. What do you play?"

"I'm the singer," I replied, trying to be light, "so I guess you could say I play with myself."

God, I can't believe I said that. I was beginning to sound like James.

"Funny." She smirked. "Is it hard rock, or..."

"Yeah," I answered. "Hard rock."

May the Metal Gods forgive me...I failed to correct her and tell her it was heavy metal that I played. Heavy metal, and I knew it. But somehow, I couldn't say the words to her and claim them as my own. In the face of Ashley's cashmere, I played it like a presidential candidate and caved in to moderation.

"So...do you play around here very often?"

"Whenever we can," I replied. "We've been doing gigs in Denver--the money's better down there..."

Money? What money? Was this my best attempt to impress? As soon as the lie escaped my lips, I found myself asking why Ashley Whitmore would be interested in hearing about dive-bar money.

"But you live in Boulder?" she asked, now seeming very interested.

I felt a bit like a case study for her developmental psych class.

"Yeah, with the whole band," I lamented. "Five guys in one house. I'm the only one going to school."

Ack! I was full of unimpressive statements.

"That sounds like fun," Ashley said with disingenuous affect. "Fun, but chaotic."

"Yeah...it's hard to get a minute alone sometimes. People are hanging around all night. I had to get accustomed to sleeping with a little noise."

"And you're an English major?"

"Well, undecided...but yeah."

She flashed me a 'wow' look. "I'd think you'd have a hard time trying to read Ayn Rand with a rock band in the next room…"

I would have made a clever Ayn Rand quip, but I was unsure how to pronounce 'Ayn' and didn't want to risk the shame.

"Very," I said, grinning, soaking in the sympathy. "My bandmates aren't exactly worried about my academic success."

"I bet," she returned. "I have to go to the library to get things done sometimes--and that's just to get away from the normal distractions. So why aren't you a music major, then?"

A reasonable question. Again, I had no rational answer.

"In my kind of music," I replied, acting big-britched, "a degree wouldn't really do you any good…"

"It would always do you good," she answered maturely.

Great. Friggin' great. Now I was downplaying the value of a good education! I'd always been the opposite of the 'who needs school' guy, and now here I was, the personification of the ignorant and uneducated! I began to wonder who else was looking at my snakeskin boots and promised myself not to wear them again.

"I know…I mean…I guess I just preferred the English department," I said, stumbling to get it out.

"I can see that," she nodded. "Not that any of the liberal arts degrees are that different--they're all worthless in their own way, I suppose. I think of switching majors all the time."

"Yeah, but what's the alternative?" I joked. "Engineering school?"

"Eeek!"

"No doubt…"

Ashley looked down at her expensive watch, pursing her little pale pink lips. "Well, Mark--it's time for me to go. Good luck with the band…"

Ooof. Regardless of my dubious success, I was just about to ask her for a phone number when she said this. The alternative was asking her to a gig...but somehow, 'good luck with the band' didn't exactly sound like the words of a future groupie.

"Yeah, thanks," I said without hesitation, remembering to smile at her. "We'll be playing around town sometime--I'll let you know if I see you."

Ashley stood with her backpack, shrugging her cashmere shoulders. "Yeah...okay. I usually study in here after my ten o'clock, so I'm sure I'll probably see you again."

"You can't miss me," I said.

She smiled. "That's the truth..."

And with that, classy Ashley Whitmore stepped away from the table, walking with an educated gait. She saw me watching her and flashed a half-smile.

I grabbed the pack of Twinkies and tossed it in my backpack, my taste for snack-cakes now absent. In fairness, I couldn't get upset about that last crack. After all, I'd served it up on a silver platter with the 'you can't miss me' line.

It was true--you couldn't miss me.

I looked down past my split ends and leather jacket to my faded jeans and snakeskin boots, realizing the loudly voiced statement that was my daily wardrobe. I'd been walking the campus for a few months, but until I met Ashley, I never felt awkward or embarrassed to be a longhair.

These are the moments when you're supposed to steel yourself against the system, fly your middle finger and say you don't care about what the world thinks. When you're living in two worlds, it's harder than it sounds.

LOSING MORE THAN YOU'VE EVER HAD

The recording studio was cloistered away in the suburbs, cleverly disguised to look like a single story house. It was a scraped out suburban pumpkin, filled with enough equipment to make a rocket scientist drool. Or so we'd heard.

We pulled up that morning expecting landmark architecture and high-tech coolness and found only a messy family room and a mulleted shirtless guy in bare feet and sweatpants.

"Hey guys…" Soundman Steven reached out to push the screen door open. He wasn't what we expected, but at the time we were still too green to realize what a prototypical soundman Steven was.

"Got your gear then? Cool." He pointed to the stairs. "Right down there--to the basement."

Recording in a basement? Had Ozzy started this way? I doubted it. Then again, all the best myths surrounding studio work are gritty. I'd heard tales of Sun Studios and Abbey Road, so I kept my reservations to myself as I helped carry Randy's drums down the stairs.

At the bottom of the staircase, the environment changed from homey domestic to reassuring dive bar standard--dark walls, blocked windows and the tell-tale contoured foam soundproofing we'd been longing for. Down here, the place looked genuine, and I had no doubt that we'd be able to capture the mood.

Steven the recording studio guy was the sole employee of Sound Ideas, Inc., a one-man conglomerate. A typically odd dude, Steven had worked for years in the local club scene and preferred sitting behind the board and playing god to mixing with the masses. Barely professional, he provided the much needed bridge between home recordings and the harsh expense of real studios. His prices were ultimately reasonable, and the recordings fell in the quality category of 'you get what you pay for'.

It didn't matter to me. Personally, I wasn't even thinking of recording quality or high-performance sound gear. I wasn't looking to record a number one single or conscious of any future beyond the next year. I just wanted something to stick in the cassette player and be proud of.

"Okay, gentlemen," Steven directed, his voice juiced with authority, "we go with the drums first, so let's get the hardware set up. Your time starts now."

A time crunch. The studio charged by the hour, and we possessed a limited number of quarters to plug into this jukebox. When the cash ran out, so did the session. We would be finished, regardless of the status of the demo. This topic had been discussed at length, and the songs duly rehearsed to maximum tightness.

We were ready. Or perhaps I should say, we felt ready. Our fifteen original songs had been contentiously whittled down to four songs--three demo-tape finalists and one 'if we have the time' track.

As Steven and Randy set to miking the drum kit and working out the bugs, we set up the guitar amps and ran through our mental lists of apprehension, waiting for the first play through. James had written down his setup in case any of the knobs were inadvertently turned, and he sat, paper in hand, fine tuning his amp head and preparing his unwieldy string of effect pedals.

Derek was uncharacteristically sullen and quiet, still smoldering from an argument at practice the night before. Thinking it best not to pick at the source of irritation, I'd been playing up the day and hoping the hard feelings would disappear when we hit the studio. Still, Derek hadn't made a single comment since we arrived. I walked over to where he stood tuning and punched his pick arm.

"Sup, man."

He didn't look up.

"So what do you think?" I asked.

He offered a shrug. "Seems pretty cool, I guess. Should be good..."

The tone of his voice told it all. Derek rarely played the self-pity card, and I knew from his reaction that the resentment was firmly planted this time. I sympathized. I was beginning to see Derek as the whipping boy for James' insecurities and wished I'd said more. But I'd missed my window--there was no time to psychoanalyze.

"Do you feel okay?" I asked him. "You don't sound very psyched..."

"I am, I am," he replied, faking a grin. "Don't worry. Just sleepy, that's all. You ready to sing?"

"I think so. I'm not sick or anything, so I don't have any excuses. I've just got to hit all my notes right the first time."

Derek rolled his eyes. "Pshht--just jam, man. Don't worry about all that technical crap!" He shook his head. "It would be a damn shame for me to stand there watching you sing and know that you're thinking about hitting your fucking notes! Think about something else, dude--think about big tits or something."

I chuckled at the thought.

"No, I'm serious," he continued, tapping me on the chest. "Do you think Bon Scott ever worried about hitting his notes? Hell no, man! He just grabbed his nuts and went for it!"

"True…but Bon was always drunk."

"Well--there you go! Maybe you just need a drink to help find your tone…"

"Nah." I shook my head, knowing a drink was the last thing that any of us needed. "I'm cool with the twenty-ounce Slushy. Besides, we didn't bring anything alcoholic."

"I did," Derek said, motioning toward his jacket. "Go ahead and get some."

I waved it off. "No thanks, man. It's still too early for that. I want to be ready to go. We should be jamming soon, right?"

"I guess so," he shrugged, looking over his shoulder at Steven and Randy. "Though this drum setup may take a while."

"No way. This guy does this stuff all the time. They'll probably be done in a few minutes…"

My estimate was wrong. Horribly wrong. In fact, had there been a word that was an extreme version of wrong, a word that meant very, very wrong--uberwrong, perhaps--I would undoubtedly have been that. Uberwrong. A few paid minutes turned into a dozen, and then more. We all sat helplessly and watched as Randy and Steven spent valuable moments discussing the best place to put a mic. After forty-five minutes or so, we were all getting our own ideas.

The wait matured. Nearly an hour passed, and still they didn't have a drum sound. They'd been moving around mikes and tuning heads for far too long and were just now dialing it in. Derek was beginning to lose faith in the credibility of Steven's basement studio. James watched intently, blaming Randy for the hold-up.

"Do you think his drums are out of tune?" James asked us.

We stood behind the soundboard in the glass-encased room, listening as Randy cracked his snare repetitively.

Crack, crack, crack, crack.

"They're getting snare buzz," I said. "They don't need tuning, though."

Crack, crack.

"I don't mean the snare. I mean the toms."

Crack.

"The toms sound fine." Derek commented. "They went over it like fifty times. Shit, man--it's just a demo! Why don't we just let him play and quit worrying about perfection?"

James shook his head, apparently displeased with the 'just a demo' statement.

"So what song do we play first?" Tommy sat with his unplugged bass, plunking the inactive strings.

"'Skin Tight', like we talked about..."

Soundman Steven walked back into the booth, frowning a bit. "Can I give you guys some advice?"

"Well, yeah. Sure..."

He sat down in his puffy soundman chair and swiveled to face us. "Okay--I can tell you guys haven't really done this before, so unless you want to waste a lot of time and money, you're better off to do it my way..."

"Cool."

"Yeah."

"I've done this so many times I can't count 'em," he told us, "and trust me, I've seen bands come in here and blow their whole wad without getting a single decent song down. No smoking in here, man."

Tommy shrugged, putting his smokes back in his pocket. "Sorry."

"You guys can smoke your brains out in the lounge, just not around the gear."

"No problem," James answered for him.

"Okay--so basically, I'll call for the bass or guitar or whatever, and you guys do your stuff. A little trust goes a long way here. Best of all, you'll come out of here with a recording you can all be proud of. The goal is to leave with a decent demo, and that's what you'll do."

We couldn't argue with such a straightforward declaration of expertise. We needed all the guidance we could get and eagerly nodded our heads in agreement.

"Good. We'll record scratch tracks first, with everyone playing together," Steven told us, now in his element. "All songs. Scratch tracks for all the songs at once. Then we go through and play your scratches while your drummer records his keepers. After the drums are down, we go back and record your parts for real, one at a time, in this order: bass, rhythm, lead, vocals, solos. Got it?"

"So we can't go back and record an extra song if we have the time?"

"Nope," he answered flatly. "Decide now. Dialing everything in is the tough part. All the songs at once, on drums, on bass, and so on. And trust me, you won't have the time for four songs. Not even. If you want any time for mix-down, then three songs is probably pushing it. I'd shoot for three and come back again some other time."

A minor difficulty, seemingly. We'd planned on a three-song demo, and losing the fourth song didn't seem to cast any particularly large wrenches into our plans. When we'd negotiated for the top three choices, we had no idea that the runner up would be so troublesome.

You see, the fourth song was Derek's creation, a grinding flurry entitled "Devastator." He held special affection for his only original and, despite the fact that it ran thematically contrary to most of our other material, we kept it on the list. We all enjoyed playing it, and it received a decent response at the bar--so we added "Devastator" as the fourth song.

Now, in one disastrous moment, "Devastator" had been effectively doused with a bucket of cold water. I could see the reaction on Derek's face, the contrary light in his eyes fading.

"Three songs then, I guess," James said, looking around the circle. "We can always come back sometime down the road. We'll record more in like a month or two."

"Yeah," Derek exhaled sarcastically. "Sure."

James turned on him. "What?"

Derek bit his lip. "I didn't say a thing. Three songs, whatever. Let's record."

"You don't have to be pissed, dude."

"I'm not pissed," Derek lied, his eyes betraying him. "But you were bullshitting me when you said we'd do 'Devastator'."

James rolled his eyes. "Oh man...here we go..."

"Yeah, whatever, James..." Derek was angry, but I could see him trying to rise to the circumstance. The look of defeat was already upon his face, as though he'd lost the argument long ago.

"We don't have time for this." James turned to pick up his guitar and lifted the strap over his head.

"I agree," Derek seconded.

"So let's record, then."

"Fine."

And we did.

The tension was still reverberating off of the padded walls, but as we began to bash away at the scratch tracks, I thought the frustration might have been a good thing. Good metal always includes a bit of raw aggression, and the angst was coming out honestly.

We began by pounding our way through "Skin Tight," our most commercial and simplest effort, a song which, like many of its predecessors, addressed the timeless subject of hot chicks. I liked it, but it bounced so much that I felt like a bit of a poser when performing it. Still, it was, as its name suggested, tight, and sounded the most radio-worthy.

The second song on the demo was a song called "Love Ain't Mine," a repetitive riff-heavy power ballad that, like its predecessors, addressed the subject of, well, breaking up with hot chicks, I suppose. The others didn't really enjoy playing the ballads, but all the big artists did the power ballad thing. No matter how rugged or crunchy the band, they all made at least one attempt at heartfelt headbangerness. Something within us warned that it would someday be required of us.

The final song on the demo was to be our best effort technically, "G-String," a song about the dangers of…yes, hot chicks. Admittedly, my songwriting perspective was drastically narrow at that point but, in my defense, the work was truly inspired.

"G-String" was a showcase number for Randy, including some of his best drumming. Somehow I knew he'd rise to the occasion.

The scratch tracks went quickly, and we sat down to wait our turn, all eyes now focused on Randy. Headphoned and sitting at attention behind his kit, he mugged a lizard face, catching imaginary flies with his tongue.

"Okay Randy, you'll hear the click track in your headphones two bars before the song begins--"

"Click track?" we heard his voice through the monitors, bleeding from the drum mics.

"Yeah. Like a metronome sound, just so you don't lose your meter."

"I can keep time…"

Steven sighed. "I'm sure you're awesome, Randy. You shouldn't have any trouble with the click track, then. This is just the way it goes--for everybody. You'll get used to it."

Randy's jaw clenched. "Okay, fine."

"Remember--trust me."

Randy launched into it, playing as though he had something to prove. Click track or not, he barely made a single mistake. To Steven's ultimate surprise, the drums were all down in two takes. By the end, I think Randy was almost enjoying the company of the metronome.

"So who's next? Bass player?"

"Bass next."

Tommy stepped forward. We still had four hours left in our wallets, and things were looking good.

Ugh.

An hour later, Tommy was just laying down his first notes on "Love Ain't Mine," having struggled through fifty minutes' worth of memory lapses and bad takes. Just watching was painful, and it seemed that when the red light went on, Tommy's IQ would drop about fifty points. Having never been through it ourselves, it was impossible to empathize with him.

We excused ourselves from the booth and held an impromptu band meeting in the hallway.

"He's got red light fright," James said immediately. "We should have booked more hours. We're not gonna have enough time."

"Pshht--we'll have enough time," Derek returned, shrugging. "As long as we don't let this guy Steven get too picky. I mean, some of those takes were good, and he made Tommy do 'em over. If I think it sounds good, I'm gonna tell him to move on."

"He knows what he's doing," James said. "Tommy's the one who's screwing up."

"This Steven guy seems kind of picky to me," I said, wavering in my attempt to agree with Derek. "Of course, Tommy didn't nail it like Randy did, either..."

"Well, the fact is, none of the rest of us can screw up, or else the clock is gonna kill us."

Derek waved him off. "He's just worried about not having enough time to record his solos. Right, James? Hey, tell you what--if we don't have time, maybe you can come back and record them 'sometime down the road'!"

"This is bullshit, Derek."

Derek was starting up again. I knew James wouldn't lie down.

"What's bullshit, dude?" Derek sneered. "You mean, you're not worried about being able to do your solos?"

"No," James answered with venom, holding Derek's attention. "It's pure bullshit that you would even start this. Of course I'm worried about my solos--just like Mark's worried about his vocals and Tommy's worried about his bass. Randy thinks he's too good to worry, and you, Derek--you don't never worry about nothin', do you? You don't give a shit if you play good or not, or if the demo comes out, or if we make it. As long as you catch a buzz, you don't care!"

Derek scowled. "Fuck you, bud. I've put as much time into this band as you have!"

"Oh yeah?"

"Totally," Derek responded, fuming. "Only I don't bitch and moan all the time like you do. I don't spend every day and night beating myself in the head trying to figure out how we're going to make it--so you think it means I don't care!"

"You care about beer, I know that..."

"Shit! I care about this just as much as you, James. We founded this fucker together! I show up at practice, I learn the songs, I jam at the gigs. I just don't ache on it like you do. Excuse me for living, bud, but I thought we were all here to have fun!"

This, I realized, was the biggest dilemma.

"That's just it," James spat back, now on fire, "all you do is fuck around and have fun! You never take anything seriously."

"And you need to lighten up, dude. You can't hold us all to your high fucking standards until you can live up to them yourself. Look around, man. This is pretty damn fun! We're gigging, were partying, we're getting laid! Who gives a fuck if we ever make it? I'm going to enjoy it anyway. I'm not going to waste today worrying about tomorrow."

"You'll never be shit with that attitude," James said, shaking his head like a disappointed schoolteacher. "I should have known you don't have what it takes."

Derek froze, utterly offended. "I don't have what it takes? I should hit you…" He balled up his fists.

"Why don't you, then?" James stood his ground.

"Why don't I? Why don't I?" Derek's fist unclenched. "For the same reason that I don't bitch at you about fucking up the solo on 'Rainbow in the Dark' every time! For the same reason that I don't sit around crying about our trouble! Because we're supposed to be friends, man! None of this shit is supposed to matter compared to that! This is unbelievable. So you really think I don't have what it takes, is that it?"

Derek was giving James a chance to retract the statement, an opportunity to end the whole thing. James could have said something halfway cool and ended it right there. He didn't.

"I guess not…" he said, shrugging his shoulders. "I guess you don't."

"Oh, so that's how it is?"

"I don't know. You tell me."

"That's how it is?" Derek repeated, on the verge of physical damage. "And you know better than I do, is that it?"

"I just want you to pull your weight, dude."

"Pull my weight?" Derek's lip curled in anger. "You little dick! You think you could find somebody better than me, is that it?"

"You know it!" James paused, smoldering. "In a week, I could find ten guitarists better than you!"

Ouch. James had crossed the line. Totally.

Frozen in place, Randy and I would always regret not having stepped in. If they were throwing punches, my first reaction would have been to break it up. Odd, then, that I didn't have the same reaction when they were bashing each other with words. The whole thing happened so quickly, I could never have foreseen the results. As in the mob, band vengeance is messy, quick, and exacted by your best friend.

"Go do it, then," Derek answered, backing away and heading for his guitar case. "Go find another fucking guitarist, dick. I'm outta here. Fuck you, James. Fuck all you guys…"

Before anyone could offer protest, Derek grabbed his axe and walked out of the studio.

We stood, for that moment, speechless and rooted in place.

The soundproofed door scraped open, startling us. Tommy appeared, holding his bass. "That's it," he said. "I'm done, dudes. Tell Derek it's his turn."

We continued staring, unable to put the tale into words.

Tommy's head tilted. "What's going on?"

Uncomfortable pause.

"I'll play Derek's parts," James announced, gathering his guitar and stepping inside the door.

Randy and I looked at each other, sharing the same thought. We made a dash for the stairs, leaving Tommy asking questions in our wake.

Heaven's on Fire

We didn't catch Derek.

By the time we reached the front door, his car was gone.

Some people make dramatic exits and then hang around a bit, hoping for an apology. Derek wasn't like that. If he made an exit, it was because he intended to go.

"What now?" I looked at Randy.

"What happened?" Tommy asked, trailing us.

"Your car!" Randy burst out. "We'll chase him down."

"Chase him? And do what when we catch him? Kidnap him and make him come back? We know where he's going!"

"Just an idea."

"Dudes, what happened?" Tommy pestered again.

"We'll go back to the house," I told Randy. "He'll be there. We can talk to him and get him to come back."

"And what are you going to say to him?"

"I don't know," I replied honestly. "I'll think of something."

"Pshht--there's like major shit to work through before he'll even talk to James again. You know Derek doesn't go for the drama shit unless it's real. Oh, and James is down there laying down Derek's rhythm tracks right now. I'm sure he'll be real happy to hear that!"

"DUDES!" Tommy shouted, finally drawing our attention. "You're gonna tell me, right now! What the hell happened?"

Randy and I stared back at Tommy like two outfielders looking up at a fly ball, each waiting for the other to call it.

"James and Derek started fighting," I said.

"Well, duh--I figured out that much."

"No...this one was bad, dude."

"Derek's still angry about 'Devastator'. They got into it, and James busted out some really harsh shit."

"Like what?"

We did our best to enlighten Tommy in as few words as possible, trying to be fair to both James and Derek. However we tried to phrase it, James came out looking like a prick. Before we even finished telling him, Tommy broke into a repetitive chorus of 'Oh Man!'.

"So I guess we head home to get Derek," I told them, wondering what I'd say when I got there. "We'll leave his amp and shit here."

Randy shook his head. "No way. Dude, you can't go."

"He's right," Tommy seconded.

"What do you mean?"

"You're up next, Mark," he told me. "You still gotta sing."

"I can't do it now," I said, hesitating. "What about Derek?"

"You have to," Randy urged, his tone regretful but infinitely serious. "This is for the band, man. You gotta do it for all of us. No vocals, no tape."

The clock was still ticking, and I knew it. Admittedly, my selfish desire to sing in a studio was contending with the instinct that told me to bring Derek back. Randy's rationalization only fueled the fire.

"This fight crap will blow over soon," he continued. "Derek and James will make up, eventually. You know it. Everything will go back to normal. Then, the question will be: Do we have a demo tape?"

I began to rationalize. Looking back, I wish I hadn't. Never trust your mind.

"Derek's really going to love having a demo he didn't even play on..."

"He won't mind," Tommy said, trying too hard to contribute.

"Yeah, sure he won't!"

"He'll have to come back and record his parts," Randy suggested. "We'll all chip in and pay for him to come back. We'll do what we have to. Look man, you have to sing! My parts are done, so I can go. Gimme your keys and I'll go talk to Derek."

I hesitated for a moment, rationalizing even more. Randy always seemed to side with Derek, and he would likely have a good shot at bringing him back.

"Don't just talk to him," I said, handing him the keys. "Bring him back here. We'll pay extra time if we have to--I know for a fact that we can stir up enough money for a couple of extra hours."

"I'll bottom out my checking account if it will help. Hell, I can bounce one if we need to..."

"We'll work out the damn money. Just go get Derek."

"Alright--laters, dude. Sing good."

"I'm coming with you," Tommy announced, moving for the door.

"No, man. You wait here and get something done."

"You sure?"

"Totally."

"Ok, cool." Tommy shrugged. "Whatever...later."

A moment later, both Randy and Derek were gone. James was downstairs laying down tracks that weren't his. Tommy was busy slapping me on the back and telling me not to worry about it. To top it off, the house smelled like cat urine.

My temper was twisting in its shackles. Anger, disappointment, apprehension and pride were square-dancing and drinking cheap beer behind my eyes. Little Jim trashed hotel rooms in my head, shirtless and tripping, shouting pulp-style as he put the heel of his boot through the television.

Bad kung fu. I was slipping into the dark side. At that moment, I could have written an entire notebook of devilish lyrics. My perilous angst needed a target.

James was stepping out of the recording room when I reached the bottom of the stairs.

"What happened?"

"Question of the day," I answered. "What do you think happened?"

James caught the vibe immediately, frosting over. "I'd say Derek ran away. I'd say he let all of us down!"

"Really?"

"Yeah!" he shouted. "Hell yeah! Do you think I liked having to record his parts?"

"I don't think you hated it…"

"Shit." James shook his head, acting as though it were funny. "Like always, I'm the one making sure we get everything done. For that, you guys get all pissed!"

Tommy sneaked downstairs behind me. For the moment, at least, he was unwilling to join in the conversation.

"It's not like that, James! Why'd you have to push him so hard?"

"He was the one pushin' ME, man."

"I just think you need to talk it out, that's all."

"You want me to apologize," his eyes narrowed.

"Well…it would help."

"Fuck that," he said simply, complicating everything with two words. "Why should I? Where's Randy?"

"He went home to get Derek," Tommy said, finally speaking.

James shook his head again, acting like a disappointed father. "Derek won't come back. At least Randy's parts are finished…" He looked to me. "So are you ready to do some singing, bud?"

And so I sang. I went in there with flames in my gut, breathing fire. I put on the headphones and didn't even bother to marvel at the sound of my amplified voice. I was so frustrated that I forgot to be nervous and belted it out like Michael Bolton on crack.

I don't remember too much about the rest of the afternoon, though I know we didn't see or hear from Derek or Randy, and all my calls to the house went unanswered. After a cursory mix-down, we left the studio with a demo tape and a master reel.

We should have stopped recording when Derek walked out. We should all have dropped the guitars and set out in search of him. In the days and weeks following, I would experience these regrets hundreds of times. Had I gone with Randy, Tommy would have tagged along. James would have been alone and unable to finish the demo until he dealt with Derek. By staying, I'd made everything more complicated.

The demo, in case you were wondering, sounded decent. Not great, not bad. Not that I listened to it much in the weeks after Derek left.

Die With Your Boots On

"I appreciate the effort and everything," Derek said, coughing, "but I'm not coming back. It's as simple as that."

We sat, parked in Lonnie's truck near the Boulder mall, passing a bowl and speaking heavy words. I'd tried every argument I could think of, but short of delivering a written apology from James, I knew I wouldn't budge Derek.

He was done. Just like that, he was finished with the band, the house and everything. I'd done my best to get them together, but a switch had flipped off within Derek somewhere, and his time as our guitarist was at an end. I was struggling with devastation, but decided to give it one last try. After all, we were friends--all of us--and some things are more important. What was a band, after all?

"I think you should go back," Lonnie told him, more than willing to support the cause. "It won't be the same without you, Derek."

"No doubt..."

"Yeah, right," he chuckled. "I'm just a rhythm guitarist. I'm not even the lead."

"It doesn't matter," Lonnie returned. "People like the BAND, man. You're part of what they like. It's a chemistry thing...like when they switched Darrins on Bewitched, or like Shemp on the Three Stooges."

"I'm so high that you're making sense, Lonnie."

"We can re-record your guitar parts on the demo," I told him, hoping to bargain. "We've got the master reel, and Steven said we c--"

"It's more than the demo," he cut me off. "Way more. Hell, I don't even care about that compared to the shit he said to me. James loves that 'don't have what it takes' bullshit, you know? But did any of us ever say anything when he jacked up his solos or couldn't learn his part? No way. You know it, Mark."

I nodded. Derek was right, and as much as I wanted to disagree, I couldn't. For a moment I wavered, questioning my own persistence. My conscience was telling me to join him, to pitch in with Derek and pray that James would see the light. I contemplated quitting, my sense of right and wrong embroiled in a battle with my ego.

"More than that," Derek continued, his tone betraying his calm, "I had Jeff Eggerton come up to me at the bar and tell me that our lead guitarist sucked! He said we should get a new guy if we want to compete! And do you know what I said? I told him to fuck off! I told him I'd give it up before I'd play with anyone else! And it's true, man. James may not have been the best guitarist, or even the best guy to be around all the time...but that fucker was my friend. Our friend, OUR guitarist, and we all started this together. That was supposed to be good enough. It sure used to be. You know it, Mark--we could both find a better guitarist in ten minutes at The Tank...but neither of us would even THINK it, much less say it!"

"But you know how James is," I offered, trying to repair what I could. "He pulls his hair out worrying about all that soloing shit."

"It's no excuse though--"

"Yeah, but he's insecure, man. He can't help himself--and he didn't mean what he said--"

"Like hell he didn't!" Derek shook his head sadly. "He DID mean it, dude. That's the problem--and has been for a long time. So don't be thinking that I freaked out and left because of one argument--it's way bigger than that. It's the way we think, James and me. I used to think we were the same, but we're not. We're different, you know? I wasn't jamming in this band because I was dreaming of some bright future."

"And James is all about the dream..."

He shrugged. "Or planning for it, at least. James is a good guy, but there's something in me that can't stand to see him take everything that was important to us and turn it on its head. Screw that, man."

"He's not trying to--"

"He lost sight of everything real, you know? At least what's real to me. Personally, I think all this competition pressure is bullshit--straight bullshit, and I just can't take it anymore. This shit is no fun for me now...

"Look, bud," he continued, exhaling, "you guys will always be my brothers, no matter what--James, too. But I'm done, Mark. Just done. If I'm not having a good time, it's not worth it. That's the easy part to figure out..."

There was so little I could say. I understood and agreed with him. I couldn't begin to know what his life had been like before or blame him for not sharing the dream. I had trouble forming anything that seemed like a logical response. To change his mind, I would have been going against more than just my conscience.

And though I sympathized with Derek, another part of me was mad--at both of them. Mad that they'd screwed up such a cool thing and had done it over pride. I remained bewildered by the fact that the two of them declined to even SPEAK to each other. All the years, all the practices and gigs, every shared joke and new set of guitar strings…poof! Done, just like that. Apparently, both of them were quite content to proclaim their differences unresolved and leave the other behind.

This, more than anything else, disturbed me. Surely, the two were just playing stubborn, begging for me to step in as I always did and patch things up. It seemed impossible that they would bluff so broadly. The threats were merely cries for help…

But neither one of them wanted my help. Derek and James were both kind and regretful, but neither ever let the conversation stray from the theme: no reconciliation, no contact, no offense. They were matter of fact about it, acting as though their friendship was a horse with a broken leg, posing like men as they pulled out their guns and took aim to plug it in the head and end the misery.

They seemed to want it. That was the thing that bothered me. I was beginning to wonder what friendship really meant, to search for the point where the band began and the friendship ended.

We talked for a long while in the parking lot that night, but as hard as I tried, I couldn't arrange a cease fire much less an armistice. And the more I talked to Derek, the more I became convinced: it had to happen. Derek and James could no longer occupy the same life. Derek would miss the band, but he'd be just fine. James would miss Derek, but not for too long. My belief in the greater truths seemed to be the only casualty. That, and the magic.

"Look, dude--don't worry about me," Derek said finally, not a trace of self-pity in his tone. "I don't have any hard feelings, and I don't expect anyone to pull any bullshit like quitting the band. I'm not gonna be an asshole about this--seriously. I wanna see you guys jam sometime down the road. We're still gonna hang out and party, right?"

"Yeah--of course we will."

"Cool, then," he told me, trying to wrap the topic up. "Just promise me one thing--remember that you're supposed to be enjoying yourself. Alright? Don't get all caught up in the bullshit."

"We'll miss you, dude…"

"Likewise, fucker." He punched me in the arm, harder than ever before. "You're the man, Mark. Let's go get some beer…"

Partying with Derek would be problematic. The band was always together, and I knew that pride would keep Derek away from James. The two would barely speak again.

I got drunk with Derek and Lonnie that night, bar hopping and cruising the Denver clubs. I'd always remember that night being colored by a nostalgic grey feeling, as though it were two hours after midnight on New Year's Eve. As we reminisced and toasted Sherrie Smith with shots of tequila, I realized that nothing would ever be the same. The Rock Honeymoon was over.

ACE OF SPADES

The rehearsals felt flat and sounded odd.

Without the second guitar, the mix was decidedly weak and diluted. As the only guitarist in the band, James' playing fell under even more scrutiny. No longer was there an accompanying buzz to cover his mistakes, and the result was worse than expected. When the solos arrived, James would squeal his way through, backed by only drums and bass, his guitar work laid bare.

It just sounded wrong. Thin, and wrong.

Not that there's anything wrong with single guitar bands--some of our all-time favorite bands sported only one guitarist. But when we played without Derek, it was evident that our sound lacked the crunchy goodness of a second guitar.

Chunk-a-chunkless. We were accustomed to the sound--to having Derek there.

At first, I actually supported the single guitarist idea. I was still hoping Derek would change his mind and didn't want to fill his spot too soon. Admittedly, I was also enjoying the view as James carried the burden he'd created. Two months later, however, the Derek situation was a foregone conclusion, and James' burden belonged to all of us.

The gigs at J.R.'s were still rolling and we showed up without Derek, working our way through the set, knowing it sounded like shit. The song list alone was good enough to hold a certain percentage of the audience, but Bladderburster Night was losing its appeal.

I was gigging and singing, but felt absent. Morale had taken a serious hit, and the hatchets were still far from buried. Without Derek, the mood felt a little more like business and a lot less like pleasure. Business, with alcohol.

Still, the dream survived. The Denver club scene was exploding with hard rock venues, and the Boulder band house now swarmed twenty-four seven with glam girls and hangers on. The taste of the deep water at The Tank made us thirsty, and we wanted nothing more than to return there and lay waste.

To do this, we needed another guitarist. A new one.

Band auditions at the bottom-feeder level. The gigs at J.R.'s would give us credibility. We posted flyers in the music stores and placed want ads in the local music rag, hoping to attract the best and brightest the town had to offer.

In addition, we spread word via Nikki throughout the entire stripper community, letting the bimbo power work for us. They were on intimate terms with some of the best guitarists in town and would get the word out.

The gigs at J.R's kept coming, though alcoholic Jay had been dropping veiled hints that he was considering other bands. To our ears, 'considering other bands' meant, at best, fewer gigs. At worst, we'd be dropped from the rotation entirely. The curse of Derek.

Gigs, once acquired, must be jealously defended. We began learning new covers and waited for the phone calls from prospective auditionees to come pouring in.

The calls came, but dribbled rather than poured.

Four calls in the first week.

The process was nothing specific. We asked the aspiring head-bangers to show up during practice and casually sit in, figuring that if it clicked, we'd know. We promised each other not to get too excited and offer the job to the first good prospect; all decisions would be made the following day.

Contestant number one was a student, a third-year music major with wicked skills but zero previous band experience. He was a virtuoso-type and, by the looks of him, a tablature freak. He seemed serious and played one of those ultra-difficult classical pieces. 1 Yea, 3 Nay. Far too good for us, and his hair was tragically short.

Next.

Contestant number two looked promising to begin with, passing the skinny and long-haired criteria immediately. His name was Lee and, despite his odd orange-tinted face, he seemed to be working out. Things hit a snag, however, when we played "Mob Rules" and he didn't know that Dio had been in Sabbath. I suppose you could say he failed the verbal portion of the audition. Not knowing his history, he was labeled a poser and never called back. 0 Yea, 4 Nay.

Next.

Contestant number three was a bit older, married, and wore a world class mullet. It parted in the middle, was feathered over the ears, then dropped like homemade spaghetti straight down his back. He played well, seemed to know the songs, and even gained a few brownie points by pulling out a spliff and sharing it after rehearsal. His downfall? His face. We couldn't picture ourselves standing next to the guy on the cover of *Rolling Stone*. 0 Yea, 4 Nay.

There was always something. The more we auditioned, the more we realized just how stringent our requirements were. Where was Malcolm Young when we needed him?

Number four was too fat. Number five was too prissy. Number six could barely play, and number seven insulted Randy's kit. Eight and Nine had no amps. Ten was too pushy, and eleven was forty.

Another week passed, and another gig at J.R.'s. Thanks to the ongoing recruiting efforts of Sandy and Sara, the crowd held up well. The advantage of dating two girls who didn't know each other was that the band could pull from two different friend pools when seeking audience plants. Both Sara and Sandy possessed their own respective flocks of party monkey girlfriends, and we were rarely at a loss for dancing flesh magnets.

The male plants were the band's responsibility and were largely composed of our close friends, new Boulder party buddies, and hangers-on. I probably shouldn't be calling anyone a hanger-on because, in reality, they were our friends. Yet there were some people who had a tendency to hang around too much and for too long. They partied hard and delivered praise in payment for the leftover beer and groupie rejects they collected. They acted like friends. Still, we knew that if the band broke up and moved out of the house, the hangers-on would be gone in an instant. Some friends are more real than others.

Welcome or not, the planted crowd pulled us through that rough stretch, maintaining a presence in J.R.'s and tirelessly cheering the same songs again and again. We were finally growing accustomed to playing without Derek. Not that it sounded any better.

"I got the perfect guitarist for us," James announced one night as we started rehearsal, beaming with premeditated confidence. "I got the guy."

"Who is it?"

"Who, dude?"

"Have you ever heard of Twilight?"

I shook my head. Tommy didn't seem to know, either.

"Didn't they open up for Metal Church at the Rainbow Music Hall?"

"Good memory," James told Randy. "They had a record deal and everything."

"Oh yeah…that's Ray Sharp's band, isn't it?"

James was about to hemorrhage with excitement. "That's it, dude. Only Ray isn't playing with 'em anymore. Twilight broke up."

"And they had a record deal?" Randy shook his head. "How stupid."

"Yeah, but it wasn't Ray's fault. I guess the record company screwed 'em over somehow, and they had to break up the band to get out of the contract."

Knowing nothing about contracts, the story sounded believable.

"So Ray's looking for a band?"

"Hell yeah," James answered. "He said he saw us play at The Tank."

"I didn't see him there."

"We just didn't know who he was. He was there, and he said he likes our act. He's coming over tonight."

"Tonight?" Randy was showing a touch of irritation. "Why didn't you tell us?"

"I'm telling you now," James replied. "Look--this guy not only fits the job perfect, but he's got connections. We're talking real gigs, and a shot at a contract."

"Cool."

Tommy was sold.

"A contract? Yeah, right."

Randy wasn't.

"What's up, man?" James turned on him, questioning. "How come you have such an attitude all of a sudden, Randy?"

Randy looked back, his eyes cold, as though he were channeling Derek's spirit. "I don't have an attitude. I just don't want this to wind up being Ray Sharp's Band...that's all."

"Oh--pshht! Right, man. That'll never happen," James reassured, wearing a salesman grin and sounding as though he believed himself. "You know as well as I do--all these lame-ass auditions are getting us nowhere! And you remember what Gary from Lyon's Pryde told us: If you want a good guitar player, you have to steal one from another band! Face it--Ray is perfect, and we don't even have to steal him! You're gonna freak, dudes. He's got like five guitars! Besides...we need a roommate if we want to make rent."

It was worth a shot. James' pipe dreams had a strange way of coming true, and despite Randy's cynicism, we were willing to believe. We ran through a few tunes, anticipating Ray's arrival.

Twenty minutes later, Ray Sharp made his entrance, the heels of his snakeskin boots clopping on the stairs.

Ray looked like a fire at a circus. He stood just under six feet, but his heels and big hair added at least five inches, making him appear tall and lanky. His clothes were poser perfect, a trademark muscle shirt and leather pants, accented by a studded leather belt with a Morrison-style buckle. Both his forearms were covered with silver bangles, and a fat chain wristband circled his left wrist. Tattoos adorned both arms, and a green dragon's head emerged from beneath his shirt, creeping out of the shorthair jungle toward his neck.

His dominating feature, however, was undoubtedly the work of art that sat atop his head. Ray's hair was epic. L.A. perfect, exploding from his head and falling away in professionally bleached strands to his waist. It had form, height, and spontaneity. It had theme, and a professional cut that rivaled the best.

Ray's face was acceptable if not enviable. He bordered on stud. A poor woman's Jon Bon Jovi, it was obvious that Ray scored more than his share of chicks.

However shallow, this was important. The chick factor could never be underestimated; they represented two-thirds of the metal audience and could be powerful allies. In payment for their loyalty, the chicks demanded cute band members. Ray would be a more than adequate sacrifice.

Poser-esque, perhaps. But he'd rubbed elbows with greatness, and this was undoubtedly what one looked like after recording an album. To add to this enticing brew, Ray also carried with him the obscure promise of the future, the magic word that was to carry us to the top…

Connections.

"Sup, Ray?" James unplugged and walked over to shake his hand.

"Hey James. Not much, man."

"You find the place all right?"

"Yeah, yeah."

"Ray, this is Tommy. That's Mark, and Randy behind the drums."

"Hey man."

"Sup."

"Sup, dude."

"Sup, Mark."

We all shook hands. The process took a while.

"Is Behindadrums your full last name?"

"Actually, it was originally Kikenash-behindadrums," Randy chuckled, "but I had it shortened to use as a stage name."

"Ahh," Ray grinned. "That's Belgian, isn't it?"

"Slava-slobodnian, actually."

The mood lightened. I think we were half-expecting Ray to be a condescending prick. At the time, he didn't seem like it.

We helped him load in his amp, a sweet Marshall half stack with an effects rack that could choke a pink elephant. Kick-ass equipment? Check.

He carried in two guitars. The hard shell cases looked new.

Ray popped open the first case and produced a shiny black B.C. Rich Warlock, the guitar which, more than any other, symbolized the struggle of our people. Jagged and angled, the body resembled a sharp, pointed X.

"My ex gave me this," he said, chuckling.

Gasp. We nearly applauded. Equipped with his own personal supply of guitar stands, Ray set the Warlock out to be admired.

"But this is my baby," he told us, popping open the second case. From this one, he pulled a vintage Les Paul black beauty with gold hardware and custom pearl inlay on the fret board. American made, genuine. Easily a two-thousand dollar piece of work.

Bigger gasp. The axe was undeniably cool. We had to admit, the guy had taste. Guitar requirement--check.

"I've also got a Kramer at home," Ray said in an 'oh, by the way' tone. "I try to break out the Les Paul only on special occasions."

Ah, the luxury of having a 'special occasions' guitar. I could see the admiration building in James' eyes.

I was equally impressed and already thinking toward the future. For Ray, there remained only one final hurdle. If he could play, my vote would be yes.

So we jammed. We started with the easy stuff.

Ray seemed to know it all. What he didn't know, he faked well. His timing was good, and he played with confidence. Again, the painted walls rang with the power of dueling guitars.

The following day, the vote was three to one. Randy was the sole dissenter, voicing his concerns over Ray's poser look and stating his general mistrust. After a short but notably civil discussion, Randy relented, agreeing that we would be hard pressed to find somebody better. He changed his vote, and it was unanimous. Derek had been replaced.

The Zoo

The Ray Sharp era began with a boom. We decided to have a house party to welcome Mr. Sharp and tighten up our song list before the next gig at J.R.'s.

No invitations would be necessary. We'd thrown enough hundred-count 'get togethers' to land ourselves on the short lists of party hoppers and student alcoholics alike, and our house was routinely checked for activity. One phone call at 5 p.m. could easily yield a hundred guests by ten-thirty. By midnight, the front yard, the back yard, the main floor and the basement would be packed with a gross-plus of our closest friends.

And the friends of our closest friends.

And the dates of the friends of our closest friends.

And complete strangers.

It's a unique feeling, standing in your basement singing "Runnin' With the Devil" while the local stoners go through your fridge. It's even more odd when you realize you don't care and keep singing.

How to deal, then, with a house full of strangers? These situations required preparation. Experience told us that during the course of the party, something would be broken, stolen, damaged or destroyed. Inevitably, this would prove true. A doorknob. A window. The ceramic lid on the toilet. We never seemed to be around when the offenses occurred, and with the inebriated culprits long gone, the bill would be ours to eat.

In a stroke of genius, we devised a plan to make the house party proof.

First, we gathered the furniture, the television, the knick-knacks and loose appliances--basically everything that wasn't nailed down--and deposited the lot in one of the upstairs bedrooms. All personal effects, including shoes, jackets, hair-dryers and pets would be placed in our respective rooms. All bedroom doors would then be locked for the duration of the evening.

Our house became a blank slate. With the exception of the stereo and the musical equipment in the basement, the place would be literally empty and, therefore, virtually theft proof. Only the refrigerator sat vulnerable--there was usually very little food to steal. We warned guests about the risks of storing their beer in the fridge and kept our own stock in a cooler behind Randy's drum kit.

The empty house theory also proved beneficial when it came to clean-up. The morning after the party we'd simply sweep and mop the floor like a warehouse and break out the furniture and pets once again, leaving no sign of the previous night's festivities.

Aside from the emotional trauma incurred by our furry friends, the system worked well. We hated to lock the animals up, but adopted the practice when we found a stripper leaving with one of our Persians in her jacket.

Ray seemed to be getting along well with Lonnie and the girlfriends. Word was spreading about the cute new guy in the band, a rumor which brought in the full henhouse of Sandy's flock and a few of their fellow chicks.

Ray mixed like orange juice, joking and getting along with everyone.

"So…do you like him?"

Sara and I stood across the room, watching Ray and Nikki flip their hair and flirt, trying their best to charm each other. As Alpha female, Nikki was first of her pride to hunt. They looked like they'd met before.

I shrugged. "I guess so. Yeah."

"You don't like him, then?"

Another shrug. "I wouldn't say that, either...Ray actually seems pretty cool, I guess."

"Ahh," she said. "So you feel guilty for liking him?"

"Well, yeah. That's pretty much it."

"You think too much," Sara commented, pecking me on the lips. "Look--you're not disrespecting Derek by getting along with Ray, and he's not the one to blame anyway. I guess the most important question would be: Does the music sound better?"

"Better than it did with one guitar," I replied honestly. "But not better than with Derek playing. Don't get me wrong--Ray's a good player. It's just...different now, that's all. It's..."

"I'm sure you sound fine," she told me, her dark eyes softening. People were oddly intimidated by Sara's stare; at first, both Randy and Tommy were convinced that she hated them. But I never saw the hard look she gave the rest of the world. For me, her eyes were always soft.

Sara looked incredible, and I hated the thought of having to leave her to the wolves while I sang. Not that I didn't trust her. Where infidelity was concerned, I trusted her more than I trusted myself.

"I guess I need to know if it's just me thinking too much. You can tell me. You'll see, tonight--and I really need the truth. You have to give me the harsh evaluation, okay?"

"Of course," Sara replied. "Don't I always?"

"I guess."

"Trust me--if you guys suck, I'll be the first one to tell you."

"I'm sure you won't say it like that, though."

"No," she mused. "I'd probably soften the blow a bit for you."

"Hey, thanks."

"That's what I'm here for." She beamed a reassuring smile.

Sara had a wonderful way of countering without being cruel. When the time came to jam, she was there, smiling at me from the back of the room.

The basement gigs were the best, bar none.

Here, far from the petty pressures of the bar scene, we thrived. Neatly tucked into a corner of our dude-designed Shangri-La, we gave blowout performances every time. The home crowd belonged to us. Our venue, our hospitality, and only one band on the program. A taste of the old days.

James juiced the crowd with a couple of power chords, grabbing a little attention and sending a rattling buzz upstairs to announce the set. The already crowded room became increasingly tight as more of our guests came whooping down the stairs, brews in hand and ready to rock. They piled into the crush of people, screaming out their requests.

"Play some Maiden!"

"Sabbath, dudes! Sabbath! Iron Man!"

"'Highway to Hell'!"

"Play 'Freebird,' man…"

James teased them with the intro from "Highway to Hell," chuckling at the moans when he stopped mid-riff.

He amiably flipped them off. "I got a free bird for you…"

Ray was attracting all the attention as he strapped on his guitar, shaking down the bangle bracelets and coolly grabbing a pick from his amp. Sandy's friends were committing felonies with their lustful gazes, and it appeared that Ray was fielding as many of the amorous stares as he could.

Tonight, Ray's ensemble included tight faded jeans tucked into little white boots, and a light blue sleeveless half-shirt that read 'You Look Mahvelous'. He flipped his hair with a twitch of his neck, sending the chemically enhanced mane drifting into space, hovering for a moment then settling back down, bigger than before.

Tommy was watching, too. Tommy's hair flips were rough and amateurish compared to Ray's, and I wondered how our bass player felt about losing his 'best hair in the band' status. No offense to Derek, but the coif-quotient had definitely gone up--we now put the normals to shame.

I grabbed the mic and surveyed the horde.

A hundred drunks in the basement, crammed together like Brazilian soccer fans, sucking down beer and passing joints, every single one bearing a grin. Laughing, shaking hands, shooting the shit, all without a semblance of personal space. A beautiful thing.

A hundred drunks who didn't care how good we were or what song we played. They just wanted to have their eardrums fried and battered, and to escape into the kind of group chaos that can only be provoked by live music. Two hundred sheets to the wind, and an eye for every one of them looking back at me.

I brought the mic to my lips and grinned.

"I don't have the figures yet," I told them, my amplified voice trumping all others, "but by the looks of things, this is record attendance. I guess everyone got the memo."

Whoops and whistles.

"So, you guys get enough beer, or what?"

Randy rumbled quads then cracked his snare, right with me.

Flugada-blug-blug. Blllllluggada.

Bigger whoops and whistles.

Flug-uh.

I grinned through my bangs, waving them in. "Keep it coming, that's right. Squeeze together in the back. Boy, girl, boy, girl. Listen up! If part of you is touching part of someone else, I want you to make noise!"

The flock sounded off, raising their beers.

Ray looked over at me. "Ready when you are, Mark..."

I turned and looked to Randy, who had Tommy and James cued. The first song was already agreed upon. House party meant garage-style artistic freedom, the ability to play whatever we wanted, as badly as we wanted, without regard for time. Hard, soft, silly--rehearsed or not--anything went.

In the basement of my brain, Jim Morrison staggered forth from the wings and grabbed his mike, tossing the stand aside. He whooped and brushed the unwashed locks from his eyes, pointing at me.

'Do your thing, man...'

Two, three--

We kicked into Van Halen's "So This is Love." Tight sound exploded from the P.A., rattling the window wells. The basement cheered as soon as they recognized the tune, reacting like a stadium crowd. With my voracious audience churning less than four feet away, I hit it hard.

I could see Sara and Danni peering around the staircase, caught in the crush as I belted. The basement bounced before my eyes.

We hit the chorus perfectly. Pure nitro coursed through my throbbing heart. I looked over to see James making a guitar face, holding his axe at an angle, his hair flipping in time.

Ray was grinning like a cartoon hyena. He backed into Tommy, mugging.

The solo arrived and James stepped boldly forward, throwing it down without the slightest sign of self-consciousness. I heard Sandy's trademark whistle over the din.

I punched my fist and kicked back into the final verse, seeing nothing but love and inebriation before me.

Bam. Bam-bam.

The ending was tight, but it didn't matter--the basement erupted before we ever finished.

Screaming drunks, pumping their fists and yelling at the top of their lungs. Earsplitting rock, and jiggling local girls. Peace, love, and the glorious feeling of group oneness.

I grabbed my beer and raised it in salute. "Drink 'em if you got 'em!"

Still immaculately coiffed, Ray looked ready to burst.

"So...what do you think?" I asked him, grinning.

"Hell yeah," he said, using Derek's words. "Hell yeah is what I think! More--more! What next?"

We jammed non-stop for the next hour and a half, pausing only when the police arrived.

Dude Looks Like a Lady

"So how is school going, dude?"

I shook my head. "That's a tough one to answer."

Randy and I drank nightcaps at J.R.'s. Our third gig with Ray was in the books, and the crowds were only getting bigger. I didn't want to think about school.

"Explain," he said, as though knowing I needed venting. "Are you flunking or something?"

"Not yet," I told him, still not entirely willing to talk about it. "But you don't get many D's before they boot your ass out."

Randy looked puzzled. "Wait a minute--you mean to tell me that you pay them all that money and it doesn't even guarantee you a spot?"

"Nope," I sighed. "They boot your ass right out if you don't perform."

"And...you're not performing?"

"I'm doing okay," I answered, lying a bit. "I'm there, you know? Going to class and keeping up with the work, but it's getting tougher. I'm having trouble thinking about school, and I have to force myself to get the assignments done."

"And you think about jamming all the time?" he asked.

"Right."

"And you find yourself thinking how pointless it is?"

"Totally."

"And no matter how long you've been there, you just want to get the hell out?"

"That's the feeling," I said.

"Yep," Randy nodded, sipping from his beer. "That's pretty much what everybody's job is like, dude. Most people hate their fucking jobs. We're talking like ninety percent of 'em. Work sucks, man; that's one of the greater truths of life. So the trick is doing something you love...like me playing the drums. That's why we have to make it. So we won't have to work."

"We all have to work, but when we make it, we get paid for doing something we love, right?"

"The American fucking way, dude. The land of a million pipe dreams. Everyone here gets a shot at doing what he loves. Every idiot gets to pretend he could be something. Every dumb-ass poser in this place actually thinks he's really gonna make it. Pretty cool... in a sad kind of way."

"We get hope for free," I commented, waxing philosophical.

"Hell yeah. That's why we pay taxes, dude."

"No doubt...I guess deluded is way better than hopeless."

"Truth." We clinked our bottles together in wordless toast, drinking down the domestic light. Onstage, the soundmen packed up for the night, wrapping cords and de-miking the drum kit.

"You know dude, drums are the one thing I really kick ass on," he told me. "Maybe the only thing."

"That's why we can't give up," I told him, trying to turn the conversation to suit my purpose. "Look, Randy--I know you don't like Ray too much..."

"It's just with all the bullshit he talks! I haven't seen a single thing yet, you know? Have you ever heard a single tune off that album he supposedly recorded?"

"Well, no," I answered.

"Too weird--it doesn't make any sense. I mean, if I had an album, then I'd sure as hell keep a copy lying around somewhere. I'd have a hundred of 'em. You know?"

I shrugged. "I think the recording probably exists, but there's something about the way he brags--it bugs the shit out of me. And then that thing with the KISS concert. He was acting like he knew Paul Stanley--told us all day how he was going to get us backstage. Then the day of the show he said he'd called the hotel but couldn't get through…yeah."

"Stupid, man. It's like he lies about things that make no difference."

"The more he bullshits about Paul Stanley," I said, my confidence waning, "the more it makes everything else smell."

"Exactly. He's a cool guy and all…he just seems to have some kind of power over James…and don't even get me started on the whole spandex thing!"

The spandex issue was heating up. Ray's pro-spandex stance was pushing the fulcrum.

"Did James say something to you?" I asked.

"Well, James kept bugging me about what I was gonna wear in the photos. I told him 'the regular shit', and he gets on that big trip about image, and talking how Ray said this and Ray said that. I guess now Ray thinks we all need to be in spandex."

"And James said that?"

"Well, in so many words, yeah. Only I'm not into it."

"How do you think I feel? You get to sit behind the kit, dude. Your legs are hidden--not like me. They want me prancing around out there with no cover!"

"Prancing," he repeated, chuckling at the image. "We don't want that."

"Neither do I, trust me. Do you think Bruce Dickinson or Dio ever feel stupid in their tights?"

"I doubt it," he said, ordering another round with a silent gesture. "They're famous, so any ridicule gets countered by people kissing their ass all day."

"True."

"Plus, somehow Bruce always looks like a badass. Course, he's English."

"Also true."

"Look," Randy reasoned, "I don't care if you all want to do it, but the spandex thing doesn't work for me."

"And you told James this?"

To my surprise, he nodded.

"James started out like he does, you know, giving an argument for everything, coming up with reasons why I should 'be a team player' and all that shit. I didn't let down, though. Once he finally got it through his head that he couldn't convince me, he caved a little. He said I should go with massively ripped jeans, or shorts, even."

James and Tommy were already committed to Ray's fashion vision, and Randy's vote had apparently been secured through negotiation. I was now the lone dissenter in the 'new look' push and, as lead singer, I knew I would never escape with a spandex exemption. My case of poserphobia was reaching a critical junction, a fork in the road where I would have to make a decision:

To spandex, or not to spandex. That was the question.

"I just don't think I'd look good," I told him, thinking out loud, realizing that my rationale was growing simplistic and weak. I'd intended to open Randy's mind and had only managed to close my own. There would be no spandex revolution. The king would live.

"I know how it sounds," Randy commiserated, "but once we're all dressed up, you won't have a problem."

"Easy for you to say--you don't have to wear them!"

He laughed a bit. "Okay, point taken. But if you think about it, the whole thing goes back to what you were saying about hope, you know? I was sitting there bitching and moaning and holding my ground against James when I thought to myself--what am I doing? I want the band to succeed, right? And in reality, I don't know shit about what will sell and what won't. So maybe we DO need more of a look. Couldn't hurt to be more professional, and I figure it's all part of being in the band--part of the commitment. I mean, why go nine-tenths of the way?"

Cornered by my own logic. Corralled by an irresistible concept like hope. What he was saying made sense, but I still couldn't picture my little butt covered in zebra stripes.

Had the greats ever struggled with such a dilemma? Did the Beatles really like those uniform bowl haircuts? Did Bob Dylan bristle when someone asked him to comb his hair? Did Ozzy balk when they stuffed him into a red, white and blue jumpsuit?

Yes, probably not, most likely, and apparently not. These things can get complicated.

THE SPIRIT OF RADIO

I stood in the bathroom at the photographer's, staring at my red and black leopard legs in the mirror. Accented by a pair of Ray's short boots and a blood red half-shirt from his closet, I looked rockin' ridiculous.

As it was her chosen profession, Sara had been in charge of my hair. She cherished the opportunity and never stopped talking about what a good decision it was to let her do her thing. In preparation for the band photos, my brown mane had been washed, styled, blown dry in zero gravity, teased and schpritzed, all by her loving hands. She insisted that it looked good.

Exiting the bathroom, I saw Ray's special friend Thumper applying eye-liner to Tommy. Thumper came along as a fashion guru, on a mission to keep our eyes lined and our hair perpetually fluffed. She, too, was a cosmetologist.

Hairdressers and musicians…a match made in heaven.

"You're next," she said, pointing at me with the eye crayon.

"I don't need any makeup…"

"Sure you do." Thumper resumed her work on Tommy, back-combing. "You'll look really bad if you're the only one without it. Trust me, you won't even notice it much."

"Did Randy do it?" I asked.

"Yep," Tommy answered, nodding.

Makeup. Good God. I'd gone from spandex to makeup in one easy step. Poserdom was a slippery slope indeed. The domino theory of fashion. I looked inside for Jim, but he declined to speak to me.

"What happened to James and Ray?"

"In the other bathroom," Tommy pointed.

Two guys in the bathroom. There was, of course, only one reason for this: Ray had scored some blow and James was joining in.

I never really liked coke--it always seemed too cold and incommunicative. When someone had a bowl of weed, they'd share it. Joints were passed around at concerts and somehow always managed to boomerang their way back home. People sat in a circle and connected, just as they'd done hundreds of years ago smoking peace pipes. I assume they called it a peace pipe because you immediately like the people you smoke with. It's mellow and friendly like a nightcap. Weed was about sharing, a group activity--a togetherness thing.

Coke, however, was the yang to weed's yin. Coke was coveted and personal, dealt out to select people in locked bathrooms. Coke had motive behind it and brought out the greedy selfish bastard in everyone. The whole thing seemed contemptible.

I may not have been in a position to throw stones, but I knew where to draw the line.

So I didn't partake, hoping the novelty would wear off. And despite my inclinations, the very thought of hypocrisy kept me from saying anything to James. I suppose I came to the decision that we all destroy ourselves in different ways, and I'd never stopped him when he ordered double cheese on his steak sandwich or told him to slow down when he was speeding. At the time, I couldn't see much difference between doing lines and drinking yourself into a stupor.

Still, it pissed me off that James, taskmaster James, would be the one snorting with Ray. I found myself thinking of Derek and the first night we ever played The Tank.

I kept walking. Randy and Lonnie were waiting with the photographer, sipping a new homemade concoction called 'Hotfoot' from a two-liter bottle. Randy looked uncomfortable in his eyeliner and leather pants.

"Whoa dude--look at mister vocalist!" He couldn't help but laugh at me.

"I need a drink…" I chuckled, looking down at myself.

"Go for it, dude." Lonnie handed me the bottle.

"What's in here?"

He scratched his chin. "Let's see…cinnamon schnapps, peppermint schnapps, vodka and Dr. Pepper. And my secret ingredient."

Well, at least it sounded tasty. A potent mix, indeed. I took a sip, shaking off the sugary kick. It tasted like Christmas cookies and jet fuel.

"Yap. A little dab'll do ya!" Lonnie enjoyed the sight of my recoil.

"You ever think of tending bar, Lonnie?"

He scratched his furry chin. "I should, man. Though I'd bet money that I'd be a raging alcoholic within like a month. You like the 'Hotfoot,' eh? You wanna know what the secret ingredient is?"

I considered the question, taking another sizeable gulp of the high octane and shaking off the effects. "I think I'd rather keep it a mystery. It helps, though."

"So you ready for this thing?"

"Yeah, I guess. I feel kinda ridiculous…"

"You'll get used to it," Lonnie told me, unfazed by my attire. "It's just part of the game. You guys are gonna be doing photo sessions all the time when you're big. That's what pros do. And, of course, I'm gonna be your stage manager."

"No doubt, Lonnie." Randy liked the idea.

"Don't get me wrong," Lonnie added, "I don't want to do anything technical. I'll just do shit like lining up the party supplies and picking groupies out of the audience to come backstage. Shit like that."

"They got to get through your screening process first. Right, Lonnie?"

He grinned. "Hell yeah! I'll be the first line of harassment. I'll be the one to make sure they're suitable for everyday consumption. Groupie inspector. Nothing but the best for you guys. Of course, the rest are mine!"

"What time is it?"

"Almost eight."

"We have to make a trip to the car," I told him. "Tommy, go get James and Ray--and hurry! It's time for Metal Mart."

We piled into the car, breathing clouds of vapor into the cold dashboard. Randy turned the ignition and I dialed the radio in. James and Ray finally followed us out, pausing at the window.

"You guys smoking a bowl?"

"No, man--get in."

Ray frowned. "We gotta do these pictures. What's going on?"

"Get in," I told him, formulating my own Christmas grin. "I've got a surprise for everybody."

James rubbed his nose, shrugged, and hopped into the back seat alongside Ray and Tommy. I turned up the radio.

"It's time for Metal Mart, the local music show that bites back! Tonight we're bringing you the best new metal from the Front Range, kicking off with the sounds of Jack Squat."

Lonnie pulled a joint from his coat pocket and examined it. "Don't tell us you brought us out here to listen to Jack Squat…"

"Who the hell is Jack Squat?"

"You know--they play that one song, 'Last Devil on the Left'."

"Pshht…"

"Shh! Just wait," I told them.

Lonnie lit the joint, his face crunching up as he passed it on.

"Dude, did you get us on Metal Mart?" Randy asked, catching on.

I couldn't help but smile.

James leaned forward in the seat. "You did?"

"I'm not sure," I told them, knowing the surprise wouldn't keep. "Could be…"

"No way, dude!"

"Seriously?"

"Seriously, dude."

We smoked the spliff and juiced the car heater for everything it was worth, fogging up the windows with warm breath and smoke. Jack Squat droned on, ending predictably.

And then, just as if I'd written it into a story, the opening riff of our song leapt through the speakers.

"And here's a hot new band from Boulder…this is Skin Tight with 'Channel 13'…"

My stomach went rollercoaster. My hair actually moved. It would take three days for the swelling in my ego to go away.

"That's us! Hell yeah!"

Tommy and Randy started whooping and banging their heads.

"Way to go, dude!"

"Right fucking on, man!"

James' jaw was hanging limp. "How did you do it?" he asked me.

"Ancient Chinese secret, bud."

I cranked the stereo, closing my eyes and listening. I'd heard the demo hundreds of times, but never like this.

We came hurtling out of the car like we were wearing flubber Underroos, bounding back in to have our photos taken, all the self-consciousness erased by three minutes of radio play.

Just Between You and Me

" So how did it go?" Sara asked as soon as I got in the car. Danni was waiting for Randy in the back seat.

"Pretty good, I guess. Did you hear Metal Mart?"

"Of course I did." Sara smiled at me. "Congratulations, slick. Radio, photos--damn, you guys are moving up in the world...is that eyeliner?"

She looked carefully at what remained of my makeup, seeming amused.

"Probably," I said, rubbing at my eyes. "Ray's girlfriend went Viet Cong with that eyeliner stick. I didn't get it all off?"

"Not quite." She touched her finger to her tongue and wiped at the corners. "There--better. Where's everybody else?"

"James and Ray were all live-wired," Randy said, "so they took Thumper and her friends out for a night on the town."

Sara frowned, looking at me. "Thumper?"

I shook my head. "Don't ask."

"She answers to Thumper?"

I nodded. "Yep."

"She's Ray's ex," Randy clarified.

Sara rolled her almond eyes. "Sounds like a hooker name to me."

"Totally." Danni nodded her agreement, returning her attention to Randy. After discovering that he was astrologically perfect for her, she had unleashed the full-blown come on. The two had been dating for weeks.

"Where to, guys?" Sara asked, wrists on the wheel with her long fingers dangling. For some reason, the sight of her behind the wheel was incredibly sexy to me.

"Hello! Attention K-mart shoppers: I look like crap-ola to-night," Danni announced with a wave of her hand. "So, no bar hopping. I've got some beer back at my apartment if you guys want to go there."

Sara looked over at me. I reached out my hand to touch her denim clad thigh.

"If you guys don't mind," she said to them in the rearview mir-ror, "I'll just drop you off at your place, Danni. I think Mark and I just want to hang out alone."

Message received.

They didn't protest, and soon Sara and I were back in my room at the band house, drifting atop a sea of warm waterbed.

Being alone in the band house was rare treat; usually our time together was accompanied by the muffled thump of stereos or the clomping of boot heels on the kitchen floor. Other times, we were fortunate enough to catch the rhythmic sexual stylings of James and Sandy in the room above us. His headboard would knock against the wall just often enough to cue the beat, the pauses signaling posi-tion changes. The guy was inconsistent at best, and it was impos-sible to get your own rhythm down when you're dealing with an unsteady drummer like James. Usually Sara and I would ride out the storm and wait for James to finish.

Tonight, however, we had the house all to ourselves. We turned off all the lights and lit a candle in the bedroom, closing the door behind us. Privacy within privacy. Once in bed, I was eager to kiss her soft lips.

"So tell me about this Thumper chick," she pulled back, apparently not yet in kissing mode.

"I told you--she's Ray's ex."

"Ex what? Ex-girlfriend? Ex-wife?"

"I don't know. I assumed it was ex-girlfriend. She could be his ex-wife for all I know..."

"Is she pretty?"

Is she pretty? One of the questions to which men should always know the answer. Hmm, let's think. Is she pretty? The truth has no place here. There are many acceptable answers and only one very wrong answer, so you'd think it would be easy. Still, it can be difficult for a man to understand the concept of a correct 'no'.

Question: Is she pretty?

The answer: Keep the focus on your girlfriend, keep it sweet, and whatever happens, do not say 'yes'. Remember, the truth is irrelevant. Recommended replies would include things like: 'Not compared to you, honey' or 'She's not even in your league'.

I decided to take an interesting route.

"She's older," I told Sara. "She's really bossy and thinks she's quite the little hairdresser to the stars."

"She didn't touch your hair, did she?"

"No way," I insisted, acting as though it would have been a crime. "I told her you'd done it."

"And did you tell her I was your girlfriend?"

"Yes, of course. I said: My girlfriend did my hair. When you see her, you'll laugh, babe. She's a big'un. A grehht big'un."

Sara chuckled, breaking free of the inquisitive trance, apparently satisfied. "I'm glad we're here," she said, finally kissing me.

"Mark?"

"What?"

"Wouldn't it be nice to be alone like this every night?"

Every night? The phrase scared me a bit. I knew what she was getting at and didn't want to go there, especially before sex. She always seemed to pick the most opportune moments to talk relationship. With my libido hunched and waiting for the starting gun, I was liable to say anything.

"You mean, like, living together?"

Like, of course she did. I was stalling a bit. Okay, more than a bit.

"Well, yeah," she said. "It doesn't make much sense for me to have an apartment when I'm spending every night over here with you. I'm barely even there. You never come sleep at my place."

"I did!"

"Oh, right. Twice, Mark. You've only spent the night over there twice."

It didn't seem fair; I mean, Sara had an apartment before she met me. Why would it be my responsibility now? Suddenly my feet were ice cold, and the realization struck me. Was I really one of those non-committal guys?

"But I thought you liked your apartment…"

Bad thing to say. I wanted that one back as soon as I uttered it.

"I do like my apartment," she raised her voice a bit, moving out of regulation conversation volume and approaching argument-level decibels. "Only you're never over there! I know you're totally into the band house thing, but I'm starting to get a little bit sick of having to hang out with all the Thumpers and Nikkis all the time. It's a circus here, Mark! I want us to try and take this relationship to another level, and I can't very well move into this little room."

Good God, she'd said it. The 'taking the relationship to another level' statement had been made.

I really cared about Sara and probably could have handled another level or two. Why then, were the hairs on the back of my neck standing up?

Little Jim took center stage behind my eyes. He grabbed the microphone, pulled off his sunglasses, and pointed at me. 'Mark. You know where those levels lead you, brother…'

Marriage? I couldn't even conceive the notion. I was going to be famous soon, and I certainly didn't want to be dumping my 'ex-wife from the sticks' like all those other celebrities. Eventually I would go out on tour, and I didn't want to leave poor Sara behind to cry in my absence, looking after the kids and explaining why daddy missed the recital and the Little League game. Besides, having a child meant having a real job, which lead singer is not.

"Do you want me to move into your apartment?" I asked her. "Is that it?"

"You hate my place," she snapped. "So, no. Honestly, I think we should find one of our own. Something we can move into together."

Warning lights flashed in my head. Gigantic, carnival-sized spotlights flooded the grounds red. The fun house clown looked down past his red blinking nose, the corners of his cherry lips bending upward into a sharp-toothed grin. He laughed, opening his arms to welcome me.

"I'll spend more nights at your house," I told her, trying to sneak back a level. "I'll take my school stuff over there and do all my studying at your house."

"Great," she threw up her hands. "I get to sit around and watch you rehearse over here, then sit around and watch you study over at my place. We need our own place, Mark. I've got all the furniture we need."

I had to be careful and avoid the furniture topic entirely. Once I started talking about end tables, my agreement would be implied.

When I argued with Sara, I always felt like she was one step ahead of me.

"Let's not talk furniture just yet."

"You don't want to," she stated. "I can tell. Just forget it."

I was tunneling to China and couldn't think of a way back up. Here, the only acceptable answer was 'yes'. No variations, no grey area. You don't 'kind of' move in with somebody, or 'sort of' sign a lease. I wanted to make her happy, but I couldn't.

I loved her--or at least I thought I did.

And yet, I couldn't even think about leaving the band house. I was already committed to four other people, dreams included. I'd already signed up for the full journey and was intent on seeing it through. Hope would prevent me from saying yes.

We heard the locks turn on the front door upstairs and heeled footsteps in the hall.

"James and Ray," Sara said, still chilly. "Do you want to go up and talk to them, or something?"

"No! Of course not. Don't be mean…"

"You're the one being mean," she said, pouting uncharacteristically.

"Because I won't move in with you?"

"Well…yes." She pouted harder, then burst out with a threshold laugh, unable to take herself seriously. This time, she accepted my kiss. "You're so damned stubborn."

"Is that what you like about me?" I asked.

"Umm…no. Huh-uh."

"Didn't think so."

"James and Sandy," she said.

"What?"

"It's James and Sandy up there," Sara replied, pointing at the ceiling. "I recognize her voice. I guess Ray must have gone home with his Thumper."

The headboard began to sound on the wall upstairs.

"Wow--James didn't waste any time."

"Damn, I guess not. Do you have any cigarettes?"

I patted my naked chest. "Hmm…not on me…"

"Mark…"

"No, actually," I answered. "I was bumming from James at the photo thing. I'm totally out."

When the banging subsided, Sara stood out of bed and grabbed my robe. "I'm going upstairs to bum a cigarette from Sandy."

"You're going like that?"

"Oh God, Mark. You're funny. Should I put on a dress? My bar clothes show more skin than this robe does."

"Alright then," I chuckled, feeling dumb. "Get me one, too."

I was in the wrong neighborhood to be casting jealousy stones. I didn't even really mind her endless questions about the other women I knew. I did the same thing sometimes, and we both just accepted it.

Did I think she would cheat on me? No. Did I worry about it? A little.

The relationship clock was ticking. Now that the 'other level' proposition had been made, I would have to step to the plate or risk being dismissed as non-committal. At the very worst, I could be considered hopeless and downgraded to friend status. She would write me off and find some guy who wasn't scared of 'other levels'.

I genuinely hoped it wouldn't come to that…but I could see the spray paint on the wall, a 'me or the band' ultimatum awaiting me somewhere down the road. The sad thing was, I already knew what the answer would be.

I had a future awaiting me. Rocking was my business. And if I was going to bomb out of college, then the rich and famous thing would have to be my main gig.

The door opened, and Sara walked in slowly. Her hands were empty.

"What?" I asked. "They don't have any?"

"Oh my God, Mark," she moved to the bed, wide-eyed. "I don't know if I should even tell you..."

"Tell me what? Sara?"

She closed the door behind her and jumped into bed, listening for sound upstairs.

"Sara, what?"

"It's not James and Sandy up there," she said finally. "It's Tommy and Sandy."

MORE THAN WORDS

This was bad. Really bad.

DEFCON-2. Potential band Armageddon, with my finger on the button.

To someone else, this might have been a small offense. To me, it seemed beyond huge. Granted, my sense of honor may have been a bit inflated, and I know it would be easy to say that Tommy's fling with Sandy was just one of those things...

But this was the band. The BAND. By screwing James' girl, Tommy had committed the worst kind of sin. He'd broken his headbanger oath and betrayed all of us.

Tommy's fate rested in my hands. I was the keeper of the dark secret, and he realized it. Had I been the blackmailing type, I might have been happy.

I deduced that I could make one of two choices: 1) Be a friend, tell James and risk band implosion; or 2) Forget about it entirely, spare the band and Tommy's sorry butt along with it. Trying to imagine the possibilities, I began to rationalize.

Sandy and James didn't exactly have what you would call a magical bond. Sure, James seemed to care for her, but she was far from being first in his life. Saying she ranked fourth would have been a generous estimate. James rarely acted jealous or needy and never let himself appear to be whipped.

Sandy, then, was replaceable. James could and surely would find someone better. Given her blatant offense, I had little remorse about the prospect of destroying their endless love.

Had there been no band, I would have told him in a heartbeat. I owed more loyalty to James than I did to Tommy. Besides, Tommy was wrong.

As wrong as he was, however, I didn't see Tommy as replaceable. Things hadn't been quite the same since Derek left, and I wasn't about to consider booting Tommy and admitting a second stranger into the band.

I didn't want to deal with it. I avoided Tommy the next day, hoping that a little distance could make me feel better. It didn't. By the time Sara arrived, I was in serious need of some conversation. We cloistered ourselves away in my room, taking the discussion to bed.

"It's not about the girl," I explained to her. "It's about the friendship."

"And the band?" she asked, leading.

"Band or not, friends don't do that shit," I explained. "Ever. Once your friend dates somebody, she's totally off limits to you, now and forever. Period. It can be three years after you broke up, and it will still feel fucking weird when you find out your friend is dating your ex. That's bad. But this? Doing it with Sandy…in James' bed?"

She shook her head. "Did you talk to Tommy today?"

"Not really," I replied. "Just small talk."

"And he didn't say anything to you about it?"

"Not a word."

"Did he act like anything was wrong?"

"Not really," I replied, remembering the look on Tommy's face when he first saw me in the morning. "He seemed…hesitant, I guess, but I don't think that he knows that I know."

"Does he know that I know?" she asked, playing along.

"Who knows? Seriously, though--did you and Tommy see each other face-to-face?"

She nodded. "They both looked right at me. The light was on and everything."

"That destroys that theory," I replied. "I guess Tommy must just think I'm going to cover for him. That, or he thinks you decided not to tell me."

"Maybe you'll get lucky, and Tommy will confess the whole thing to James," Sara said, trying to find an optimistic path. "Then James will dump Sandy, forgive Tommy, and you'll all get famous. The end."

"Yeah, I wish. If this were a movie, maybe. This is Tommy, though. I just don't think he'll ever admit it."

"He's afraid of James?"

"It's not that," I replied. "He could confess, but even if he stayed in the band, James would never look at him the same way again. By just keeping his mouth shut now, I guess he figures he has a fifty-fifty chance of taking no damage at all."

"You're not going to let him do that, are you?" she asked me as though the answer was obvious. "Tommy and Sandy can't just walk away from this…"

A difficult question. At the time, I didn't know the answer.

"I don't want to destroy the band," I said in reply.

The comment brought an angry flush to Sara's face.

"The band?" she snapped, rolling her eyes. "Come on, Mark! James is getting completely taken for a ride, and you're worried about the band? You're the one who's always talking about friendship!"

"I know, I know. But if I tell James, one of the two is going to quit the band! James always has the best interest of the band at heart."

"It's not right. James would tell you, Mark. If he caught me with Randy or Tommy, God forbid, he would tell you."

I wasn't so sure. I knew James much better than she did and, from my perspective, he came off as a what-he-doesn't-know-won't-hurt-him type of guy.

"You have to say something," she continued. "If the band breaks up, then so be it. Seriously."

I understood. Sara would have loved for the band to fall apart. I'd be sorted into a quaint little apartment within a week, taking out the trash and hanging my keys on a little hook. And yet, despite her motives, what she said made sense.

"Damn, Sara. Why are you always right?"

"Because I'm a woman," she smiled, tilting her head.

Now I knew the right thing to do. The wrong thing still seemed a pretty good option, too.

"I'm right about moving in together, too," she added, changing to an even riskier subject.

"Do we have to talk about that now?"

She put her hands on her hips, the vibe changing. "It's not like I'm asking you to quit the band, Mark."

"That's a good thing," I replied crustily.

Mistake.

"What are you saying?" her tone fell dead away. Sara backed off, and I saw genuine anger in her glare. "You don't think our relationship is worth sacrificing anything for?"

Befuddled by her question, I mistakenly resorted to honesty. "I didn't say that. I just said it's a good thing you aren't asking me to quit."

"Is that so?" She scowled at me. "Oh, okay, I see. You're saying that if you had to choose between me and the band, I'd come second?"

She was making me say it. Had my ego been a bit smaller, I would have known enough to lie.

"I thought you knew that..."

The words brought tears to her eyes.

"I guess I did," Sara looked back at me, her bottom lip quivering a bit. "I guess I always knew I was second best with you, Mark. Your dream always comes first, right? So I might have known it... but you know, it hurts just a little bit more when I hear it come out of your mouth."

"Sara, I didn't mean it like--"

"Forget it, Mark. Just worry about your little band fight..."

Sara began to gather her things. I felt the sudden despair of regret, as though I'd just dropped a diamond ring down the sink.

"What are you doing?"

"I'm going to Danni's," she said, pulling on her clothes.

I slid out of bed and moved to stand between her and the door.

"Sara, why?"

"Look, Mark--I'll call you later." Dressed, she pushed past me and reached for the doorknob. No time to think. I went for the premature apology.

"Wait. Sara, I'm sorry, baby."

She looked up, her face streaked with watery charcoal trails. "You can't say that. You can't say you're sorry yet--it's too soon."

"What?"

Hand on hip. "Mark, you can't just say you're sorry five minutes after you do something and expect it to mean anything! It sounds like you're just apologizing to get out of trouble."

"But I AM sorry," I replied. "Should I lie, and tell you I'm not?"

"No," she said, glaring. "You're supposed to tell me later, so I'll think you've had time to reflect on it."

"But I already reflected," I told her, "and I'm sorry! Really! I'm a really fast reflecter. A speed-reflecter!"

"You're making jokes now," she scolded, her eyes narrowing. "And you're not sorry about how you feel…"

"Well, I'm sorry you're angry, then…"

"I bet!" Sara reached for the doorknob, and I didn't try to stop her.

"I'll call you?"

No answer.

I wanted to run after her, but couldn't. This would require more than a simple apology, and I couldn't think of anything substantial to concede without turning myself into a liar. It's not that I didn't see what was happening or understand what she meant…but I was beginning to have trouble separating the 'what is' from the 'what is yet to be'.

When she met me, I was in the band and little else had changed. And yet, by some unwritten relational commandment, I was now required to move to another level.

My feelings were genuine--truly. I had as much affection for Sara as for all the rest put together. But every part of me was cringing in anticipation of a crisis, a moment where I would be required to proclaim the next level and swear my love forever. As much as I loved her, I knew it would be a lie.

Perhaps I was wrong for thinking I could love her without promising everything. Or for thinking that I could work part-time, juggle fifteen credit hours in college and still play full time with the dudes. Or perhaps, just perhaps, I was wrong for thinking I could juggle them all at once.

I was running, my obligations piled in my arms and the weight of expectation strapped to my back, knowing that if I stumbled I'd surely drop something. Running toward a light, an unknown but brilliant destination that awaited me if I could just keep moving. My pace lagged, my focus more enrapt on carrying my burden than on taking the next step, my eyes straying from the road ahead. And looking back, I realized that I was running toward many lights and not just one, and that by running toward all, I was reaching none.

Sara pictured me working nine-to-five and raising the kids.

Mom and Dad envisioned me directing corporate takeovers.

And James saw me on stage, riding out the headbanger dream for life.

There I was, knowing only that I was running toward a brilliant future and that I couldn't dare stop. I'd been angry at them all for expecting too much of me, but I was beginning to suspect that these expectations were monsters of my own making.

Too many promises, to everyone. Promises like love and loyalty. Things I really meant.

I did want to be a rock star. I did want to graduate college, have a good job and marry a classy woman. And I did love Sara. All at the same time.

Was it so wrong for me to think that I could enjoy the now? After all, I'd never intended to let any of them down...except maybe Sara.

This was the part that hurt me the most. After everything we'd been through, I was telling her I couldn't commit and claiming that I didn't want to lie to her.

In truth, I suppose I'd been lying to her all along.

I'd lied to her every time I let her believe in the dreams that she had for us. She'd been running toward her own light, truly believing I was beside her. Admitting now that I wasn't--this was no noble act.

I couldn't blame her for being angry. There was no excuse for my dreaming and the promises I'd made...but I didn't intend to alter my course. I had to keep running and hope that I'd arrive. I'd come too far to quit now and, though shaken, still genuinely believed that my airy castles could hold together.

Well, at least some of them.

Sara was gone.

MIRACLE MAN

"So what's this guy's name again?"

"Paul Pressman," Ray answered from behind his shades. "He looks like Burt Convy--you can't miss him."

"Burt Convy?"

"You know, the actor on *The Love Boat*. He hosted *Password*, I think."

"Ahh..." Tommy nodded, acting as though he remembered.

We sat five in a booth at the Waffle Hut, drinking too much coffee and waiting for a promoter named Pressman who had no office but apparently had the *Love Boat* look going for him. One of Ray's dubious connections, Paul was presumably going to offer a spot in his massive festival concert.

Local promoters. The delinquent CEO's of the river bottom. Shameless men with alliterative names who deliver hope and huge promises.

Promoter is one of those self-appointed titles, like Agent, Manager, and Consultant. An assumed career. Any one of us can wake up in the morning, make a simple decision over coffee and toast, print up business cards in the afternoon and lay claim to an alleged career by five o'clock. The charade can only continue so far, however, because these titles are earned after they're assumed. Still, anything free will be taken, and the pretenders were everywhere.

Pressman was something of a poser himself. A business poser.

It seemed almost reassuring, knowing that posers existed in other fields as well. Once again, dude philosophy plays out. The concept is universally known and generally despised in varied cultures and religions. Of course, there is a great difference between looking like one and actually being one.

That bleary-eyed morning, we were simply crossing our fingers and hoping that P. Pressman was the real deal.

Three coffee refills and still no sign of him. The table was littered with empty sugar packets, and the waitress was showing repressed rage after not being able to take any food orders.

"Aren't businessmen supposed to be on time?" Randy commented, halfway through his second tabletop drum solo. Randy simply had too much energy to sit still; the diagnosed 'hyperactivity' of his childhood had actually been unrecognized talent.

"When you've got as much money as Paul does," Ray said coolly, "you take your time."

"He'll be here," James seconded, speaking as though he actually knew.

We got lucky, and mere moments after the complaining began, the promoter walked through the front door, briefcase in hand.

Burt Convy all the way, with just a dash of Huckleberry Hound.

Well-dressed? I didn't know a good suit or an expensive watch when I saw one, so I couldn't really tell. The suit was dark. Suit-ish. Businessey.

"Should we, like, shake his hand?" Tommy whispered.

"Duh," James nodded, and five headbangers awkwardly squeezed their way out of the tight booth and stood, ripped-jeaned and fluffed out in the family dining atmosphere to shake hands.

"Hey, Paul."

The promoter showed teeth. "Hello, fellas."

Thinking on our feet, no one offered him the dude handshake. We shook flat-handed, like civilized men, behaving as though we were conducting actual business.

"Mark Magruder," I said, offering him a hand.

"Mark? Paul Pressman." He tested me with a stiff squeeze.

"Tommy."

"Tommy? Paul Pressman."

"Randy--drums."

"Randy? Paul Pressman."

And so on. When the odd round of civility subsided, we stuffed back into the booth. The amazingly tan Paul pulled up a chair to head the table.

"You want some coffee, Paul?" Ray took the lead.

"Yes, actually. I think I will."

"You can have mine," Tommy offered. "It's a new cup and I haven't drank out of it yet..."

James rolled his eyes at me.

"No thanks," Paul politely waved off Tommy's offer. "Actually, I think I'll skip the coffee. So let's see...you boys are Skin Tight. Now, which one of you did I talk to on the phone?"

Ray leaned forward, taking off his sunglasses. "That would be me."

"That's right--Ray Sharp. Well, guys, I guess I should begin by saying that I've heard a lot of good things about your act. The demo is great, but I'll be even happier to hear the album when you've finished with it."

Album? Apparently Ray was doing a little excess promotion.

"You've built a good following, which always helps," Pressman continued, leaning back and crossing his legs politician-style. "And Ray here tells me you're even getting some radio play."

Some? Does once count for some?

"We're pretty psyched about it," Ray nodded.

Paul grinned back. "That's good. I know the feeling. You know, I used to play a little bit--nothing as intense as what you do, but I had my day. Yes, yes. Bass player. Hair down to my ass and everything..."

"Really?"

"Wow."

I pictured a long-haired Burt Convy.

"I go by the sound," Pressman resumed, "and I think you guys are just what I'm looking for. The event is this--an all-day rock festival at an amphitheatre just outside Denver. I think you'd fit great on the card. I'm calling it 'The First Annual Rocky Mountain Rock-fest'! There will be eight or nine bands, and we should be pumping from eleven a.m. to midnight. We're talking about a huge crowd here, guys. In my estimation, I'd call fifteen hundred people a disappointment. I'm thinking more like three thousand. Probably."

Three thousand people? Randy and I exchanged skeptical glances.

"So...you're gonna be serving beer?"

A critical element, granted.

"You bet," Pressman answered, smiling. "We're all set up with a beer sponsorship--two stands at least. We'll be advertising on the radio and in the Sunday paper--I expect advance ticket sales should be huge."

"We're definitely interested," Ray said, displaying his masterful skills of negotiation. "Where exactly on the card would we be playing?"

"Okay...let's see..." Paul opened his briefcase and looked at his notes. "I have you guys warming up Bad Froggy. You'd be on about eight-thirty and off at nine-thirty. By that time, we should have the place rocking. The job pays a thousand."

A thousand? Dollars?

Paul Pressman made 'rocking' sound like a nursing home activity, but his offer made our mouths water. The band went into grateful butt-kissing mode.

"Sounds like a great show."

"No doubt, Paul."

Pressman knew he had us. "So, do you think you fellas would be interested?"

We stared at each other, realizing that with a thousand bucks on the table, no band discussions were needed. We would have played Chernobyl for less.

"Definitely, Paul." Ray stuck his hand out and shook with Pressman again. "I'm just curious--who else is on the bill?"

Pressman returned to his briefcase and shuffled around a bit. "Ah, yes, here it is. So far we've got Red Moon, Tomorrowland, Satan's Stepkids, Doomtown, Hot-n-Nasty, Vandermeer, you guys, and, of course, Bad Froggy."

Vandermeer?

"Did you say Vandermeer?"

"Yes." Pressman nodded, surveying his notes. "They'll be on right before you--seven-fifteen until eight. Write down your address, and I'll send you the contracts within the week."

"Contracts. Cool."

Our eyes widened with repressed satisfaction. Vandermeer would warm US up. Todd Vandermeer would be our opener. Surely this was a mistake in judgment. And though it likely destroyed Paul's credibility by itself, we weren't going to be the ones to point out his error. I couldn't wait to see the look on Todd's face when he realized who he was warming up.

Derek would have enjoyed that moment. He should have been there.

Juiced on caffeine and a bump of anticipation, we said goodbye to Paul and ordered food, singing Ray's praises. Finally, our fortune seemed to be turning. Ray's half-truths and claims of friendship were forgotten in wake of big exposure and a thousand dollar payday. Even better, we'd be topping Vandermeer.

I held on to my dark secret that night, still gator-wrestling with the moral dilemma. After such a long stretch of strained hope, it was good to look forward to something again. James was as happy as I'd ever seen him, and Tommy's routine had returned to normal. Things were finally recovering, and I couldn't bring myself to rain on this much-needed parade.

So I rationalized. Maybe Tommy had learned his lesson. Maybe he'd had an attack of conscience after he'd been caught and was recanting his sins! It would have made things so much simpler if I could have believed it.

To be honest, I was hoping Sandy and James would self-destruct over some unrelated topic. This was the simple answer. The secret would die with their relationship and the band would continue. We'd be rid of Sandy's treachery, and Tommy's secret would be classified in the interest of band security. Wishful thinking. Sandy had a good thing at the band house; she wasn't going anywhere.

And just as I'd decided to keep the whole thing quiet, another horrifying possibility came to mind.

If James happened to catch Tommy and Sandy in the act, my goal of protecting Tommy would be meaningless. Not only that-- James would ask a hundred fire-breathing questions and, to lighten their culpability, Sandy and Tommy would give away Sara. The trail would inevitably lead to my own implication in the cover-up.

I knew the facts but pushed it. I gambled that the veil of secrecy would be maintained. I gave myself until after the Rock-fest to decide, then crammed my worries deep down, trying not to think about Sara, college, or cheating bass players. It would be all about the band now, and I was doing the best thing for everyone involved. Fluke or not, we were topping Vandermeer.

Dirty Deeds Done Dirt Cheap

We'd realized going in that Ray was a well-known figure in the local rock circles. Without question, it was one of the key factors in his passing the audition. We wanted some recognition, some connections---and playing with a notable local rocker would lend associative credibility to the rest of us.

Ray Sharp. Eighties metal guy. The epitome of the scene. Our golden goose.

As for the connections, the jury was still out, but the Rock-fest thing would help. As for credibility, we were, admittedly, being taken more seriously as a band, and thus considered better musicians. Odd, how without ever practicing, one can gain musical clout. Apparently, you're only as good as the people you play with.

And recognition? Oh, we were getting recognized. Or perhaps I should say: Ray was getting recognized. By ex-girlfriends, ex-wives, and all the new men in their lives. He was also being recognized by rival band members, soundmen, and guys whose sister had been dumped. Everyone in the big bad world knew him, and we were realizing that they all seemed to use the same word to describe him:

Asshole.

Luckily, he'd never lived in Boulder before, so Ray's anonymity was far more secure at the band house. A trip to the Denver clubs, however, was an invitation to disaster. Inevitably, we would be flipped off or shouted at by a drunken lioness. The vixens from his past were seemingly everywhere, most of them war-painted squaws who started beating the war drums at the mere sight of him. If a convenient biker boyfriend was available, then Ray would have a guy in his face, primed and ready to kick ass. At just over a buck forty, Ray would back down every time.

Each time it happened, we'd drill Ray with questions, curious to know what he'd done to infuriate the world. He'd routinely lower his head, shrug, and tell us it was 'just a bunch of bullshit'. When we did get an explanation, it would be vague and dubious, and Ray would come out looking like the unfortunate victim of bimbo treachery. Apparently, the guy had horrible luck where 'a bunch of bullshit' was concerned.

As the band, of course, his bullshit was our bullshit.

A month earlier we had some unexpected guests, two utterly brutal looking bikers who were quite plain about wanting to see Ray. He bailed out the bathroom window just in time, not returning till morning. The bikers sat in on a long rendition of "Smoke on the Water," but never told us why they'd come. We let them play Ray's guitar.

Odd, really. Despite the outrageous clothes, Ray always seemed like a pretty mild mannered guy to me. As it turned out, he was a habitual heartbreaker.

A romantic sociopath. A man too pretty for his own good. We'd all committed a few amorous errors, and no one I knew, male or female, could say that they'd treated everyone as they should have. But I never had an ex defile me the way that these women cut at Ray. They hated him with the kind of scorn Shakespeare wrote about.

The guy was infamous. Hated. Hunted and pursued. You don't really understand infamy until you're connected with someone who's come down with a case of it.

The night before the festival, Ray said he had a confession to make. We braced ourselves.

Here's the gist of it: Two or more members of a death-metal band named Satan's Stepkids wanted to do permanent damage to Ray's face. Coincidentally, the Stepkids were booked to play the Rock-fest.

He doubted there would be any guns or knives involved, but he wanted to warn us.

What do you say to that? Thanks? Okay, dude? No problem, man, I'll wear my bulletproof half-shirt?

Had it been Derek, James would've freaked. But Ray was still technically the new guy, and he represented something different to James. We all told him not to worry about it and resumed rehearsal, more than a bit distracted.

We'd worked hard for this gig. We'd overhauled our new originals and practiced the hell out of the old ones. We'd whittled our song list down to the absolute best shit we had and sorted strategically. If Vandermeer made us look bad, at least we'd know we went to the wall. With any luck, we'd manage to remain a couple of steps ahead of Ray's reputation.

We got to the site around eleven a.m. as instructed.

"This place is like a horse ring," Randy commented as soon as he stepped out of the car, already disappointed. "Bonanza city."

"It's a rodeo pen," I commiserated. "Some amphitheater."

The arena was located in rural prairie country, looking more suited to barrel races and bronco riding. Little more than a high-school football stadium with no grass, the place smelled like horse-shit and fresh air. The crowd was still quite small, just specks of glitter on the dung-colored background.

"So...where are all the people?"

"Nobody comes out this early," James looked the place over, nodding. "The crowd will keep growing as the day goes on. By the time we hit the stage, I guarantee the place will be packed. Damn... nice setup..."

Admittedly, the stage looked impressive. Elevated, twenty-five by twenty, already loaded with sound equipment and amps. Above the floor a glorious lighting rig loomed, and beside it stood two Stonehenge-worthy stacks of booming cabinets, book-ending the stage with twin speaker towers. The first band was finishing their set-up to the strains of Sabbath's "Heaven and Hell."

We walked to the rear of the stage, finding a congested dirt lot filled with vans and stuffed trousers where eight bands were attempting to load-in simultaneously. Bangers and bangettes flitted about the place, some unloading trucks while others waited behind to guard their gear. The drums and amps sat in line on the open ground behind the stage, gathering dust and warming in the sun. The place looked like a Saudi music store.

"We probably don't have to load out yet," James said. "Tell Lonnie to park it. We'll wait for some of these bands to clear out."

"So we're waiting to load in?"

"Yeah, might as well. I don't want my shit getting all dusty."

"It's getting way hot out here," Randy announced. "Lead me to the beer trucks."

"No doubt."

We searched the horizon, finding no beer trucks. From the stage, Red Moon began their set.

"Man, I feel sorry for those guys." I looked again to the front of the stage. "No crowd at all."

"No doubt," Randy chuckled. "They're gonna get so sunburned up there..."

"So where's Paul?"

"Who knows," Ray shrugged, looking a bit timid as he scanned the area.

Lonnie and Tommy approached, having found a spot for the truck. They looked massively baked. Lonnie drank from a two-liter bottle of his latest concoction, 'The Nectar of the Metal Gods'.

"Sup, guys?"

"Enough fresh air out here, or what?" Lonnie chuckled.

"I saw Sara and Danni on the way in," Tommy told me.

"Oh yeah?"

"They'll be down front, I'm sure. Are you guys still broken up?"

It struck me the wrong way. Tommy, the guy who couldn't seem to keep it zipped up with his friends' women, was asking me if Sara and I were broken up.

"You looking for a date?" I asked him, snipping.

"Oh, no, man. No way," he replied, catching my drift. "Nothing like that. I was just curious…"

"Well, we're not broken up yet," I said.

"So…you think Vandermeer is here already?"

"They'd better be," Randy mused. "They gotta get their asses up on stage and warm us up! Man, it's wicked hot out here…"

"No doubt, dude." I squinted up into the wide blue sky, wishing for a cloud.

"Hey Mark--speak of the devil."

The lovely Todd Vandermeer and his drummer strolled by, blonde and butched out, not even acknowledging our presence. Todd didn't utter a single word, but I could recognize the unpleasant smell of resentment. The advertisements had been out for weeks, and Todd was aware of the billing order.

"He must be burning up," James commented as soon as he stepped out of range.

"Oh, he's pissed alright," I commented, feeling the glow. "Now all we have to do is kick his ass!"

So far, no sign of Satan's Stepkids. Ray was being cautiously quiet, his eyes continually searching the crowd. He seemed genuinely and understandably spooked, and as I looked over at Ray, I wondered how we'd manage to get him through nine hours of close calls. Eventually, his speed metal enemies were bound to find him.

I was right. As it turned out, 'eventually' arrived only ten minutes later. We never saw it coming.

The blow came from behind, clocking Ray in the side of the head.

Ray went down immediately, covering up.

Satan's favorite stepkid, a monstrous leather-clad thug named Dirk stepped forward and began throwing down fists. With a name like Dirk, it was bound to hurt.

Thwap-thwap-wup-thwap!

In films, fights seem to last forever. In reality, they're sudden and short, messy little explosions of rage. The guy delivered at least five good blows before we could react.

Lonnie and James moved to pull Dirk's flailing leather bulk away from Ray.

Stepkid number two, an unnamed chapped mosher, grabbed Randy's arm to hold him back. Not appreciating the gesture, Randy turned on him and pushed.

James caught one of Dirk's zippered elbows in the mouth and subsequently fell on his ass.

The sight provoked Lonnie, who leapt up to throw a muscled arm around the bleached behemoth's throat, choking him. Putting all those gym reps to good use, Lonnie squeezed.

The fists stopped flying. Dirk's hands came to his throat. Ray scrambled out from under the assault, his big hair streaked blood red.

Stepkid number three counted the numbers and decided to back away. Tommy and I weren't imposing individually, but two on one was a different matter. I felt fortunate that the other two stepkids were absent.

After choking out Dirk for an appropriate amount of time, Lonnie threw him to the ground, poised and ready to continue if necessary. The big guy didn't challenge him.

"This isn't over, Sharp," Dirk shouted, sounding like a bad actor. Excluding Ray, the numbers were still five on three, and the behemoth wisely backed away, rubbing his tattooed throat. Randy broke his death-stare, rejoining us around the battered Ray.

Slowly, Satan's Stepkids crept back to the mini-van from which they came, grumbling profanity and promising a rematch.

"Next time, they'll bring the whole band."

"Bring it on," Lonnie shouted, bristling with testosterone and nectar. "That guy is a pussy."

"You okay, dude?"

Ray staggered to his feet, blood dripping from his nose. A gash under his right eyebrow bled in a steady drip down his jaw. I'd seen him take two blows to the head and countless others to the body and arms as he tried to defend himself.

"Ray...man, you okay?"

He spit, reaching up a hand to check his teeth. "Yeah. Just fuckin' great."

"Here's your shades, dude. They're broken."

"I know," Ray winced, touching the gash and looking at his finger. "They got drilled into my head…"

"Where did those guys come from?" Randy's switch had been flipped as well, and now he wanted to fight. "I should have raged on that little fuck."

"Tell me about it," Lonnie shook his head. "We should have gone for it, dude! They deserved it for taking a cheap shot like that!"

We all began bitching at once.

"Settle down," James shouted finally. "We're attracting a crowd here. Let's go back to the truck. Ray, can you walk, dude?"

Ray was still on planet gone. "Yeah, yeah."

Tommy helped Ray take his first steps and soon we neared the refuge of the truck, eager to find some shade. Good old Paul Pressman was waiting for us.

"Great…it's the promoter…"

"So? What can he do to us?"

"Why else would he be waiting at our truck? He heard about the fight."

"We don't know that," James reassured us. "He could be dropping off our check for all we know. Or the contracts."

"You mean, the contracts never came?" I asked in vehement whisper, handing my shades to Ray.

"No," James confessed.

Paul was on us before I could complain.

"Hey guys!"

"Hey, Paul," James did the talking. "Just checking out the stage. The setup looks great."

Paul cleared his throat. "Yeah, thanks. It's coming together. Ooh, what happened there? Are you okay, Ray?"

Ray grunted and nodded, giving Paul a half-salute.

"What happened, guys?"

"Just a little altercation," I said. "Unintended, of course. We'll be fine by gig time..."

"But you have all your band members present?"

"Yes."

Paul nodded at me. "That's good, because that's what I wanted to talk with you guys about...you see, Tomorrowland isn't here yet, and they're up next. I need you guys to swap spots with them and head up to the stage now."

N-now?

Getting cracked by Dirk would have been more pleasurable than listening to promoter Paul say these words. The rug had just been snatched from beneath us, and even James was speechless.

"I hate to do this," Paul tried to be sincere, "but I want you to know you'll still get paid the same amount."

"What about the other bands?" I asked. "Can't one of them switch?"

"Well, Doomtown isn't even here yet," Paul said, looking at his hands as though he were adding numbers. "And I already spoke with Todd from Vandermeer and Kim from Hot-n-Nasty, and both bands are still missing members. Other than Satan's Stepkids, you're the only complete band here. They just told me they needed time to re-string their guitars. They'll play after you."

I was stunned. Vandermeer would get the prime spot after all.

"Wait," James stepped forward, his cool nearly blown. "Why can't we play after the kids?"

"Because I'm sick of screwing with this lineup," Paul raised his voice, his bronzed features frowning. "So you guys either play now for the original price, or I give you two hundred dollars to go on after the Stepkids. How's that?"

"What about the contracts?"

"The contracts and the check are in the mail, and I'll take that as a yes." Paul looked at his watch. "Now get your asses up to the stage. Have fun, guys."

We didn't know whether to scream, bitch, or get in the truck and get the hell out of there. It didn't take long for the scent of money to lure us over to the stage.

Caught in a Mosh

Accompanied by a downpour of sunshine and the smell of fresh dung, we took the stage. No sound check, no waiting time, just 'set up and play'.

James started the first tune, hammering out the riff to "G-String" and taking his position stage left.

I walked to the microphone, the drums kicking in behind me. The bright sun drowned out the colored lights, searing my club-anemic skin.

Twenty or thirty in the crowd, maximum. I could have counted them on my fingers and still hit my cue in time for the verse.

I started singing, the massive monitors spitting my voice back at me. They were mixed to the perfect volume, the point where I felt as though the sound was coming out of the speaker instead of my mouth. I leaned on Jim and tried to get into it.

The first song ended with a polite golf clap from the picnicking crowd. I turned to Ray, checking on his condition. He gave me the okay sign and stomped his pedal board a couple times.

"Alright Rock-fest!" I said into the mic, my amplified voice booming out and then dissipating in the wind.

How to rouse the crowd that doesn't exist? Professionalism seemed to suggest that I should act like a crowd actually existed, do my normal thing, and ignore the fact that I was playing for an audience of dung-beetles and earwigs.

It was just as well. Ray still staggered with the aftereffects of blunt force trauma, and James' lip had swollen to the size of a steak fry. There's no telling how big it would have grown by nine.

We played on, focusing on our parts. By this time, our friends realized the timing error and were appearing in the crowd. Sara and Danni stood with Lonnie, arms crossed and observing. Sandy and her bimbo bunch seemed nomadic, apparently trying to find a sexy place to stand.

We'd just finished "Skin Tight" when I heard the heckling begin. I looked over to my left and saw Dirk and Satan's other stepkids massing near Ray's side of the stage.

"Fuck you, Sharp! Your band sucks!"

Ray was past the point of further cowering. He held out his middle finger, spitting at them and starting the next song.

Dirk lunged for the edge of the stage, but was intercepted by the bouncers. Ray stared menacingly as the massive security dudes escorted Dirk and his clones back to the staging area.

"He's real brave when he's got bouncers to hold him back," Tommy said in my ear, his voice barely audible above the mix.

I nodded, thinking about how Satan's Stepkids would be loading in as we loaded out.

"Get ready to rock!"

The set plodded on ineffectually, the crowd never getting any bigger. I still hadn't spotted a beer truck, and the parking prairies were virtually desolate. It didn't feel so bad knowing we could pin all the blame on Paul. At the time, however, my thoughts were primarily focused on the five leather-clad poser Satanists who were waiting offstage to strike.

To be honest, I still don't know why they wanted to hurt Ray so badly. You'd think the 'why' would have been important to us, yet I don't recall anyone ever asking about it. I guess, after the bathroom window thing, we just accepted it as par for Ray's course and needed no other explanation. The guy was simply a health hazard.

At least the fight didn't happen on stage.

Satan's Stepkids were waiting by Lonnie's truck. Dirk saw us and immediately began striding forward, growling like a Gallic berserker. The clones fell in behind him, wide-eyed and snarling. All talk and no action, this guy.

It was like a medieval battleground, without armor. It was the O.K. Corral, without pistols. It was West Side Story, without singing and snappy dance moves. Without saying a word, we all sat down the equipment and stepped forward, lining up.

The two lines collided, with Dirk heading straight for Ray, arms swinging. Ray held up his arms and deflected a blow. Lonnie intervened with a fist of his own, cracking Dirk in the ribs and swinging up at his chin.

The shit was on.

Randy's nemesis leapt at him, and the two fell to the dirt. I looked over to see Tommy and James, similarly occupied with dance partners of their own.

Thwack.

A fist connected with my cheek, sending me to a knee.

I should have been paying attention to Stepkid number five. Regaining my feet and expecting a flurry of fists, I looked up to see a black-spandexed, ebony-haired, tattooed, high-heeled speed metal chick.

Satan's fifth stepkid was female. What's worse, she wanted to fight.

"Come on, dick!" she taunted with blackened lips, fists raised and ready. A crowd was beginning to gather.

I didn't want to. I tried to ignore her, moving to help Randy.

Thwack.

Yet another shot.

Thwack.

Followed by another.

Bright pain erupted from my nose. I was getting my ass kicked by a metal diva. My eyes watering, I turned on her.

I never hit a woman before, and I haven't since. But, with the jeers of the crowd and her verbal abuse ringing in my good ear, I willingly chose to step across the line and rid myself of this devilish vixen once and for all.

I ran up intending to swing at her, flaking out at the last moment and merely pushing her to the ground.

She snarled, examining the split in her tights.

"Chill out," I told her, turning back to Randy and the others.

Again, I underestimated the resolve of a vixen.

I heard the leather creak as she stood up. By the time I turned around, she was whacking me with her spike-heeled shoe.

"You tore my best pair, you dick!"

Relentless pecking that left a distinctive square heel mark. I tried unsuccessfully to subdue her weapon hand.

"Cops!" I heard someone yell.

The fight dissolved. Stepkid number five ceased hitting me and offered a few choice words before backing away into the lot. I looked around, finding only Randy. We could hear the sirens now.

"Where to?" he asked.

"Back to the stage, to load out the rest of our shit," I said, shaking it off, craning my neck to search for authority figures. "Just walk normal and do our thing. Everybody here looks alike."

Sara walked up to me just as we were reaching the staging area.

"Mark, are you okay?" she asked with a wry grin.

"Don't be funny," I told her, looking away. "I've got to help load out so they can get the next band on."

"I'm not here to hold you up," she said. "Go ahead. I just wanted to say hi. I must say, I thought it was cute how you kept trying to ignore her and she kept beating on you…"

She laughed.

My head pounding, I couldn't help but smile. "Don't rub it in. Did you see the set?"

"Of course."

"And?"

"And how about I tell you later?" she offered. "I'll come by your place and we can talk…"

"Yeah," I replied absently, my attention stolen by a glimpse of blonde hair and familiar cheetah spandex. "Okay…"

As though suffering the continued wrath of the metal gods, insult was literally added to injury. Todd Vandermeer and his band of prissy grunts approached, gloating with poser amusement. They were strolling by on cue, killing time before their eight o'clock slot.

"Rough set, huh?" Todd asked, staring directly at me, his tone dripping with jerk.

I wanted to tell him to piss off, but given my humiliating circumstance, I was held speechless in concession. I took a breath and turned away, headed for the truck.

Ray was already in the passenger seat, slouched down and unresponsive.

I expected a gloom of defeat from the others as well, yet they didn't seem too affected by the ordeal. Instead, they chatted like cops after a big bust. Randy was already making jokes, and Tommy was laughing. Even James seemed oddly content--perhaps he was feeling guilty about his contractual lies. Whatever the reason, I caught surprisingly little grief about my run-in with hell's stepdaughter. The jokes would come later.

Sunburned and bruised, we loaded the remainder of our gear into the truck, eager to leave the Rock-fest behind. Soon we were free of the cow-pie air and headed back home, nursing our injuries and expecting a paycheck that would never arrive.

HERE I GO AGAIN

The post-fight discussion lasted for hours. The consensus held that we were winning the fight when the cops arrived…and that I had been laughably assaulted by a speed-metal bimbo.

Lonnie suggested that we go out and hit the clubs, diagnosing alcohol as the cure for Ray's ills. Despite his swollen lip, James agreed to go, unwilling to allow Ray in public without some kind of supervision.

I remained behind to wait for Sara. For some unknown reason, Tommy stayed home as well. It felt odd sitting there, watching videos with Tommy, thinking about how much was left unspoken as we bullshitted about meaningless things. Half-pickled and nursing my sunburn, I couldn't think of how to begin.

He stood to make a phone call and re-entered the room wearing a smile. "I got a surprise for you, dude," he said, strutting. "You're gonna freak."

"Oh yeah? What's that?"

"Tabitha's in town," he said proudly. "And she's on her way over here."

The words held me motionless for a moment. Everything in my world shifted slightly to the left. Jim toasted me with a fresh bottle of Jack.

"Seriously?" I asked, in need of confirmation.

"I'm serious, dude," Tommy returned, flipping his hair and checking it in the hall mirror. "Yeah, I guess her marriage didn't work out or whatever. Anyway, she says she's here to stay. Moving to Denver, actually. Asking about you, too."

"How is she getting here?"

"Uncle Pete's bringing her, then I'm going out with him. You guys can come if you want, but I expect Tabitha will decide that."

Tabitha's desire to see me was genuine, no doubt--but judging by memory, Tommy seemed a bit too happy to be setting us up.

"Oh yeah?" I shrugged. "That's cool, Tommy."

He tilted his head, looking at me. "Shit, dude--I thought you'd be psyched."

"Oh, I am. I'm way psyched. It's just that things aren't, you know, finished yet with Sara. She was saying something about coming over tonight--"

"I thought you two were broken up."

"We are, technically," I replied, not knowing how to explain it. "This is just one of those 'talking' things, you know--just working things out…"

"Ah," Tommy nodded, "the post-relationship booty call."

"Not this time," I shook my head. "If Sara says she's going to talk--"

"If she wanted to talk, she wouldn't be coming over at midnight, dude. When did she say she was coming?"

"She didn't say a specific time."

"And when did you talk to her?"

"At the gig."

He smirked. "That was hours ago, man. She would have called by now. Anyway, if you want to wait for her, I understand." He stared at the television. "I guess I'll just have to tell Tabitha you're taken, because once you and Sara sleep together, you'll be back together again."

He was baiting me with Tabitha and trying to lure me away from Sara with talk of commitment. My defenses weakened and wobbled, bombarded by newly restored images of Tabitha.

"If I was you," Tommy continued, "I'd just blow off Sara tonight, dude. You guys are broken up, right? So you don't owe her anything. Seriously. It's not even like you're cheating on her!"

"Oh yeah?" I asked, my mind shifting. "Not like some people…"

He looked away, breaking the stare. "Look man, I know we haven't talked about this whole Sandy thing, but I want you to know, I appreciate you not telling James…"

Just like that, he mentioned it. He apparently considered my silence a personal favor. The thought made me angry.

"You do, huh?"

"Sure," he replied. "I mean, you could have told him, but you know just as well as I do that Sandy's a total whore, right? I mean, I couldn't resist. You know, there are some things that are more important than friendship. The band is bigger than all this little shit. Besides, chicks are chicks--you and I know that."

"So…you're not even sorry about it?"

Tommy paused. "Sure, I'm sorry about it…only I don't think it's such a big deal."

Not a big deal? I wasn't liking the answers I was receiving.

I turned on him. "That's bullshit, Tommy."

"What?"

"It's a really big deal, and you know it!" I was angry now, and spouting. "First of all, James is your friend. But more than that, you're risking the band, dude--and that involves all of us! Shit, dude--you might as well have been fucking ALL our girlfriends!"

"Come on, man--James is better off without her. Sandy's a little bitch, and I'm not the only guy she's screwing around with. When you think about it, I was doing him a favor."

"Don't even start with that shit!" I yelled, stepping toward him, intent on making him see. "It's not about Sandy, dude! It's not about girls at all! It's about being able to fucking trust each other--keeping our promise. You made a promise, man--we all did. And to make it work, we ALL have to keep it straight. It's bigger than just you--"

"All right--shit!" Tommy put his hands to his ears. "You're right, dude! Fine! But don't go thinking I was screwing with the band. I love the band, man."

"I know you do...but this shit is harsh."

He slouched, shaking his head. "I didn't get any chicks till I started jamming with you guys. You know that, don't you? I was a total loser, dude. Now I'm like beating 'em off by the dozen, and I got the band to thank for it! I know it was stupid to do Sandy, but you gotta know I wasn't trying to screw over James, or hurt the band or whatever you think, man. So I get carried away some-times...so what? And I swear, Sandy was the one putting the moves on me!"

"Yeah...but you kept going..."

"Shit, Mark! I said I was sorry! What the hell do you want from me?"

I don't think I'd ever really unleashed on Tommy, and I didn't expect him to be arguing with cousin Tabitha as a shield. But some-how, I felt like I was serving my purpose.

"You should tell James," I said to him, watching his hesitant reaction.

"I can't man," he looked down. "That won't help anything...I thought you were worried about the band..."

I'd stirred his remorse. If I intended to tell James, now was the moment to reveal my intentions.

Rarely was I able to pinpoint one of life's crux moments--much less to understand it as it was happening. But at this instant, I realized that my next comment had the potential to alter our futures. I tried to keep cousin Tabitha out of the equation.

"He'll find out somehow," I said, leaving the rest to horrible chance. "You should tell him yourself."

Tommy smiled at me like I was his blood brother. "Thanks, Mark. I know this kind of shit makes you mad, but it'll be history soon. I'm just glad it was you and not Derek. He would have told James for sure…"

This last bit was what really got me. And even though I knew I should say something more, I held my tongue under the strictest of orders from my libido. By the time Tabitha arrived, I felt pitiful.

Freewheel Burnin'

Tabitha arrived just after midnight at 12:06.

After a few minutes of small talk, Tommy and Uncle Pete left at 12:17.

Sara arrived with a bottle of wine at 12:41.

But I get ahead of myself.

Tabitha still looked baberiffic. She wore one of those little bitty leather jackets and an even smaller T-shirt underneath. Trailer-made silver hoop earrings and bombshell cherry lips. Her jeans were painted-on-perfect, and her expertly blown locks fell demurely past her shoulders. She'd dressed with a purpose tonight.

Tabitha explained that she was supposed to come to the Rock-fest. She'd been called off by Tommy after the gig went to hell.

"Do you want something to drink?" I asked her as soon as we were alone, feeling ugly and awkward. "We've got beer."

She followed me into the kitchen. "So I hear you had quite the eventful day…"

"Yeah." I put a hand to the sore spot on my forehead. "Brutal, actually."

"I hope I made it a little better."

"Most definitely," I replied, fetching the brews. "To tell you the truth, this is the best part of my day."

"I'm glad," Tabitha cooed, moving too close for talking. "Tell me something, Mark. Have you...thought about me at all, over the years?"

"Of course," I inched backward, steeped in the smell of her perfume. "You were the one who never returned phone calls."

"I know," she said, looking down. "I'm sorry about that, Mark. Really. I was just too close to my wedding to be tempted--and you were tempting. I guess it was selfish of me, not telling you. I just wanted to enjoy a night without having to be...me. You know?"

"I understand," I said, her divinely scented skin telling me that bygones were just that. "I was more disappointed than mad..."

"There was no escape for me," she lamented. "You know, when you get married like I did, you find out that weddings aren't about the bride and groom. Nope--it was about my mom's dress, my grandma's ring, my dad's truck...it's like your wedding day is the one day that everyone gets to totally nose into your relationship. I swear, everyone else was more excited about it than me! What was done was done, though. I just had to give my marriage a try."

"So...it didn't work out?" I asked, fishing for information. "Tommy said something about your getting a divorce."

She nodded dramatically. "I just couldn't live with him anymore. He was SO possessive, Mark. You wouldn't believe how jealous he got. I was his perfect little wife, and it was like he wanted to keep me locked in the bedroom all day!"

I could have guessed that one. Gorgeous woman/insanely jealous man--the formula was legendary. Knowing Tabitha, the guy sounded pretty normal to me. She possessed the kind of beauty that could regress even the most evolved of our gender.

"Really?" I said blankly, not knowing how much to ask. "How terrible for you."

"I thought he would change, you know? I thought it would get better, but it didn't."

I suddenly felt like a character in a soap opera. Tabitha's dialogue seemed cardboard stale.

"Once a dog, always a dog," I answered with the stock talk-show response, wanting only to touch her and wondering how much history I'd have to listen to. My eyes were doing laps on her chest between sympathetic glances into her eyes.

"And then," she said, coming in for another close pass, "the day I left him, you know who the first person I thought of was?"

Let me guess...me?

"Who?" I asked ignorantly.

She exhaled in my ear and moved in to kiss me. "You, of course."

Her lips felt different than Sara's. Not bad, necessarily, but different. Good, actually. She felt good in my arms. I kept kissing her, moving my hands around and down her back, stopping when I got to her--

Boom-boom.

A knock on the front door.

The only person who ever knocked was--

Sara.

Sara!

Shit.

My libido shrieked, threw on a robe and hid under the bed. Jim laughed, zipping up his pants and looking for a cigarette.

"Oh shit..."

I wondered how I could be so stupid.

"What?"

I turned, ignoring the California scent. "Tabitha...I know this is fucked up, but you've got to hide. Err, not really hide--just go downstairs, okay? Go downstairs to my room and close the door. I'll be down there in a few minutes. Okay?"

It didn't take Tabitha long to figure out what was going on. She'd been to dental assistant college, and she knew a thing or two about painful extractions.

I waited for her to complete the high-heeled journey down stairs before opening the door.

Sara.

Of course. She looked amazing.

"Hey you," she stood on the porch, cradling bottle of wine. "I'm from the Post, and I'm looking for the inter-gender kickboxing champ…"

I smiled, touching my tender eye. "Hey now, I didn't kick her!"

"What took so long? Were you asleep?"

"Uh, yeah," I rubbed my eyes a bit. "I'm really wiped out."

"You look really sunburned. I'll put some lotion on it for you while we drink this wine…"

Sara moved to step into the house. I blocked her way.

"What are you doing?" She looked at me, laughing. "Let me in, mister."

"I just don't feel too good," I said, doing my best to seem tired. Already I sounded as guilty as I felt.

"You've been sick before. I think your pride is bruised." She smiled a what-a-cute-little-boyfriend-you-are smile. "Don't worry, I'll make it better. Come on. Move…"

"I just really think maybe we should do this another night."

Her smile vanished, and her eyes leapt up to meet mine.

"What's going on, Mark?"

She scanned my face, and I looked down. "Nothing, nothing. I just think we should wait…after all, we have to talk and everything…"

"We don't have to talk tonight," she answered, her tone drooping. "I just wanted to be with you, that's all. I missed you, Mark."

I felt like a piece of shit. My heart was shrinking inside me, and my conscience was bearing far more than its maximum burden. I was king hypocrite, righteously damning Tommy with one hand and waving Tabitha inside with the other. And worst of all, I was now hurting Sara. Like everything else, I regretted it immediately.

"I miss you too," I told her, the only honest thing I'd said since she arrived. "I just can't do this right now."

I'm not quite sure what it was, but at that moment, Sara's suspicion went into overdrive, her sixth sense bursting out into dissonant song.

"You've got somebody in there, don't you?"

I gave her the 'surely you're joking' face.

"Of course not. Don't be ridiculous."

Apparently, I wasn't very convincing

"Let me come in, then," she said, calling my bluff immediately.

"I told you--I'm tired and I want to go to sleep."

"And I told YOU," she shouted back, raising her voice to neighborhood watch levels. "Let me in the damn house, Mark. I'll only be five minutes. I need to use your bathroom."

"You don't trust me," I said, digging myself deeper into hypocrisy. "I can't let you in just to satisfy your little jealous fantasies! It's the point of the thing."

"You're pissing me off, Mark. And you're fucking hiding someone in there! So let me in!"

She tried to push past me into the house, but I had a foot wedged and she couldn't get through. Then I said yet another thing that I shouldn't have.

"This is dumb, Sara. We're broken up anyway...aren't we?"

She stopped fighting and backed up, pushing the dramatic pause.

"Trust you…shit!" She looked at me with a melancholy glare. "You know, you've got a good heart, Mark, but you never take a stand. You sway with any little breeze as long as it feeds your dream! You'd sacrifice everything for it, wouldn't you? You'd give up school, and friends, and me…"

"Sara--"

"I love your dream, Mark. I do! You may not know it, but I love you for being that kind of person. But if your tomorrow doesn't come, you've got to be content with today! And today, you're damn lucky I'm here. You used to think so, at least…"

"Sara, I don't wa--"

"Shut up!" she snapped, hardening again. "Now I don't know who's in there with you tonight, but if you ever want to see me again, you'll tell her to get her little bitch-ass out of my bed and send her home! Listen, Mark: If my phone rings within a half-hour, I'll answer it. If not, then don't ever bother calling again."

Sara turned her back and marched back across the lawn to her car, leaving me speechless in the doorway. As she reached her car, she turned back toward the porch.

"Oh, by the way, here's a little present for you and your girlfriend. Enjoy!"

With that, she hurled the bottle of wine at me. It landed on the porch and shattered, sending purple streams creeping down the cracks.

Sara's car shrieked out into traffic, carrying her away.

My conscience stepped down from its podium and took three thunderous strides across my personality, sending my libido scrambling for a dark corner. Jim pointed at all three and laughed even harder. He shrugged at me and staggered off to find the bar.

I turned and stepped inside the door. Still reeling from her words, I looked at the clock and headed downstairs, prepared to tell a few more lies. It wouldn't be the first time, but it might have been the last.

"Tabitha?"

She was sitting on the bed, beer in hand, looking through my photo scrapbook. "Hi. Everything okay?"

"Sure, it's okay. But I have something I need to talk to you about..."

"Well, it's pretty obvious you have a girlfriend, or at least a jealous ex," she looked moist, as though she'd applied even more lipstick.

"Well, yeah. I was going to tell you--"

"It's okay," she said, closing in again, reaching up a red-nailed bronze skinned hand to touch my hair. "I don't mind."

She didn't mind. Good Lord, I was having a wet dream and a nightmare at the same time! Jim stepped forward, bottle in hand, looking over his sunglasses and grinning a king-snake grin. 'You'd better hurry up, man...'

I glanced at the clock. 27 minutes left. Tick tock.

My conscience roared, tying my libido to a chair and asking Jim to hold it at gunpoint.

"Tabitha, I can't."

"You can't?"

"No--I don't mean I 'can't' can't. I guess I mean I don't want to..."

She thought I was teasing, and turned on the smile again. "Are you sure about that?"

I didn't have time to play semantic games all night. Beautiful or not, I decided to lay it all on her at once.

"I'm sure. Look--here's the deal. I'm with this great girl, and we've been together for a while now. I just found out, here tonight, with you, that she's the one. You know you're beautiful, Tabitha, and I swear this has nothing to do with you..."

"Mark. Mark. Mark, I understand." The smile changed, but remained.

Partial relief. Tick tock.

"That's good," I told her. "Because you're going to need to understand just a little more. You see, she gave me an ultimatum, and if I don't call her in twenty-five minutes, I'm going to lose her."

"Go ahead, call her," she said. "I'll be quiet."

"No, see--you're supposed to be gone when I call her."

"She won't know I'm here."

Sara would know. She would use her supernatural girl powers to find out the truth. She'd hear it in my guilty voice. And I expected the conversation to go on all night if necessary. Future or not, I could still fit Sara in--a little quiet convincing would change her mind about the co-habitation issue and put us back where we were.

I desperately wanted Tabitha out of the house.

"Well," I said, "It's really the point of the thing. It's great to see you and all--just bad timing. Really bad timing, actually."

Tabitha was finally getting a bit miffed. She cocked a glossed lip in scowl. "Well, I don't have a car. How am I supposed to get home?"

I looked at the clock. 24 minutes and change.

Tick tock.

"I could take you back to your Uncle Pete's in my car."

Her gorgeous eyes narrowed. "You won't make it back in time."

I would. I had to.

"Sure I will. Again, I'm really sorry."

"Whatever..."

I drove with desperate focus, like A.J. Foyt on crystal meth. I pushed the car and myself to the limit, one eye glued to the clock as it tick-tocked my reality away.

Streetlights and traffic cooperated, blurring into rainbows in my wake.

I dropped Tabitha off at Uncle Pete's, keeping it short. She seemed bothered, but didn't offer any parting shots.

Now, to get home. I looked at the clock. 10 minutes and counting.

My throat tightened a bit as I realized the odds were against me. It would take an amazing display of driving to get me back in time. But, like the mother who finds the strength to lift a car, I was in possession of some pure, heroic, page three of the Post adrenalin. The good stuff.

I cranked the Megadeth and hauled ass. Parts of the trip are still fuzzy; I still seem to have event amnesia from an adrenalin overload. Like a drunk who can't remember finding his way home from the bar, I have no recollection of how exactly I made it. I only remember sprinting up to the front door, running into the house and grabbing the phone.

One minute left. By my clock, that is. As I dialed, I wondered if hers had already expired. Surely she would spot me a minute…

Ring. Ring. Click.

"Three minutes late," was her greeting. "You're cutting it close, don't you think?"

"Too close," I said, my heart still pumping. "Don't I get a hello?"

"Hello, Mark." she replied, bittersweet. "We need to talk…"

In a band, these four words signal the beginning of the end. With Sara, I knew it would be the same.

DREAM WARRIORS

apologized to Sara for an hour before hanging up and crashing to the hypnotic strains of Pink Floyd's *Wish You Were Here* album. I awoke with an oddly optimistic perspective, eager to forget my armed combat with the she-devil and my high speed episode.

When I walked upstairs and saw a half-clad Sandy cooking eggs in the kitchen that morning, I realized that the decision had been made. This trailer-park Yoko was not going to be our downfall. One of them had to go, and Sandy didn't play bass.

She didn't, by the way, make any eggs for me.

I resolved to tell James and somehow maintain Tommy's security within the ranks. I would urge James to forgive and forget, to dump an undeserving Sandy and move on. If things got desperate, I would pull out the heavy artillery and talk about the dream and the music--his sense of duty would do the rest.

Granted, Tommy didn't deserve immunity. And yet, he didn't warrant expulsion, either. The strange thing was, I'd been leaning in his favor that night, ready to keep my mouth shut and forget everything. But Tommy said something that stayed with me, something I remembered that morning, a phrase that would affect many of my decisions in the coming weeks and months:

"I'm just glad it was you, and not Derek."

That one did it. The stage fog was clearing, the air moved by the rhythmic vibration of a huge woofer. Jim sat atop the speaker, bearded and swaying, barefoot, his glazed eyes staring through me.

'Listen to the music,' he said, closing his eyes and leaning his head back. I listened.

The truth was as clear as a simple melody, and my path as obvious as a country beat. My rock Karma had been scarred. I'd strayed too far, leaned too much on pretense and deception. I would find the right time, when James was in the right kind of mood. I'd tell him the truth, and let the cow chips fall where they may.

Speaking of bullshit, Ray was recovering slowly.

Having been stoned and drunk at the time of his 'accident', he declined our offers to take him to the hospital and went to the clubs to drink off the concussion. When he woke up alive the following morning, he apparently took it as a sign of his improving health and avoided the doctor bills entirely. Like many of his fellow uninsured musicians, Ray chose the widely practiced and rarely documented 'Hopelistic' healing, in which the patient avoids the doctor, drinks a lot, and hopes like hell he gets better.

A little bruising wasn't going to stop the Ray parade, however. He wore his wounds like tattoos, enjoying the reaction when he removed his sunglasses and revealed the damage. Almost as soon as he was injured, Ray began using the wounded soldier bit to work chicks.

And I don't just mean working them for attention. Ray was cashing in. Within a week, he netted four homemade meals, three new albums, one bottle of Jim Beam, and countless sexual favors. Blondes, brunettes, blondes.

No one ever knew how he did it, and Ray never revealed the hypnotic combination of words he used in those private moments.

I've met many self-proclaimed Casanovas, but none of them could ever touch Ray's career numbers. Five years after he retired, Ray's statue would be erected in the Pick-Up Artist Hall of Fame. It was charisma, and a confidence that bordered on egomania. Coupled with intelligence or compassion, he could have really been something.

Ray's ultimate failure was just as certain as his initial success. Remarkably, the pattern would repeat itself. The new girlfriends would idolize him for two or three weeks, and then hate him with a passion for the rest of their lives. It was like a Greek curse. Ray Sharp was doomed to possess both an irresistible charisma and a stark fear of commitment. He could attract any woman, but could keep none of them.

Something had been broken inside Ray, and it wasn't his ribs.

The Rock-fest had been a financial disaster, but proved to be a dark horse promotional victory, as word of the battle royal spread across the metro area. In two weeks' time, our crowd doubled. As a bonus, we were suddenly in possession of a new, gritty reputation. Of course, most of the grit was still lodged in Ray's forehead, but we were willing to ride the wave.

Lemons turned themselves into lemonade. What seemed a step backward was actually a shining opportunity. You see, few people actually witnessed the show. Paul's advertising, however, had been extensive. While we were pouting about no one seeing us play, thousands of others heard our name in the frequent radio ads.

If a gig falls in the forest and no one hears it, it DOES still exist. You're only as good as your last booking--whether you actually play it or not.

Finally, The Tank summoned us for another dunk. Over a year after our first appearance, we would be returning. This time, however, would be different. We were now armed with the infamous Ray Sharp and a puncher's chance.

In preparation we scoured the set lists, determined to take the place by force. James was practicing more and was discreetly taking private lessons to improve his game. After the resentment following Derek's exit, James seemed eager to prove that everything really WAS better.

King Ray showed up late for rehearsal, wearing his trademark sunglasses. We were talking about him when he walked in.

"Oh hey--sup Ray."

"Sorry I'm late, dudes." Ray extracted a new guitar from its case, admiring it for a moment before plugging in. "Check out the new axe…"

"Whoa."

It was a Jackson. Crimson, and spanking new. Active pickups, custom inlays, immaculately clean. The guitar was far too sweet to have been purchased by Ray.

"Sweet, man. Is it yours?"

Ray nodded, playing a few chords. "It is now. Crystal bought it for me," he grinned. "Damn nice of her, too. I always wanted a Jackson."

"What?"

"Crystal bought that?"

"Truth," he beamed.

"Damn!"

Ray nodded again, quite proud of himself. "Looks like I don't have to break out the Black Beauty anymore…"

"Are you gonna play that at The Tank?"

He shrugged. "Guess so. Though I was really hoping we'd have our act together outfit-wise by then…so we could get the colors right…"

Randy huffed audibly.

The spandex wars continued. Lately, Ray had been lobbying for color scheme. He'd been listening to Stryper and thought the yellow and black thing was cool.

"And your point is?" Randy asked.

"This guitar doesn't match my blue outfit," Ray answered, looking down at it. "If we're all going to wear blue, then--"

"Wait," I protested, choosing Randy's side and jumping in Reeboks first. "When did we agree that we were all wearing blue?"

"Well, we talked about colors," James offered. "And me and Ray thought that blue was--"

"That's the trouble right there," Randy interrupted, obviously in the mood. "It's always you and Ray deciding everything. I never even heard about this!"

James bristled. "What do you mean? We talked about doing the color thing the last time we talked about this!"

"Huh-uh," Randy replied, now resolute. "Ray just brought it up, that's all. He brought it up, and you said you thought it was cool. I didn't agree to shit, though. I never got to vote on that lame-ass idea!"

Ray rolled his eyes and flipped his hair. "Oh, okay, I get it...I think. So now we have to vote on everything instead of doing what's best?"

Ray was pissing me off--on so many levels.

"No," I told him, staring. "We have to do better than vote because we don't need a simple majority. We need a unanimous decision. That means everybody agrees or it doesn't happen."

"I agree with Mark," Randy said.

Ray smirked. "Oh, college shit, right? Well, no wonder you weren't getting anything done..."

Randy and I glared in unison as Ray turned toward his amp and began tuning the Jackson. Tommy shrugged.

Without warning, Randy thundered into an angst-inspired thirty-second drum solo, unleashing his aggression into his toms in a statement that spoke a thousand words.

Blug-a dug a dugga CRACK blug thwap!

Blug-a dug a dugga CRACK flacka-dug-a dug!

The rhythmic din packed the walls with sound, so loud that words became irrelevant and thoughts difficult. Randy's statement was not lost on Mr. Fabulous.

"Get it out of your system, Randy?"

Randy nodded, wiping his forehead. "I feel better."

"I suppose you're all right," Ray said, leaping back to the topic with a new strategy. "There's really no need in worrying about our look when the musical side still needs so much work…"

"What?"

Now he was treading on dangerous ground.

"So, what exactly is your problem musically, Ray?"

"Not a problem, really," Ray shrugged, his nonchalance stuffed with sarcasm. "Just things we need to work on if we want to be professional."

That word again.

"We've all got to keep improving," James added, sounding like an Ab-roller infomercial host. "As a group, and by ourselves. And if there's something we're doing wrong, then we need to help each other out."

This sounded rehearsed. I was getting the feeling that Ray and James had come to practice with an agenda.

"Who or what are you talking about?" I asked, snapping. "What's the big problem?"

"It's not a big problem, really. I just think Randy could be a little less…busy on the drums."

I double-taked in disbelief. I was certain he'd been referring to either Tommy or me.

"What?" Even Randy was chuckling at the thought. "You think I'm too busy?"

"Don't get me wrong--you're good and all…"

"Shit. Fuckin' thanks…"

"But I just think you could play with a little more discipline."

James nodded his agreement. Randy was visibly floored.

"What do you think, Tommy?"

Tommy shrugged, "I don't know…I guess you guys have a point…"

Sacrilege. I kept expecting Rod Serling to walk out from behind a curtain and tell me I was in *The Twilight Zone*. And yet, it was real; it was actually happening. Randy's drumming was coming under fire.

"We didn't say that," James answered for Ray. Suddenly it was 'we'. "But he doesn't have to overplay all the time."

"Overplay is a harsh way to put it…"

"We're not playing fucking elevator music here," Randy snapped. "Funny--I thought I was playing in a metal band, and not some fucking joke glam band! Look--I do what I do, man. I play the damn drums. I've always done the same thing--I've played this way since you met me, so it couldn't be that. I think this has to do with me, and not with my drums!"

"Oh great," James frowned. "Don't take it all personal, dude."

"But it is fucking personal!" Randy shouted back. "How am I not supposed to take it personal? Shit, man--when you talk about my drumming, you're talking about me. I don't criticize your shitty guitar playing…"

I thought James deserved that one. Maybe I was just feeling hurt.

"You have problems with my playing?" James went into aggressive mode. "Is that it, Randy?"

"That's not the point..."

"No, I asked if you had a problem."

Randy glared. "So maybe I do."

"Well, why don't you tell me then? I'd really like to hear it!"

"Don't get me started, dude..."

James gnawed his lip. "Go ahead! Unlike you, Randy, I can take criticisms! Do you got something to say too, Mark?"

"Sure!" I snapped back, driven to defend Randy. "I could say something about your guitar playing, or Ray's, or Randy's drumming...but what good does it do me to rip on you or anyone else? Does it really make us better? Is that the point, or not? Is the point to have fun, James--because this isn't fucking fun! Is it going to help you if I yell at you more?"

James stared, blank but finally listening.

"You guys could hack on me just as easily," I continued, calming. "My singing's obviously not perfect. I know that. So maybe I can't be throwing stones, but here's a fucking clue for you: I know when I screw up, James. We all do. You do, Ray does, Tommy does, Randy does. When I hit a bad note or my voice goes out, or when I say something totally fucking lame on stage--I know it. I remember it, and of course I don't want it to happen again. So there's no reason to bitch about it."

James shook his head. "We weren't bitching at Randy."

"Sure you were. If you wanted to talk about his drumming, there are a hell of a lot of other ways to bring it up. Ray was mad at Randy for the little drum solo, and so he cut into him about being busy."

"What you don't seem to realize," Ray said, reverting to the mentor act, "is that this is a business. Get it? Show business? You dudes really have to learn to have more of a professionalist attitude."

Ray Sharp, the professionalist.

"Which 'dudes' are you talking about, Ray?" Randy asked. "I guess I can assume you aren't talking about James."

James turned. "What do you mean?"

"You know what I mean," Randy's wounded pride provoked his instinct to lash out. "You guys are all tight now, making decisions without telling anybody and doing your fucking coke together…"

"Fuck you," James spat out.

"Oh, what, James? Am I wrong?"

"You're way out of line, Randy."

"Whatever," Randy threw his drumsticks down. "Whatever. Yeah, I may need to be less busy, but I know that this thing is NOT just business. If this is just business, then we're all fucked! We might as well go out and get real jobs, because as a business, this shit isn't making any money! It's about jamming. It's about the music, dumb-asses. It always was. Oh, and fuck you too, James."

Randy made his exit without listening to another word, storming up the stairs and out to his car. Apparently rehearsal was over. I wanted to go with Randy, but didn't think I could top his dramatic exit. I wound up creeping off to my room, leaving James, Tommy and Ray to shake their heads and pretend they were professionals.

LAY IT DOWN

waited two hours for Randy's return, ultimately deciding that he'd gone to Danni's to blow off some steam. His exit didn't ring of finality like Derek's had; there was no doubt in my mind that we'd still have a drummer in the morning.

Scars, however, were inevitable. Randy didn't like to be criticized, and the insults would linger for a long time. James seemed married to Ray now, and the fight was likely to further strengthen the bond between the king and his Svengali champion.

I don't quite know how James came to take the reins. We didn't vote him in. It wasn't a bloody coup or a single defining moment of leadership. We didn't even hold him in any special regard or believe that he was the one most deserving. Instead, James' power was gained by attrition, a gradual wearing down of our resistance through consistently applied bitching and mothering. We'd submitted because he was always willing to assume the role and through nature or necessity was well-suited to keep the rest of us in line.

I'd always considered the band to be the height of democracy--five members, five votes, and the knowledge that no one truly claimed the role of boss. It seemed wrong for a rock band to adopt the methods of the same authority figures we were trying to piss off, and none of us took orders too well. But more than the rest, we were friends--dudes. Like the Soviets, I'd been foolishly believing in the ideal, thinking I was one among equals. But it was now painfully obvious that James was the captain of the ship, a spandexed Ahab in search of his own pink and black whale.

As I sat in the front room channel surfing, I could hear James and Ray talking business in the basement, their voices kept purposely low. Being the only other person in the house--it was Sandy's bar night--I had to assume that the whispered comments were directed toward me.

Talking behind my back. Well, murmuring, actually.

Murmuring behind by back. Just as hurtful, but somewhat harder to understand. If they wanted to rip on me, they should have kept their voices down.

Secrets. It's an odd thing to be sitting in one room and know that people are back-talking you in the next. Knowing it, realizing it, and yet remaining calmly in the chair--thinking to yourself how ridiculous it is, wanting so badly to march in there and yell at them...and remaining in the chair. Saying nothing despite your every instinct. Realizing that if you're a topic of cloistered conversation, intervening will do you no good.

I was being indicted as an accessory to Randy and that was fine by me. I supported him because he was right and because it was hardly fair for a fuck-up like Ray to be musically strong-arming someone in the band. But beneath all the justice and honor stuff, down at the base of my soul, I was feeling like Derek.

Our ravenous dreams were eating everything. I could see it now.

So I waited it out, feeling resentful as I flipped channels. The band angst swirled with thoughts of Sara and my upcoming exams, leaving me newly resolved to settle with James. It seemed a spiteful moment to be delivering such bad news, but my course had been set since early that morning and I wasn't going to let a little treachery steer me astray.

Fortune intervened when Ray's generous new girlfriend Crystal arrived and the discussion downstairs ended. Tommy and James avoided me entirely, creeping off to their rooms without comment. I waited another ten minutes before heading down the hall to James' room.

I knocked, and the door cracked open.

"Hey dude," James' face appeared, looking much calmer. Seeing him made me wonder what had just been said in the basement.

"Hey, man…can I talk with you for a minute?"

"Yeah, well…I'm kinda burned out," he replied, rubbing his neck and yawning.

Fortunately, I was prepared for this eventuality. I'd been pocketing a gift joint from Lonnie, and I held it up for James to see. "I got something for that."

"Okay." It didn't take him long to answer. "Let's go out on the back porch."

"Cool."

Yes, I'm sorry to admit I lured him with drugs--something I knew James wouldn't turn down. Not the most notable or heroic of efforts, I know. However, in all fairness, I should be exonerated of any contempt. It was dope for a good purpose. Strictly altruistic enabling.

We sat out on the porch, passing the joint and listening to the flapping drone of a distant Harley.

"So Randy isn't back yet?"

"Not yet," I answered.

James huffed, shaking his head. "Well, I hope he doesn't get all pissy like Derek did."

"You and Derek never talked it out," I clarified.

"Pshht--it wouldn't have done any good," he coughed. "Derek wasn't going to come back. I knew that much. You know, sometimes I felt like he wanted to leave, but he couldn't do it on his own. Like he wanted to piss me off--just enough to give him a reason."

The thought had never crossed my mind.

"You think?"

"Shit, Mark. Why do you think he got drunk before the Tank gig? I mean, what kind of fucking sense does that make? Derek may have been the ultimate party machine, but he was smart, too. He knew what he was doin' that afternoon when he started knocking back shots before the gig, dude. And I've thought about it a million times, but I can't figure out why.

"I know you think it's my fault," James continued, clearing his throat. "I know you guys blame me for Derek leaving. I can see that. But you gotta understand--I didn't want him to go any more than you did. He moved out like a day after the fight, which didn't exactly give me the time to talk it out with him. He didn't want to work it out, dude. His choice. I know that. You can believe what you want..."

"I never said it was all your fault," I told him. "I just felt like we could have done way more to work the whole thing out. You have to admit, dude--you were pretty harsh."

"Yeah, but Derek needed it. He didn't have the right attitude--"

"That's the problem, James."

"What is?"

"You expect everybody to be like you--to have the same attitude as you. No offense, man, but you're a pretty intense guy. And that's a good thing--at least, most of the time. But when somebody else doesn't match your intensity, you act like they're slacking. Derek loved the band, too--just for different reasons. We're all here for our own reasons, James. That doesn't make it wrong."

"Don't think I haven't been feeling it," he said. "I know you guys have been pissed off at me since Derek left--"

"It's not like that," I told him. "I blame myself for it, too."

"Yeah, but Mark--you were on Derek's side in that argument. You were always on Derek's side. Randy, too."

I shook my head. "I'm not, though. That's the thing, man--it's not about sides with me. I've always looked at it this way: We're in the same band, so we're on the same side. Always. Rehearsals, gigs, fights, everything! That's why we all jumped in on the brawl at the Rock-fest, right? If we didn't know Ray and saw the Stepkids kicking the crap out of him, we'd probably watch like everyone else. Nope. We sided with Ray because he's in the band. Our band."

"So, you're saying that if Todd Vandermeer joined the band tomorrow, we'd fight for him tomorrow night?"

I winced. "Well...I wouldn't, because he'd have my job. But you would. Hell yeah--I guarantee it! It's like in football when they trade some guy from the Raiders to the Broncos. You've been booing this guy for years, and suddenly everyone's glad to have him on the team. They cheer just as loud. If Todd joined tomorrow, you'd be on the same team and you'd fight for him, too."

"Hmm," James contemplated. Football metaphors always did the trick with him. "Yeah. I see what you're saying and everything--but I did my part. I didn't let Derek down--he knew where to find me."

"I just know we all want the same thing, James. Maybe we all go about it in different ways, and some of us fuck up more than others. But when we get pissed off and blow off steam at practice, we've got to remember that the other guys want it, too. We all have to lighten up a little bit..."

"You're still like Derek," James told me, chuckling. "Always try-ing to get me to lighten up. One of these days you guys are gonna realize--I'm just not light."

"True." I smiled, squint-eyed. "That's one thing you'll never be accused of. And I'm not trying to make you the bad guy, either. I know you're doing the best you can, James. And the same goes for everybody else. We need to get back to the music and back to enjoy-ing ourselves, light or not."

He leaned against the house, exhaling a cloud of smoke into the starry air above us. "You know, that's what I always liked about you, Mark. Well, one of the things, at least. You're always the peacemak-er. When we argue over shit, you go person to person, and figure out what everyone wants. By the time you're done with the rounds, the problem is solved. That's what's cool. You always want to see things all happy and shit. You want everybody to get along, and you do whatever you can to make it happen."

"I appreciate that, man."

"Just being honest."

Honesty. It seemed the perfect lead-in. This was undoubtedly my cue.

"James, I've got something to talk with you about..."

"Yeah? What?"

He sat quietly and listened as I told him the story--not necessar-ily what I thought was going on, but only what my part was, serving my testimony like a witness on the stand. I offered no hearsay evi-dence. Without wavering, I revealed the details of Sara's little mid-night romp and the odd report that resulted. He remained staring at the concrete porch for a moment after I finished.

"You're serious, aren't you?" James finally asked me in mono-tone, clenching his jaw.

"I wish I weren't, man..."

He looked down, rubbing his neck. "In my own bed?"

"I didn't actually see anything," I admitted. "But Sara says that's what happened…and I heard the headboard, err, you know…"

James turned away. "Oh, man. I don't believe this shit! Damn, dude--how long has this been going on?"

"I don't know," I answered. "I only know about the one time."

"So Tommy knows that you found out?" he asked.

I froze, considering dishonesty once again. Should I tell James that I'd actually had a discussion with Tommy about it?

"He knows," I said, deciding to reveal all. "I talked with Tommy and tried to get him to come to you on his own--"

"You see," he replied, containing his anger. "There you go--trying to make things better again. So I take it he didn't want to tell me face-to-face?"

"I don't really know what he wanted," I replied honestly, feeding Tommy to the wolves. "But I got the feeling you weren't going to hear it from him."

From inside, the ringing of the phone. James moved to answer it, then stopped, his hands balling into fists.

Without warning, he punched the back door, leaving a sizeable indentation.

"Whoa! Go easy, dude. You need your hands. You're a lead guitarist--break a leg or something, would you?"

He rubbed his knuckles, examining them. "Ouch."

"You see? The door wins the round, 10-9."

No way was I getting a smile out of him. James was locked in and focused, on a slow bus ride through the land of Testosteronia. I hoped Tommy didn't end up looking as bad as the door.

James offered a hand, his eyes bearing prideful fires. "Thanks, Mark. I appreciate you telling me. Looks like I've got some business to take care of. Just do me a favor and keep out of it while I talk to Tommy, okay?"

"I just don't want to see--"

We heard a wailing sound, indistinguishable at first, then taking on the distinct quality of Ray's backing vocals.

"Everybody! Get your asses down here!" The voice was clear this time, ringing through the window wells.

"What's up?" James shouted down the hall, waiting for an answer.

"Just get down here!"

James and I headed for the basement, shrugging and curious. Tommy appeared out of his room and followed behind us. I made certain to position myself between the two as we tromped down the stairs.

Back in Black

R ay waited for us in the basement looking both excited and worried, as though someone had wired his shorts. Still no sign of Randy.

"Well, it's just the four of us, but that's gonna have to do," he said, the elation palpable in his voice. "You guys heard the phone ring, I'm assuming."

I was keeping an eye on James, who was fixed and glaring at Tommy. Tommy immediately caught the bad vibe and glanced at me.

"I'm tired, man," James said, lighting a cigarette. "How about we just jump to the point, okay, Ray?"

Ray shrugged. "Sure, why not...but you're gonna feel bad for acting like a dick when I tell you. This is big shit."

"What, dude?"

Ray paced a bit, brushing back his hair. "I just accepted a gig at the Rainbow...as the warm-up band for Juggernaut. Now, is that fuckin' big enough for you?"

Juggernaut?

Good god, they were huge. Anthem rock with a Nordic theme. Their videos were all over, and I even owned two of their albums. They weren't just a dinosaur band, or a group at the top of the local scene. Juggernaut was nationwide. They bad, they nationwide.

"You mean THE Juggernaut?" Tommy asked, on the verge of spasm. "As in 'Soulstealer'?"

"There's only one," Ray responded, beaming. "Fuckin-ay, dudes."

"Whoa…"

"Dude."

"Holy shit, man!" I was pacing now, too. In a moment, everything had changed again. "A real gig!"

"Damn right." Ray beamed. "The band they had booked quit on 'em, so I guess we get the gig. Don't ask me how or why he chose to call us, but I'd say the promo had something to do with it. I told him we'd do it, of course. I accepted without asking you guys--I figured you'd agree."

"You figured right."

"Hell yeah!"

"You're not kidding, are you?" James looked about to implode, as though having trouble reconciling this glorious news with the knowledge of Tommy's betrayal. The gig seemed the perfect remedy for his anger.

Ray shook his head, chuckling. "Of course I'm not kidding. I wouldn't do that to you guys. No lie, honestly. Shit, guys--I thought you'd be happy about this thing!"

"I am!" Tommy whooped, curls bouncing as he hopped in place. "This is too sweet! No way! No way! No fucking way! I can't believe this."

"So you're sure?" James needed more confirmation. "You're totally sure?

"Yeah, man, it's all worked out. You'll see. I'm not bullshitting you. Would I do that?" Ray looked around the group, making eye contact with each one of us. "Now you guys might think I'm full of shit or whatever, but I've been through this whole thing before, and

I'm not letting it get screwed up this time. Take it from me--this is it, dudes. This is fucking IT. If we kick ass here, I can practically guarantee we'll get some kind of record deal."

The words themselves lifted me up, feeding the smoking fires of ambition with premium grade gasoline.

The ultimate gig. A chance for bottom feeders to crawl, even if just for a moment, from the muddy water into the sunlight of the shore.

We didn't even bother to ask Ray how much it paid; money was irrelevant. Had he told us it cost a hundred each, we would have emptied our pockets on the spot. This, after all, was the mother of all local gigs. And gigs keep bands together. When the gigs are regular and good, everything is sunshine and daffodils. When gigs are scarce, arguments prevail.

This particular gig, however, was huge enough to gloss over any problem. In a single moment, we'd gone from cursed to blessed. The room got rosy.

Ray wore an inspired scowl. "Looks like we've got work to do. Man--we'll have to practice these ten songs until our fingers fall off! This is the big league, and we can't sit back and think... What's the matter, James?"

"I think he's still in shock..."

James still wasn't smiling. "I guess it hasn't sunk in yet."

"It will," Ray said, "once you're standing on stage in front of ten thousand people!"

In a somewhat delayed reaction, the room exploded with high fives and hugs, pumped fists and raised voices. It was elation on top of expectation, like having someone tell you they'd added a second Christmas in June. It was the pure rush of grabbing hold of something you'd long considered out of reach, then looking down and being unsure of how it came to be in your hand in the first place.

I was close to the mirror now. So close that it seemed I only needed to step through and greet my audience on the other side. I could see them out there, thousands of them, lighters raised in tribute and waiting for me to take the stage. Jim waited as well, stirring the crowd with poetry and shouts, singing "Soul Kitchen" and fumbling with his belt buckle.

These thoughts consumed me, and for a moment I got lost in a daydream.

When I turned back around, James was throwing punches at Tommy, unleashing the angst of three years' good behavior and finally doing something that wasn't in the best interest of the band.

Out of respect and a keen sense of chaotic goodness, I allowed James get in a few extra shots before pulling him away.

SUICIDE SOLUTION

After assuming the role the pivotal informer and star witness in the case, I never even got a chance to listen to the testimony. Following the initial cool-down phase, James met with a swollen-lipped Tommy privately to discuss the situation, excluding the rest of us. Surrender was imminent.

So as not to waste rehearsal time, James was forced to officially accept Tommy's apology and oath of fealty less than a day after he heard the news. With Juggernaut in our future, James knew better than to boot the bass player.

And like that, it was officially over. All the aching and mental anguish, all the questions resolved with one long conversation and twelve or so swift blows to the head. Still, we all knew it wasn't the belated confession or the battery that swayed James to be so forgiving. It was the gig and the gig alone that saved Tommy.

The metal gods had seen my plight and sent down their leather-studded Deus ex Machina to save us.

Unofficially, the hard feelings would linger for a long time. For the moment, however, the ship had been patched and set sailing. The open seas were much rougher than the peaceful harbor we'd departed from, and it would take five sailors pulling together to reach the New World.

Elation, however, has a shelf life. Anticipation tends to get stale in the heat. Once the initial excitement died down, the Juggernaut gig metamorphosed from a blessing to a constant worry, leaving us questioning everything. We fell into endless rehearsals, second-guessing ourselves and repeating tunes, writing new songs and then discarding them as inferior. There would be no cover material allowed--we would have to wow the arena solely with our own tunes. As it neared, the gig became increasingly intimidating.

The politics of the band were getting complicated. There were five victims and five villains in the band, and with all the loaded comments flying around the room, it became hard to tell who was upset and why. When I sorted it out, I realized that each of us had at least one other person up our ass.

Here's the rundown:

Randy was angry with Ray for what he'd said, at James for backing up Ray, and at Tommy for proving himself a lousy friend to James. James, in turn, was angry with Tommy for doing Sandy, at Sandy for doing Tommy, and at Randy for denying that he was doing too much drumming. Tommy was furious with me for telling James, but had little other room to throw stones. And Master Ray was angry with Randy for making comments, disappointed in me for insulting his sense of professionalism, and mildly peeved at James for 'letting his personal life affect the band'.

I wasn't angry with anyone, really. At the moment I wasn't exactly too fond of Tommy or Ray, of course, but I didn't think anything was beyond repair. The gig would pull us out of this, and like elation, the hard feelings would soon dry up and fall away. Apparently, everyone else agreed. The personal crap was being honorably set aside in favor of the common goal. The band was being civil and workmanlike, practicing hard and contributing to the new material. We jumped on the fulcrum and rode it from the 'too personal' side of the spectrum all the way into the 'strictly business' category. A new work ethic was born in our lazy longhair hearts.

In other words, the enjoyment had been completely drained out of it. Like blood drawn with a syringe, our fun was extracted and placed in a tiny vial, labeled and put on the shelf for better days. Hating the deflated feeling, I tried to rationalize our attitude, figuring there would be plenty of time for fun after our big break. For now, we would simply have to get by.

Artistic differences. That was it--my Pollyanna rationale. The whole thing could simply be explained as artistic differences. It made everything sound so much more refined and...professional. The drum debate? Artistic difference. The spandex wars? Artistic difference. One longhair sleeping with another longhair's girlfriend? Sure, why not? Chock it up to A.D..

So we argued, pretending not to argue.

We maintained a decorum of veiled dude civility, going our own ways at the end of rehearsal and not thinking twice about it. I suppose that, like the rest, I figured the gig would be a stepping stone. After our ultimate triumph, none of the hard feelings would matter anymore. At the very least, we'd be rich and famous while we were fighting. Regardless, the reconciliation would have to keep for a better day. We burped our emotional Tupperware and fresh-locked our true feelings.

The arguments were dropped and the issues avoided, as we held faith in the ultimate power of the gig, praying that success would soon come and lift us above all these petty problems. We waited, practicing with intensity and the fire of our suffocated feelings.

The music itself was getting better. We were as tight as ever, snapping through the songs with focus, repeating them so many times that the breaks became second nature. We found we could hide from the arguments inside the joy of the jam, realizing that it was genuinely difficult to maintain a pissy attitude when you're banging away. In the midst of the music, it was much easier to forgive.

Who's Behind the Door?

"This will be an open note exam. Bring a bluebook with you, along with whatever else you need. No textbooks, of course. Good luck then, and we'll see you Thursday."

Professor Hale backed away from the auditorium crowd, bowing slightly to indicate that we were all dismissed. My Psych classmates stood up around me, gathering their backpacks and heading up the aisles like passengers escaping the Titanic, eager to be away from the stale air and out in the warm spring sunlight.

I hesitated in my seat, staring down at the study guide and wanting to throw up. Four final exams to go, the first in less than two hours. I was unprepared and out of time, my leathered back to the wall.

I was smart enough to know I'd been stupid.

My apparent mastery of the educational system was hitting the wall, landing me in academic purgatory. Like some pitiful Greek hero who should have seen it coming, I was seeing the fruits of Mom's prophecy, living out the curse of my own pride. The days were flying by, and I'd fallen short on too many small assignments.

Like a battered fighter in the final round, I needed a knockout to win.

As I walked from the classroom and headed for the smoking section of the University Center, I tried very hard to forget about the band and Sara, even if just for a moment, and concentrate on the task at hand. With luck, I could cram a few more tidbits between the snips of song lyric in my head and pull through on the final.

Sad, to think that I needed luck. I'd never needed luck before, and didn't know how to rally the muses of fortune. A bit of last-second studying, however, couldn't hurt.

I skipped the chocolate milk and Twinkies, finding a seat and immediately diving into my notes from class. The names and dates leapt up in endless succession, only half of them as familiar as they should have been. What had seemed a benign little history class was turning into a recital of Edwards and Louies, a mishmash of swords and crowns that suddenly didn't seem all that interesting to me.

"You look very…focused."

I looked up from my notes to see Ashley Whitmore, looking decidedly sharp in a pale yellow spring outfit.

"For what it's worth," I replied, shrugging cutely.

I hate to say it, but my libido awakened at the sight of her, nudging a sleeping Jim.

"I won't demand too much of your attention." She set down her herbal tea and took the seat opposite me. "Big exam?"

I nodded ruefully. "Exams. Plural."

"Oh, I know! I've barely had time to do anything else but study."

"Yeah…"

In truth, I'd done very little actual cramming, forced by necessity to focus on the two term papers I'd had to submit. The actual schoolwork had been done between classes or very late at night when the rest of the band was sleeping. Compared to a girl like Ashley, I was looking more and more like a scholastic delinquent--smart enough to hack it, but dumb enough to spend my time practicing the same ten songs over and over again instead of studying.

"I have two of my finals out of the way already," she said, blowing on the cup with unglossed, beautifully plain lips. "What final are you studying for?"

"Survey of Western Civ," I answered, looking down at the page.

"Oooh, tough one. Who do you have?"

"Professor Aweida."

She nodded knowingly. "I had him, too. That class is almost enough to turn you off on history."

"Yeah, it sounded like fun. A few kings, a few battles...easy, right?"

"I know. That's one of those freshman boot camp classes..."

"What?"

"They're trying to weed out the weaklings before their junior year. The hundred level classes are no mercy. Trust me; you'll love the professors when you get to the better classes..."

"I hope so."

I looked up at the clock, the minutes fading. I was feeling like a weed.

"I should probably stop bothering you and let you study," she said, apparently noticing my distress. "What time is the final?"

"Two o'clock," I told her, looking again.

"Hmm, well, I heard that your long term memory can't really recall anything that's less than a couple hours old...so, technically, studying right before a test doesn't do you any good. In fact, you're likely to rely on your short-term and remember JUST what you crammed. It can be bad for you..."

I didn't really need to hear this. Her words had me picturing myself sitting blank in the classroom, unable to recall anything but the words to "Love Gun."

Ashley had planted a vicious seed in my subconscious--given me a rational reason to blow off the cramming entirely and chat with her instead. It was nice to talk to someone who could sympathize with my scholastic plight, even if she didn't know the horrid extent of it. Admittedly, I'd be gaining little by reviewing what I was unfamiliar with in the first place. And, of course, there was a chance that she'd be running along any minute. She'd be gone soon.

Well...

Ashley was in the mood to talk, and she didn't leave until my time was almost up. And though I realized the gamble I was taking by closing my notebook and opting to chat, there was something in me that needed the conversation more than I needed the knowledge. We sat there like adults, without beer or joints, talking about literature and politics, sharing our views on Perestroika and Solidarity, enjoying the kind of 'my dinner with Ashley' afternoon I'd rarely experienced before.

I enjoyed being with her there--conversing with someone who didn't care about my hair or my band, listening as she spoke without pretense on whatever subject pleased her. Ashley may have been a little rich girl, but she possessed a depth of awareness I didn't encounter often, and wanted more of. The few carefree moments were working a number on my romantic sensibilities...and though I was yet to verge on a pickup line, I began to think that she and I might have more in common than simply Professor Aweida.

Different worlds, perhaps. But girls like Ashley were supposed to be intrigued by guys like me. I'd seen the movies...classic Olivia Newton-John. As rocker guy, I naturally represented everything she'd never had in a guy, and she was bound to be attracted.

This was the theory...and by the time I had to leave for the exam, I was believing it. There was still room for one small victory amongst all the recent defeats.

"Time for me to get out of here," I announced, shrugging regretfully.

"Good luck on the exam," she answered, smiling. "You should do well if you studied."

"Yeah." I stumbled over my thoughts. "I guess you're staying in town over the summer?"

Ashley nodded. "I'll be working. I'll probably see you back here again in the fall."

I was loaded up and ready to move away from the table. My time to hesitate was through. I gave it a shot.

"Hey, Ashley--since you're going to be around, you know--maybe I can get your number and call you sometime. We could go out to dinner or something…"

She looked at me oddly, tilting her head as though she'd just smelled something strange. A flattered grin parted her lips.

"You're sweet, Mark," she said without hesitation, looking straight at me. "But you're just not the type of guy I date. No offense, but the whole rocker thing seems a little…ridiculous to me. Though, you should ask me again if you ever decide to drop the look. You're a nice guy…"

Ka-boom. I could feel my pride imploding inside me.

"Thanks," I said, choking on her frankness. "Have a good summer."

Thanks. I'm an idiot? Oh, yeah--thanks.

I wasn't angry. I couldn't blame Ashley for telling it like it is. After all, I was a lead singer. I was the man.

At the moment, I felt more like a circus clown, a juvenile little rocker who still wore his high-school rebellion like a gaudy badge of honor. The disappointment was more par for the course than astounding, but I stomped into my final with a bad attitude and a head full of distraction, knowing that the worst was on its way.

Bringin' on the Heartbreak

"So how is school going?"

"Don't ask," I told her, closing my eyes in feigned agony. "Pretty brutal…"

I sat with Sara in the smoking section of Benny's, regretting my choice of restaurant and thinking that our final memory together would be that of stale coffee. We met that night as part of the obligatory 'exchange of personal effects' that follows failed relationships, a ritual in which we'd each gathered all of the others' wayward stuff and met to trade. I'd come to the meeting thinking that I could win her over again…but all it took was a word from her to know I was wrong.

Tonight, her caring tone was tempered with distance. I could tell by her red-tinged eyes that she'd been crying, but we persisted with the obligatory small talk.

"What were your grades like?" she asked.

I shifted in the booth, reaching for the sugar. "Not very good--I don't really want to talk about it…"

Which was a lie. I wanted, needed to talk--to dump my kingdom of problems on a friendly ear. I was longing for the kind of sympathy that rocker dudes are simply unable to provide. Sara, however, was now out of reach; everything from her posture to the short regretful glances told me that she'd drifted away. It would re-quire a genuine wooing effort to regain her.

"You might as well tell me. It can't be that bad…"

"You're right," I replied, less than reluctant. "It's worse than that. Academic probation."

"What? Oh no, Mark…"

"Yeah, no shit. They sent me this nice little letter that says if I don't bring up my GPA by fall, I'm out. As in, OUT of college! Do you know how humiliating this is for me? I never got so much as a C before, and that's the truth! I swear, I don't know how this happened!"

"The band," she returned immediately, without contempt. "That's what happened."

She was right…in part. But as much as I would have liked to blame my crisis on the rest of the guys, I knew who ultimately claimed the role of culprit.

"It's not just the band," I said in my defense.

She smirked. "Mark, you know damned well that none of those guys gives a crap about your school! And why would they? Trust me-- none of those guys wants you to be anything but their lead singer. I mean, honestly, it's a wonder you got this far living in that house. I remember how hard it was for you to study…"

I shrugged. "Yeah, but I'm good at school--I always have been! There's no way this should have happened. I don't do this…"

She smiled at me as though remembering some distant moment we'd spent together, then looked at me with the amiable, warm con-descension that only a lover can deliver. I felt childish and defeated.

"You know what I've always liked about you?" she asked, paus-ing rhetorically. "You think you can do anything. You don't just hope in things, you believe--and that's beautiful. That's why I don't question that you meant it when you said you loved me. But sometimes, Mark--a lot of the time, actually--you're so confident that you take on too much. You have all this important stuff competing for your time--trust me, I know. And I also know you're a little genius and a sweetheart and a good person...but you can't do it all, no matter what you think."

I listened to her, knowing she was right, thinking how great she was to deal with my crap at this point in our relationship.

"I shouldn't be bothering you with all this."

She smirked, tapping me on the hand. "And who else would you bother? I have the best perspective. I do know this...you're gonna miss me someday."

"I know I will..."

She looked down at her cup. "So what did your parents say?"

I shrugged. "It was weird. I thought they'd freak, you know? I figured they'd go ballistic, but it wasn't like that. In a way, it was worse--they were really quiet, giving off this kind of 'hands-off disappointment' vibe. It sucked. I have to take summer classes and get A's in everything to bring up my GPA, so that's what I'm doing."

"I'd think they would blame it on the band..."

"Well, they did, but nothing epic. I'm sure they'd like me to quit the band, but--"

"But you'd never do that, would you?"

I noticed a tinge of bitterness in her voice and kicked myself for speaking without thinking.

"It's not like that. It's just that this Juggernaut gig could be something really big, you know? After this, things could change--"

Sara flashed the pity-filled smile again, as though I were an alcoholic swearing off the bottle for the hundredth time.

"The dream never ends, does it, Mark? You'll waste another three months and maybe your entire college career this time, right? And what if nothing happens? You lost me because of it, why not college? Why not everything? You've got your dream, right?"

I withered at the sight of the tears in her eyes, watching without response as she raised a hand to wipe them away.

"I didn't want this, Sara."

"What?" she replied angrily. "For me to cry?"

"To hurt you any more than I already have…"

"Don't give yourself so much credit," she replied, sniffing. "I'm just confused that's all. I sit around and think about all these things and…were you embarrassed of me, Mark?"

"Why would you say that?"

"Well, you never took me to meet your parents. You never even suggested it! Did you even tell them about me?"

"Of course I did."

Which was true. Barely. I'd told Mom and Dad as much about Sara as any of my other prior girlfriends, a meager report which usually began and ended with a name and the fact that they weren't in college. Beyond this, my parents weren't interested. I'd been saving Sara grief by not bringing her around them. Or so I thought.

"Why would I be embarrassed by you?" I continued, repeating nothing, defending myself without ammunition. "I think you're amazing! Really, Sara…"

"Just not amazing enough for your dream," she said in reply, the words ringing long after she said them.

I couldn't lie anymore. As shallow as it might seem--as difficult as it was for me to admit, I was faced with the humbling truth of her statement. It wasn't that I considered myself better than Sara or wanted a supermodel with a Ph.D. instead…but everything, every fiber of my rocker body and rebel soul was telling me that my destiny--my achievements, my marriage, my life--was awaiting me somewhere else, sometime later.

Jim stood by the tour bus in a fringed leather jacket, beckoning me. 'She'll go crazy with a guy like you, bud...let her down easy, and let's go...'

"I'm sorry, Sara," I said to her, trying to vocalize what I was thinking. "I made the commitment to the band so long ago...everything gets wrapped up in it, you know?"

She nodded curtly. "Yeah--I know. I always knew which commitment came first."

"But it wasn't like that...Sara..."

"I don't know what it is that you're really chasing," she began, talking through her tears, "but I hope for your sake that you find it, Mark! For your sake, I really do! You're letting everything else fall apart, and I hope when it's all through that you can still enjoy whatever it is you have left. I told you before that I loved your dream, Mark--and I meant it. I still do. But if you think about tomorrow all the time, you'll wake up one day and realize you've wasted all the todays."

Her words reminded me of Derek, and I felt ashamed. Was I really wasting todays? After all, I was doing exactly what I wanted--what I loved--and enjoying every minute of it. Wasn't I?

"I want you to know how much--" I never got the words out.

"I don't need to hear that right now," she cut me off, looking away. "I've got all of your stuff out in the car..."

I looked out the window, searching the lot.

"I didn't see your car when I came in."

"I didn't drive my car," she answered, wiping her lined eyes carefully.

"Whose car did you drive?"

"A friend's," she answered reluctantly, the words singing with meaning.

"A new boyfriend?"

"That's a question you can't ask. I didn't come here to fight with you…"

I nodded my acceptance. She was right. The time for personal questions was at an end. This was our last 'us' conversation--the next time we spoke, there would be a chasm of emotional distance between us. We'd see each other somewhere down the road and offer a polite hug, or maybe just a handshake. I grieved at the thought.

"So…maybe we can still hang out?" I offered, feeling pitiful. "You know, as friends…see a show or something…"

She looked into my eyes and shook her head slightly. "I don't think so. Not just yet. It's too soon for that."

"Too soon," I said, holding it back with a forced smile. "Like that apologizing thing…"

"Something like that," she said.

We couldn't leave right away. Sara and I talked for another hour before exchanging items and pausing awkwardly for one horribly final hug. She leaned in and kissed me just once, softly, and wished me luck at the Juggernaut gig. As I drove out of Benny's parking lot and away from her forever, I wondered just how many eggs my Juggernaut basket could possibly hold.

Ten Seconds to Love

Ray fixed his hair for the hundredth time, allowing big-hipped Thumper to fluff him up in the back. As our 'hairdresser', she was the only girlfriend to make it backstage.

"Nothing worse than flat hair," she commented, adding more spray and sculpting the strands individually. Thumper teased and back-combed, scowling crimson, her very presence enough to command follicle rigidity.

"These fluorescent lights make everyone look pale," Ray announced, pinching his cheeks. "They should have red light in here."

We sat in the ready room, waiting for the stage manager to cue us, less than twenty minutes from our destiny.

The load-in had been particularly mild, and the sound check was utterly professional. Not just two or three soundmen, but an entire team descended on Randy's kit and fixed him up right. The microphone was wireless and cost more than I did. My voice leapt from the monitors at divinely ear-crushing volume.

The sound check was done with prompt efficiency, and we only got through the first verse of "G-String" before the soundman cut us off and said he'd see us at gig time. Wham, bam, thank you band. Too smooth.

After dutifully accepting our last minute instructions, we retreated to the waiting rooms to sweat away the three hours until show time. We had a beer or two, and some of the guys sampled the catering. Knowing my propensity for anxious nausea, I stayed away from the food and only sipped my beer.

We neither saw nor heard from Juggernaut, but it was just as well. I was far too wound up to pal around with greatness. Ray, understandably, was a bit disappointed that our fellow musicians didn't pay us a visit.

"Ten minutes, guys," the stage manager yelled into the room, her voice startling me.

"Shit--I thought they said twenty..."

"Ten minutes ago."

"Shit."

"Relax, dude," Randy said, shifting absently from foot to foot.

"I'm trying," I said, taking a deep breath and picturing that yoga lady in her purple leotard. No effect. "Are you relaxed?"

"Hell no," he said.

I held back the heaves. "Well, at least I don't feel like puking."

"So you got that going for you..."

"Hey Randy, do you remember what that guy from Bad Froggy said--remember how he told us he played for huge crowds for years, but then once the single got hot, they went on tour with Razorback and got booed every night?"

"It happens. Shit, we've seen our own share of on-stage deaths. Remember when The Cult opened for Metallica and everyone was throwing shit at 'em? That singer got all pissed and walked offstage, remember? We booed even harder."

"That's what I mean," I told him. "It's pretty much tradition to boo the opening act."

"Not necessarily," Randy replied. "You're thinking about it too much, dude. Stop worrying! We're gonna kick ass, just like we did that first time, back on the Andersens' deck! That night, we were all nervous--you were sick that night, too. So we just jammed, and it fuckin' worked out. That's what's gonna happen tonight."

I thought about our beginnings. "I hope you're right, dude."

"Just get your shit right," James said, turning to point at each of us. "We screw up here, and we can just cash out..."

"Five minutes," the announcement came. We looked to each other, gathering in the center of the room.

"James, do you want to say grace, or what?"

James looked to me. "You do it, Mark."

I stared around the group, then looked down at my snakeskin boots, trying to formulate a last-minute Gipper speech. Did we really need inspiration, and was I the one to deliver it?

My college career was scheduled for the guillotine. My love life was unquestionably in the toilet. I'd failed twice in two tries, proving myself a bad student and a worse boyfriend...

But just as I was sure that it was all bullshit, I saw them all look at me--and knew that this was my job. I was the glue and the rehabilitator of spirits. I was the source of the unity, and the friend that would always be there. I was a damn good front man and could still snatch one dream from the wreckage of the other two.

Could I say grace? Hell yeah. Derek would have had it no other way.

"This is it, dudes," I began reverently. "This is the place we've been beating ourselves up to get to. All the trouble and the fights, all the asshole bar owners and long rehearsals...we made it all this way, thinking that this place--that stage right out there--was the ultimate. But it's not dudes! It's nothing! No more of this nervous bullshit. We've beaten tougher crowds than this. We can do this gig with our hands tied behind our backs!

"Shit, dudes--all I ever wanted was to jam and have fun. I trust in every one of you guys and I know we're gonna kick ass. But listen to me, just this once. We know these songs backwards and forwards--all the work has been done already. Whatever else we do out there, I want to see you guys jamming like we used to--I want to see your fucking heads banging like you mean it! We've climbed our mountain, dudes. Let's plant a flag on this mother!"

Tommy whooped, bouncing in anticipation. James and Randy began a vociferous round of 'you da man', high-fiving and loud. Ray grinned from beneath his sculpted strands like an electric peacock, geared up and ready for battle. For a moment we were all acting ridiculous, amped-up and ranting as we'd done in high school, feeding from our fear and turning it into reckless exaltation. For a moment I felt happy and confident again, as though everything were somehow going to work out.

Randy turned to me, reaching out a hand. "This is it, bud."

I shook with him. "I'm glad you're back there, Randy."

"Listen--we do this gig for Derek. Right?"

"Totally," I nodded, sorry I hadn't thought of it myself.

We pumped our fists and ranted, praying one final time to the metal gods before turning for the door.

I'll See the Light Tonight

The house lights came down.

As we walked up the short staircase leading to the stage, I could hear the crowd react to the darkness, the swell of cheers rising to meet us.

"Right through there, guys," the stage manager pointed. "Break a leg."

I'd been through it as a spectator dozens of times--that prodigious moment when the lights come down and the silhouetted figures of the band first take the stage, stirring the hungry crowd without playing a note. I'd watched in envy as they strolled out, whiskey in hand, motioning to the sound of their chanted names. And suddenly, here I was, walking out on the smooth floor and into the subdued light, looking up and gazing out over the sea of faces for the first time. The arena looked just as I thought it would.

I had crossed into the mirror. I was finally there, living and breathing within its confines. Jim Morrison stood beside me, clean-shaven and grinning, pointing me toward the audience.

'Welcome to the inside, brother,' he said. 'Whatever you do, enjoy the ride...'

I nodded to Jim and approached the microphone, remembering I'd been told not to touch it until the music started.

Randy counted off the first song, and we were off to the races.

The lights came on, blistering the stage in warm red and yellow light, a spotlight following James through the opening riff.

Another spotlight targeted me, shining in my eyes like a flashlight at ten feet. I flipped back my hair and began belting it out, doing my best to move around and perform the obligatory singer gestures.

'Fried eggs, burnt toast, elemental overdose
Right brain, left lane, tell me why do you remain
Strapped in chains like a fool in the acid rain'

The sound was loud and beautiful. The stage was easily twice the size of anything we'd ever set foot on. Determined to use every inch of it, Ray was hopping around like a clown at an aerobics class, banging his pre-formed hair and proudly displaying his tattoos. Ray was from the Gene Simmons school of stage presence, and he liked to make faces while he played. Tonight, he was at his poser finest.

'Win some, lose more, wonder why you're on the floor
Give, take, shake, bake, push it till you're bout to break
Give me the remote and I'll show you all what's at stake'

'It's all attitude, man.' Jim pushed me, and I raised my arms to the crowd, trying to pretend it was just another night at The Tank. The first few rows seemed indecisive, but I didn't let my gaze linger.

'On my big screen – I see everything
Ain't no pipe dream - just channel thirteen'

The tricky break came and went without incident, and James took center stage for his solo. The blinding light ceased for a moment as the spotlight shifted places.

Still banging my head, I walked back to where Randy worked the drum kit, his hair pulled back and out of his eyes. His arms and legs moved in cyclical flow, jumping and striking with effortless grace, the deep wet reverberation from his kick shaking the stage.

He looked up and grinned at me, crushing the cymbal closest to my head.

I stepped back upstage and hit the chorus a couple more times, the band working hard on either side. Bright color filled my eyes again, and I could see very little beyond the first ten rows.

I looked up into the lights, singing to the scoreboard and feeling the first beads of sweat seeping from my face and neck. The end of the song approached.

Buggada buh buh, buggada buh buh bom... (three, four) *Bug-uh!* Blackout.

Straight into the second song, as tradition dictated. I listened in vain for any sign of audience response, yelling the always popular 'Come on!' into the microphone and vocalizing the next lyric.

A new light scheme on this one. The spotlight hit me like a plutonium sunlamp, and I began to understand why female performers dressed so scantily. I put the microphone back on the stand, brushing a slab of melting hair back from my face and belting away.

Volume. Mega volume. So loud that my lips were the speakers themselves, and I heard my voice from outside and not from within. The stage seemed huge.

It didn't seem huge--it was huge. I was accustomed to the cramped confines of J.R.'s and the equipment-laden three-band bookings. Now I looked over to see Ray's mike stand ten feet away, dull black empty stage stretching out beneath us.

Tommy flashed in and out of sight to my left, and Ray started moving behind me. I picked up the microphone stand with the classic two handed grip and walked down the stage front, trying to exude coolness in my spandex.

Again, the song sounded nice and tight. Randy was commanding the tempo, playing steadily and without hesitation, working like a machine and sounding better. I walked back to my monitor, setting a foot up on it as I'd seen my idols do, pointing at imaginary people in the audience and letting my voice fly.

Unlike the music videos, there weren't any beautiful girls crushing the front of the stage, or desperate hands reaching out to touch me. There were people in the front row, but they weren't desperate at all. I longed for the basement crowd.

I looked past the front row. A couple of small mosh pits were developing, spinning like flesh whirlpools to either side.

The gig was moving smoothly now. We chunked faithfully through the well-practiced material, anxiously awaiting the first opportunity for crowd response. But as I banged my head through the instrumental part, I began to realize something I would never have believed to be true. A king-size revelation, with pillow-top mattress.

Opening for Juggernaut was no more satisfying than playing a drunken kegger in the basement.

More intimidating? Yes. More prestigious? Of course. But more fun?

I always assumed that the bigger the gig, the bigger the fun. And yet, there's no such thing as 'more fun'. The best days of this band had already been lived through, and we didn't even know it. To my ears, three thousand in a venue sounded no better than thirty in a basement.

Did I mention that things were going smoothly? They were. And to steal an unofficial quote from a famous captain…we were making good time until that iceberg jumped out at us.

It began with an ill-advised leap.

Ray was getting adventurous by the middle of the second song and jumped up on the Juggernaut drum riser, chunking out chords and pumping his fist at the crowd. At the moment, it seemed pretty cool. We chuckled at the sight of him, loosening up as we worked our way toward the end of the song.

Bom, chunka chunka chunka- De-dipp. Bommm.

As we hit the last note, I caught a glimpse of Ray flying off the drum riser and attempting a mid-air high kick.

Air Ray.

A headbanger in flight.

Defying the laws of physics, his hair never lost its shape.

I don't know exactly what he was thinking as he leapt, but as he returned to earth, I could see that Ray wasn't going to nail the landing.

Crash.

Ray faw down and go boom.

Right there, center stage, with everyone including baby Jesus and his band-mates watching, Ray hit the ground in a groin-rending half-split.

He flapped his arms awkwardly before falling backward and landing firmly on his ass.

The crowd erupted, but not with applause. From where I stood, it sounded more like the sound of a cheap sit-com laugh track. A mocking cheer spread like melted margarine through the thousands, the front row bursting into a litany of taunts and insults.

Our jaws hit the stage. The laughter was like poison poured in our ears.

I turned to Randy, about to signal him for a drum solo when I saw Ray scrambling back to his feet. From the annoying rumbling in the monitors, I assumed his guitar was still operational.

"Next song, Randy."

"Aren't you gonna introduce it?"

"Just play it!"

Randy scowled at me and counted off the third song. We stomped into it, our fate already having been sealed. The boos continued to multiply.

Jim Morrison's flops were poetic and premeditated. Jim fell on purpose. Infamous Ray's crash landing, however, was merely ludicrous. This kind of fuck-up was an unforgettable act and would no doubt be remembered long after the show. Down the road, it would inevitably take its place in the legend of Ray Sharp, the first metal aviator.

Ray joined in the riff without looking back at us, but I could tell by his gimpy stance that his leg was injured. Like a wounded zebra trotting back to the herd, he banged his head and flipped his hair, attempting to resume where he'd jumped off. The only face he made now, however, was the defeated glare I'd seen the day of the Rock-fest when he was cowering in the dirt.

I hit the lyric on cue, feeling guilty for not having created more of a distraction in Ray's time of need.

Smelling blood, the crowd was beginning to swarm. The front rows booed outright now, shouting colorful insults. I looked out to see several middle fingers extended and heard every gracious word of commentary.

I tried to ignore them, struggling to focus on the lyrics and hoping that after a couple of songs, the novelty of Ray's crash would wear off. Tonight there would be no encore. I pumped my fist during the guitar break, dreading the silence that would come at the end of the song, knowing that my lead singer banter would sound stupid as hell now.

The dogs were loose. No longer was it our yard. We'd made the fatal mistake of showing weakness, and now the rabid bastards were going for our throats.

The guys nailed the ending perfectly, thanks to Randy. I suppose it didn't really matter; no one was listening to the music anymore.

The respite of relative quiet that followed the song lasted for only an instant, as a ground-swelling moan of group discontent rose from the crowd. Not just a casual golf boo, but a genuine, all-inclusive expression of boo-ness, a resounding personal rejection intended to stick with us for a long time.

I looked out to a sea of middle fingers, the fuck you's and you suck's raining down on me like chunks of hail. On Ray's side of the stage, the guests began throwing actual objects. He was limping, and pointed down at his ankle.

I put the mic back and stood center-stage. Here I was, in the midst of my life's dream, about to reason with a pack of barking dogs. What was I supposed to say?

"Mark!" I heard James' voice, and turned.

"What?"

"Ray screwed up his ankle!"

"I saw that," I said, hearing the boos multiply as we huddled on-stage. "Look, let's just roll through the rest of the list without pausing…"

"Maybe we should quit," Tommy said, speaking sacrilege. "This is fucked up anyway."

"No doubt," I said.

And then it hit me. With the crowd raging at my back and my band wavering before me, I suddenly understood what Jim was talking about.

Enjoy the ride. Listen to the music.

Moments before, I'd seen the dream gasping at our feet, mortally wounded. All our hard work seemed an utter failure. We'd made it to the big game and lost miserably.

Suddenly, it didn't matter. This gig was for Derek.

It took me until that moment to realize: Rock and roll was never about popularity. It was about sound and fury. It was about difference, and rebellion, finding the music that could tap your emotions and then letting them out. It was about jamming in the basement with my four closest friends, no audience, no compensation, doing it just because it felt good.

Enjoying the ride.

The ride is the thing.

Within, Jim nodded slowly. 'All about the ride, man.'

Dude nirvana. I'd discovered the mystery of the golden rule.

For the first time, I recognized the dream for what it was. My ultimate success would never again be measured in gigs or babes or contracts. Life was the action. Living and loving and jamming were the victory. Success and ambition were merely motives, and not the dream itself. As a chant of 'you suck' took root in the crowd, a wave of contentment was sweeping over me, washing away the fear and leaving no doubt that hope would remain.

"We're not walking off of this stage until we've played eight songs," I told him, looking over to see if James had any complaint.

"Damn right," James said, fire in his eyes. "They'll have to kick us off..."

"It's out of our hands," I told him. "Fuck it, man--let's have fun."

"Fun? Are you fucking crazy, Mark?"

Not a reasonable question to ask a guy wearing cheetah spandex. "Well, duh…"

And then, when I least expected it, I saw James' face crack, the disappointed look splitting down the middle and falling away. The corner of his mouth turned up, and James smiled the way he had that first day in Derek's basement.

"Can you make it, Ray?"

Ray nodded.

I turned toward the crowd, running a hand through my sweaty locks. The spotlight streaked back into operation, covering me in white light. I held a hand up to my eyes as though I were looking for someone in the crowd. I leaned into the microphone.

"Sup Denver…"

The place responded with a booming shout of boos. The front row resumed their chant. I opened my mouth to talk again, and laughed.

I laughed out loud. At the moment, being roundly booed just seemed fucking hilarious to me. Ray was glaring incomprehensibly, and the sight of him tickled me even more. Someone yelled something about Ray's mama, and I turned to see the corner of James' mouth turning into a grin.

Suddenly, pressure was gone. It was like the oddly calm feeling that overcomes you moments after you puke, as though the worst had passed.

James chunked a single chord. "So what now?"

I didn't have to search my soul. The answer seemed obvious.

"Let's jam, dude."

"What?"

"Like the basement man. Let's fuckin' JAM. 'Whole Lotta Rosie' dudes!"

James grin was spreading into an inspired punk smile, and for a moment he looked just like Derek. Randy was nodding and glaring like a hungry linebacker, eager to quiet the boos.

DA nana nana da chunk

James' riff resonated through the smoky air.

Da nana nana da chunk!

Again. This time, the crowd recognized the riff, and responded.

Da nana nana da chunk

(click click click click)

Da nana nana da chunk

(click click click click)

Da nana nana da chunk.

In time-honored tradition, the crowd began to yell 'Angus' between riffs in homage.

Da nana nana da chunk!

Hobbling but determined, Ray had straightened his headband and was ready to go.

Da nana nana da chunk!

I pounded my fist to the Angus chant, letting James ride out the riff a good twenty times before grabbing the mic and singing the opening line of the old AC/DC song. I closed my eyes at first, focusing on the lyric, my lids widening as I heard the crowd clapping along in time.

I squared myself with the crowd and delivered. A sea of hands sprung up before me, adrenaline and inspiration drag racing in my veins.

Dude.

Words can't come close, so I'll leave the rest to imagination.

I will add that as James screeched into his guitar solo, I turned away from the mic to see a familiar figure standing in the wings, naked and grinning, arms outstretched in exaltation. His lips only mouthed the words, but even within the glorious din I could hear Jim's voice reverberating in my head.

'Ride on, man...'

Ride On

I t was less than a week later that Ray left, stealing away in the middle of the night with his wounded pride, his wounded leg, James' amp and the contents of the refrigerator. The humiliation of that night had been too much for him to bear, and after skipping rehearsal twice, he was gone for good.

At the time, we figured Ray was replaceable. After all, he'd been a second-generation member, a poser, and a rhythm guitarist. He also proved to be a convenient scapegoat for a majority of our woes, and so none of us really sweated his departure. A new guitarist would be found and life would continue.

Until the second shoe dropped.

We were preparing for rehearsal when Tommy walked in, dragging a guilt-ridden Sandy by the hand and announcing that the two were in love.

In deference to sensitive readers, the touching scene should not, and will not, be included here. Suffice to say that Tommy handed in his resignation and carried her out, trading the band for a woman. James, surprisingly, wasn't very angry. He'd already done away with Sandy and admitted to having doubts about continuing on stage with Tommy. Dream or no dream, I understood.

Within two weeks' time, the band had dwindled to three people and zero bassists, forcing us to cancel the gigs indefinitely. The dream, postponed. We still met regularly in the basement, but we'd reverted to our prior form, jamming with no responsibility or repercussion. Tempered optimism still reigned.

No one expects a third shoe to drop. But it did.

Randy took James and I out for dinner, offering to pick up the tab. When the burritos arrived, we were happily discussing new bass players. By the time I was through with the delicious little bean-filled sucker, Randy was explaining that he had passed an audition with a speed metal band and wanted to take the job. I don't remember how the conversation reached that fatal point--the middle is a blur of green chili and sour cream--but I do remember thinking that the band was history. Someone needed to stick a fork in us, because we were most certainly done.

Unlike Tommy, Randy was very apologetic and reminisced with us for hours about all the better days. He'd considered Tommy's defection a godsend, confessing that he wanted to play a harder brand of metal than we'd been writing. He was so honest and straightforward about the whole thing that James and I were left with no choice but to pass on our collective blessing. After all, Randy was our brother. He'd been there through it all, and if he wanted out, we had to let him leave.

And once again, it was the two of us.

I thought James would be crushed. I was ready and willing to call the suicide hotline on his behalf, wondering how he'd ever cope with the thought of the band's collapsing in such a short time. But in the days and weeks immediately following Randy's departure, James seemed more relieved than distressed, almost happy to get some release from the burden of the future. He continued his private lessons and devoted himself to improving, determined to read tablature by the time he was thirty.

Away from the pressure, James seemed his old rocker self again. He could walk away without blame or regret, and could manage his disappointment with the notion that he'd been a victim of circumstance. He steeled himself with the reassuring notion that there would be another gig waiting somewhere up the road, believing that a dedicated guitarist could always find a band. James had experience now and would embark on his next mission with plenty of supplies.

And as for the journey of your dude narrator?

With my back, elbows, and butt against the wall, I had confessed to James that I'd be moving out of the band house and going on a short life hiatus. He took it well, knowing my college crisis simply demanded attention. This was my choice. I had no intention of failing at something I knew I could accomplish, something I'd intended to achieve. This time, I would do it because I wanted to--and because I could.

So I moved to a small loft apartment within walking distance of campus, a Spartan little place that served my purpose perfectly. Mom and Dad were happy to see my new resolve, though I knew that they'd never really understand what brought me to that moment or know the extent of the reckless journey that had carried me to my new world. In truth, I was the same guy I'd always been--headbanger, friend, bookworm--but the perspective had changed. And perspective, I'd realized, is important where dreams are concerned.

I worked at it. I studied my little tight-jeaned butt off, diving into the work as I'd never done before. I had something to prove and was realizing that the best I could possibly do in life was to try without regret, and strive to do just a bit more than I believed myself capable of doing. When I finally earned my Bachelor's degree, it would be for me and not them--and it would signify something.

I was walking now, my eyes open and aware, still chasing the light but doing so at a pace I could stand, for a reason I understood, trying my best to enjoy each moment as it arrived. The dream had been re-defined but not diminished, this airy castle now secure enough to support the weight of my hope.

"Hey, dude?"
"Yeah?"
"Do you ever think about that night?"
"What?"

James and I stood together in the basement, re-painting the practice space. We were on our third coat already, and still the faint outlines of graffiti faintly showed through the white.

"You know." He rolled his eyes at me. "Juggernaut. You ever think about it?"

I chuckled. "Yeah, of course I do."

"No, I mean, like, a LOT."

"Sure--it wasn't that long ago," I reminded him. "You shouldn't be worrying about the past, man. You're way too hard on yourself."

"No, it's not like that," he answered, sounding inspired. "Nothing bad. Seriously. In fact, the more I think about it, the better it gets. It may sound strange coming from me, but I'm cool with everything. It's like time washes away all the bad shit. Like, I can walk around saying I played with Juggernaut and it means something. It STILL means something. In a year, it'll mean even more. No one cares how we played...it just matters that we did."

James' revelation hit me in a good way. Personally, I didn't use the Juggernaut gig for clout; the college girls were spooked enough by my hair. But, like James, I was already hooked on the memories, the irrevocably burned images of the world as seen from the lip of that massive stage.

"Makes you want to go back, doesn't it?"

He nodded. "Hell yeah. It could happen, you never know. Whatever. Juggernaut's more than most people do…I guess I'm just saying that I'm cool with everything. Everything. I was just checking, you know, to see that you're cool with it, too."

I looked up at him. "Without question, dude. I'm right there."

"Cool."

"Cool."

I reached out a hand and we shook, successfully past the final hurdle. Now more than ever, I realized the importance of befriending our past. With luck, our memories would grow to sustain us.

As was our custom, the dramatic moment passed quickly.

"Look," James said, pointing to the wall. The black 'To Hell' sign persisted beneath the layers of white, refusing to be dismissed with a simple stroke of the brush.

"The realtor will love that one…"

"I know…maybe we should put up paneling," he suggested, dabbing at the wall with his finger. "Then again, considering the rest of the house, we're not going to get our damage deposit back. We might as well just let it go like this."

"Paneling sounds like a lot of work."

"Yeah. Or we could wallpaper…"

"Yeah."

"Seems a shame, you know? Covering it up, I mean."

"Don't worry--no matter how much white paint we put on the wall, it'll still be bad-ass underneath. We're not erasing the past, we're just, painting over it. The spray paint is still there."

He offered a mildly confused look before agreeing with me. "Yeah. No doubt."

"Did you get the dent in the door fixed?"

"Yeah."

"Well then, I wouldn't worry about it. This is good. The wall looks white enough for me."

"One more coat," he said, reaching for the roller, the ashes from his cigarette scattering into the paint tray. "So...how's school going?"

"Better," I answered, pausing to think. "Good, even. I like my classes now, and there are some cool people...it's work, of course, but I'm kicking ass, long hair or not. I'm enjoying it, you know?"

James shrugged, baffled at the concept. "Well hell, that's cool, man...even with school, I guess that's what counts. I always knew you could do it."

It sounded like something Derek would say. I remembered what I'd been forgetting to tell James.

"Hey, I got a call from Derek, man..."

"Oh yeah? Shit--what's he doing?"

"Marines," I answered, picturing Derek with a gun.

"No way..."

"No, seriously. He says he likes it!"

James shook his head, chuckling. "Yeah, I guess I can see him liking it--actually, the military is kind-of like a band that shoots people and frees stuff, right? I wouldn't want to be on the other side, that's for sure. Why is it that the punkers always join the military? Where's he at?"

"California," I answered, the word summoning images of Tabitha. "But he said he's going overseas somewhere."

"Really? Damn..."

"He asked for your number, so I gave it to him."

He smiled a bit. "Oh yeah?"

"Sure, man. Nothing serious--he just wants to talk, you know."

James looked pleased. "Yeah, that's cool, man. If you talk to him again, be sure to tell him to call me."

"I will." I nodded, surveying our handiwork. Considering the damage we'd done, it looked surprisingly civilized. The beer-stained carpet had been shampooed and de-candle-waxed, the broken windows repaired and the cat-turds collected. The synthetic paint smell chased away the lingering scent of cigarette smoke and cheap incense, leaving only the enamel-meets-ammonia show-ready 'fresh' smell that new-used houses were supposed to have. Like most headbangers, the band house cleaned up pretty well.

"So what about that new chick you're seeing?" I asked him, curious to find out what life after Sandy was like. "How's that going?"

James shrugged, chuckling. "Good, I guess. She's cool. She works at a tanning salon, so she's pretty hot..."

"Nice."

"We're not all screwed up in love or anything, but it's good."

"What's her name again?"

"Laura," he said, pronouncing it as though it were French.

"Laura, not Lori?" I asked.

"Right."

"James and Laura. Real soap-opera."

He shrugged. "Yeah, well, we try to keep the grief to a minimum. How about you? Any new girlfriends?"

"Nothing too exciting," I told him. "Yet..."

"Well, that's by choice, dude."

I grinned, mugging. "You know me...I do okay. It gets strange talking to women when I'm not the lead singer."

"Yeah, uh-huh, I have no doubt you manage, dude. Just don't cut your hair."

"I've got to be myself," I replied, carefully misquoting Sammy Davis Jr. "I'll cut it when I feel like it."

New perspectives.

I'd been quick to agree when James called and said he needed someone to help clean up the band house in preparation for moving. With none of the other culprits still present, the job was left to the two of us. I didn't mind too much--I wanted to see the place one last time, for nostalgia if nothing else.

"Lots of good parties here," James said as we were finishing, hands on hips and surveying the room like a contractor. "You don't forget nights like those."

His words sounded like a poorly written beer commercial, but I was feeling the vibe. Admittedly, we were both overcome with a case of mover's remorse and had been reminiscing all afternoon. It seemed like too brief an ending.

"Of all the gigs we played," I answered, "and that includes The Pit and Juggernaut and everything--the basement gigs outshined them all."

He nodded. "No doubt."

"A hundred drunken strangers in the house, the basement packed and us turning up, screaming loud and feeding them no-miss jams--"

"Hell yeah!" James' eyes blazed with memory. "The front filled with hotties, the cymbal crashes blasting in our ears…it was the shit, period. And you can quote me on that."

I took a deep breath, calming the siren song that continued to wail within me.

"We'll put it on your grave," I told him, grinning. "It was the shit, period."

"No way," he waved me off, smiling. "They're gonna put 'rock legend' on my grave...no, I want to be cremated and then they can do something honorable with my ashes. You know, like having 'em made into guitar picks for third-world children or something. Bizarre, but cool, you know?"

"It's you, man."

We locked the front door and stood for a moment on the front lawn, paying our last respects.

"Too bad." James shook his head. "This place was perfect. My new practice space is roomier, but not as cool."

"The new band is sounding pretty good?"

James looked down, shrugging. "Well, not really. I mean, instrumentally we rock out. Guitars are good, Ron Mallory's gonna play bass--"

"Oh yeah? He's pretty cool."

"Yeah."

"You're not jamming with Randy, are you?"

"What?" He shook his head. "No way, man. Randy's speed metal thing broke up, but I hear he's jamming with some dudes from Lakewood. He's delivering pizza, from what I hear. No big gigs or anything."

"They broke up? Is he disappointed?"

"Yeah, I'm sure. It's tough to land a good band. I'm playing with Terry Thompson now. Do you know Terry?"

"Sounds familiar," I replied, wishing I had a band to brag about.

"He was the drummer with Lions' Pride in Denver. Totally cool, kick-ass drummer with no drama. Works."

"You can't ask for more than that."

"No, I guess not. We've written a bunch of tunes, you know, but it's hard without a good singer."

Instinct told me what was coming next.

In the desert of my minds' eye I could see a distant figure, slumped and staggering, approaching from a distance.

"To be honest," James continued, now in full diplomatic voice, "we can't find anyone who can sing near as good as you, and you know all the songs. Everyone always asks where you are man--I tell 'em you're taking care of business at school so you can come back and kick some ass..."

I waited to speak, knowing he wasn't finished. If I were to become a singer again, I wanted to be invited.

"You know I have respect for your studies, man--I'm not trying to screw you up or anything." He paused, running out of words. "Anyway, I guess I was just wondering if you want to come jam with us sometime..."

The figure moved closer, clearer in my view, kicking up sand as it stumbled toward me. I knew immediately who it was.

My long lost friend Jim stood before me, shirtless and bearded, looking as though he'd just crawled through the desert on his hands and knees. Grinning, he showed me his palms.

'I'm back, brother--couldn't stay away. So...are we jamming, or what?'

EPILOGUE

It was almost the nineties. And it wasn't exactly the suburbs anymore. Metal was everywhere. With the scores of bubblegum bands soaking the airwaves, the saturation levels redlined, and heavy metal became terminally popular. With this news, the 'genre' title was removed, and heavy metal officially became a trend. The jagged writing was on the wall.

The country was afflicted with sensory overload, and the pretty-boy metal routine was feeling as tired and redundant as a slasher movie sequel. Something had to give.

Soon, it did. A scrawny genius from Seattle had written the disenfranchised anthem of the 90's, a song with meaning and purpose. Heady and real, "Smells Like Teen Spirit" decimated an entire genre in mere weeks. Suddenly, the muddy hammer of grunge was swinging wide with style and purpose, allowing the pent-up headbangers to loosen their pants, open their minds and stop with all that bothersome hair washing.

The Cold War was over, and apparently everyone was depressed.

Like a tomato in a microwave, heavy metal eventually exploded, scattering messy bits of juice and meat into everything near it. With the seeds safely planted in other forms of music, the original genre mercifully rotted away. The insignificant trend of the insignificant decade was replaced with something more substantial. Less fun, perhaps, but more serious, and important.

That was cool with us. Grunge seemed to make sense. It was organic.

We weren't fifteen anymore, but we were still rockers at heart. We donned our flannel, grew out our bangs and played on devotedly, our sound evolving, our own tastes changing as the scene changed around us. The dream lived on in its own way, now redefined by time and temperament, metamorphosing with each new band and performance. I never again truly believed I would be famous, but it no longer mattered. Not really. If it happened, I would be ready. If it didn't, I would still be jamming.

For success, like so many other dreams, is relative. Wanting is sometimes more important than getting, and sometimes wanting is all you'll ever have.

When the band was finally laid to rest, our eulogies didn't speak of gigs and recordings. Instead, our reminiscences were filled with stories of keg parties, hot girls and late nights, basement jams and believing the improbable. The headbanger years. The days when hope reigned and everything sounded good.

We were headbangers, rockers who just wanted to be legends. We were little shits who believed that wanting something could make it real. We were basement visionaries and hedonists, lovers and fighters. Dreamers...just like everyone else.

Kirk Anthony Vollack lives in Colorado where
he teaches music and writes.

www.ingramcontent.com/pod-product-compliance
Lightning Source LLC
Chambersburg PA
CBHW051312250626
47155CB00007B/2285